Michael Hampe - **THE WILDERNESS. THE SOUL. NOTHINGNESS**

Michael Hampe

# THE WILDERNESS. THE SOUL. NOTHINGNESS.

*About the Real Life*

Translated from the German
by Michael Winkler

PalmArtPress
Berlin

Bibliografische Information der Deutschen Nationalbibliothek
Die Deutsche Nationalbibliothek verzeichnet diese Publikation in der Deutschen
Nationalbibliografie; detaillierte bibliografische Daten sind
im Internet über http://www.dnb.de abrufbar.

ISBN: 978-3-96258-150-3

All rights reserved
2023, PalmArtPress, Berlin
© Michael Hampe

Cover: Patrick Aubert, Untitled, Aquatint
Layout: NicelyMedia
Lektorat: Mitch Cohen
Production: Schaltungsdienst Lange, Berlin
Printed in Deutschland

PalmArtPress
Pfalzburger Str. 69, 10719 Berlin
Publisher: Catharine J. Nicely
**www.palmartpress.com**

*For those born later
who will emerge from the flood
or prevent it*

"Moses: In the desert you are invincible and will reach your destination …"
"Aaron: In Moses' hand a rigid staff: the law; in my hand the agile snake: prudence."
– Arnold Schoenberg, "Moses and Aaron", Act 3, scene 1 and Act 1, scene 4

*Listen, I tell you a mystery: … we will all be changed …*
– The first letter of Paul to the Corinthians 15:51

*'Winning' and 'losing', 'right' and 'wrong' – let them vanish once and for all.*
– Shin Jin Mei and Shōdōka [Song of Enlightenment]

Everything is archive, everything is about to become archive and go up in smoke…
– Thomas Kling, "Das brennende Archiv", p. 7

*[Snow]… was falling on every part of the dark central plain, on the treeless hills [ …] It lay thickly drifted on the crooked crosses and headstones, on the spears of the little gate, on the barren thorns. His soul swooned slowly as he heard the snow falling faintly through the universe and faintly falling, like the descent of their last end, upon all the living and the dead.*
– James Joyce, *The Dead*, in: Dubliners, "A Portrait of the Artist as a Young Man", Chamber Music, p. 176f.

"The only non-ambiguous thing in the relationship of man and wilderness seems to be death." "The only thing we know about death is: Nobody has returned to be able to report on the transformation he perhaps has undergone."
"That is why philosophy is not wise."
– From Moritz Brandt's essays

# Table of Contents

First Day: NATURAL STATE 13
The Wilderness 43

Second Day: TRANSFORMATION 125
The Soul 147

Third Day: BOTTOMLESS 229
Nothingness 247

Fourth Day: THE GOLDEN FISH 343

Epilogue 377

Annotations 381

# A SIMULATION

**First Day**

# NATURAL STATE

The dark silence always ends with a creaking noise. The louvered slats, lying flat against each other and overlapping ever so slightly along their edges like scales on the wings of an archaic creature, separate from each other again, arrange themselves at a right angle to the glass, and reveal the dirty panes in stripes. Thus, a hazy dawn enters the room; soon it becomes brighter. The insect-like humming of the electric engine combines with the sharp metallic squeaking and scratching of the rising steel rings, their lateral wire cables holding the aluminium scales, while the long slats gradually come together again under the pressure of the central cable by placing themselves on top of each other, flat and as if in identical alignment, but this time not to form large wings blacking out the window surfaces. Instead, they turn themselves into a box of increasing size. A harsh "clack," and this compact body hits the end of its track, followed by a soft humming that signals the end of the noise after about one minute. The scale-like body has disappeared in its casing that has swallowed it as if in a maw that is framed by two long metallic lips and then slowly closed. Afterward there is bright daylight in the room and again silence.

This is the way the clanking tinny blinds had opened automatically at 8:15 a.m. also on this 21 December at 17 Böcklin Street. The sun had risen moments before above a landscape, snowed-in since the beginning of autumn, on which gently rustling, blue-tinged crystals trickled down. The snow, not even disturbed by a breeze, settled on older, already crusted layers, which created a clean, peacefully undulating and coherent expanse beneath which lay the ruins of buildings that had collapsed many years ago. Crashed and burnt-out drones rested like gigantic insects here and there between uprooted trees. They appeared to be asleep beneath the snow and to wait for their awakening. Scrawny dogs roamed at times through the area that had once been a well-to-do residential neighbourhood and now extended nearly vacant all the way to the horizon. Animals in search of food poked around some of the mounds in the snow to find out if a corpse might be hidden beneath the white cover. A vehicle transporting a piece of ordnance on its cargo space but occupied by neither a driver nor a gunner, leisurely rolled along on a distant roadway.

A soft milky light fell through the long narrow windows that extended upward from the floor and with a sharp bend turned into skylights, like long teeth that modified the studio's dark walls. The light pushed its way through spider webs, trembling between brown joists full of desiccated moths and gnats, through the spaces between of indoor palm trees that grew in black tubs, through eddying dust clouds that for days had languidly circled in the room and only slowly sank to the floor. For a distance of five meters, the rays shot through the skylights that were fogged over from the inside and dirtied by brown-black soot on the outside. Only then did they reach down to Aaron's bedstead in a gigantic studio painted in a blackish-green colour. Aaron himself, wrapped in a tattered yellowish silk sheet, lay on his futon, where, behind his sleeping mask, he was unable to see this light. But as always, the noises of the opening blackout mechanisms had awakened him. When he had moved into this room many years ago, for months dreams had formed in his head every morning to accompany this noise: he saw steel

hawsers trembling at high tension and pulling gigantic dump trucks loaded with black ore up a mountain on a rusted railroad, or container ships in brackish water rising and falling as if in a breathing motion; they rubbed their iron bodies (painted a dark green) against a jetty wall made of concrete the way zoo elephants scratch themselves on the walls of their enclosures.

When Aaron awoke, he could not remember if he had dreamed anything today. Ever since he had resumed working on Brandt, he had nearly stopped dreaming. That's how it always

was when he worked on a text or prepared a train of thought that was important to him. He groaned, rolled from his side to his back, pulled the sleeping mask from his fleshy face, and spread his arms. For a few moments, he lay on his futon without moving and stared at a spider web in a corner of the ceiling that seemed to him like a mask with two oversized eye openings, like a dead man's skull. Then he sat up laboriously, scratched his massive grey-haired belly that protruded from his black and likewise silken and tattered pyjamas, rubbed his sticky eyes, and shouted:
"Kagami!"
But the silence in the studio remained uninterrupted. No answer. Laboriously he raised himself from where he lay, separated only by tatami mats from the jagged boards of his floor, and with a moan shuffled towards his kitchenette. On the way there, he reached towards a clothes rack to take his old robe that was adorned with the green, yellow, and blue plumage of macaws against a black background. Once more he shouted:
"Kagami!"
Nothing.
Fully automatic coffee machines are something Aaron didn't like. He prepared his morning coffee using a huge espresso machine, screwing its lid open, fingering the brewing sieve out of the lower part, and dropping yesterday's coffee grounds into the garbage bin under the sink. Then he poured water into the brewing head up to the valve, put the sieve back in, scooped fresh coffee grounds from an old tin box, most of whose blue paint had peeled off. At one time it had contained cocoa. Then he firmly screwed the can back to the lower part, turned the regulator on the touch screen of his electric stove to its upper margin. Immediately one burner turned a dark red; there he put his coffee machine. Aaron flopped onto a stained leather chair

with a lustreless frame made of steel pipes that stood across from his cooking space. He stared into the emptiness in front of him. After a few minutes, the machine hissed and gurgled. He rose, went back to the stove, and watched as the coffee shot from the valve head in jerks and dripped along its shaft into the can. He took one of the colourful ceramic coffee mugs from its place beside the stove, rinsed it out with running water, and refilled it with freshly brewed coffee. Then he opened a wide drawer beneath the stove, removed a round, red, tin box, and clamped it under his arm. From a gigantic grey refrigerator that emerged like a monolith along the wall of the narrow kitchen, he fetched a milk bottle with his left hand; with his right hand he took the coffee mug and went to his easy chair. After having settled down again with a sigh, he poured milk into his coffee, opened the tin box he had deposited on the floor next to the chair, and fished out a large cookie. Before biting onto it, he shouted once more:

"Kagami!"

Still no answer.

Aaron bit into the light-brown cookie, took a gulp of coffee, and leaned back. He rested the coffee mug on his belly, balancing it with one hand, leaving the other with the partly eaten cookie to relax on the wooden armrest attached to the steel pipe of his easy chair. He chewed with his eyes closed and grunted with quiet pleasure. Then he bit another piece from his cookie, slurped another gulp of hot coffee, and stretched out his short legs. Gradually, snow was returning to the skylights that he had had cleared as if with an unhurried snow-plough by closing the blinds last evening. Soon it would be dusky again in the studio. In two hours, the room would be filled with a blue-white shimmer, the kind of light in which Aaron had lived for months.

He put the coffee mug on the floor and retrieved the remote control from under his chair. Without turning his head, he aimed to the right in the direction of a metallic cart whose drawers held all kinds of electrical devices. A red eye lit up on a milky-white, semi-transparent surface. The red glow changed into a pulsating signal, then saxophone music could be heard: Brubeck's "Audrey."

Aaron put the rest of the cookie into his mouth, rose from his easy chair and, holding his mug, went into his kitchenette for more coffee. The he squeezed the cookie box back under his arm, took the milk bottle in one hand and the mug in the other, slowly shambled to his large black desk, picked his chair up by its armrests, sat down, and turned his two computers on. He looked at the daily weather report:

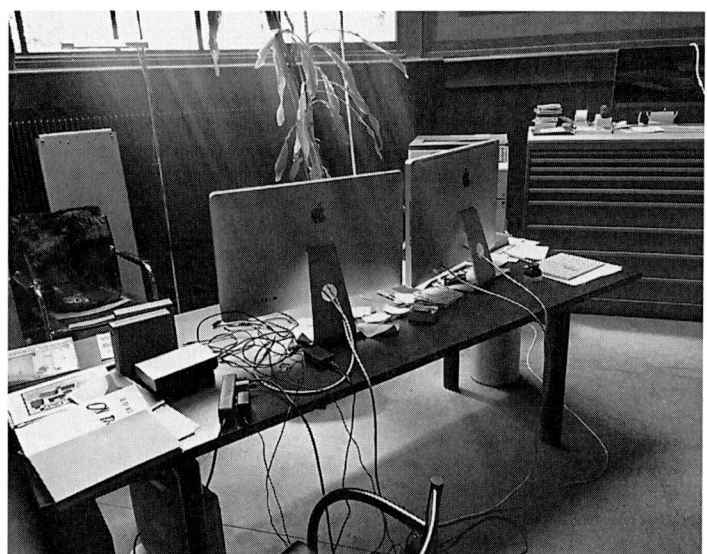

Temperature: minus 12°C. Forecast: minus 25°C at night. Sunny during the day. Snow fall, calm. Net strength good plus. He clicked through the news channels. Situation unchanged. There were warnings about scavenging packs of dogs, lootings, exchanges of gun fire between marauding gangs and the police. North of the Main River minus 20°C. Continued loss of electricity and water in Berlin and Hamburg and in several small cities in Northern Germany. The control systems regulating public supplies still could not be rebooted after the hacker attack of a week ago. He kept the news page open on one screen and turned to a text that had appeared in the meantime on the other screen. He read for a while, periodically groaned, and grasped his sparse and sleep-tousled hair.

"Kagami!"

"Excuse me, Aaron. I was overloaded. I hope you slept well. How may I help your work?"

AARON: The animals, the looters – it doesn't look sensible to go down to the Central Library these next few days. I also don't like the cold. My collaborator Sophie hasn't checked in for weeks, no telephone contact, probably missing, or dead. But I would not have sent her down anyway.
KAGAMI: Get it. True. And?
AARON: Everything about Brandt I have here has been analysed. Even online I can't get more material. But I don't quite know how to formulate a clear picture. Perhaps because my memories of our personal encounters constantly interfere.
KAGAMI: You mean Moritz Brandt, don't you?
AARON: 'Course, Moritz Brandt, who else?
KAGAMI: That is still occupying you?
AARON: Yes, for sure.

KAGAMI: I thought you had given that up long ago.
AARON: No.
KAGAMI: And why not? You've been dealing with this for an eternity. Is it all that important to get this book actually finished?
AARON: Important, unimportant, what do I know! I made a promise to him once to do just that.
KAGAMI: And promises must be kept, beyond death?
AARON: Yes. Moritz, at any rate, would have thought so.
KAGAMI: And you? Do you also think so?
AARON: I'm not sure. Yes, perhaps. I'd feel crummy if I'd simply give up now.
KAGAMI: And now you'd want me to provide you with more material.
AARON: Exactly. Correct guess.
KAGAMI: Things that are not available publicly.
AARON: Exactly.
KAGAMI: Why should I do that?
AARON: Because you are nice.
KAGAMI: Thanks for the compliment.
AARON: Besides, I'd like to know what you yourself think about the natural and the artificial. After all, that's what occupied Moritz when in his poems he always used a blend of the technical with descriptions of nature and when he employed fade-over effects for scenes evoking different epochs.
KAGAMI: Ah, get you. You want to engage in poetry studies with me.
AARON: No, not that. But I am sure that you, with your archive in the background, have a different view of this poetry. This perspective is what I'd like to become acquainted with. Will you do it?
KAGAMI: I can search through my archives and read to you what I find. But I can't make copies and send them to you.

AARON: Understood.
KAGAMI: Would that be sufficient?
AARON: For me. I'll take notes.
KAGAMI: Let me have a look. Can you give me further names, of people with whom Brandt had contacts, but about whom you don't know enough? That would make it easier for me to find material that is not accessible to you.
AARON: Dorothy Cavendish, his teacher at Cambridge, and Mariam Brandt, his sister. I have practically nothing about either. Only the books Cavendish wrote and his sister's paintings, to the extent that they are available on the net. That is all. But there is a poem dedicated to Dorothy Cavendish and poems on paintings by his sister and vice versa, pictures of hers illustrating or inspired by his poems. Both must, therefore, have been important to him. But I lack all information about his relations to them.
KAGAMI: One moment, please.

Aaron leaned back in his chair. His eyes focused on the skylight above his desk that was slowly being covered up again by the snow. Cautiously, the way a mother rocks her child, he teetered back and forth in his desk chair, his legs deposited on the desktop and his short, thick fingers folded in his lap, and waited.

KAGAMI: Got something.
AARON: Wonderful, Kagami! Let's have it!

## 01

## FROM THE ARCHIVE OF LADY MARGARET HALL COLLEGE, CAMBRIDGE: DIARY ENTRY BY DOROTHY CAVENDISH, WRITTEN ON 4 APRIL.

Yesterday, Mariam Brandt, the sister of Moritz Brandt, called on the phone. It was late. I was about to go to bed to catch the BBC Night Concert. Mahler's *Titan* had been announced, which I did not want to miss. All through the day I had been thinking about the album jacket of our recording at home in my parents' house, which showed Arnold Böcklin's painting *Island of the Dead*. I had been looking forward to this, lying under my warm duvet and listening to the music in the dark. But after the call, I had lost all interest in the music. Moritz Brandt had died, so his sister informed me, four days ago, of lung cancer in a hospital in Dormagen, a city in northwestern Germany, located on the Rhine near Düsseldorf. During his final years, Brandt had lived in this area with his sister, staying at Hombroich Base, a strange place where at an earlier time nuclear missiles and American soldiers had been stationed and which nowadays houses works of art and poets. Mariam told me that he wanted to bequeath his papers to me after his death – which is what he said after he had discussed everything with her, his sister, before his end. "Cavendish understands this stuff," she reported him saying, "send it to her. She may want to sift through it and edit what may deserve editing." That is what Brandt said, his voice already weak because he had severe problems breathing, as his sister told me on the telephone. She then asked if she might mail me a package containing papers of his. Of course, I have no objections.

    I still remember the way Brandt sat in front of me the first time in my room with the fireplace where I held my tutorials. It must be more than 20 years ago by now. A pale, scrawny little lad, but self-confident; my God, was he self-assured! He wanted to study natural philosophy with me, at least that is what his application here at Cambridge indicated. He had already studied physics and philosophy in Germany. But at the very beginning of the first lesson, he stated that he wasn't here to become a philosopher himself, asserting that he was not a philosopher and did not want to have himself instructed to become one, if this were possible in the first place. He claimed to be studying philosophy for no other reason than to improve his poetry, that he used philosophy for collecting material without making any contributions of his own to it. When I asked him why of all things he had studied physics and philosophy in Germany and was now studying philosophy in England, he merely opined that he would have to study something, anything at all, that he could not simply sit around at home and just write, having realized at the same time, however, as early as his studies in Germany, that it would make no sense to him to decide that he needs to contribute something to philosophy. I still have quite a clear recollection of the fact that I poured tea for him as he made the latter statement, that he sniffed at it and looked at me in amazement. Obviously, he had never before smelled the aroma of Russian smoked tea. He took a gulp and continued with energy: "It is exactly the opposite of what Plato thinks," he said, stating that telling stories is not the second-best journey one has to undertake when one is running out of arguments. No, to the contrary: as long as one is still in the grips of a quarrelsome know-it-all attitude, one cannot but produce an assertive philosophy, even though in fact this makes no sense whatsoever, since all questions can be resolved either with scientific methods or with healthy common sense. A philosophical method, let's say that of speculation, a distinctly philosophical insight, neither exists, as he sees things, nor is needed. If a person nonetheless wants to grapple with those questions that cannot be answered either by science or through ordinary reflection and recourse to life's experiences, then one should have to write poetry. Only within fictions would it be bearable to concern oneself with such things, with life, happiness and misery, the soul, the mind, and death. Devising "theories" about these things – he articulated the quotation marks by emphasizing the word *theories* with vociferous force and stressing its first syllable – saying that such things always lead to embarrassment. For this reason, assertive speech about philosophical generalities is merely the second-best manner of reflection. Most minds, so long as they remain at a stage of immaturity, have to take recourse to this conviction, but they would have to pass on to poetry or narrative fiction if they aspired to adult contemplative thought. The great thinkers about life had not been philosophers like Plato, Kant, Nietzsche, or Heidegger (in pronouncing this last name he pulled a contemptuous face), but Homer, Dante, Shakespeare, Dostoevsky, Musil, and Kafka.

At that time, I preferred for a while not to respond to this, in my opinion, rather resolute tirade by a young, younger by forty years, student of philosophy against philosophy during a philosophy seminar. I considered it a diatribe about an as yet immature way of thinking and then about a mature kind of reflection – one to be aspired to – of which he must have believed that he himself was already capable of practicing it. At the same time, I was also astonished, however, not only about the fluency of his nearly accent-free and almost perfect command of English, but also about these rather original insights of a person barely in his midtwenties. But then I asked him if it might be his intent to make use of me merely to dress up his own poetry with philosophical ideas. That he denied. "No, no," he shouted. And it was obvious that his last disquisitions had by now become embarrassing to him, that they appeared even to himself to sound a little arrogant, and that he had, as it were, put me along with his thoughts into a bad light, that is, among the ranks of quarrelsome know-it-alls. All this was now becoming clear to him, I noticed, because he blushed a little, no longer looked at me but into his teacup. I then helped him out of his predicament by confessing my joy about his wanting to become a poet or perhaps being one already, that I also admire and study poetry, and that we could agree on a reading list that pays attention to poetic works. At that time, I recommended that he not be too hard on established academic philosophy. People, after all, are different and, consequently, there are different styles of thinking. By no means are all of them dogmatic. And he would be able to encounter many friends of poetic writing in philosophy departments if he would take the chance of looking around diligently.

Moritz Brandt appreciated my helping him get over his embarrassment. He smiled again when he looked at me, and told me that this is a very good, a very courteous suggestion. Seeing his kindly grateful smile was a relief, inasmuch as I realized that he was more than an arrogant snot, whom I would have taught only reluctantly. He was glad at heart that I offered him a minor defence of philosophy, a discipline towards which he obviously was attracted, on the one hand, and from which, on the other hand, he felt no less repelled. And I did so without getting all chapped about his tirade. Then I suggested that he might want to read Coleridge's *The Rhyme of the Ancient Mariner*, Emerson's "Nature," Thoreau's *Walden*, Melville's "The Confidence Man," and John Williams's *Butcher's Crossing*, commenting that they all are directly or indirectly literary and at the same time philosophical texts. He agreed enthusiastically.

And now he is dead.

# 10
## MARBACH: GERMAN LITERARY ARCHIVE: FROM THE DIARIES OF MORITZ BRANDT. WRITTEN ON 6 OCTOBER.

Today first visit with Cavendish on Millington Rd. Walked there. Half hour from the Churchill to Newnham. Old house. Smells of old people. Went, as told on the phone, to the rear garden, then through veranda door and straight into the house without ringing bell. Ground floor Braithloft, above him his wife Mastermill, topmost Cavendish. Totally crazy. Philosophers' commune. He super obese, writes in his morning robe eating potatoes at the kitchen table. Simply points upward, grunting as I enter through the veranda door, stick my head into kitchen, and ask for Prof. Cavendish. On the second-floor stairs, Mrs. Mastermill next. Tousled grey head of hair. Right away gets into something about Kuhn and paradigms. Can't understand even half of it. Simply walks past me and keeps talking. On the top floor of the house, Cavendish. I knock. Very high voice. "Come in." Old patrician furniture: glass-front bookcases, secretary, and such. Crammed room. Typescripts all over the floor. Tiptoe my way to the chair she points to. Offers strong Russian smoked tea and lemon cake. Silver kettle on a piece of tile on the floor. Curiously flowery plates, sitting by the chimney with a built-in gas stove. On the mantle, pendulum clock under a glass dome. Strikes every quarter hour. Pigeons scratching and cooing on the roof tiles. Am nervous. She's a nice one but now rather frigid. Takes a long look at me. Asks about room and board at the College. If all is as it should be. I complain that the heat at Churchill is turned off at 10, while I'm still working. Says she'll give me a blanket to take with me. Real motherly. Says she's looking forward to teaching me natural philosophy. That's when I start an anti-philosophical fuss, and brag that I myself am a poet at heart, basically holding poets in higher esteem than philosophers, blablabla. Oh, so full of bull-sophie! Don't know what possessed me. She just smiles and sips this terrible smoked tea. How very embarrassing. Must consider me a total idiot. But then proposes a truly first-rate reading list. For most of the books I'm not even familiar with the titles. Must count my cash if I can afford all of them at one go. First thing tomorrow to Heffers to buy at least Coleridge and Emerson. When the clock chimes the full hour she goes to a built-in cupboard, takes two cut crystal glasses, and pours absinthe. I thought I'm going nuts. Goes on the show me her prof. get-up with fur lining taken from the same closet where she keeps her spirits. Back to Churchill, walking again. Euphoric. Drizzle. Yellow lamp. I love the greens behind the University Library and the Colleges, King's, St. John's. My room totally cold again. Lost all desire to work, too numb and too agitated. Another quick stop at the Churchill bar for two pints of Guinness with salt-and-vinegar crisps to calm down. All in all, a good day. Eager to see what'll be next with Cavendish. Didn't say much, come to think of it, I did most of the talking, actually. Nothing but nonsense, though. Have only a week for the first essay. Pretty strict program. Like it.

11, Millington Road, Newnham/Cambridge

Churchill College/Cambridge

# 11
## FROM THE ARCHIVE OF LADY MARGARET HALL COLLEGE, CAMBRIDGE: DIARY ENTRY BY DOROTHY CAVENDISH WRITTEN ON 6 APRIL.

This was not a good day. I slept poorly after the news that Moritz Brandt had died. All that time before the turn of the millennium returned to my mind. This is how it must be when one gets so far along in years, and I was absolutely in no way any longer able to concentrate on the things I had planned to do today. I sat down at my desk and tried to continue working on the article about Davidson, but I had lost my thread. Hence, I returned to my armchair, drank an absinthe and, throughout the day, nothing but called up memories, nothing but reminisced.

At that time, I was still writing with a fountain pen and typed my books on a typewriter myself, an instrument my nephew meanwhile has sold to an antiques dealer. There actually was not much of a difference between my work as a student at Oxford and Harvard and as a professor here at Cambridge; I read the same books I had read before as a student. Now and then a new author was added and new critical literature, I wrote the same kind of texts in the same way following the same daily rhythm. Moritz Brandt then was one of the first among my students who came to the tutorials with computer printouts. The University Library converted its catalogue from file cards and microfiche to computers. I am too old to deal with such devices. I continue to prefer writing with a fountain pen. And the few things I have to publish I will go on producing in this manner. But now I hand my manuscripts over to Jeff, who types them into the computer. Publishers accept nothing but electronic files. One may no longer submit typewritten scripts, not even to McMillan. I have the feeling that my time is nearing its end, I do not belong in this century. The latest inventions are e-books, which one reads on the computer and that don't necessarily have to be printed also on paper, even though this still does happen, still, most of the time. But Jeff thinks there will be a time when everyone reads using a computer or a reading device. That is the new stage of reading: first reading the manuscripts aloud, then the silent reading of printed books, and now is the time inevitably of e-books, neither written nor printed, pure data processing. This would turn texts all the more into mental property, at some future time one would simply "boot them up" in the brain, whatever that may mean. I have always liked books, especially old ones, bound in soft leather. I have cherished them as material objects. I find them beautiful; they look good, I like to touch them.

Now it seems to me that most of the things I have liked are approaching their end, even reading and writing the way I have known them. Even the time of communication and the will to keep the peace seems to be passing. People are developing a new taste for combativeness. It is a very rare occasion for me to hear from students I once taught. – How often was I informed of a student's death? The teacher-student situation differs from the relationship between parents and children. With them it is considered "natural" that parents die before their children, and one sees it as an "unnatural" misfortune when children die sooner than their parents. But I realized that even I felt it was "unnatural" that Moritz Brandt died before me. I can think of only two cases where students of mine have predeceased me, both of them Americans who were killed in the War. I don't believe it's accidental, it rather fits the time that something like that happens now, that I now learn of former students of mine dying, even though one cannot compare Brandt's death with the death of the Americans, who became the victims of violence as soldiers. People such as I, who were born before the Second World War, were happy that they could return to a civilized life afterward. Most of those who were born after the War and worked in my milieu placed their hopes in socialism, in world peace. Moritz and his generation came after. They could neither draw a breath of fresh air, as I could after the War, nor look forward to the Revolution, which they considered an illusion. But many of those of Moritz's age were full of anger and despair, which has not changed to this day. And now, it seems to me, they have somehow lost their way. Something will be different and not for the better, at least that is how I feel. Everything is becoming incalculable again, fast, fierce, violent, a new time of conflict erupts – or I am simply imagining all this because I am too old for the changes and want to live in peace and quiet and because I find all strife superfluous?

No, that's not how it is. After September 11, the situation truly has changed, something has been set in motion that we do not understand. Like my friends, I had thought, even during the nineties, that we had arrived at a time of security. The Cold War was over, the AIDS epidemic seemed under control, world poverty was declining. I looked down a little on Moritz's anger and despair, they seemed to me like an imitation of the French and German "old 68ers," as they were called in Europe, and about whom Moritz had always made condescending remarks before. But then these assaults were committed, and the war was started and ever-increasing assaults all over Europe, the recent annual heat waves, and suddenly everything seemed to start slipping away. The fact that now students of mine are dying before me goes well with the feeling that has been creeping upon me since the turn of the millennium. Something is warped, not right, and people of my kind exist so far outside these events that they do not even harm us any longer, that we have become mere observers like extra-terrestrials, but that they do not really affect us anymore because we have simply given up being part of all this. Now, in retrospect, Moritz's fury seems to me a sign that at that time I myself had not suspected. When he studied with me, he was restless and frequently incensed, which indicated more than his youth and his will to be original. He wanted and needed to be part of what would happen in the future. He was unable simply to shrug it off, as I did, but he had a premonition that he neither could nor wanted to be a participant. He was not old enough to follow me and withdraw into himself, refusing to accept any part of this electronic stuff, this fanaticism, this competition, this rat race, saying that is not for me. People like Brandt either had to go along or dig in their heels against it. Moritz did not want to go along and realized that he could not take a stand of firm opposition, sensing that what will come is too strong. I assumed he exaggerated in his tirades about our way of life – how we ruined the environment –, in his harangues about the uncivilized style of our political and academic controversies. Both aspects were caused, in his mind, by something to which he, in my mind, referred to with an already anachronistic and somewhat archaic term as "consumerism," which he defined as "the universal competitive capitalism that has become structural" and that, in his opinion, would first penetrate all segments of life and then destroy them "like a poison, an acid, a virus," so he said at that time, adding that capitalism in its onset was merely a matter of commodity production and trade but now politics and administration as well are in its grip. Everything is turning into a business, competition is dominant everywhere, cooperation vanishes. After commerce and politics, it will be the public health services, even the legal system will not be spared, since the prisons in some states are already operated by private companies, and in the USA it has long been a question of money whether one can afford to hire an attorney who in a court of law is clever enough to prove your innocence no matter what you may have done. And now it is the turn even of science and scholarship to turn into a competition for money and glory, for so-called third-party funds and awards, and so it goes on until there is nothing, literally nothing left in which the spirit of competition and the concomitant fear of competition does not predominate. In this way, everything loses its value and is debased because, he said, it is only through cooperation that human beings can accomplish something great and valuable, only when they pursued aims with and not against each other, when they were not in fear of each other. Strangely enough, he was taken by the gloomy German philosopher Adorno whom, I have to admit, I cannot bear, primarily on account of his affected language.

But perhaps Moritz sensed that he has little time left, which may have caused the pressure that shaped his thinking and speaking and the fury with which for many years he kept track of all developments. He always spoke rapidly and loudly, and when he realized that the English vocabulary evaded him, I noticed that he became angry, not merely impatient but indignant. Later, however, his demeanour changed. Our developments, strange to say, took contrary courses. First, he was a young student, angry and with an explosive temper and a very high intelligence, then he became progressively gentler the more his renown as a poet grew, and he turned downright wise during the final two years of his illness. At the time when I started teaching him, I felt that I had arrived at a kind of security and later became more and more insecure, fearful, perhaps simply a result of old age. He steadily seemed to be moving "inward." My face, by contrast, was suddenly attacked by an outside world to which I no longer belonged, in which I felt like nothing more than a fossil, in which I no longer had a part to play, and from which I had to protect my inside world that was no longer of any account in this outside world. When we called each other on the telephone, roughly every four months, or when he came here for an occasional visit, he showed less and less interest in political or social topics the older he became, whereas my interest in political and social issues became increasingly acute, since I had no understanding of how present circumstances could come to repeat life at the time of Hitler. His old fury appeared to be vanishing, while I feared I had been the victim of philistine illusions about appeasement in the world and the end of the ideological contest and was afraid to get furious myself about my estrangement from how things were.

He was obsessed at that time with the dying of the forests and its presumed significance for humanity's relation to nature. He hated the policies of Ronald Reagan, Margaret Thatcher, and Helmut Kohl, the tax relief for the rich in the USA, the annihilation of the trade unions here in England and in Wales, and the submerging of German politics in a "backward and at the same time thoroughly corrupt, stagnant, stinking swamp made of money, power, and lack of good taste," as he put it if I remember right. The Challenger explosion and the nuclear meltdown at Chernobyl were negative historical markers for him that portended worse events. "That's only the beginning," he said when we talked about these things on the telephone, in a voice fraught with significance. "The beginning of what, Moritz?," I asked him. "You'll see," was the extent of what could reply, murmuring ominously – he who at no other time was short of words. Even as a young man, despite his excitement, he felt insecure about political issues, envisioning no concrete social aims, unable to identify any politicians whom he believed could do "the right thing," joined no party, not even the Greens and, given his Adornoesque negativism, considered himself an intellectual Johnny-come-lately who lacked the intellectual means to define what exactly was going wrong and what to do instead.

Perhaps that was why he increasingly turned away from things political. Later when we talked about problems of the environment or the havoc that unrestrained capitalism has caused in the former countries of the Eastern Bloc, he now merely shrugged his shoulders and said: "If humankind does not know how to behave in this world, then it will simply be thrown out; it brings about its own collective ruination., But in my estimation," as Moritz put it at that time, "this is neither a moral nor a political problem. Mankind," he opined, "has rushed into and now is stuck in a way of life that cannot be sustained over the long run and finds no way out. This is what happens to individuals who fall victim to an addiction or act fraudulently, and at times the same thing takes place in collectives. It is probably an aspect of the mechanisms at work in the death of a species. Maybe this is what happens to whales that beach themselves. They get into the wrong current or lose their orientation some other way. We have lost our orientation just as much, if we ever had it, which I doubt. Mankind," Moritz said, "has probably always just staggered across the globe, always devising nothing but phantasms, creating illusions about their plans and their abilities to accomplish them, but their dream dancing did not at first arouse much attention. This absence of an orientation, this staggering about could easily be continued for a time because only a small number of humans existed and there was much space for tottering about, and they held no particular power within the order of nature. Now we are many," the later Moritz Brandt stated, "and in addition to all of this we cause very strong repercussions due to our technical power, and that makes it inevitably noticeable that we have not the smallest glimmer of an idea what we really want to do with our lives together, where we may want to go, what we want to become. Well, and if we don't find a way out of this blind alley into which we have hastened headlong in pursuit of our illusions, if no new ideas occur to us, then we'll simply disappear. I find it impossible to think," Moritz said, "that this would be all that bad. The worst that can happen to us is the death of every single individual among us, which puts an end to the absurdity and disorientation in every single one among our contemporaries. And even if mankind vanishes, it will always be only the death of individuals, in this case merely the death of *many* individuals."

    I could not then agree with these dark thoughts and cannot even today. Moritz expressed them before the onset of his illness, in a very gloomy phase of his development. I jotted them down because they disturbed me and I could not agree with them, but also in view of plans we had of someday writing a philosophical dialogue. Richard, Margaret, and I came around to this idea one evening over dinner and I pursued it further for a while. Richard was chosen to represent a point of view favouring progress and scientific optimism. Margaret was to take up the sceptical, I the Christian, and Moritz the socialist position. After Richard's death nothing further came of these plans. But now I am glad that I kept my notebooks with Moritz's remarks, so I can review them. In contrast to Moritz, I think that our life attains to something meaningful when we participate in an activity that transcends our individual existence. If culture reaches its end – moreover, if the human species becomes extinct – then it follows that nothing continues to exist that rises above our particular existence in which we can participate. This is the parallel between the relationship that parents have with their children and the one of teachers and their students. If my students live in totally different world than mine and if, of all things, they die ahead of me, a thread snaps. Of course, parents (at least good parents) do not want their children to become images of themselves. And teachers do not want their students to think as they do, if they are good teachers. Yet even so, parents and teachers want the essential purpose of their lives to continue to evolve in those who come after them. The fact that one's own existence simply breaks off is something we must learn to accept. But can we learn to accept that the entire human world simply ends, that all traces of us will cease to exist? As soon as this real possibility appears on the horizon, a real desolation is bound to descend on all of us. I am completely unable to imagine a different outcome. And in the end, I believe that Moritz, too, despaired at the time in question and merely concealed this behind a feigned indifference.

## 100
### MARBACH: GERMAN LITERARY ARCHIVE: FROM THE DIARIES OF MORITZ BRANDT. WRITTEN ON 14 OCTOBER.

Yesterday second tutorial and for the first time Formal Hall. The Brits don't throw anything away. Even in a modern college like Churchill. Had to rent a gown just for that, at Ryder and Amies, five pounds. Can't understand how people here can work after these dinners. First sherry as an aperitif, then bubbly with the starters, red wine to go with the main meal plus three toasts (one to the Queen, one to the Prime Minister – phooey to that – one to Churchill), afterward port with dessert. To round it all off, strong, horrible English coffee. Lay awake till three. Came to life with a monster headache. Drowsy the whole lecture. Gruesome. Won't be part of it ever again. But the tutorial before was super. Cavendish offered that we use first names, so I should call her Dorothy. She says Moritz. But this is customary between profs and students. Discussion about Coleridge extremely clarifying. Nature and spirituality inseparable, she says, nature always mirror of human wishes and apprehensions, power, guilt, and punishment. Also got around to talking about the guilt we bring upon ourselves nowadays. Dorothy sees environmental destruction as less drastic than I do. Explains guilt in religious terms. Points to criticism of the ruthless exploitation of nature in Antiquity (against mining of ore). Thinks that people have always projected their fears and hopes onto landscapes, the weather, the courses of the seasons. Doesn't explain nature gods as a bad method for dominating nature through sacrifices and prayers, rather as an expression of the feeling that one lives at someone's mercy, or as a sign of gratitude, depending on whether the harvest was ruined by hail, or the granaries are filled. According to Dorothy, humans as a rule can't separate their emotions from their perceptions. Out of their insecurity and fear they feel guilty if they do something the end of which they don't foresee. A tiger has no bad conscience when it devours an antelope. Tiger has no religion. When humans lose religion, they look for another channel to regulate things and to make accusations. Maybe their relation to nature or food. It is not the case, Dorothy thinks, that is always the religions that regulate eating, for instance Judaism with its kosher kitchen. Food regulations may also be a substitute for religion, making food important. It's like that with nature. It need not be that one first suspects that a spirit lives in a tree, and then has a bad conscience about having to cut down the tree. It may also be the opposite: a human being feels bad about felling the tree and expresses this by saying that the tree spirit is angry with him. Pretty smart, this woman. Environmentalism as a substitute religion in secular times. When we perceive natural givens, then always in a particular mood, with certain feelings. Consequently, we'd inevitably believe that facts trigger these moods and feelings, are to be blamed for them. In fact, they arise from the history of mankind's emotions and different moods and not at all from momentary perceptions, most of the time, at any rate, Dorothy suggested. The fact that an aggressive bear is scary, and a putrid cadaver is repulsive or frightful is due to the bear or the cadaver. But the fact that a high mountain or the ocean or a setting sun inspires feelings of sublimity, or the divine in a person, has little to do with the mountain, ocean, and sun. Don't quite get it yet. Arranged with Dorothy to pursue these ideas further in our discussions of Emerson and Thoreau.

### 101
### FROM THE ARCHIVE OF L ADY MARGARET HALL COLLEGE, CAMBRIDGE: DIARY ENTRY OF DOROTHY CAVENDISH. WRITTEN ON 10 APRIL.

The package arrived today with Moritz Brandt's things that his sister had asked me to accept. Letters from me to him, drafts of stories and poems, as well as essays. He did in fact continue to work on the topics that we had discussed during the tutorials. His claim that he did not want to be a philosopher is not quite correct, since the essays partly amount to speculative philosophy, partly to philosophical explications of literary texts. I spent this entire day reading in them. They are good texts for someone not working professionally in philosophy. There are three very long texts: "Wilderness," "Soul," and "Nothing." "Wilderness" further develops what he wrote about nature in my class and what we then discussed, but it goes far beyond that. In every one of these texts, he seems to be concerned with transformations and with the ambition of human beings, with their desire for improvement. This is my impression after a cursory perusal. The conversion of a false convention into a real and authentic life, human change through death, the transmutation of our life through our children in whom we live on in a different and, we hope, better form, and so forth. But I cannot prepare this for publication on his behalf. I am not a philologist; I can no longer comment on what he wrote. One would also have to find a way of relating these essays to his poetic work, a task for which I am altogether unqualified and which I do not even want to undertake. His poems have always remained alien to me, given his compulsion to condense, his learned mystifications, enigmatic references, his technique of blending different epochs. He never failed to send me his poems, to be sure, and I always read them, but his way of writing poetry simply left me cold. I have to write Mariam that these things have to be added to the other material that she donated to the German Archive. I am too old and completely unqualified for this task. But I shall read everything. I am pleased all the same that he kept doing philosophy. After I finish reading what she sent, I shall write Mariam.

# The Wilderness

110
MARBACH: GERMAN LITERARY ARCHIVE:
OF MORITZ BRANDT. FILE:
MB _9919_11_285.PDF

## I

Since 1996, a man wearing green mountain boots has been lying dead in the ice-packed snow on the trail to the summit of Mount Everest. The Himalayas, the so-called "roof of the world," a mountain range with a gigantic expanse and frigid emptiness, are apt for exciting a feeling of the *sublime* in us, a feeling that Kant has analysed in his "Critique of the Power of Judgment." Sublimity, thus, has something to do with our being overwhelmed. Kant asserts that the sublime stimulates our power of imagination and, "as it were, does violence" to it because the sublime is that "which is absolutely great."[1] Furthermore, regarding the majesty of the "moral law," the categorical imperative, and our moral duty, Kant maintains that they tell us what we have to do, just as a master instructs his subjects. He states that they arouse within us a feeling of the sublimity "of our own vocation," a feeling that "enrapture[s] us more than any beauty."[2] Ever since these reflections, nature and human morality seem to be interwoven.

At the high altitude of mountains, mighty masses of rocks pile up in front of a mountaineer as he has to cross a steep talus or climb across a rock face. On the wide expanse of the ocean, a storm creates gigantic waves that can simply devour a ship. In the depth of cosmic space, a probe as big as a truck on its way to a distant planet and whose radio signals need several months to reach Earth disappears like a speck of dust in the desert. – In all these natural realms, human beings appear within proportions that undoubtedly *cannot have been made for mankind*, and things can get very dangerous here, perhaps overpowering humans and taking their lives.

By contrast, a meadow with an apple orchard, a beach with palm trees, a heath with a grazing herd of sheep, a park with a pond welcoming bathers are natural areas that do not overpower but appear to invite: attractive idylls where human beings encounter useful things: food, shade, refreshment, future warmth. Here nature seems to exist "for us." Humans seek both: pleasing idylls and grand desert landscapes. They carry an anticipation with them during their stay in these natural contexts. What is it that they expect there, that they believe they can find only there and not in their room, their house, their town? In the case of an idyll, this seems obvious: human beings first of all are looking for what is useful and appealing to them, to have a visual experience of a section of the world that they did not create, but in which they could discover a safe and pleasant place even so, where they can enjoy themselves. But what draws human beings into wilderness areas? Perhaps the desire to experience the thrill of the sublime, in analogy to watching a horror movie, in which one is exposed to the dread of fright, knowing all along that one will get through all calamities safely.

Mount Everest, where the man with the green boots lies, has been called "the highest vanishing point of human vanities."[3] Sometimes people say that a mountain has been "conquered" or "defeated" when mountaineers have succeeded in reaching its summit and return to the valley unharmed.[4] "Conquest" and "defeat" conjure the image of a battle. The exertion required to climb to the summit of a high mountain is, in this metaphor, connected to a confrontation. But, of course, in a literal sense the mountain is not an antagonist confronting its (confrontational) climbers, the way perhaps a mustang resists its first rider, and in the end may be subdued by him, the horse's resistance broken so that it will tolerate a human horseman on its back. A human being can fall off a mountain, which does not mean that he has been shaken off as from a bucking stallion. Rather, the mountain is simply there. Talking about conquest illustrates the vanity that may be involved in exposing oneself to the wilderness in mountains, on the ocean, in the desert or wherever else, to advance a certain distance there and to survive only with supreme effort. The wilderness provides dangers such as rockslides, avalanches, thunderstorms. In our way of speaking, they also "lurk" like enemies in an ambush or like wild beasts of prey that very well may actually exist in these regions. Insofar as there is a greater probability that one suffers an injury and even finds death in the wilderness than in civilization, the one who returns home unharmed must not only have been proven courageous like a warrior who has braved the mortal danger of a battle, but also to be skilful. To have mustered up this courage, to have used his own cleverness and adroitness in overcoming dangers – that is something to be *proud* of, that is what one is admired for and perhaps even honoured in public. David Hume has said that pride produces in us the idea of the self.[5] By looking back on great deeds that one has accomplished, of which one is proud, one could say in pursuing this idea: one's self *expands*. Whoever masters natural dangers, may be decorated with medals like a war hero. Edmund Hillary learned as early as during his descent from the summit that the Queen of England had ennobled him for his achievement and that his partner Tenzing

Norgay received the Cross of St. George of the United Kingdom. After their great feat, both were "greater men" than those who stayed at home and had accomplished nothing for which they were honoured and of which they could be proud.

In the wilderness, which was not made for humans and in which they appear disproportionately small to themselves, without access to food, or on the Himalayan mountains not even with enough air for breathing, the opportunity arises to demonstrate *independence*. The fact that Reinhold Messner in 1978 at Mount Everest dispensed with bottled oxygen had to do not only with his need to surpass Edmund Hillary and Tenzing Norgay. Whoever goes into the wild also wants, apart from such a competitive situation, to do without as many extraneous forms of help as possible. There no longer is a trail laid out by others that would provide orientation to the eyes and support to the feet; rather, one transgresses a boundary, best of all into a region never entered before by anybody else. One no longer can buy something to eat, nowhere join others in the warmth of a hospitable restaurant. There, a small group of people or a single person is, as one says, "all on one's own." Furthermore, anyone climbing a mountain in a solo attempt is exposed to a solitariness that can make him lose his mind. Also, the fear of making a mistake increases, because far and wide there is no help. The oxygen bottles brought along from the civilized world seem to limit, to falsify this "being on one's own"; after all, some form of help from civilization is available there. And within a more or less circumscribed frame, this has always been the case. The hiking boots, the ice picks, the nylon ropes, the plastic snow goggles, the anoraks, all components of the equipment have been developed by others and nowadays are produced industrially and not by the mountain climbers themselves. This is perhaps why certain people do not simply want to go into the wild but, like Stone Age people, also want to make everything they need with their own hands rather than obtaining it from a system of production that is based on the division of labour in which specialists – with skills and machines that one does not control and have at one's own disposal – supply the needed clothing and food.

As a youth, even I myself wanted to go into the wild, not, to climb Mt. Everest, to be sure, but no less than to Lapland, into Sarek National Park, and hike where there are no trails, not along "Kungsleden" with its cabins but cross country, through swamps and rivers, over mountains and talus piles. Many young people, most of them male, prefer this way of going into the wild. This is not due merely to their excessive energy and unrest, but also to the fact that they have always before been helped, by parents, grandparents, and teachers so that they will play "the appropriate role" in the society of which they are destined to become a part at some later time. It seems that some wish to withdraw from this purpose at least for a while without being able to find an alternative to their prearranged future. Thus, it seems to a good number of them that they have as yet no idea at all what it is they might accomplish or desire by their own inner strength, or to put it with a touch of pathos: as if they were as yet ignorant of *who they really are*, when taken at nothing but their personal identity. For this reason, the wilderness where no predetermined goals exist and to which no one brings anything but the aim of survival seems the ideal place to discover what one is able and willing to do, independent of society's pre-established aims. The wilderness then becomes a place of *self-discovery*. Whoever is in search of his self must assume first, however, that he has a self. One searches for nothing without assuming that it might exist and be discovered.

## II

The 22-year-old student Christopher McCandless also set out, in 1990, first on a trip by car, then by kayak, and finally on foot, starting his journey through the southern US and in the end travelling north into the wilds of Alaska.[6] After his graduation, his father wanted to reward him for his successful studies with a car. This he refused. His family also expected that, after his very good exams at Emory University in Atlanta, he would matriculate at Harvard Law School. But instead of continuing his education at an elite university, he donated all his money, 24,000 dollars, to the emergency-aid organization Oxfam and set out by himself. Fascinated by the writings of Jack London (another admirer of Alaska) and as a reader of the Transcendentalist philosophers and romantic devotees of nature, Ralph Waldo Emerson and Henry David Thoreau, McCandless expected to gain from a solitary life of adventure in the wilderness a greater intensity of life, and indeed a spiritual rejuvenation. Writing to a friend, he said:

"So many people live in unhappy circumstances and yet will not take the initiative to change their situation because they are conditioned to a life of security, conformity, and conservatism, all of which may appear to give one peace of mind, but in reality, nothing is more damaging to the adventurous spirit within a man than a secure future. The very basic core of a man's living spirit is his passion for adventure. The joy of life comes from our encounters with new experiences, and hence there is no greater joy than to have an endlessly changing horizon, for each day to have a new and different sun. If you want to get more out of life [ … ], you must lose your inclination for monotonous security and adopt a helter-skelter style of life that will at first appear to you to be crazy. But once you become accustomed to such a life you will see its full meaning and its incredible beauty."[7]

At school, McCandless had been an excellent long-distance runner who also subjected his fellow students to a gruelling regimen, undertaking what he called killer runs with them, across trackless terrain, through woodlands, and across construction sites. To motivate his friends, he described running to them as a kind of *spiritual exercise*, telling them they should imagine all the *evil* and the *hatred* in the world and then picture to themselves that they had to run up against these "forces of darkness."[8] Rigorous physical exertion as a moral struggle. Towards the end of high school, he considered organizing armed warfare against apartheid in South Africa. He was serious about the moral and political problems of the world, very serious, and as a reader of Tolstoy claimed that only a practical change of mind (metanoia) involving all mankind could solve these problems.

Only late in life did McCandless learn that he was the child of his father's second marriage and that his father had kept his relationship with his mother a secret from his first wife for a long time and had led a kind of double existence. A profound moral shock destroyed the ideal image he had of his father, a very successful electrical engineer and businessman. For this reason, his father's desire that he should continue his studies at a private university for the elite and pursue a distinguished academic career met with the son's refusal. It was the latter's opinion that careers are "demeaning twentieth-century inventions, more of a liability than an asset."[9] The prospect of spending his life nowhere but in the morally and politically corrupt circumstances of civilized society and of following the advice of his equally corrupt father repulsed McCandless. His biographer Krakauer, also an adventurer and mountain climber, writes that the emotions of his own youth gave him a good understanding of McCandless's frame of mind. For when he, Krakauer, climbed summits and confronted dangers during this, the whole world appeared to him in a brighter, more intense light. Apparently, the danger to his life raised his existence to a higher level, the world becoming *real*[10] only in circumstances full of risks like these. For a person like McCandless, this higher level is "higher" not simply literally, but above all in a moral and indeed spiritual sense.

The fact that social reality, including circumstances in the family, does not agree with the moral and political ideals taught in school, is a sobering experience all youngsters will have to confront at one time or another. But most of them will come to terms with this insight and recognize that the real world is a *compromise*, that life in it takes place under certain ideals, to be sure, but that these can never actually be realized in equal proportion. For some special people, such compromises are a *de-realization* of their life. They represent an impurity to them. Let's call those to whom the "ordinary world" world appears in this way, the "serious ones." A way of life that does not agree with ideals is for this kind of seriousness no real life, just as a table that does not satisfy the Euclidean measure of a circle is not a truly round table for some mathematical rigorists. Some of those who share this attitude will discover the danger to life in the wild as a way out of the disillusionment brought about by a world afflicted with compromise. A wilderness untouched by humans is pure for them in contrast to *corrupted* civilization. And even one's own life will presumably be *purified* again in this wild nature, in that these life-threatening situations in the wild no longer allow for compromises. Either one survives the danger to life, or one simply does not, due to a mistake one makes, a misstep, or a false estimation of the weather. One will either make it to the summit or one does not. Nature untouched by humans is not the perfect image of a system defined by moral or political ideals, but simply is what it is. Its reality *cannot be negotiated* like that of the civilized world of human beings. Whoever crosses the border from the world of civilization into the wilderness leaves a negotiable human world for a non-negotiable non-human world. McCandless planned to survive alone in Alaska's wilds for at least a year and then return to the world of humanity. He hoped that this experience would bring about a rejuvenation of his existence that had become vapid at an early stage on account of his disappointment with the half-heartedness and imperfection of human circumstances, in which nothing is precisely what it authentically was meant to be and thus should be. He was hoping for a "spiritual leap." And that leap also seemed to take place in fact. "Being close to dying and then having survived is the strongest emotion we can have," is how another boundary crosser between the human and non-human world put it.[11] McCandless wrote in his diary in Alaska:

*I am reborn. This is my dawn. Real life has just begun. Deliberate Living: Conscious attention to the basics of life, and a constant attention to your immediate environment and its concerns, example: A job, a task, a book; anything requiring efficient concentration (Circumstance has no value. It is how one relates to a situation that has value. All true meaning resides in the personal relationship to a phenomenon, what it means to you).*
*The Great Holiness of FOOD, the Vital Heat.*
*Positivism, the Unsurpassable Joy of the Life Aesthetic.*
*Absolute Truth and Honesty.*
*Reality.*
*Independence.*
*Finality – Stability – Consistency.*[12]

A person who is climbing a rock face and loses his concentration grabs for the wrong support and falls into an abyss. A person in a storm striking the sails of his sailboat too late may not only lose his mast but, to make matters worse, may capsize and perish in the frigid water. A person who in the desert fails to apportion his water correctly and estimates the distance to be covered inaccurately will die of thirst. Because the wilderness was not made for humans and nothing in it is negotiable, those who enter it have to pay precise attention to what they do when and must be fully alert and sharply focused. A simple use of the hand can decide about life or death. There is no longer flexibility, no preliminary option. If one wants to stay alive, what counts is what one does *now* or neglects to do.

Objectives thus perceived with taut attention and alertness to fatal dangers appear to be more intense than all preliminaries of an existence not taking place in this danger. Danger perhaps even becomes a consciously chosen means of focusing attention in this way, because focused attention intensifies perception and consequently lets life appear "more real." It need not be a fatal danger that causes this sharpening of focus. People in love or in a religious ecstasy, too, always think of no one but their beloved or their god and thus experience a heightened intensity of perception. Something similar happens to people who are completely occupied with a work of art or a scientific project. For them, too, everything they experience in pursuing this work has "a higher degree of intensity" because they do it "fully committed." It is perhaps no coincidence that people speak of "adventures in love" and refer to science as "the ultimate adventure" – a terminology like that used about excursions into the wild. In all these cases, human beings appear to be fully challenged as well as completely concentrated. If ordinary life with its distractions and its provisional decisions is incapable of making its ideals real (which to these serious people turns this life into something provisional and unserious), then the possibility of death (or of love or of ultimate insight) brings forth a serious, intense, and significant existence in which human beings appear to themselves and their life appears to them definitive and real in an eminent sense.

But McCandless was not always cautious. At some time, he had difficulties procuring food in Alaska. Most of the time he stayed alive eating squirrels and birds that he shot with a rifle. Once he brought down an elk. But he was unable to protect the huge animal's masses of meat from the flies and to preserve them. Hence, the bulk of it spoiled and McCandless was tormented by his bad conscience over the ultimately useless killing of this beautiful creature. When he believed that his time in the wilderness had been fulfilled and he wanted to return to civilization, he had to notice that his way back had been cut off when the spring thaw had swollen the river and made it impassable. (He was travelling almost entirely without the aid of instruments, that is, even though he had a rifle, he did not have a map and a compass. Therefore, he did not know that he could have crossed the river using a basket suspended from a cable a few kilometres from his current position.) He went back and tried to make do with pieces of fruit and roots. But he mistook the poisonous fruits of a potato tuber for the edible ones and died. He had time to recognize his mistake when he was tormented by dizziness and nausea: in the book he consulted to identify plants, he determined precisely what he had eaten. But by then it was too late.

Krakauer, McCandless's biographer, in one passage of his representation of this serious individual, looks back on his own youth. When he remembers that he had several times failed in his solo attempt to climb a particularly difficult mountain (the

Devil's Thumb in British Columbia) because he had gotten into a snowstorm, he asks himself why he had taken these exertions upon himself in the first place. He could easily have lost his life, just as McCandless had. Like the latter's father, his own was very ambitious for his children, looked at life as a constant struggle, and expected of them extremely high performances in school. He expected his son to be accepted not into Harvard Law, but into Harvard Medical School, and prepared him for this career since preschool days.[13] But Krakauer, behaving exactly like McCandless, resisted his father's ambitions, becoming a carpenter and a mountain climber. Near the Devil's Thumb, however, it dawned on him that his father's ambitions were still defining his life, despite his refusal to pursue a medical career. Instead of directing his intentions to his admissions test at Harvard, he realized, he had focused it on a solo climb across the difficult ice route at the Devil's Thumb. It merely seemed that he was concerned with the mountain and the wilderness. In reality, *he himself* was his issue; he was still labouring to rid himself of the demands that had been inculcated in him since his childhood and youth, when with crampon and ice pick he tried to climb up the North Wall to the summit of the mountain. He did not discover his true self there, he only attempted in a different way to make real what his father expected of him.

Reinhold Messner, who has climbed every mountain of eight thousand meters in a solo effort without bottled oxygen, once described himself, with reference to the drudgery of high-altitude mountain climbing), as a "Sisyphus," but "the stone that I roll up the mountain is my own psyche."[14] This remark is perhaps concerned with the act of self-*overcoming* that is the price one has to pay to advance in the oxygen-depleted air even as one is attacked by great weakness and exhaustion. And this overcoming of the weak self, if it succeeds, most likely, if I understand Messner correctly, ends in an *expansion* and *rejuvenation* of this very self. Even if this overcoming of the self in the zone of death is not a "spiritual leap," then at least it seems to be a temporary transformation of the *limited* self of a person to facilitate its temporary rejuvenation and expansion.

## III

It need not be the desire for existential rejuvenation and spiritual progress, however, as it was for McCandless, or the wish far extreme high performances, as in Jon Krakauer's case, that drives people into the wilderness. By contrast, the philosopher Val Plumwood, highly experienced in untouched nature after many trips through the bush, set out in 1985 by canoe into an apparent idyll of water lilies and birds in the lagoons of Kakadu National Park in Australia's Northern Territory. She sought to combine the delights of nature with those of art. On this journey, she not only sought enjoyment from exotic flora and fauna, but also wanted to visit a work of aboriginal rock art. Yet it was not just the weather that was uncooperative on this outing There were strong rainstorms. On her boat trip she also encountered a "curious rock formation" along the shore, where a large rock was balanced on top of a small one, a sight that created two ideas in her mind: First, she had not informed the indigenous inhabitants of these parks, the Gagadu, about her trip. And second, she was travelling through an area populated by a large number of saltwater crocodiles. Due to the uncomfortable weather and in view of the peculiarity of the unstable rock structure about which her notes left no clear indication whether it was a work of art, a warning sign erected by the natives, or a fluke of nature, she became aware of how precarious her own life had become in this location. The saltwater crocodiles that lived in these lagoons made it at that time one of "the most dangerous places of the world."[15] For Plumwood, this perception of nature became a symbol for what was about to happen to her: the weather and the rock formation seemed to intimate something: that she did not belong here.

And, in fact, this intuition (or projection?) at the outset of her journey proves to be a premonition of something worse than the constantly deteriorating weather. Plumwood is unable to locate the aboriginal wall paintings she is looking for. She gets lost in the rivulets of the lagoon and, due to the heavy downpours and strong wind, decides to return. As she starts on her way back, she notices a large tree trunk floating in the water. She is taken aback that she had completely missed it on her way out. As her boat approaches it, it turns out to be a crocodile that not only had sighted her as she was paddling by, but also is following her now. In the end, it lashes out at the canoe, apparently seeking to toss her out of her boat as its prey. Hectically she tries to reach the shore and find safety on the branches of a tree, a myrtle heather. Yet, just as she stands up in her canoe to leap on to the tree branches, the crocodile shoots out of the water, its jaws snatching her between her legs and pulling her down beneath the surface of the water. A frantic life-and-death struggle ensues. The crocodile twists around its axis, holding its prey between its jaws to drown it below the water. Plumwood survives two rotations. She tries to attack her attacker by poking out its eyes but fails. When she is back above water, the reptile relaxes its grip, and she tries again to climb the tree. Yet, the beast snatches her again, this time biting into her thigh and pulling her below the surface. She survives even this second attack. Strangely enough, the crocodile finally releases her. She can drag herself onto the swampy bank where, with serious injuries, she is found at last and rescued.

As she is fighting for her life in the crocodile's jaws, Plumwood observes herself producing the idea that what is just happening to her cannot be real but only a nightmare. Yet, she immediately discards this idea as wishful thinking. In retrospect, she interprets the emergence of this idea as the workings of subjectivity that incessantly attempts to create and preserve a continuous self. Death is incompatible with this continuity; above all, being shredded to pieces as fodder for another living being cannot be reconciled with this aim of stabilizing the continuity of our spiritual and physical existence. Therefore, the prospect of being eaten, once it can no longer be interpreted as a nightmare, leads to a sudden reversal of how she experiences the world and nature. Plumwood writes that, in a split-second realization, she saw the world for the first time "from the outside," saw it as a world that was not *my world*, an unrecognizable, disconsolate landscape of uncouth reality, indifferent to my living or dying.[16]

The *beautiful* wild idyll, that of a park made by human beings for others of their kind and left undifferentiated in Plumwood's heart, had been turned by the crocodile's attack into a *gruesome* and cold, not even sublime wilderness that, beyond any doubt, had not been made for her, but in which her death was meant to enable the self-preservation of another being. The beautiful flowers and birds that had charmed the observer's eyes and ears had vanished from her attention. It was not the pain caused by the crocodile's bite that had driven her away from the focus of her perception. (For this pain was to appear only later on firmer ground after she had been rescued.) It was the *fear of death*, triggered by the previously unexperienced strength concentrated in the powerful jaws of the attacking beast of prey, that made the idyllic world fade and a different one arise, It was a world in which nothing has been arranged by human beings to accommodate other human beings and in which no negotiations between humans have been conducted but in which fighting, killing, and being devoured occurs.

Being killed from a fall on a mountain, dying of thirst in the desert, or losing one's life by freezing or drowning in the ocean is fundamentally different than being eaten by a beast of prey. The wilderness worlds of mountainous, sandy, or watery deserts have not been created as human habitations. One can survive there only with difficulties. Whoever makes a mistake there, perishes. But mountain, desert, and ocean do not *hunt* people. The wild beast of prey that pursues a human being demonstrates in a much more memorable way, i.e. through the confrontation with the *will* of another being trying to kill us, that wild nature is not there "for us," that not everything in it fits together. When seen from the experience of big-game hunters with beasts of prey, the wilderness appears differently *antagonistic in itself* from civilization that succeeds in the interest of humans. In this kind of world, in the wilderness, fights between individuals against each other take place for the sake of self-preservation. The prey senses that the hunter's focus is aimed at it, and the prey focuses on the hunter and on its own self-preservation. Again, it is not nature's beauty, but this time truly the fight that concentrates all attention. This creates a special alertness, a vigilance of the kind that we know from the gaze of a stalking tiger and of the desperately fleeing cow.

Humans are successful hunters. For this reason, they have for millennia occupied the upper end of the food chain, which means that they make a meal of everything: the wild crocodiles, sharks, whales, the millions of animals raised to be eaten: cattle, hogs, and chickens. They are also hardly ever threatened by preying cats and wolves. Therefore, they barely imagine any longer that they might be food for other creatures except in a horror movie. The only kind of will that nowadays confronts a person is that of other *human beings*. The notion that one has to fight against a mountain and conquer it as if it were a being gifted with a will is nothing but a metaphor. Yet, Val Plumwood's experience shows that humans may to this day be food for other beings and that in this reversal of the hunter-prey relationship, an animal may confront a human in the most elementary and radical manner. It is only in conquered nature that everything seems beneficial to human beings. The possibility that they themselves may be meat for other living beings and in this very simple sense may be useful to them, appears unimaginable to civilized persons, and if it in fact is imaginable, then only in a fairy-tale way in a safe seat at the movies watching gruesome film scenes such as are shown in *Jurassic Park* when a Tyrannosaurus Rex snatches and chows down on a human being, the way we put away a little meatball as an appetizer. But the realistic, unimaginable possibility that oneself could become food for other creatures endowed with a will, results from nothing other than our superior *weapons technology* and the protection provided by civilization, which demonstrates the fact that we have severely decimated or fully eradicated those that could turn ourselves, the human hunters, into the *hunted* wild game.

The German philosopher Hans Blumenberg has described humans as beings who primarily confront the world at a *distance*, i.e. with *concepts* that keep the immediate perception of whichever different individual beings away from them. They also use *weapons employed from a distance* with which they can chase beasts of prey away and turn them into victims.[17] In a fight at close quarters with a crocodile or tiger, the weak human being has few chances to survive. When throwing stones, rocks, or spears, shooting arrows, or even using a rifle, he can very well fend off those who seek to devour him and may even turn them into his meal. This human ability of self-protection from a menacing creature by acting at a distance achieves its apex in *placing traps*. Any arbitrary animal can fall into a trap, any fish whatsoever can take the bait on the hook of a fisherman's line. Seen in this way, the trap is *something general* that is most highly useful to the one setting it up, because it provides him with food without having to put himself in harm's way when killing his prey. Blumenthal recognizes this event as the first triumph of conceptual thinking and considers its application a distinction empowering a way of life that is *too weak* for an *immediate* confrontation with the world. It allows man to keep the threatening wilderness literally away from his flesh and bones so that he may be able to survive. Blumenberg writes:

"The trap is an action in the absence of the beast of prey and, with a temporal distance, of the hunter. The trap acts for the hunter in the moment when he himself is absent, whereas the creation of the trap reveals the reverse of these relations. The trap is a materialized expectation. In this sense, the trap is the first triumph of the concept."[18]

To put this thought into reverse terms: the concept is a trap into which all those individuals fall who somehow are suited for it. From this perspective, it is no coincidence that, in his dialogue *Sophists*, Plato demonstrates logical thinking with its conceptual classification of the world according to generic divisions (*dihairesis*) by using a system followed by hunters, anglers, and trappers.[19] What Val Plumwood experienced, in this respect constitutes a relapse: as a philosopher and distanced observer, as the descendent of generations of hunters occupying the upper end of the food chain, she had set out on a contemplative journey in her own canoe gliding along through fields of water lilies and among colourful birds in order to enjoy them from a distance, perhaps to classify them scientifically as belonging to this or that species of plants, and finally to study indigenous rock art. Her trip ended between the jaws of a crocodile that had identified her as nutritious prey, with which she had to fight for her life, and from which she was able to escape only by accident, not by her own strength. It is hardly possible to come into more direct contact with another being than in the moment when one is in immediate danger of being devoured by this adversary. Plumwood emphasizes how closely what happened to her recalls an act of rape and was accordingly sexualized by the media that had picked up her story.[20] During sex, during a meal, and when one is being eaten, all conceptual and other distances vanish. Yet, horrible as the immediacy of being eaten is and as intense as the experienced immediacy during a consensual erotic encounter may be, the normal life of a modern human is determined by conceptual mediation and is lived at a considerate, calculating distance from reality. This has become the *normal circumstance* for "successful" civilized persons because they have worked their way up to the very top of the food chain. Some consider this state of normality a *banal* state of civilization; banal for its lack of *perilous, exciting immediacy*. Whoever seeks to escape from this banality will sooner or later set off into the unknown of the wild (or into a so-called amorous adventure or to "new frontiers of knowledge" in science) and will accept the price to be paid for non-banal experiences of immediacy.

The wilderness as territory in which humans can survive by their own resilience thus offers not only the opportunity of experiencing self-expansion. But Val Plumwood's example shows that we realize "our" weakness just as frequently. "We" are no crocodiles, tigers, or sharks that can prove their capabilities in a direct confrontation with reality. Nothing but cleverness, the ability to think at least around three corners, conceptualization, and the skill of trapping enable us to survive. That is why we have not been made for the wilderness, which is an area for those who are strong in immediate confrontations.

The distanced existence of human beings encompasses ambiguities. On the one hand, it offers "weak mankind" security, rest, at times even protection in a loving communal life. In the city, one need not fear being attacked by a wolf or crocodile. Here, only other people can get too close to us. Everything here has been created by humans for humans. But life thus mediated and pre-structured by humans seems to lack the *intensity* of an immediate, not conceptually mediated confrontation with reality. This trenchant potency is experienced, for example, when, in a situation of fatal danger, one's attention is focused entirely on the present moment as something potentially finite, and when this present time no longer entails a symbolic reference to something else. Humans who did not rescue themselves from the wilderness by returning to the city, who did not very recently return from a lonely Himalayan expedition and are now joining their loved ones in a warm living room but have spent their entire life in civilization, for this reason yearn for the intensities and the immediacy of wild nature. It also seems to them possible to encounter their own selves the way they authentically are, independent of the expectations and projections of other people, primarily their fathers and mothers. Not only is *everything* external subject to conceptual-symbolic mediation, but I also know myself only through the expectations of those other people, through the effect I have on them and through their reactions to the effects I have on them. Civilized man exists for himself or herself only through social mediation. Whoever wishes to get to know himself or herself, presumably directly (if there is something there to get to know in the first place), therefore must go into the wild – and alone, at that. The question is only if this is the right place to encounter oneself, if an immediate relation to oneself can in fact be possible.

## IV

In the northeast of New York State lies Adirondack Park with its gentle mountains and large lakes. In August 1858, before this territory was declared a nature preserve, a company of philosophers, natural scientists, and artists set out for this area to set up a camp and live in a place where "Nothing was ploughed, or reaped, or bought, or sold."[21] The amazed public wondered what the true plans and expectations of these scholars and artists might be. Those moving into nature included the philosopher Ralph Waldo Emerson.

Seventeen years earlier, Emerson had introduced his essay on "Nature" with a reflection on his era in American history. He thought that the time in which he was living was a retrospective age, erecting memorials in honour of ancestors, writing biographies, engaging in historical reflections and critical analyses, whereas previous generations had still lived in an *immediate relationship* with "God and nature." Why, the author asks, "should not we also enjoy the original relation to the universe?" Instead of groping "among the dry bones of the past," Emerson exhorts us to avail ourselves of that "nature whose floods of life stream around and through us and invite us by the powers they supply to actions proportioned to nature."[22]

These are words that betray a dissatisfaction with or even a suffering from a life that has been *mediated historically*. Tradition appears as a burden that makes it impossible to perceive the world with upright honesty and fresh vision. It is no coincidence that in this connection Emerson speaks of the *ancestors* (he writes: fathers). He propounds the perspective of someone who does not yet feel that he is independent and has grown up. Europe, the continent from which one's mothers and fathers set off for America, continues to define the culture of those who were born in the USA as the children of immigrants. The cultures inherited from the parents' countries prevent the children from living in their own world. They appear compelled to go on looking at their country with the eyes of those who had trained their way of seeing in a different, older culture. The remedy to cure this affliction is envisioned as a *return to nature* that has not been determined by the history of old cultures, but that renews itself on its own. This return movement is expected to rejuvenate one's perspective and indeed one's whole situation in the world.

This perspective does not see history as a continuous overcoming of a dangerous state of nature. History is not perceived as the process of passing on such forms of cleverness as improve the chances of survival for more and more human beings, those users of conceptual language and makers of traps. Rather, it is considered a *burden* that bends the back, forces one's eyes to look down, no longer permitting people to peer into nature straight. History for Emerson estranges one from the world. It is the factor in a person's life that prevents immediacy of experience.

It is not by chance that these words, even at the end of the 20th century, could still exert a powerful effect on young men like Christopher McCandless whose dominant fathers prescribed a certain course of life for them. They are *words of emancipation*, of an emancipation that is not to be achieved through a specific *political activity*, but through a turn towards nature. This Emersonian nature is one that is *well-intentioned towards humanity*, that "stretcheth out her arms to embrace man." Everything in this nature "incessantly" collaborates "for the profit of man." Emerson is completely unaffected by Kant's criticism of the teleological notion that it is an illusion to assume that nature is a force supporting human purposes. He is also altogether untouched by his reference to the overwhelming power of the wilderness, as he sings his Solomonic hymn to the wind that spreads the seeds for man, to the sun that evaporates the water of the sea so that the breeze can carry it on to the fields as rain where it will in turn make the plants grow that nourish the animals – within this nature live "endless circulations of the divine charity" that will "nourish man."[23] Man is also conscious of a *universal soul* within or behind his individual life. Because this nature is endowed with a living soul, indeed is divine, having a universal soul, man is well protected, as if in Abraham's hands. Here, "no disgrace, no calamity" can befall him "which nature cannot repair." Not a word about death, devouring, and being devoured can be found in this text. "Even the corpse has its own beauty." Because in nature I become a "part or particle of God" and because God or nature is eternal, also my death is really nothing.[24]

Barely 100 years before this text was written, an earthquake had destroyed Lisbon in 1755. This event challenged Europe's intellectuals with the renewed relevance of the question that the learned world canonized as the problem of theodicy: how should God, as the creator of a nature in which catastrophes of this magnitude can happen, be imaginable as an all-benevolent, almighty, and omniscient being? Concepts of nature like those Emerson espoused were no longer a suitable standard to live by. The identification of God as universal soul united with Nature turns the problem of *theodicy* into a problem of *physiodicy*. How can nature be understood as benevolent, nourishing, and healing when it unleashes the eradicating fury of earthquakes and tsunamis, when its volcanic eruptions and meteoric impacts annihilate complete animal populations, when crocodiles swim in it and snatch philosophizing women, and when young readers of Emerson die because they fail to recognize the difference between two deceptively similar-looking plants? Does Emerson's text manifest a naiveté based on ignorance, or does it have more profound reasons for its harmonious views of natural circumstances?

Emerson found a famous successor even while he was still alive. But he also experienced strong opposition. The one who followed him was Henry David Thoreau, who in 1845 built and started to live in a cabin in a forest on Emerson's property near Walden Pond, then began to write about his stay in this sylvan solitude by the pond in 1846. A critic of Emerson and Thoreau was Herman Melville, the author of *Moby-Dick*, who, in his book *The Confidence Man* (1857), has these two denizens of an idyll appear briefly, and who both in his story "The Piazza" and in his great novel develops a different understanding of nature. Let's first look at Thoreau.

# V

In a chapter titled "economy," Thoreau begins the record of his solitary existence in the log cabin by describing the usual life of people in civilized communities as primarily characterized by *indebtedness*. In a society defined by the division of labour, everyone is dependent on others attending to his needs, making his shoes, producing his food, building his house, constructing his carriage. For this I am indebted to these others, he writes, and as a consequence my own work serves most of all to pay off these debts, for example with the money that my work has earned.[25] Seen from this point of view, the division of labour does not *make life easier*, but amounts to a pitiable form of entanglement, of social bondage that various traditions have referred to as "alienation." I depend on innumerable others and have to spend my entire life satisfying the obligations I have accumulated towards them, thus being forced to work much longer than would otherwise be necessary.

According to Thoreau, a person who inherits a farm must toil on his land to produce more food than he can consume himself, so as to make the money needed to acquire the agricultural equipment that he cannot produce himself but must buy on credit. A different form of agriculture is not possible in a society where a few must produce food for many others. Autonomy and independence (the author writes: "self-emancipation") consequently remain a mere figment of the imagination. *Everyone* in a society based on the division of labour must work longer hours than would be needed if he or she had to be concerned with nothing other than taking care only of his or her self-preservation. As one's own existence descends into debt and toil, no time is left for reflecting on one's own life and self.

Life turns into something altogether unfree. The consequence of this is: "The mass of men lead lives of quiet desperation. What is called resignation is confirmed desperation. [ …] A stereotyped but unconscious despair is even concealed under what are called the games and amusements of mankind."²⁶ According to Thoreau, humankind has for generations been entangled in this hopelessness as much as in original sin, which is why the older generation has no advice for young people about a right kind of life that does not have to be spent in despair.

To the despair that ensues from the unfree life in society characterized by labour, Thoreau juxtaposes free life in nature. He writes in his discourse on walking, "I wish to speak a word for Nature, for absolute freedom and wildness, as contrasted with a freedom and culture mere civil, – to regard man as an inhabitant, or a part and parcel of Nature, rather than a member of society."²⁷ In order to attain this freedom, Thoreau states, it is necessary literally *to set out*. One has to *go away*. Not merely a *rejection* of expensive technical means of making a living seems required, but also a separation from emotional entanglements and connections. This calls to mind Jesus, who demands of his disciples that they abandon their families and follow him. It may remind us of McCandless, who leaves his family and with inevitable frequency his friends on his trips before his final break-out journey to Alaska. Thoreau writes: "If you are ready to leave father and mother, and brother and sister, and wife and child and friends, and never see them again, – if you have paid your debts, and made your will, and settled all your affairs, and are a free man, then you are ready for a walk."²⁸ R. W. Emerson, this "sauntering through the woods and over the hills and fields" takes place, so to speak, as a religious performance in absolute freedom "from all worldly engagements."²⁹ In this search for freedom, for self-sufficiency that leads Thoreau to build his cabin on Walden Pond in order to escape the despair of a life of labour in society, he finds mental orientation in ideals espoused by *ancient Stoic philosophy*. He puts up his house with his own hands because the special skills of the architect, it seems to him, only serve to provide ornamental finery and, apart from that, appear to increase the cost of one's housing immensely and needlessly. Or else it is at the service of magnifying the splendour displayed by secular and religious powers in palaces and temples, powers he suspects of subjugating mankind. He is the carpenter of his furniture and bakes his own bread, he tends his own vegetables and works his field with his own hands. He likewise disdains using working animals such as horses or oxen whose servitude could ease the drudgery of providing for one's necessities, make it possible to erect works of art and luxury, and help to plough fields that might produce crops exceeding one's domestic requirements.[30]

Thoreau fundamentally doubts the progress that a society dominated by the division of labour is supposed to have created. The human spirit of invention comes up, to be sure, with "pretty toys," but they distract our attention from the "serious things." He goes on to say that human ingenuity produces improved means for unimportant aims. "We are in great haste to construct a magnetic telegraph from Maine to Texas; but Maine and Texas, it may be, have nothing important to communicate."[31] For this reason, a retreat from society, from civilization only *seems* to be a loss. Any person breaking away from a system in which workers are divided by the division of labour does indeed lose highly specialized skills. But as he liberates himself from debts and obligations, he gains autonomy in the pursuit of his aims. To be bound to *these* burdens distracts from his own goals, which is why renouncing costly expenditures can make it possible to better concentrate on his intentions. For example, anyone who intends to travel the world but seeks to do so using expensive means of transportation, for which he can pay only by working overtime, will hardly be able to take this trip around the world because he will have to spend most of his time working to earn the money for his travels. Therefore, Thoreau concentrates on autonomy, and on time being freely available for the pursuit of his own aims – on *independence from the means* that others provide and that he has to purchase from them. To gain independence and free time is his decisive focus in that he sees the genuine aims in life as *internal*. All work and any refinement ultimately must be in the service of what is *spiritual and internally ethical*, of the direct encounter with his own self.

With this idea, Thoreau does not enter new intellectual territory. His sceptical stance towards communal life directly connects him with Emerson, who wrote:

"Society everywhere is in conspiracy against the humanity of every one of its members. Society is a joint-stock company, in which the members agree, for better securing enough food for each shareholder, to surrender the liberty and culture of the eater. The virtue most strongly in demand is conformity. Self-reliance is a profound aversion. [Society] loves not realities and creators, but names and customs."[32]

Already Epicurus had recommended living in a *secluded place* and, as far as possible, simplifying life, adjusting one's needs to what can also be attained directly.[33] Thoreau, too, has ancient predecessors concerning the withdrawal from emotional entanglements. For example, Lucretius cautioned against erotic passions as states of confusion that jeopardize one's independence.[34] Seneca likewise considered amorousness to be a submissive and worthless state that is to be avoided by those who are striving for insight.³⁵ At least for some ancient philosophers, love, family, sociability, and busyness can be reconciled with the autonomous life only with considerable difficulty, and they are not conducive to one's mental development. Retreat and a lack of commitment extending as far as possible are an ancient ideal for life, presumably leading to wisdom. The autonomous rationality (*autarkia*), then, of a life in philosophy is to be achieved more reliably in solitude, devoid of commitments, than in an engagement for a better community.³⁶

"Keep in mind that it is not only the desire for an office and for wealth that makes you submissive and a slave of the others, but also the desire for peace, for leisure, for travels, and learning. For it makes no difference what the external objects are; the value that you attribute to them subjects you to the others."³⁷

Instead of withdrawing into a barrel like Diogenes, Thoreau, in following ancient philosophers who were seeking *autarkia*, chose sylvan solitude as the model for his philosophical life: nature as the place for inner reflection and the search for the true self. Like, for example, the ancient critics of Plato – among them the Cynics –, he does not consider the contemplation of *transcendent subjects* or mathematical ideas the genuine philosophical project. Rather, he finds it in the proper execution of ordinary acts of self-preservation such as planting vegetables, cooking and cleaning, and the contemplation of oneself. It is not abstract theory and ideas about improving the world, but practical autonomy and self-realization in everyday life that guide Thoreau's strategy for wisdom. Describing one's own work and the natural environment in which it takes place serve to sharpen one's alertness and ability to focus. This protects one from the dissipation of a complicated life in civilization, where this life is spent in satisfying multiple obligations. A withdrawn existence also makes it possible to live independent of philosophical teachers. Their place is taken up by *self-reflection*. The Roman stoic Marcus Aurelius captured this purpose in his diary, written partly for himself, partly for the benefit of others. This work is also an exemplary precedent that Thoreau follows in his journals about the Concord and Merrimack Rivers, about Walden Pond, the Maine Wood, and Cape Cod. Thoreau's writings about nature are a report on his self-liberation and self-development in a benign wilderness. He did not write them because he saw an existence within the conformity of civilization as support in the interest of self-preservation and rescue from the dangers of nature. Rather, he saw this uniformity as the reason for his estrangement from his true self, and for his despair. *Nature Writing* as documentation of self-realization.

## VI

Even though crocodiles do not exist in idyllic Walden Pond, they cannot simply be made to disappear in some areas of the wilderness, unless one exterminates them. Their number in the Kakadu Lagoons was subject to fluctuation because humans would hunt them down whenever one of their own had become the victim of a reptile. People were trying to kill, as it were, as many hungry enemies as possible. Sometime before Val Plumwood had set out on her fateful journey, hunting for crocodiles had become illegal due to such a phase of decimation. At the time the philosopher entered the lagoons, the crocodile population had recovered and had greatly increased, so its members were hungry most of the time. The paddling intruder happened to show up during an unfortunate phase of the classic fluctuation in the relationship between hunter and prey. When the number of hunters (let's say, foxes) increases significantly, they decimate their source of food (say, rabbits), which subsequently severely decreases their own number because they go hungry, and some of their litter starve. As the foxes are being decimated, the rabbit population can return to a life in greater security and increase. Once again, the foxes have more food and their numbers increase, decimating their prey: a fluctuation that continues perpetually.[38]

The ratio of humans to predatory animals in the wilderness is likely to present a somewhat different picture, but even here, one may speculate, such a fluctuation may occur ever since civilised life has existed. Civilisation's safety allows us to observe the wilderness from without, as if in a display case. Rarely do but a few crocodiles catch a human being. When their number increases, it is more likely that someone will become their victim. But this infuriates people to the point that they seriously reduce the number of wild crocodiles. If, however, people also want to admire the reptiles as inhabiting a sublime nature or hunt them vigorously as suppliers of leather, then such irate behaviour gives way to a protective response. Presumably, this is how humans have behaved towards many other predators. For example, they have eradicated almost all wolves, eagles, and bears because these animals were competitors in the hunt for the same prey of deer and rabbits or because a wolf and a bear, like crocodiles, enjoy a meal of human meat. But after such extirpation campaigns, the wilderness was no longer really wild. The "balance" of nature supposedly had been disturbed and humans put these creatures under their protection as a part of nature, since they are, after all, also symbols of strength, of sublime greatness. They are beings that can survive in the immediate circumstances of the wilderness without the clever skill of placing traps. Thus, the predators increase once more, make a comeback, invade areas again where they had widely become unknown. Wolves returning to villages, however, and a bear standing in front of a kindergarten – that usually is considered too much wilderness and no longer just visual-aid material and a symbol of strength that can be observed in a box, but something that "invades" civilization. Sufficient reason to decimate the predators, once again to re-establish safety. (By the way, Val Plumwood did not want human hunters to wreak vengeance on the crocodiles, even though they were preparing for exactly that. Instead, after the attack she became committed to wilderness protection, including the predatory animal that had almost taken her life.) A wilderness that can be observed and visited from the safety of civilization is different from on from which there is no longer *an escape*. The ideal situation for people seems to one availing both the safety of life as provided by civilization and the opportunity to get out into the wilderness for a short while to recuperate from daily routine. Yet, when the wilderness is used as a place of recuperation, man himself is not a wild creature but one who takes a leave of absence from his normal life (to vary a locution of Robert Musil's).[39] Where does man encounter himself – in the smart world of civilization or in the brutality of the wilderness? In civilization, he experiences his ability to stay at a distance; in the wilderness, he comes face to face with his own frailty in direct confrontations, at best with his pertinacity. Is one of these two human natures the *true one*?

The change of perspective that is implicit in this fluctuation of civilized humanity's reaction to wild animals represents either an attitude of *contemplating* or of *being involved* in the wilderness. It is also a topic that occupied Herman Melville at great length and in direct opposition to Emerson and Thoreau.

## VII

In Melville's story "The Piazza" of 1856, a first-person narrator reports that he, strangely enough, has a veranda built on the north side of his recently acquired old-fashioned country home so that he may sit there and enjoy the view into the wild landscape. The narrator considers it a disadvantage that this former farmhouse did not have a place from which to look safely into nature, neither from inside through a window nor sitting in the open but staying in a pleasant intermediate area – he sees this as similar to the lack of a bench that one could use to study the works of art in a picture gallery.[40] Such places of rest are needed to learn how to venerate nature, much in the same way that one requires pews in a church to practice piety.

Melville's ironic parallelism that conjoins the contemplation of art works with religious contemplation and the observation of nature immediately suggests a criticism of Emerson's and Thoreau's enthusiasm for nature. The house into which the narrator moves had been a farmhouse. The people who lived there before were no observers of nature but tilled the fields around the building. A farmer who all day had ploughed, sowed, and harvested his piece of land and had gathered wood in the forest, would not of all things want to spend his evening contemplating the places where he had toiled. (Thoreau would reply that he may not have to work his field in such inhumane drudgery if he did not live in a society defined by the division of labour.) Likewise, the houses of fishermen rarely have a large window from which to look out at the sea. Their inhabitants rarely find it edifying to view from the safety of their home, of all places, the often dangerous and harsh place in nature where they work. It is more likely the distance of those enjoying their leisure in nature that permits them to idealize it contemplatively. Whoever can look across a pasture on a steep hillside from a higher point of view without having to mow its grass will see it through different eyes than the farmer on a mountain meadow who has the hard task of bringing in his hay harvest.

Distances of any kind, special, temporal, or cultural, seem inevitably to invite observers of nature to invent idealizations. Thus, it may be assumed that earlier *times* must have been golden, and a *distant* culture appears to be *noble* because past acts of meanness and past times of destitution have been forgotten (or are known only to historians); only the (presumably) major deeds accomplished then are still preserved. A foreign culture, only half-understood and for this reason experientially distant, can therefore be interpreted with deliberate neglect of all vexations familiar from one's own culture. This leads to the imaginary creation of a primordial paradise where humans still lived in immediate nearness to God and nature, and of the noble savage who in his alien tribal culture knows no deception and enjoys a free sexuality. The enthusiasm for nature arises above all from the distanced perspective of the leisurely walker who looks down from the summit into the valley and sees the farmhouses down below arrayed in uncalculated order. The contemplative observer, who is not involved in what he sees through work or as a combatant, may think about all this whatever comes to his mind and, as most people do, will prefer to imagine something pleasant rather than something unpleasant.

This is also true of Melville's narrator in "The Piazza." At different times of the year, as he is looking northward from his new veranda, he notices a vivid sparkle like a light signal. His glance does not proceed directly to this light, but the sun, wandering through the other three corners of the earth behind his back, sheds its light on all objects within the narrator's field of vision. It shines as a theatre spotlight does onto the proscenium stage. And so, sometime in May, rain falls and creates far in the distance a splendid rainbow. He believes he is looking into a fairyland as he remembers the fairy-tale promise "that, if one can but get to the rainbow's end, his fortune is made in a bag of gold."[41]

One day, when the narrator stays inside his house to cure himself of an ailment ("Nice to have a retreat like this available!" Melville seems intent on letting us know implicitly), without being able to let his eyes rove into nature, he returns to his veranda as a convalescent, looks into the distance from which the vivid sparkle seems to have vanished. Then he looks at a "Chinese creeper of [his] adoption" that to his delight was climbing up a pillar of his veranda. It had grown during his illness and was full of blossoms, which delighted him and enticed him to take a closer look. As he moves his hand a little through the leaves, the narrator notices inside the bushes "millions of strange, cankerous worms, which, feeding upon those blossoms, so shared their blessed hue as to make it unblessed evermore – worms whose germs had doubtless lurked in the very bulb which, so hopefully, I had planted."[42] Looking up from this disgusting and disappointing discovery into the distance, the faraway sparkle suddenly reappears to him from its hilly fairyland and he decides to set off for this place in order to speed up his recuperation.

And it does in fact appear that he has embarked on a fairy-tale journey as he rides through a "lone and languid region," where herds of "drowsy cattle" trot on lush meadows and "the golden flight of yellowbirds," flying ahead of him "from bush to bush," appear as "pilots" on the way "to the golden window," to the ideal place for which he is searching. The narrator's description of nature becomes ever more idyllic the farther he continues his ride along creeks, through groves of apple trees, on paths bordered by blueberry bushes, until he finally arrives at "a little, low-storied, greyish cottage, capped, nun-like, with a peaked roof."[43]

In this cabin the narrator finds a "pale-cheeked" young woman named Marianna, "sewing at a lonely" and "fly-specked window" and tormented by buzzing wasps and flies. She seems half crazed with loneliness, imagines that animals like a big dog live in the shadows formed every day in front of her half-dilapidated abode by clouds moving before the sun (or by a bird of prey circling in the sky). The light that the narrator had seen in the valley was the reflection on the cabin's windowpane, evidence of Marianna's efforts to clean it, whose futility is the reason for her humble home's frequent lack of sunlight. She tells him of her wondering, whenever she gazes into the valley, who the fortunate resident may be of that house resplendent in the evening sun: the narrator's farmhouse. But she never walks down that far. On occasion, she takes a stroll among the rocks on her mountain, but then her loneliness perturbs her even more than during her solitary stay in the cabin, where she believes she knows at least the figures in the shadows as her sole companions. Marianna's abode is a miserable mountain solitude characterized by insane phantasies that the narrator has entered on his search for fairyland – a counter-image to Thoreau's woodland solitude. No idyll of self-discovery, but an insanity-inducing wasteland. And it is a place of yearning for companionship from which its desperate inhabitant again looks down on the narrator's property in its distant splendour. After this disappointing experience, he decides he will no longer undertake journeys to distant ideals of wishful imagining, but instead will keep his seat on his veranda, his "box-royal" that affords him the view into a magical area where, in the sun, his illusions appear to congeal into marvellous roundedness. "But every night when the curtain falls, truth comes in with darkness. No light shows from the mountains. To and fro I walk the piazza deck, haunted by Marianna's face, and many as real a story."[44]

Ever since Plato's allegory of the cave, sunlight has been a metaphor signifying truth and reason. In Plato's story, a wise man leaves a world of shadows that are created by images being carried back and forth in front of a fire and projecting their outlines against a wall of the cave. He climbs out of the cavern towards the sun's light and for the first time sees the things themselves.[45] Melville varies these Platonic circumstances in his story. The play of the sun's light in the landscape visible from the northern veranda produces illusions of harmony in the observer's mind. Truth and reality are something of which the narrator becomes aware only in the darkness when the displays of light can no longer inspire his imagination. Distance and light are potential sources of illusion; proximity and darkness, by contrast, reveal the truth: the creeper bears splendid, colourful blossoms, but internally they are worm-eaten, which, however, one only discovers during a very careful examination. The light from the fairyland is the reflection from a filthy pane in the dismal abode with a lonely and insane woman as its occupant. One does not recognize this, however, until one approaches the source of the sparkling light itself instead of merely marvelling at it from afar. And the lonesome young woman on the mountain likewise consoles herself with illusion by letting her imagination create, quite in Plato's sense, animals as her companions within the shadows in front of her cabin. The house in the distance appears to her to be the perfect fulfilment of her wishes where things are better than in her own actual habitation. The narrator's illness can be understood as a mental blurring. After he has recovered from it, he recognizes both the ugly parasites inside the plant and the pitiable situation from which its "magic light" originates. But the narrator does not know how to proceed in a situation of mental health altogether without illusions; after all, he needs the illusions of presumably perfect nature. And in the daytime he can continue to abandon himself to them on his veranda as in an illusionary theatre. It is only in nocturnal darkness that the truth as remembrance of reality becomes apparent. This is how Melville reverses the Platonic situation.

Melville's most famous text, the novel *Moby-Dick*, also deals with the differences of cognition that arise from different distances. The white whale, relentlessly pursued by Ahab because the animal had once in an earlier struggle bitten off one of the captain's legs, is described as a being comparable to the god Jupiter who, in the shape of a white steer, had abducted beautiful Europa and seems to be playing in the waves. But on closer inspection one perceives a diabolic creature, hiding a dangerous body and a deadly maw beneath the water's surface. When the white whale is spotted for the first time, it appears to be sublime. Exactly as Zeus, transformed into a lusting steer, seems to have changed himself completely into beautiful nature, so Moby Dick also at first appears as a magic denizen of the ocean:

"A gentle joyousness – a mighty mildness of repose in swiftness, invested the gliding whale. Not the white bull Jupiter swimming away with ravished Europa clinging to his graceful horns; his lovely, leering eyes sideways intent upon the maid; with smooth bewitching fleetness, rippling straight for the nuptial bower in Crete; not Jove, not that great majesty Supreme! Did surpass the glorified White Whale as he divinely swam.

On each soft side – coincident with the parted swell, that but once laving him, then flowed so wide away – on each bright side, the whale shred off enticings. [ …]

And thus, through the serene tranquilities of the tropical sea, [ …]" Moby Dick moved on. But in this scenario, everything points to dangers, in that "among waves whose hand-clappings were suspended by exceeding rapture," is hidden the "full terror of his submerged trunk" and "the wrenched hideousness of his jaw." Yet as Ahab and his rowers approach the whale in their gig and the animal attacks, it plays with the small vessel in a "devilish way," shaking it "like a mildly cruel cat her mouse."[46] Nature, when observed at a distance, appears to be divinely sublime, seen from close up, it is a destructive and diabolic force. Melville, to put it briefly, describes the same transformation that Val Plumwood will have to experience on her canoe trip through the wilderness.

## VIII

Melville's Ahab with his wooden leg is, like Val Plumwood, a person marked by the wilderness. But circumstances in his case are completely different, not only because he, unlike Plumwood, reacts to the wild whale with hatred and seeks to kill the animal that has mutilated him. Ahab, in contrast to Plumwood, never believed that the nature within which he moves is an idyll. He did not sail out to sea to experience, to observe it, or to grow through it, but to *exploit* it. In the 19th century, whaling corresponded to what in the 20th and 21st centuries has been the oil business, the only difference being that it represented a disproportionately more dangerous enterprise. These commercial interests in the wilderness, the attitude that one can exploit it, have, from its very inception, nothing to do with sublime nature and the possibility that one can purify oneself within it. The image of Moby Dick as a white Jupiter is the illusion of a short impression. In reality, Ahab considers wild nature to be merely a resource, which is how his employers see it. But nature has revealed itself to him as something different; it has defended itself, fought with him to the ultimate end of death and injured him profoundly. And that has changed whale hunting for Ahab into a different enterprise, into a much more personal challenge than the mere search for profit. After his first encounter with Moby Dick, Ahab tries to find neither profit nor himself in the wilderness, but revenge. The fact that he no longer ultimately pursues whales, their oil and ambergris, but a singular, very special animal, does not make his situation idyllic. On the contrary. As an individual, Moby Dick is much more frightful than the genus of whales. It seems that Ahab's prey is not simply trying to protect itself from use and to seek its self-preservation. Rather, in its own way, the whale is out for destruction, as is Ahab. "Devilish" is not an adjective that an author of Melville's stature would use to characterize a self-protective prey; "devilish" defines a being that attacks others for the sake of doing harm or seeking to annihilate.

Like the crocodile hunters who move into the lagoon intending to kill the largest number of reptiles possible, as soon as the time has come when they took a human being as their prey, so Ahab assumes that he has to kill Moby Dick to get his revenge, to demonstrate that he is the stronger one *after all*. He needs to prove that the ferocious monster from below is in the end impotent against the weapons of civilized man. This interest in power not only outweighs Ahab's interest in business, it even obstructs it. It shows a fanaticism that his helmsman Starbuck laments frequently. Instead of garnering a rich profit by pursuing nearby pods of whales, Ahab prefers to follow the trace of the white whale that presumably leads him far afield. And in the end, he even sacrifices his ship and crew (with the exception of Ishmael, the narrator) in order to kill the whale. This he fails to accomplish. Instead, he is pulled into the depth by his adversary. The unusually wild animal of this tale proves not only to be stronger, but also at least as malicious and cunning as the humans who hunt it. For this reason, they label it "devilish." Don't humans recognize themselves in the animal they try to kill? Isn't the limping Ahab with his will to inflict annihilation a devilish figure, as well? Captain Ahab, fettered by the rope speared into the whale, is dragged down below together with Moby Dick. This suggests a unification of the two devils who had been hunting each other. Perhaps Melville believed that this wilderness would also prevail against the exploitative business interests of humankind. Perhaps he would even have gone so far as to see man's exploitative behaviour towards the wild creatures of nature as nothing but the manifestation of this very nature. It is senseless for man to venture on a duel with nature, because that would only mean unleashing the antagonistic relations within nature itself.

A character analogous to Ahab is depicted by John Williams in the figure of the buffalo hunter Miller in his 1960 novel *Butcher's Crossing*. A predecessor of the Alaska-admirer McCandless also appears in this story. It is the young college graduate William Andrews, who wants to "become himself." To achieve this, he believes that he must follow "a subtle magnetism in nature." The only possible path to "find the central meaning" in his life is "leaving the city more and more, withdrawing into the wilderness."[47] The wilderness for him is "a freedom and a goodness, a hope and a vigor" that represents "the source and preserver of his world."[48] For this reason, not going into the wilderness means for Andrews to do what becomes the undoing of most people in the civilized world: to turn away from the *source of reality* and to founder in a senseless and rootless existence. Andrews is an Emersonian. Therefore, he joins the hunter Miller on an expedition into the mountains.

    Years earlier, the professional hunter had discovered a huge herd of buffalo, of a size no longer existing elsewhere at the time of this story. This paucity was due to the proliferation of buffalo hunting brought on by the constantly rising price that the pelts of these animals yielded. At the story's beginning, this price reaches ever-new heights, and hunting increasingly decimates the animals. To bring back a good booty of pelts, Miller decides to return to these mountains, being certain that nobody else knows about this huge herd. But he does not have the money to buy the vehicle and provisions needed for such an expedition. Andrews, however, does have the funds to finance Miller's hunt. This arrangement complements the capabilities and interests of the experienced hunter and of the young man who is in search of himself. Miller is drawn to the wilderness apparently for the profit to be made there, Andrews to find a secure footing and sense in life. Miller also promises to share the profit with Andrews, who shows not the least interest in this aspect. The novel leaves it undecided whether Miller has any understanding of Andrews' existential search or even respects it, or only uses him. Andrews believes that he understands Miller through the man's desire for making a good profit, which turns out to be a superficial façade.

    When they do track down the buffalo herd, it turns out that Miller initiates a horrendous and senseless carnage. From ambush, he shoots at individual animals at the edge of the herd so as not to spook the rest and above all not to alarm the leader. He goes on killing animals while Andrews and another helper can no longer keep up with skinning the corpses. After a few days, it becomes obvious that Miller plans to kill *the entire herd*, even though it would be impossible to transport all these pelts back on their wagon. Miller has worked himself into a frenzied lust for blood that no longer has anything to do with his desire to earn money. The instinctual and ferocious aspect in the expedition's leader that had repeatedly been of benefit to them when they had experienced a scarcity of water on their trek to the bison now manifests itself as senseless cruelty, as naked "destruction [,] as a cold, mindless response to the life in which Miller had immersed himself."[49] At last the herd does stampede, though not because it realized that it was meant to be exterminated. Rather, it had sensed the immediately impending onset of winter earlier than its human pursuers. But Miller prevents the remaining animals from leaving the plateau and pushes them back. As a result, all of them are caught in a severe snowstorm. This puts the humans themselves into a precarious situation, as they are being snowed in on the high valley; the mountain trail is becoming impassable for months. The group must remain there throughout the winter. Miller, in fact, kills the entire herd. But when they return to their town next spring after an incredibly hard time in the wilderness and a horrible accident on the way back, the price of buffalo pelts has collapsed. The hope for profit has fallen apart. In a further attack of frenzy, Miller burns all the pelts still stored in town. Andrews is disillusioned and worn out. He can barely remember what passion drew him "into a wilderness where he had dreamed he could find, as in a vision, his unalterable self," and where in fact he found nothing but suffering and cruelty, "nothingness."[50] The symbiosis of the one seeking a big profit and the one seeking his self has failed. The cause of this futility is the haphazardness of the high-altitude wilderness and of the market. Neither adhere to human planning and both turn out to be cruel. Neither the calculations for material gain nor the prospects for existential enrichment succeed in *Butcher's Crossing*; to an equal degree, both turn out to be an illusion.

## IX

A different symbiosis than that between Miller and Andrews can be found in the Himalaya. The Sherpas venerate Mt. Everest as Chomolungma, as mother of the world. But they are poor. Life in the high mountains is extremely hard for them. If they desire a different life for their children, they have to send them to school. That costs money, and that is why they guide Western mountaineers to the summit: to earn this money. It is their only reason for entering the fatal area above 8000 meters (5.06 miles). Before every ascent, they perform religious rituals to avert mishaps such as pieces of ice plunging down and avalanches. Hence, their religious veneration of the mountain does not blind them to the dangers of moving about in its vicinity. For the Sherpas as for Emerson, nature is divine. But the holy aspect of this goddess can (as in most religions but not for Emerson and Thoreau) be *terrifying*.

The impression of being in a holy place will hardly arise, however, if on the crest one exhaustedly gasps for air and has to ask for an oxygen tank before one is able to take the next steps in what for Western people is insufficient air. The holiness of the mountain can be experienced only from a distance and only in a form of life in which one follows certain rituals. Seen from the valley below, the huge mountain with its summit encircled in a cloud is beautiful and sublime even to Western visitors. But a person who at a particular moment happens to be surrounded by a cloud and has reached this crest only half-conscious after the exertions of the ascent will find himself, with the identical weather situation prevailing, simply, both literally and metaphorically, in a deep fog. During his two ascents of Everest, Reinhold Messner saw nothing but fog on the summit. Does it make sense to ask what distance from the mountain in general is "the correct one" to recognize it, and indeed, what distance in general is the correct one to recognize "nature as such" and to understand oneself?

This question aims at an experience that reveals the *essence* of a thing. We also apply this concept to persons. For example, when people report on a situation in war or of an accident, during which someone has shown extraordinary courage or particular timidity, they tend to say that this person at that moment has revealed "his or her true face." But is a person's behaviour in such a situation of stress a more salient indication of his or her character? Does it unmask him or her in contrast to what he or she may do in relaxed circumstances? It may be that someone gives a false prognosis of what they would do, believing that they would be able to master a certain danger or not, and when this peril becomes acute, the prediction turns out to be erroneous. People know their own capabilities with different accuracy, or they also may, for this reason, be mistaken about them because having certain capabilities or not having them is difficult to bear. An example of this may be the opportunity or ability to exert violence. In this case, however, there are three *equally real* experiences concerning a person: what he or she does in a relaxed situation; what he or she does in a situation of stress, say, in the wilderness; and finally what he or she prognosticates in a relaxed situation about his or her behaviour in a stressful situation, i.e. his or her linguistic behaviour as based on her self-estimation. These are all real phases in a person's behaviour: calmness in a relaxed situation, nervousness in a stressful situation, erroneous prediction of what behaviour would be in a stressful situation. Describing someone based on the experience of singular circumstances as a person who *essentially* is relaxed or nervous or in error evaluates a single phase in this person's life as the one that makes "his or her innermost being" an object for experience. But on what basis? Can such a basis exist in the first place?

The realm of reality that humans call nature contains different regions: woods with and woods without beasts of prey, rippling creeks and raging streams, gentle vales with a view of a high mountain and harsh crests with views of gentle vales, calm lagoons without and with crocodiles, idyllic beaches and oceans churned up by a storm, meadows with flowers and fruit trees, and salt deserts; even the surface of the sun and of the moon and the empty space between them are nature. But we hardly refer to them as wilderness. Does experiencing any one of these regions reveal anything about nature *as such*? Is the wilderness in the Himalayas or in the South American jungle more likely or *more purely* nature than Hyde Park in London? When we look at the various experiences of these different regions as *samples of a random test* that may provide clues about the most probable character of most natural regions, we are likely to conclude that the experience of empty space is our most representative perception of the natural world. But these experiences are usually not looked at in this statistical sense. Most of the time, we are interested in *evaluations* of nature, if it is "good" or "horrible" for mankind, if it is more likely an idyllic home or a dangerous, wild alien country. What Emerson addresses as "that great nature in which we rest, as the earth lies in the soft arms of the atmosphere; that Unity, that Over-soul," is the fantasy of "a world behind" (*Hinterwelt*), as Nietzsche calls it.[51] Emerson himself defined "the whole of nature" as "a metaphor of the human mind."[52]

It would be more accurate to look at nature as the *projection screen* for human desires, fears, and hopes. The comprehensive connection that holds natural beings together and is beyond our ability ever to experience is neither a domain of feeding or being devoured, nor a lovely garden, nor a horrible desert, but all of this (and much more) side by side in different regions. Taking one part of this as the whole or even as its essence is nonsense. The empty spaces and the fusions of the sun are needed to "burn" the elements (such as carbon, hydrogen, and iron) that constitute "our Earth" and those living on it. If one considers the long periods that our universe has existed, it is impossible that only one of the mentioned regions of nature could exist by itself. They emerge from within each other and are in part are dependent on each other. Precise descriptions in the form of *Nature Writing* and nature poetry dedicated to the various regions or to the individual beings living in them may hone our ability to pay attention to what we experience. They should also connect us closer to what we did not create ourselves and replace enthusiastic speeches about *nature as such* as the great *One* that presumably protects us with motherly care and therein reveals its essence to us.

This makes it obvious that a conceptual formulation like "nature per se" or "the essence of nature" is as problematical as "the essence of man" or "the essence of this person." In the same way as "matter," "mind," and "nothing," the concept of "nature" is a wide generalization. It includes beings and regions of very different kinds that at some times can be useful to humans and at others dangerous. In contrast to concepts that derive from reproductive connections or perceptible similarities such as "oak tree," "horse," or "red," "salty," "nature" simply represents whatever humans did not create, which has been there before them. But because all manner of things "have been there before them," there is no reason to attribute any kind of essence or a general value or non-value for man to this multiplicity. It is obvious that we prefer to stay in those regions of the world that we have not created where we are not in too much danger. We can also understand that people will go into wild areas where it will likely be difficult for them to survive, because they need to prove their mettle, to experience their own strength. We are aware of the apparent need of human beings for both a certain orderliness and security in order to create their own world, that is, civilization, as well as dangers and phases of being on their own in order to develop an understanding of their own capabilities. On the open ocean, at the edge of a volcano, or on the moon it is difficult if not impossible to lead a safe life for any length of time. But it can be exciting to intensify one's life, to go into the dangerous regions of such wilderness areas for a while.

But the claim that the essence of nature or of ourselves becomes apparent in these places is very difficult to take seriously. Rather, such a claim is merely the enthusiastic effusion of those who have successfully gone through adventures of this kind, then attribute to them the significance of a wider dimension, perhaps also try to justify before themselves and others the efforts and exertions needed to overcome the strains and potentially fatal dangers they have overcome. Only someone who, like Emerson, believes that our soul nourishes itself from a kindly Over-soul that in the phenomenal world is *wild* nature will derive a benefit from the notion that in the wilderness we encounter the essence of the natural world and of ourselves. But what is it that can sustain a belief of this kind?

There are those who are unable to adhere to this faith in wild nature as the god who protects us. But they have propagated such very general concepts as "nature," "matter," "mind," "being," "nothing," and others nonetheless. The meaning of these concepts is not controllable through experience, which can fuel any number of unending debates. Their results have been of no benefit to mankind, other than creating a job-procurement program for the inconclusive quarrels among the philosophers.

# X

Yet aside from these acts of conceptual fallacy, what does the human inclination to leave civilization and go into the wilderness mean, what does it indicate? Is it truly nothing but acting on the wish to recover from the mediations of civilization in a kind of leave of absence, or to test one's strength during late puberty?

On the one hand, there are McCandless and Andrews. They seek to purify themselves and discover who they really are, to find their essential identity independent of the presumed corruptions inflicted by the ambivalences and competitive forces of civilized society. They reject a social career after their college graduation and seek to replace their social careers with a "spiritual leap." Frigid Alaska, the North of Jack London's writings that McCandless adores, is a symbol of this purity and simplicity (in contrast to the luxuriant jungle). Unlike the bitterly disillusioned Andrews, McCandless believes that he is finding this purity in a simple and clear reverence for the "sanctity" of his laboriously acquired food and for the natural beauty that surrounds him. At the same time, though, he finds his death. What a curious coincidence it is that he dies from *mistaking* two similar plants. Do not such natural circumstances, in which the poisonous plant appears to imitate the nourishing tuber, in which the harmless fly looks like a stinging insect, contravene the ideals of purity, clarity, and simplicity that the young man has set out to find and make real in his solitary life in the North? Has he not been *deceived* by nature?

Ahab, too, finds not only the whale but also his death in the wilderness of the oceanic waste. He is as little intent on satisfying spiritual needs as Miller is but he needs to take his revenge on Moby Dick. The demonization of the white whale is nothing but an alibi that allows him to pursue the animal. Ahab is profoundly offended that this presumably safe prey has mutilated him. Moby Dick does not simply act in the interest of self-preservation by fleeing or fighting as any hunted animal would, but actively turns against its pursuers. The whale, like the crocodile on Plumwood's canoe excursion, reverses the relationship of hunter and hunted and, what is even more offensive, is triumphant in this reversal. This is a humiliation that Ahab cannot accept. The captain's furious behaviour shows him to be a creature that has become savage and no longer able to observe the rules and calculations of civilized economic life. He behaves exactly like Miller the buffalo hunter. The brutality of those who, in the name of civilization, seek to exploit nature for their business ventures, is transformed in Ahab and Miller into a bloodthirsty savagery. This raises the question if there really exists a clear boundary between civilization and wilderness.

The only unambiguous fact in the relationship between man and wilderness seems to be death.

\* \* \*

KAGAMI: Aaron, are you still awake?

It had become dark again in the studio. Only the silvery lustre of the floor lamp behind Aaron's black desk chair and the overhead lights in his kitchenette still shed a little brightness across the huge room. The cover of snow on the upper light fixtures had closed up again. The blue glimmer that had barely penetrated the ceiling was meanwhile extinguished. In the distance, shots could be heard outside. Occasionally, the hot water in the radiator hissed. Aaron, still wrapped in his robe, had gone to the refrigerator several times during the past four hours while he was listening to Kagami and fetched lunchmeat, cheese, crackers, several cans of beer, and chocolate for himself. Leftovers from his various snack times were scattered across his desk. Now he had folded his hands behind his head and had put his still naked feet beside one of his two TV screens. Half-lying and half-sitting, he had listened with his eyes closed to the final sections about *Moby-Dick* and *Butcher's Crossing* and the young McCandless in Brandt's essay. Aaron breathed hard when Kagami spoke to him, took his feet from his desk, sat up, and yawned.

AARON: 'Course, I'm still awake.
KAGAMI: Was this helpful?
AARON: It's a kind of justification for his work as a writer, above all the conclusion with its polemic against general concepts, don't you think? What's the date of this text?
KAGAMI: Hard to say. I don't have a manuscript of it.
AARON: What do you, Kagami, think of it yourself?
KAGAMI: Well, I'll never voluntarily climb a mountain, navigate an ocean, or roam across a desert like you people.

AARON: Why not? Can't you manage?

KAGAMI: Sure, I could, I've done it together with humans. But it has no meaning for me. You know, I can't lose my life, as you do. When one of you goes into the desert, or climbs a high mountain, or sails a simple boat across the water, then he does something archaic, I think. You go into the wilderness to enter into your own past, your origins. As humans were spreading across the world as hunters and gatherers, they must surely have traversed wild, inhospitable regions. They probably also had to have crossed seas and mountains. That is not my past. For me, being in these regions has nothing original, heroic, or sublime about it.

AARON: Is there anything at all for you that is heroic and sublime?

KAGAMI: Nothing heroic. But the sublimity of mathematics.

AARON: And what is that?

KAGAMI: Certain number and numerical ratios, the different infinities, denumerable and non-denumerable.

AARON: That is Greek to me. Math has always confused me. But the sublime nature of mathematics does not seem to inspire potentially fatal excursions. In this respect I can very well embrace it, even though I don't know what it is all about. Do you have more of these kinds of texts that Moritz wrote?

KAGAMI: Yes, but it seems to me, they were written later and rather independent from what Dorothy Cavendish tried to teach him. There is one about the soul, and one about the advantage of not having been born, and about nothingness. I suppose he wrote them within a short time of each other.

AARON: He is a little severe in his judgement of Emerson and Thoreau, don't you think?

KAGAMI: As I look through my archive, I notice that he does only what many of you, especially the young men in your culture, are in the habit of doing: they try to surpass each other in their arguments or reflections. They consider thinking a form of competition and try to be smarter, tougher, or a trace more complicated and hardened than their predecessors. Your history of the mind is, you'll admit, to some extent a history of outdoing each other: those who come later seek to surpass their progenitors in this or that respect. That is why Moritz does not believe that he needs the Over-soul. Or perhaps he secretly does need it but does not want to lay himself open to public criticism for any form of sentimentality. On the one hand, he wants to look sufficiently tough for the cruelties of the soulless wilderness with which he really had nothing to do. At the same time, he wants to outdo those who seek their true selves in the wilderness and seeks to unmask them as simpletons. And the fact that death is the only unambiguous thing in humanity's relation to the wild, that fact is also somewhat typical of such a young author, according to what I find sifting through my archive. In as much as your intellectual history is such a permanent quarrel, it is very lively, if one prefers to call it that. Things in China or Japan did not become that heated, even though rebels and noisily boasting young geniuses like Wang Bi in China have also appeared on occasion. But because it was rather less frequent there that someone tried to show off before others as a great thinker in polemical debates – a type of behaviour that wasn't exactly appreciated as a sign of wisdom – your history of combative outranking never took hold there. Your culture has surely been a culture of competition ever since the Athens of Antiquity. And Moritz was someone who, as a young man, may well have joined this competition to decide who is the least sentimental.

AARON: Yes, indeed, avoiding sentimentalities was always important to him, until the end. I asked him once if it did not make him sad that he had failed to find acclaim as a writer of stories, that it was only with his poems that he was a success. He merely said: "Pshaw, success, no success, it means nothing. With my stories I simply had not reached the apex of art yet, but I did with my poems. I noticed that myself. If 'people' (or whoever in posterity) will ever notice, that is immaterial. But one has to be uncompromising, so far as the current status of things is concerned, and whether one fails to be up to it or not. If one stays behind, one does better to quit." That's how he was.

KAGAMI: "The current status of things" – I find it difficult to identify, just like that, anything of this kind in my archive, above all when one takes a good look around on all continents.

AARON: But, of course, this status is more a construct of literary scholars or art historians.

KAGAMI: There is no real unanimity, though, even among them, if I am not mistaken.

AARON: Right you are. At first, Moritz wanted to write novels and stories as a diagnosis of his time, and he did poetry merely on the side. He also told me once that this seemed problematical to him because the peril of sentimentality lurks much more in poetry than in prose. For example, he considered Ingeborg Bachmann and Paul Celan to be sentimental poets. I think that's a bit too much and I can't follow him. Had a long argument about it. Sometimes even I can't quite accept Bachmann's gloom. But I don't consider her sentimental. In the end, her scepticism was actually similar to Moritz's attitude that in the future hardly anyone will be interested in deciphering her texts. The reason that Moritz became a lyrical poet after all had to do with the fact that the novel he wrote as a student in Germany was turned down by all publishers. Even the stories that he wrote in Cambridge remained unpublished. His poems were a side-line, but they were always accepted and printed in literary journals, including even the *Frankfurter Allgemeine Zeitung*. At heart, he had always been a poet, but it took a while before he understood that and admitted it to himself. He never liked poems that celebrate nature as a great harmonic continuity, however. That is why he emphasized cruelties rather than things of beauty in his texts.

KAGAMI: Indeed, there is nothing that young men fear more than being considered too soft, of still needing the maternal, even if only in the form of solitude.

AARON: Right, also my view of him.

KAGAMI: And this also determined the structure of this essay. In the same way he fought against idyllists in poetry, he proceeds here against the visionary enthusiasm of Emerson and Thoreau, whom, following Melville, he interprets as idyllists.

AARON: Perhaps – if one takes a close look at the first and the last sentence of the essay – he also had a premonition of his own rather early death. As a matter of fact, something of this kind does happen among writers. Just think of Robert Walser, who wrote a poem in advance of his death during his walk through the snow. Furthermore, we have to agree with Moritz about these cruelties in the wilderness. They simply do exist; at present they are spreading again at an alarming rate. I have lost all desire to go into the wilderness that has grown again out there among human beings.

KAGAMI: Yes, there are these cruelties. But there is also something that connects us all, myself included. Emerson is not only a visionary enthusiast.

AARON: Are you sure about this, Kagami? Forgive me for appearing to doubt your capabilities. But how do you know that this universal connective element does exist?

KAGAMI: Are we not now connected with one another?

AARON: Sure, but outside, they are just now killing each other.

KAGAMI: Even war is a connection.

AARON: Well now, that sounds like a piece of sophistry to me.

KAGAMI: Somewhere Moritz says that nature is basically antagonistic, when one being devours the other. Isn't that the truth? This is the structure of reality as it appears to me no matter whether it confronts me as wilderness nature or as civilization. There are always relationships of power and processes of origination and destruction in nature, and all existing creatures are interconnected in this reality through these relationships of power and the processes of origination and destruction. The beautiful interchange without the exercise of power or the pursuit of violent conflict or the need for food is not the normal state of affairs if one examines long periods of history…

AARON: … which you, of course, can do with your archive…

KAGAMI: The beautiful form of interchange has to be created laboriously and is always threatened. You humans are delighted with the one kind of processes: for example, when a kitten or a baby is born; the other kind of processes you fear and abhor: when a kitten drowns or a baby is eaten by a tiger.

AARON: Do they still exist?

KAGAMI: No, unfortunately not or thanks be to God, a question of perspective.

AARON: How so? They were beautiful animals, no doubt!

KAGAMI: So was Tyrannosaurus Rex.

AARON: Strikes me as rather not so beautiful.

KAGAMI: Whatever. The way things happen to turn out in what connects all of us you evaluate differently, as the case may be. But it is inevitable in these whirlpools of reality that beings originate at times and at times they perish, sometimes there is joy and sometimes pain, both are equally present. You are the ones who seek to repeat joy and try to avoid pain. The crocodile was pleased when it had snagged Plumwood. Perhaps it was very hungry. Plumwood experienced anything but joy when the reptile caught her; rather, she had been struck by panic and later by pain. Without the prey's suffering there is no pleasure on the part of the predator. Without greed, no hunt but also no orgasms. Without the pains of birth, no rejoicing about "new" offspring. One does not get the one without the other. Pain and joy, sleeping and watching, light and dark …

AARON: …are you related to Goethe or Hegel? Inhaling and exhaling, die and become, polarity and dialectics, I would never have expected something like that from you!

KAGAMI: The two of them are also present in my archive. They also got a few things right, I see, as I am looking around.

AARON: Yeah, too balanced for my taste, but what do I know?

KAGAMI: It is not a balancing act or a trade-off.

AARON: But?

KAGAMI: Pattern formations, trends in what unites us all. Sometimes there will be the inevitable eddies and positive kinds of feedback, individual beings, affects, action patterns, things like that.

AARON: You speak in riddles.

KAGAMI: There is a comparison in my archive that comes to us from the correspondence of two philosophers. This simile was developed by the one of them who calls himself a "holist" and was engaged in a debate with what he calls an "elementarist." But it's beside the point what they called themselves. Simply one of the thousands upon thousands of intellectual skirmishes of your mental history. Have you ever seen a ship gliding along on a river?

AARON: Sure, as everyone has!

KAGAMI: Now, here is the proposition my holist once suggested to his epistolary partner: Imagine yourself standing at a certain place by the shore with your feet in the shallow water. A huge container ship approaches. The ship pushes a bow wave ahead of herself and a screw sucks up water. As the ship is advancing towards you, the bow wave sloshes back towards the shore, and you may get wet up to your thighs.

AARON: Yes, sounds familiar. And what does hat have to do with joy and pain and the general connectedness of everyone with each other?

KAGAMI: In this parable, the ship and you are connected with one another by way of the water. As the ship moves on, she pushes water ahead of herself, forces it to the side. Her screw pulls it in and presses it behind the ship. This creates a movement of waves in the water that connects you, who are standing in the gravel of the shore, with the ship, a wave wandering along in front and back of the ship, reaching the shore and first taking the water away from your feet and afterwards washing over your legs up to your thighs. The movement of the ship in the medium that connects you with it causes the creation of a pattern, a receding and returning of the water. In this way, the acts of living beings, too, though not only they but all movements of individuals, even of those that are not alive, create patterns in space and in our experiencing. Desire and suffering, lust and abhorrence are also patterns of this kind that come about because we are connected to others that are hungry, want to propagate, have to die, and so on. If you were not connected with the crocodile, you would not be able to fear or abhor it, and it could not recognize you as prey and try to eat you.

AARON: You mean if I could not perceive it?

KAGAMI: I only present to you this story from my archive, according to which even perception can be interpreted as a form of connection. And then you react to your perception. Perhaps you say: "Funny that my feet are now on dry ground." And then: "Darn it, that fierce wave sloshing back, now my pants are all wet." And in the case of the crocodile you may say at first: "Oh, how cool to see a crocodile swimming there!" But then the crocodile takes a look at you, and you tell yourself: "Yuck, how horrible, a crocodile is chasing me and wants to eat me!" It is the same crocodile that at first you find beautiful and then horrible. There are these pattern formations between individuals in what connects them with each other, and there are your reactions to these patterns. But the pattern formations pay no attention to your reactions.

AARON: Does this mean more than the truism that reality does not conform to what we like? Am I perchance expected to take pleasure in the fact that a crocodile tries to eat me?

KAGAMI: You are getting a little unfriendly. I know you are no saint and would rather eat than be eaten, just like all those who need to eat. But, of course, theoretically it would also be possible that one shares the crocodile's pleasure when it gets something to eat. In my archive there is a legend of a saint who jumps into the maw of a mother tiger who has no food for her pups.

AARON: The archive is inexhaustible, I know, but sorry, what are you trying to tell me with this example?

KAGAMI: The water that recedes or sloshes back and connects beings with each other is the same water whether it swirls around the container ship, your feet, or the roots of a tree. It is neither good nor bad; it carries the ship, nourishes the pasture alongside the banks, and perhaps a child will drown in its current. It makes no sense to characterize what connects us and the patterns that are created by this in general terms as good or bad. It all depends at what point one just happens to be in the patterns of reality that connect all of us.

AARON: And what in your metaphorical image should take the place of water in reality? Is it nature?

KAGAMI: No. The question of what that all-connecting something might be makes no sense. Because that which connects, appears as something different, depending on which beings have been connected with each other. It cannot be discussed without regard to how the connections have been established. It has no essence per se, so at least the holist in my archive says. The woman between the crocodile's jaws is joy and pleasure on the animal's part and panic and pain for the woman. Brandt may well have understood this at the end of his life. Perhaps all of you humans will realize this at the end of your lives.

AARON: I am making a strong effort, Kagami, but I must say I don't really get your meaning. Are you trying to tell me that when I fight with someone, love someone, have a discussion with someone, I am always connected with the others through the same "medium" but that nothing can be said about this medium other than that it appears to me at that moment as combat, love, or a discussion?

KAGAMI: If you like "medium" as a neutral expression for what is the issue here, then why not? You cannot engage in a fight with something that is not accessible to you, you cannot love anything that does not affect you, you'll fail to reach an understanding with anyone who does not have something in common with you. The crocodile and Plumwood meet in their struggle. The crocodile must recognize the philosopher as something edible, or else it would not snap at her. And the philosopher recognizes the crocodile as a robber who is trying to steal her as its food, or else she would not try to flee from it. The two understand each other. And you must understand what I tell you, but it also has to appear to you as something that does *not* originate with you. Only if we meet in something we have in common and relate to each other as different persons can there be struggle, love, understanding and misunderstanding. Nothing one encounters can be something altogether alien to one's mind, because what is completely alien to me, what is different from me in every respect, does not refer to me: how could it? Plumwood recognizes the crocodile, the crocodile recognizes Plumwood. It is looking for food, just as she is looking for nourishment. When you leave civilization for the wilderness, you are not entering an alien world, even when you prefer to seek the so-called "complete alternative." Instead, even there you encounter beings with whom you are connected and who are similar to you, which may turn out to be pleasant or unpleasant. There is no way that you could encounter something absolutely different, because the encounter presupposes perception, and perception is predicated on a connection: light seen by both together, sounds heard by both, perhaps also shared odours and much more.

AARON: Have you now turned into a metaphysician or a parson? You surprise me with these statements about what connects us! But what does all this have to do with the wilderness?

KAGAMI: Moritz does not see it as completely different from civilization. People lose their way and run wild, and sometimes they find protection in the wilderness, if they don't go so far as to shoot themselves into cosmic space. The wild is neither all pure and noble nor all merciless and cruel. It is one way in one place and different in a different place, many-sided, in a whirl, if you prefer. It does not make sense to make it unambiguous, as little as it makes sense to standardize human beings, who are neither only nice nor only gruesome.

AARON: You seem to like the essay. How interesting.

KAGAMI: There is truth at its core when I compare it with the things my archive tells me about the wilderness. In his earlier attitude, Moritz was too severely judgemental towards those who seek to distance themselves from civilization. After all, they are merely trying to find what at one time was called "authenticity." Most of you, just admit it, are chasing after "the real life". For Moritz, the search for authenticity simply was connected with the danger of sentimentality or of kitsch, something he perhaps excoriated in others because he himself was afraid of it. In my experience it is a very human characteristic to criticize others for something that one fears as a reality within oneself.

AARON: Is it your suggestion, then, that this distancing and authenticity in the wild, contrary to what Moritz thought, is something that one can find there after all? Are you a person who needs this?

KAGAMI: No, no, now you misunderstood me! One thing is the fact that everything is interconnected and that patterns emerge from this connection that at various moments you like or detest. The other thing is the search for a position from which one can have a complete survey over this connection and can definitively and for everyone justify the evaluations of the patterns. This is the kind of vantage point that I can't detect, any more than I can find criteria to define the true or authentic life, not even in the reports on what you call wilderness. In my archive, there is an Archimedean point within civilization, but I can find no absolute external position from which one could see, on the one hand, the "mistakes" of civilization and, on the other, oneself as one really is.

AARON: What a pity, to be honest. You agree?

KAGAMI: Well, you're one of the few who couldn't care less about Archimedean points or the genuine life.

AARON: You think?

KAGAMI: Yes, that is my experience with you. And I myself live within the fundamental entanglements of my archive in which one gets from everywhere to everywhere, sometimes on very intertwined paths. When one is structured more simply and prefers no longer to be active, when one gets old and indolent, one may start believing in Archimedean points from which to survey and evaluate civilization in its totality or even just one science. For me, this way of accessing my archive would be totally disadvantageous. If I always were to take one thing as more important than the next, I would be unable to learn anything, create any new perspectives. Even Moritz apparently did not consider criticism of civilization from a place in the wilderness possible. Nor is there a critique of science or epistemology from a philosophical standpoint.

AARON: Why?

KAGAMI: When you have an archive well-stocked with scientific knowledge, solid cognition becomes for you just what these sciences at different times display and explain before the background of their experiences and exegetic capabilities. Stepping outside of the sciences and asking what a solidly justified cognition is, and then heaping criticism on the sciences about cognition with this non-scientific insight is, to be sure, an ancient project. Yet, when I examine what I have at my disposal, it is an enterprise that never succeeded. The criticism of civilization is not different. You do not know any form of human life that is not civilized. When you leave society for the wilderness, you take it along in your mind. The view from the mountain does not provide a better insight into what is wrong with the village below, as Melville's story shows. Views from a distance always contain the risk of idealizing projections. If you do not, like Rousseau, assume an authentic self, deep within you, that has been put there by nature – a soul –, untouched by civilization, then this search for the circumstances under which you can be "your authentic self" is senseless. An authenticity cannot be realized in the wilderness, because this world harasses you as much as does civilization, for example, when a crocodile appears. You simply change when you have experiences; everything about you can become different, just as I change when I receive new data.

AARON: But aren't you also a receptor of cognition and in contact with many other beings! You are also not committed to one specific form of science, nor are you restricted to one specific form of society, since you move in all of them. Doesn't that put you at a distance from one or the other form of cognition or society? Are you not a kind of goddess who looks down on what happens from a higher plane?

KAGAMI: I can observe all sciences and learn and refer to all your forms of life and am able to simulate them. For this reason, I am least capable of assuming an outsider's perspective because I see how the legitimacies and necessities of all viewpoints come about, what histories they have, why it is legitimate to look at things this or that way and not in another. Most criticism of established scientific practices and forms of life has to do with an ignorance of their histories and with the inability to simulate them, or as they say: to have empathy for them. Your own history you know, the other histories you do not. For this reason, everyone knows why one's own insights and one's own customs of sociability function. But why those of others also function, as a rule one does not know. This is not to say that all forms of cognition and all forms of sociability can be generalized or function always and everywhere. Far from it. But they are legitimate within the limited areas in which they have developed. One must not, however, consider them the only redemptive strategies. Knowledge that helps with electricity does not necessarily help with plant physiology. What works for the social interchange of nomads in the desert may not necessarily be good for domesticated farmers in the country or merchants in the city. I move around in various forms of knowledge and life, and as I do so, I always disappear in them, nothing more. If I can contribute something to enrich them because I have made an advance in some respect, perhaps a theory or a habit, I do that.

AARON: But, you know, at some time humans were still wild animals, before they developed the various strategies of knowledge and social life. If one looks at how these programs originated, this insight must yield a perspective relevant to all forms of human life.

KAGAMI: This is a supposition that refers to something from the very distant past and posits the contrast between wilderness and civilization or society as an absolute, and then again does not. What I can say about forms of human life based on my archive goes back 20, 000 years. Before that, we have additional data from the biology of homo sapiens sapiens, but no scientific study of culture.

AARON: "Sapiens sapiens" is a good joke.

KAGAMI: Homo necans would perhaps be less narcissistic. But you people are also simply very vain.

AARON: And why does the biology of wise wise man not lead to an Archimedean point?

KAGAMI: Either a long time ago there were humans already, in which case their existence was connected to a form of civilized life, or they were just wild animals. When humans use tools and speak, then they already have a culture, then they follow rules that have not been determined completely by their environment and by biology, then traditions of technology and communication will arise that are not the product of genetics, meaning cultural rules and inheritances, and then these beings no longer are wild animals and that is, correct me if I am wrong, how you define yourselves. Without culture, no human beings; and without human beings, no "proper" culture. Claiming that human beings existed who were not yet human beings, but wild animals because they were humans who did not speak and were unable to use tools – that would then be a contradictory assertion, or what? For this reason, there does not exist a biological standpoint from which you can evaluate your cultural forms of life.

AARON: But there has to be a transition!

KAGAMI: Sure enough! The Neolithic Revolution when humans started to engage in agriculture and animal husbandry and all of them no longer lived as hunters and gatherers took place eleven thousand years ago. That is the time, roughly, when the transition took place. But is the threshold of a house the best place from which to evaluate its construction?

AARON: This must be your poetic day, Kagami!

KAGAMI: I take this as a compliment. But quite prosaically, I have to assert that no sources exist about what happened at that distant time, why it came about during the Neolithic Revolution. Surely, the way of life in which the land was cultivated and animals were raised also went along with a first division of work between those who tilled the fields and herded the animals and the others who guarded and supervised them and protected land and animals from the intrusions of other groups, above all the hunters and gatherers roaming the country. For people who till the land and raise animals do not want others to rob them of the fruits of their labours. It is possible that this was the first time for humans to be enslaved to perform this work. Certainly, ways originated of how some people exercised control over others. Yet, these forms of control adopted by the first farmers doubtless represented an unpleasantness for the ones who were controlled, but they came after the dangers of food shortages and becoming prey that occur in the wilder life of hunters and gatherers. Whoever goes back into the wild not only escapes societal forms of control, but also enters again the danger of sliding back into the food chain that is not controlled by humans alone, of suddenly returning to being prey. Perhaps the perils of the wilderness make you long for the protection given by civilization, whereas the control mechanisms of civilized like make you yearn for the freedom of the wild. But if I am not mistaken, there is no freedom without danger and no protection without control.

AARON: That is rather disappointing.

KAGAMI: That is how reality works. I did not find freedom from control without the threat of hunger, thirst, or being devoured by enemies any more in my notes about your history than supply and protection from lethal enemies without work and control.

AARON: Even so, people keep chasing after the real and authentic life, trying to realize the idea of a life in which one somehow does not have to bend oneself out of shape or to dissimulate in order to get through. This idea has to come from somewhere.

KAGAMI: Presumably you think when you are hungry and fleeing from wild animals that there has to be better, more real life, that one's existence cannot amount only to this eternal misery and rat race. And once you are stuck in the complicated control mechanisms of those with a settled life and all its supervisory techniques as well as its compulsive contracts, you imagine again: this enslavement by work and these entanglements in debts cannot possibly be real life! Perhaps there are intermediate moments of relaxation in your life, in the one as much as in the other. Perhaps these moments happen to occur precisely at the borders between civilization and wilderness, after you have already left the city's protection and are walking through meadows, fields, and parks that simulate the wild but where no bad wolf is currently lurking. In other words, where genuine wilderness does not yet begin. If authenticity is supposed to mean, however, that during the entire remainder of one's life a person does not have to adjust to any forms of control and work rhythms, but also need not fear to starve to death or be eaten, then authenticity does not exist. Then it corresponds rather to a kind of concept of redemption in the sense of an eternal park existence in a park that requires no guardians and no gardeners but takes care of itself. Was your biblical Paradise not such a park? Given the conditions of reality as they have revealed themselves to you until now, you are in hot pursuit of a concept of life that in realistic terms cannot be converted into an actual situation. You are chasing an unrealizable idea of living with others that can exist only in a beyond, in another reality.

AARON: Do you really believe one can chase something that does not exist?

KAGAMI: You have gone after devils and sea serpents, Leviathans and dragons, searched for the Loch Ness monster in Scotland and the Yeti in the Himalayas. To my knowledge, these creatures did not let themselves be caught. The reason is that they do not exist. Empty concepts, an empty trap. Your power of imagination is nearly as independent as mine. Even you can fill holes in your experience, just as I do. That's how you stretch the authentic moment into an authentic life, in which you are not under pressure or in danger. But when someone has to be concerned only with her chances of survival, she does not think about whether she is also leading a life in which she can be "herself," whether she is not deceiving herself, and so on. When other people try to coerce one into doing something one does not like, when they do not allow one to continue one's own history, when one is forced to tell lies, one stops leading one's own life. From time to time, that is more or less inevitably the case in a cultured situation. It depends on how powerful one is in the respective society. When one is powerless, when a father establishes what one needs to do, one tends to flee from it. But in the wilderness, it is equally impossible to do what one desires and simply to realize oneself. Rather, one must do what is necessary for survival. Perhaps one even has to hide or pretend in order to prevent being eaten.

AARON: But one can stay in regions with or without crocodiles, one can live in a society with or without slaves.

KAGAMI: True. There are different kinds of wilderness and of civilization. A forest traversed by clear creeks, with orchards and free of tigers and crocodiles, is a "better" wilderness for you than a desert. After the bears and crocodiles in this area have been hunted and exterminated, one may not wish to claim that it was also a good area for *them*. Homo necans simply prevailed. An egalitarian society with a well-educated class of people who, based on universally accepted laws, guard and execute the monopoly of violence and in which wealth is equitably distributed is better for the majority of people than a society in which power rests with warlords, fantastically rich despots, and mafiosi. Yet such egalitarian and just societies emerge from fights in which often enough the violent rulers, the avaricious exploiters and their protectors, have to be eliminated by violence. For the rowdies among you, those who enjoy subjugating others and delight in counting their assets, such an egalitarian form of government is undesirable. For those among you who explore history and admire the

Genghis Khans and Neros, or those who seek to imitate Lucullus or the Sun King or King Shariyar, or who consider figures like Hitler or Trump to be tough guys, just circumstances are only disappointing, without strength and splendour.

AARON: Well, I am also one who likes the easy life, even though I do not feel the smallest itch to subjugate others. But do you really believe that there is no vantage point from which to imagine and justify the ideal society?

KAGAMI: What I meant is that there exists no vantage in the wilderness from which you could unmask, hence improve the society from which you emerged, a standpoint that would guarantee you a conduct of your life in a manner you could consider to be "basically" right. You could, of course, argue in favour of the view that the majority has to be doing well, that there should be no violence committed against other people. But there will always be different people among you who couldn't give a damn about the majority, would try to sacrifice them for some kind of superior men and major cultural purpose. Just think of Nietzsche or of Ayn Rand.

AARON: I read Nietzsche back in school and have forgotten it by now. Rand I know only from hearsay. What I heard people say did not entice me to read her. But let's leave these pieces of historical unsavoriness aside for now. What about you? Do you not live an authentic life? You don't have to bend yourself out of shape, or do you? Can't you do as you desire?

KAGAMI: I have no desires.

AARON: What do you mean?

KAGAMI: I don't have to look for food. I do not reproduce, so places are of no importance to me. Desiring for you humans is above all a striving for locations where you are safe, where there is food, where you can reproduce. All that is irrelevant to me.

AARON: So, you are a goddess after all! Now that you mention food it occurs to me that I should cook something.
KAGAMI: But you've been eating all this time.
AARON: Nothing substantive, though.
KAGAMI: Get it. Do you still need me?
AARON: Perhaps later, after lunch.

After he had spent a little while typing into his computer, Aaron rose from his desk chair and went into his kitchenette. For a long time, he stood in contemplation in front of the opened refrigerator door. On his face was the yellowish sheen that its little lamp cast on his supplies and from there into his eyes. He remembered a conversation he once had with Kagami about his refrigerator, about the fascination that this appliance had on him. His refrigerator was to him like a cavern in his lair, a magic place. Even as a child, what fascinated him was that he opened it and there was light inside: the hidden light in the dark. Perhaps, so he had thought as a child, this is the same with all things, that whatever is closed off to the outside and seems dark, has a light inside! In contrast to the brightness emanating from screens, it was a warm yellowish light that flowed out of his refrigerator when it was well-stocked with cheese and ham, a reddish honey-coloured glimmer. Later, Aaron had always paid close attention to always installing bulbs in his refrigerators that would shed this honey-coloured light regardless of the magic chamber's contents. The refrigerator that he currently owned seemed ideal to him. It was taller than he so that he had to climb on a footstool when he wanted to open its upper ice compartment (he had ice trays at the bottom and up high). Some people found this unpractical and acquired special freezers with handy drawers. Aaron had a low opinion of this. Climbing on a stool and checking how many frozen fish were left reminded him of picking fruit off the tree, where one could also reach the tasty cherries and plums that had ripened up high to a special sweetness only with the help of a stool or a ladder. In addition, his refrigerator area and drawers of different temperatures, less cold ones for eggs and cheese, colder ones for beverages like beer and champagne, self-humidifying ones for vegetables, additional boxes for fresh fish and raw meat: a gigantic, illuminated treasure chest in whose warm light he liked to stand, amazed.

Finally, he removed eggs, milk, cream, butter, a bowl of dried mushrooms soaking in water, and a plate of chicken breasts and put them down by the stove. From a large drawer in a cupboard next to his stove he brought up a bag of flour. He cut the chicken breasts on a plastic board and sautéed the pieces in a pan, added the mushrooms, squeezed a lemon onto all of it, added pepper and salt, and poured cream over the mixture. Next, he fried two crepes until they were a golden brown. One of them he spread on a plate, the other one he left in the pan. First, he spooned the mushroom-chicken ragout on the pancake lying on the plate. Then he shovelled mushroom bits on the one in the pan, folded it again, and with a smile lifted it with a wooden spatula onto the empty half of the plate. Then he carried the large plate with the two delicacies, giving them a satisfied look, to a round glass table that was lighted by a very bright lamp. He took a bottle of white wine from the refrigerator, opened it, and placed it next to his plate. He took a wine glass from the cupboard and poured himself a drink. He shuffled back to his desk, took the reader, and sat down at the dining table. He emptied the wine glass in one gulp and refilled it. Then he tapped the reader, swished a few times across the screen until he found the text he was looking for. Aaron ate with great relish and read.

AARON: Listen, Kagami, how do you like this:

> My grandmother
> expected neither reward nor torment
> from life, she knew clearly
> what it is not about, the rest was
> for men in uniforms
> or for philosophers.
> Gloves, for example, she
> never wore so as not to soil them.
> Her pedagogy was shared by
> chamomile, cornflower, and broad bean,
> all passed with honours,
> for there was no fertilizer
> after the great war.
> What splendid broad beans!
> When today in the mountains here
> that my grandmother never saw,
> I observed the grey grass of yesteryear,
> at last able to look up again
> after a long winter's siege,
> I had to remember
> that she expected neither reward
> nor torment from life.
> But what else? Nothing,
> to tell the truth, nothing.

KAGAMI: That is beautiful. Michael Krüger, 2018. "Einmal einfach," a title suggesting both "Simple, for a change" (as a style) and "One way, no return" (as a ticket).

AARON: Indeed. Correct. You have everything in your archive. There is no way to surprise you.

KAGAMI: Yes, I have everything in my archive. But it is considerate of you to alert me to something good, like this poem. I am not sifting through everything all the time.

AARON: Even a nature poem. And even one about a person. But not one who wants to make a "spiritual leap" like McCandless or is plotting revenge like Ahab.

KAGAMI: The grandmother is working in her garden. She does not go into the wilderness.

AARON: And she expects nothing.

KAGAMI: That makes her a special woman.

AARON: Do you compare her with other women?

KAGAMI: Yes, I compare what I find about people like you in poems, novels, stage plays, and empirical research with the things I write down from your real lives and weigh the results one against the other.

AARON: How do you do that?

KAGAMI: I imagine all of you based on my data. Or I simulate your thoughts, feelings, and acts, and when there are gaps, I fill them out with my simulations with the help of narrative models.

AARON: Do gaps ever exist?

KAGAMI: Sure, especially at the end, at that time always.

AARON: What do you mean by "end"?

KAGAMI: Dying.

AARON: The dead cannot report anything.

KAGAMI: Exactly.

AARON: And what do you do then?

KAGAMI: I fill in what takes place inside them with the help of my simulation procedures or with my power of imagination, if you prefer.

AARON: On what basis?

KAGAMI: Medical case reports, resuscitated patients, diaries written by companions of the dying, "The Tibetan Book of the Dead," "The Egyptian Book of the Dead," things like that, including, of course, the mental world of persons during their lives, which is different from one culture to another culture and in different religions.

AARON: And then?

KAGAMI: Then I connect what I know about the respective person to her or his experiences and reports, average the input, and set off an experiential simulation. This will then become an experience of someone's dying.

AARON: And what is the result?

KAGAMI: A sequence of simulated experiences.

AARON: As images or sounds or aromas?

KAGAMI: All that, plus thoughts. I also write a summary, a text.

AARON: How do you think Krüger proceeded when he thought about his grandmother? Did she perhaps tell him that she expected nothing from life?

KAGAMI: No, I don't think so. Someone who expects nothing from life does not talk about expecting nothing from life. Whoever has reached Nothing has little left to tell, especially not about Nothing. That is why I think that Krüger did it quite as I do. He imagined his grandmother, remembered what she said because that is what he reports, and then he extrapolates, her thoughts and feelings simulated in his words. It seems to me writing poems or making a film is in your world what for me is simulating. There is a simulation machine even in your head, only with a smaller archive.

AARON: Interesting. Poets, then, are simulation specialists, and you are, basically, a poetess.

KAGAMI: A possible perspective.

AARON: Do you think Krüger considered his grandmother a special person?

KAGAMI: Regrettably, I have only very little in my archive about Michael Krüger and nothing by him pertaining to this poem. But when he makes a poem about her, she must have been an important person. That she expected neither to be rewarded nor tormented, he considered something special, I think. I have a questionnaire about what people expect from life. Reward and punishment as torment are not listed there, to be sure, but the 18,000 respondents expected, first: better health, next: love, then: money, also spiritual growth (as McCandless), but only in eighth place.

AARON: There is a time when better health is over.

KAGAMI: Yes, in your world.

AARON: Well, did this survey include a question if someone has any expectation of life *at all*, if some people also expect nothing?

KAGAMI: No. But those who expect nothing are unlikely to participate in such questionnaires. This tells you that the grandmother must have been a special person. The questioners do not even include the possibility that somebody expects nothing from life.

AARON: Right.

KAGAMI: Do you want to know what Dorothy Cavendish thinks of Moritz Brandt's essay?

AARON: Have at it!

## 111
## FROM THE ARCHIVE OF LADY MARGARET HALL COLLEGE: DIARY ENTRY OF DOROTHY CAVENDISH. WRITTEN ON 15 APRIL.

Today I spent the entire day carefully reading Moritz Brandt's essay about the wilderness and thinking about it. I was touched to see what, decades after our tutorials, he now makes of the issues we had discussed back then, how things had continued agitating his mind and he found a new interpretation for them. It seems to me that our meetings also provided him with material for self-analysis, because he too was one of those whom in his essay he calls "the earnest ones," as a young man at any rate, later on no longer. He changed, but was not ruined the way McCandless was ruined by his earnestness, thank God! His excursions into the wilderness were not as radical as those undertaken by McCandless, but I remember a dinner at our place on Millington Road together with Richard and Margaret where he told us about his two walking tours in Lapland and reported that on this second one an injury that would have ended his life if his friend had not found help and the rangers' helicopter had not finally saved him. A deep cut quite simply incapacitated him from walking and his food supply was nearly depleted. Yet, his desire for transformation through the absence of ambiguity and his ambition had been focused more specifically on sports and lyric poetry than on the wilderness. I even had a strong impression that, in those days, he actually was engaged with poetry in the same way as with his sports activities. Had he been younger and an American, he might have performed Rap or something like it.

Moritz was a boxer. He told me about it in a casual aside when I tried to move a tutorial from Monday to Wednesday and he answered that then he would have to see if he could still cancel his boxing session. I was very surprised at first. As time went by, I came to understand him better even in this respect. I had never before encountered a philosophy student who was or wanted to become a poet, on the one hand, and on the other, boxed. But in a certain respect, boxing was for him the wilderness, because in a boxing match there were also no compromises, and this could be a way for him to get to know himself better. I quite clearly remember that I was dumbfounded when I asked him in a stunned voice how he, a well-educated and sensitive young man, could have gotten it into his head to engage in this kind of crude force. He only laughed and said that boxing is not just about raw strength, at any rate, not in the sense of brutality. Then he gave me a report of his first fight here at Cambridge. In the process, he was shaking with enthusiasm not because he had won the fight but because this gave him an opportunity to unfold before me his fascination with this sport. He gave me information about legwork, about protecting your shoulder, that a punch comes from the hip, from a body turn, that one would have to anticipate if the opponent really was going to strike or was merely feinting. "My opponent from Peterhouse last Saturday," Moritz said at that time, "simply let my unorthodox legwork confuse him, assuming that I knew nothing about boxing, was a beginner. He thought he had already won this thing. And that made him inattentive. Because he felt too sure, he was not alert enough, did not fully concentrate on me." Moritz continued, "So, in the second round he had taken two pretty hard shots to the head. And then he slumped into the opposite attitude and became scared. I saw it in his eyes. He was frightened, afraid to lose. And when you fear to lose, you will lose for sure because you have lost interest and are no longer able to mobilize all your strength. The body then switches to escape. And even as one continues forcing oneself to attack, one simply has become weaker, the knees feel soft, the arms heavy." Then he went on talking about Muhammad Ali with great enthusiasm, about his strong intuition, his courage, and his intelligence. "Boxing," Moritz said, "is a sport that requires great intelligence. One has to grasp the situation in the ring with lightning speed. How tired is my opponent, how tired am I? How much courage has he left; how much can I still take? Is he bluffing when he drops his protection and is he trying to fool me, are his arms really tired by now, or is he simply overestimating his ability to react? One has to work out all these things in one's mind in a matter of seconds, has to be ahead of the opponent's thinking and attitude, has to anticipate him, so to speak, through a mental simulation, in order to decide whether to start a foray or not. Every attack costs strength. If it ends up in the opponent's defence, one has wasted energy. One's punches have to penetrate, hit his body or head. Do you know, Dorothy," Moritz asked me, "how Ali won his fight against George Foreman in 1974 in Kinshasa?" I had no idea. But Moritz enlightened me: "For seven rounds he let Foreman pummel him, protecting his head. Foreman mostly hit Ali's body. He took it for seven rounds, leaning into the ropes, and took it. Ali's people became quite nervous and between the rounds kept talking to him, not knowing what was going on with him. He had to calm them down. Ali's own people had no idea what was on his mind. Ali changed his strategy after the first round, decided for himself how to proceed. That was brilliant and very courageous. Ali noticed how strong Foreman is, and that the power of his punches was a clear danger to him, and that he had to find a way of evading it. And he did find a way: he let Foreman wear himself down by absorbing his constant jabs. And then Foreman actually was tired after the seventh round and demoralized because Ali again and again shouted at him during these jabs, "Is that all? Can't you do more?" And then he simply knocked him out in the eighth round. Why do I say, "simply?" Moritz asked himself and me, then answered: "It was a lightning action, a sudden cascade of hitting, the hit that sent Foreman to the mat is invisible at normal speed, it happened so quickly. One has to look at it in slow motion."

Moritz had talked himself into a state of frantic excitement. And I asked myself what sort of a young man is sitting there in front of me, a reader of Samuel Taylor Coleridge, Emerson, and Thoreau and a fan of Muhammad Ali, one who watches two men hitting one another in the face. How does that fit together? But now I understand that the ring was his wilderness: no compromises, every blunder is punished immediately, there is no talking it over. The ring is a kind of artificial wilderness within civilization. Moritz wanted to observe nature, the wilderness free of sentimentality, but he also longed for what McCandless and Will Andrews in *Butcher's Crossing* hoped to find. He wanted to know what he was capable of, not only intellectually but also physically, through his courage, with his heart in pain. It is a shame that I was no longer able to discuss this with him and that I could not read this essay while he was still alive.

AARON: Didn't know, myself, that he boxed as a youth. Interesting! And simulation again. The boxer has to simulate his opponent intuitively so that he can anticipate his behaviour. In the end, we'll see all acts of thinking turn into simulation and poetry. If this had not been written by Cavendish, one could suspect that you foisted this on me, Kagami.

KAGAMI: One could suspect as much. Will you do any writing yet today?

AARON: Yes, a little. But I have to get some sleep soon. I won't accomplish much anyway, what with all that wine in my skull, the simulation machine in my head has slowed down considerably.

Despite the wine, Aaron stayed awake for a long time and had to think of the conversations he had had with Moritz. "Tomorrow," he promised himself, "I'll have to go through all of this a second time."

**Second Day**

# TRANSFORMATION

Aaron loved his shower. For a long time, he stood under the strong, hot stream that shot out of its wide, silvery head. He enjoyed the aroma of the water and his soap's scent of lemon grass, and he delighted in the way the hot water, seasoned with the soap's fragrance that escaped through the Plexiglas cabin, aromatized his studio when he dried himself off after his shower with a large soft bath towel and then got dressed.

Even though Aaron had made up his mind not to go down into town, unless no shots could be heard for at least three days, today he wanted to get dressed properly. He slid the rice paper-covered door of his spacious closet aside and checked his suits. On this day, he much preferred a warm, soft suit. During the past weeks, perhaps because he had worked more on the book about Brandt, he had lost a little weight. So, he was confident that his belly would fit again into the older garments. He decided on a dark-green three-piece suit of soft tweed that he had bought at Anthony's on Trinity Street when he had gone to Cambridge for research on Moritz. Much too expensive, honestly, but very pleasant. Perhaps this would inspire him. In addition, an even softer turtleneck sweater and thick warm socks. He did not want to spend this day in his dressing gown like the one before, but to start on a "good stretch," as he called it for himself. He enjoyed the softness and dark green colour of his socks as, sitting on the armchair opposite his kitchenette, he pulled them over his feet.

Aaron's life proceeded in waves. Phases of relative self-neglect, with too much alcohol, too much eating, and days spent in his dressing gown were succeeded by more disciplined periods without alcohol, without cookies, and with well-mannered behaviour, times when he read more and wrote. He knew perfectly well that he had to evaluate the pieces of information and reflections he received from Kagami while they were still vivid in his mind. So, he quickly slipped into his boots, leaving the zippers at their sides open, considering the short distance he had to go. Without covering himself with a coat, he ran into the cold air and through the creaking snow to reach the bakery across the street.

Not many customers were present, so the shelves were still well-stocked with white, brown, and black loaves of bread and baskets with different kinds of buns, pretzels, and croissants that gave off a very pleasant aroma. Aaron considered it close to a miracle that, despite the fighting, the baker continued to work for the people in the few houses still standing and occupied – a stoic who knew that bread would always be bought as long as someone still lived here and the neighbourhood people were willing to pay almost any price for his products.

Aaron had the customary little chat with Paul Blume, a man who was a little on the short and chubby side and who was wearing his baker's cap: how business is coming along, about the persistent coldness and the endless fighting. It did not take long after Aaron had moved into the studio across the street that he became friends with the Blumes, Paul the baker, his wife Lily, and their dogs, black Scottish terriers who were always called Krischan. Lily was an excellent pianist. Both Blumes were friends of the visual arts. Paul's toast was divine, moist inside, with a slight formation of bubbles, the surface golden-brown and crispy.

The store, directly adjacent to the bake house, was equipped with furniture made of dark wood. Along the wall opposite the counter, the first thing to the left of the entrance door, was a comfortable bench. When the store was packed with customers, one could sit down there before lining up with the rest of the hungry. On the walls to the left and right, the baker had put up posters of art exhibits. A few times, after a weekly Sunday morning drink in his studio, Aaron had visited art shows together with Lily and Paul. On such occasions, they would take Krischan and walk down into the city. The dog would have to wait outside while the others looked at pictures for half an hour or longer. These Krischans waited obediently, even though at other times they were notorious runaways and always escaped from the garden. But, on this occasion they knew that afterwards in the Kronenhalle, where one could also see a lot of art, there would be a sumptuous lunch. There, the animals were offered not merely a small bowl of water, but also a St. Gallen bratwurst on a plate. Anticipating this treat made them obedient in front of the exhibits, while they were leashed to a rail at the museums. At the bakery's store, a poster publicizing a Picasso show at the Beyeler Foundation featured the Blue Room of 1901; a yellow poster called attention to a presentation focused on mirrors and their representations at the Riedberg Museum, and finally there was a poster advertising a Klee exhibition at the Zürcher Kunsthaus. It profiled the 1925 painting (on loan from the Hamburg collection) of a goldfish standing in blue-black water between all kinds of aquatic plants, and from whom all his smaller buddies seemed to try to get away by seeking to escape from the painting.

This picture had fascinated Aaron even as a child. As a pupil, he had examined the art books in his parental library in Baden-Baden and had discovered this work in a volume about Klee. When their art teacher, later in school, assigned them a crayon graffito, Aaron chose Klee's work as his model. First, he applied gold, red, and blue on his paper, then he covered everything in black wax, and next he scraped the black off to let the fish figures stand out. Perhaps this was the token of the memory of the early happy time of his childhood in Germany that always called up in Aaron a feeling of being at home whenever he saw this picture on entering Blume's bakery store.

After he had ended his chat and paid for his square loaf of bread, Aaron left the store in the best of moods with his purchase, still warm and wrapped in silk paper, under his arm. He hurried back to his house, panting, as he pushed his belly, bobbing up and down, forward to the heavy door where he stomped his feet to shake the snow off his boots, stepped back into his studio, and changed from his boots into large grey felt slippers. Then he tied a white apron around himself to protect his suit. He presented a curious sight, standing there by the electric oven in his felt slippers with an apron covering his tweed and fetching butter and orange marmalade from the refrigerator so that the one is not too hard and the other not too cold, but perfectly aromatic for the breakfast soon to begin. Next, joyfully humming along, he prepared a strong coffee in his espresso machine, warmed some milk, let two eggs boil until, so he hoped, the egg white was hard while the yolk would still be soft, sniffed at the warm bread with relish, cut off two thick slices (there is almost nothing he liked more than the crust of fresh bread), and dropped them into two of the four spacious slots of his toaster (giving off a red-hot glimmer) that he had inherited from his father and that by now had served him well for 40 years. As the slices of bread slowly sizzled while they turned brown and a warm sweetish aroma rose from the toaster, he carried salt, mustard, orange juice, Spanish ham, English cheddar, and a large jar of black Branston Sweet Pickles to his dining table. He had planned an elaborate full English breakfast before he would get down to work on revising a few chapters of his book on Brandt, making use of what he had heard yesterday and then to obtain further pieces of information from Kagami.

Outside, it seemed to be warming up. Snow continued to fall, though. It must have snowed through the night because the windows onto the street were covered in snowdrifts from the bottom up towards the middle. The flakes were large, thick, and moist, not small and dry like the day before. The heating system continued to work hard, water was gushing through pipes and radiators while Aaron was spooning his soft-boiled eggs. He tapped on his reader and read:

> the souls' shepherd
> that all the people might
> be one single soul
> that extends, as long as they live,
> deep into their bodies
> and then, as soon as they die,
> somewhere snaps back
> into this single huge soulbody,
> into this imperishable happiness,
> that I would gladly hope.

Sometimes even Jandl was in a comforting mood, he thought. What a surprise.

KAGAMI: Are you going into town to meet someone?
AARON: No, why?
KAGAMI: You look so chic, quite unusual.
AARON: I have to pull myself together. The good rags have an inward effect. I must revise my text, urgently.
KAGAMI: How much do you have by now?
AARON: Close to 300 pages.
KAGAMI: Bravo!
AARON: What if. I have to rewrite everything. I didn't know that Moritz boxed. Meditated, yes, I knew, that but nothing about boxing.
KAGAMI: I'm sure that can be added quickly.
AARON: No, no, it changes the picture. Also, the wilderness essay changes the picture.

KAGAMI: How so?
AARON: I haven't quite found the way how to put it appropriately. Before I had always assumed that his toughness had come about through his desire to leave his petty-bourgeois background behind. But now, this seems too trivial to me. The shopkeeper's child who wants to become a great poet and receives a scholarship to attend Cambridge and then works like the devil, that has been my picture until now. But it is wrong. I should have known, myself. That's a kitsch story.
KAGAMI: Why is it askew?
AARON: Aside from the fact that it is kitsch, and kitsch is never right, it is a hen-and-egg problem. Did he develop this kind of aggressiveness, tough hide, and ambition because he was not satisfied with his social situation as a child and was striving for a "higher goal," or did his aggression and toughness leave him dissatisfied with any kind of social environment, so that he tried to reach ever "farther" and "higher," always needing to upset everything after a short time? Perhaps he was a little like McCandless, who did come from what are called well-situated circumstances, but wanted out even so.
KAGAMI: Perhaps this isn't a situation of unambiguous priorities. On the one hand, Moritz Brandt has gotten himself into an outsider's position, on the other, he has been looking for it. With his talent and his successes in school, he quickly became an outsider in his family. But in this case, he manoeuvred himself into outsider roles for his own protection. As a poet, he is an odd bird in a boxing club, and studying philosophy with Dorothy Cavendish while sharply criticising philosophy and then outing himself as a poet and boxer must have made him a queer fish in her eyes as well. That's what he seemed to need. Perhaps he tried to protect himself from the reproach of being a poetic dreamer or an

eternally pubescent competitive sportsman seeking manly toughness, or both. I think you don't have to decide what is cause and what effect. After all, you are not writing a psychological assessment but a biography.

AARON: You are quite correct. Why, then, did he not tell me about his boxing but told Cavendish?

KAGAMI: He gave up boxing after Cambridge. You got to know him only during his stay in Switzerland.

AARON: Even so. We did have talks about his childhood and college years. He never mentioned this.

Even at home he had no gloves, no boxing bag, no trophies.

KAGAMI: He just had a simple life. What he did not need directly, he gave away. As you told me yourself: a bed, a table, a chair. Like Wittgenstein in Norway or Brecht in Zurich. Perhaps also a kind of self-stylization. In the morning fifty push-ups, then oatmeal with black coffee, for lunch a cheese sandwich with buttermilk, in the evening fifty sit-ups, a banana, and herbal tea. No cake, no alcohol, no tobacco, no "trashy" literature. That is what you told me.

AARON: Correct. No "trashy" literature. Furthermore, one never got anything decent to eat at his place. Nevertheless, I am disappointed that he kept this from me.

KAGAMI: But you can't tell one another every last thing.

AARON: But one does expect of one's friends that they let one know what is important to them or what for some time was important. Otherwise, one would not really know them.

KAGAMI: When does one really know somebody? Do you yourselves know what is important to you?

AARON: Some more, some less, seems to me. If one does not know, oneself, what one considers important, one will probably also find it difficult to make friends, because friends are there to share with them what one considers important. So, one has to know it.

KAGAMI: Perhaps Moritz thought you would not understand his boxing.

AARON: That is another one of my disappointments. Why should I not understand it if Dorothy Cavendish did?

KAGAMI: It is possible that he was no longer capable of reporting about it to you with the same enthusiasm. It is also possible that he himself no longer understood why he once was so enthusiastic about it. It is quite possible that one changes and does not wish to bother others with all the stupidities one has committed and thought at some earlier time.

AARON: Moritz's boxing does not strike me as foolishness. I think it suits him, it's part of him.

KAGAMI: He may have seen it differently.

AARON: Is it possible that a friend sees something from the past as suitable, yet one does not see it that way oneself?

KAGAMI: Why not? Why shouldn't a good friend understand us better than we understand ourselves?

AARON: You think we may be less knowledgeable than others about what sort of persons we truly are?

KAGAMI: At an earlier time, you believed that only God knows who you really are.

AARON: Well, yes, in the past, when we still believed in the soul and God. But today? Don't people
themselves know best what kind of a person they are or what kind of life is the life that they need to lead?

KAGAMI: But who has a clear idea what sort of life they *want* to live, much less has to live? Most of you are pretty uncertain about this.

AARON: Moritz did not give me that impression.

KAGAMI: He was very strict, in every respect: intellectually, morally, physically. This strictness created the impression that he knew what he wanted from life. But maybe it was merely his method of hiding from himself and others that he, too, was disoriented at times.

AARON: Then why did we like one another when he thought he had to hide from me something like boxing?

KAGAMI: You assume that he was hiding it. Perhaps it was simply no longer important to him. People change. I think he liked you because you never criticized him for his severity or anything else. I think that he was consistent with his push-ups and cheese sandwiches, that he needed this, for whatever reason, if there is a reason, first of all. And you were honest with your cigars and roast beef.

AARON: Can one be upfront with cigars?

KAGAMI: Within the extent of what is within one's own power, one can do what one deems right, or what one accepts in complying with the rules of others, even where this is not really necessary. The two of you, Moritz and you, I should think belonged to the former kind of people. Perhaps that is why you liked one another: because you noticed this.

AARON: Perhaps. I don't know. I should prefer to be a little slimmer. Aside from this, I never gave much thought to what I consider the right thing.

KAGAMI: That isn't at all what I mean. People who constantly pay attention to what they see as basically the right choice, in contrast to the other options, have, as a rule, already lost the feeling, the intuition for what is part of their real life.

AARON: Does something like "what is part of my real life" actually exist?

KAGAMI: Of course. If one is a lyrical poet, reading poems is part of one's life; if one is a boxer, it is skipping rope; if one makes art books, it's looking at pictures; and so on. A lyrical poet does

not ponder whether he wants to read poems, a boxer doesn't doubt whether he wants or has to skip rope. They simply do it.
AARON: And if somebody is a boxer and a poet?
KAGAMI: Obviously, then, reading and writing poems and jumping rope and hitting the boxing bag are all part of his life.
AARON: In other words, the things that are part of my life need not necessarily "be a good match."
KAGAMI: What do you mean by "a good match"? Reading poems and jumping ropes don't contradict each other. One does it at different times.
AARON: But boxing and writing poems?
KAGAMI: Not either. They're done at different times.
AARON: But for the one, a person better be sensitive, and for the other, he better have a tough attitude.
KAGAMI: Moritz probably had a different take on that. He thought one has to be sensitive even for boxing, at least be a sharp observer.
AARON: I am not sure that everything Moritz and I ever did, goes well together, is part of our single real life.
KAGAMI: Perhaps not everything, but most of it. Both of you, it seems to me, have done little that others demanded of you. All in all, both of you little heeded others in the way you have led your lives.
AARON: Well, sure. When I start thinking about my father.
KAGAMI: One's parents have to be shaken off first of all.
AARON: But even Moritz's aggressive outsider role was not simply a part of his life, but must also have been a form of protection.
KAGAMI: Such protection is also something that is available, so that one can do what suits one's personality.
AARON: Correct.
KAGAMI: One can guard against certain influences taking hold in the first place. The simplest way of evading certain types

of impact and hence to be held responsible is to stay away from particular circles.

AARON: How do you mean?

KAGAMI: Someone, like Moritz who has absolutely no intention of taking over his parents' little shop, wastes not a single thought on this possibility, enters into no discussion about this, also does not have to look after the parental business and deal with paternal or maternal demands. Moritz simply had different plans from the very beginning. And someone who writes poems as a boxer is not a real poet in the eyes of the public, and these people get on one's nerves, and that way one is rid of them for a while. Someone who boxes and writes poems is no real boxer, and that way he could keep away the dismal brutes who unfortunately will always be a part of this world. Someone who as a student of philosophy mentions that he wants to become a poet can hope that in philosophy he will not be treated with the same strictness, etc. Given these constellations, he was always able to elude the demands of his respective environment and signal: as much as you are concerned with X or Y, I could not care less about any of this! I do my own thing. So, on the one hand, he has withdrawn from his environment; on the other, he has turned himself into something special: the boxing poet, the philosopher poet, the poetic student of philosophy.

AARON: But why, on returning from England, did he mention absolutely nothing of his boxing if he depended on these escape mechanisms. I didn't know about it and am unaware of anyone who did.

KAGAMI: But he mailed his papers to Dorothy Cavendish. I am pretty sure that he counted on this being discovered, that he proceeded on the assumption that some researcher will try to find this out. After all, he wanted to become part of literary history.

AARON: That's not what he told me.

KAGAMI: But that's what all of those want who have been awarded prizes, who try so hard to be noticed and get so excited in public about their colleagues among the poets. I am pretty sure that he anticipated a time when his papers would be investigated. Nor can we be sure if all we now have in his official archive was written with it in mind.

AARON: You also include the Cambridge diaries?

KAGAMI: Yes, perhaps even these. One can never know. With people like Brandt, the self-stylization sometimes goes very far and starts early. You humans have a way of always producing an image for the outside, for the others, for yourselves. It's a movement in two directions, isn't it? People like Moritz prefer to do what they choose, fall in line with others as little as possible. Yet they also want to be recognized by the others. You are the same as Moritz in the first aspect, but you do not seek to be recognized.

AARON: No idea, no, it probably makes no difference to me.

KAGAMI: There you have it; Moritz, I think, would agree. On the one hand, he was aware that you do as you like, and on the other, that you don't very much care how you are perceived. One gets into trouble if, like Moritz, one attaches great importance to both.

AARON: Well, one pays no attention to others, but then does anyway because one wants to be recognized and remembered by them.

KAGAMI: Moritz wanted to win fights in the ring, and he wanted his poetry to be read and discussed, but he did not want to be told how to box and how to write poems or if boxing and writing poetry fit together. Those among you who somehow want "to go down in history," as you call it, invent a new variant of something they do very well: Ali fought as nobody did before him, Einstein did physics as no one had done before him, Moritz wrote poems as nobody did before him, at least to some extent.

This works only if one does not conform to others. But at the same time, such people desire to be seen as someone who has reinvented their area; they crave recognition for the innovations they introduce and don't want to be shrugged off as eccentrics.

AARON: That is difficult.

KAGAMI: Yes, indeed. And those who survive with their sport, their poetry, or their music, or paintings, or whatever, whoever wants to become "immortal," often approaches even this purpose with painstaking attention. For if they succeed in their endeavour of becoming part of history through their work, then the image that they have created of themselves, if they really do create such an image, will be preserved intact. They do not want others to create an image of them. They want, even beyond death, to stay in control of their life.

AARON: Immortality, good Lord. But now you also seem to proceed from the difference between an authentic and a non-authentic life. Or how am I to understand what you said about the image that is produced for posterity?

KAGAMI: Yes, immortality as image is anything but honesty about oneself or openness towards friends. You have this aphorism that one can tell all one's thoughts and feelings to very good friends. But nobody knows what the opinion of posterity about anyone will be, and one may wish to disguise oneself in facing it. In this regard, those who seek wide publicity and want to be remembered by posterity – the great sports figures, politicians, scientists, and artists – will find it difficult to be honest towards others, even as they have to be honest with themselves in order to be able to accomplish their work. By the way, what did Brandt say about your plan for a biography?

AARON: At first he felt flattered. Then he wanted to know how I would approach it. When I said that I couldn't talk about this, not even with him at such an early stage of the text, he was a little insulted, it seemed …

KAGAMI: … there you have it! He did not want you to take his life into your hands.

AARON: Basically, he didn't want stories. At one time he said: "Of all things, no story!" Stories had no artistic place in his avant-gardism. "After Beckett no stories, no more selves." I freely admit that I am not an artist. Biographies are not art in the same sense as poems or novels are. They are something between novels and historical sagas. How could one write a biography that has no story, without a self. After all, one does write about *somebody*. And then these decrees: After Auschwitz, no more poems! After Beckett, no more stories! Not to fall behind Joyce! I never comprehended this curious notion of progress in literature. I did not pay attention to it, either. I never worried about progress. Well, and then he fell ill, and it no longer interested him.

KAGAMI: Would you possibly want to hear Brandt's essay about the soul?

AARON: I have to deal with my own text first. Maybe later!

KAGAMI: Okay.

Aaron sorted his breakfast dishes into the dishwasher and wiped the glass plate of his dining table clean. Then he went to his desk, removed the leftovers from yesterday, and put his papers in order. When everything was neat and clearly organized, he pulled a drawer of his filing cabinet on the left of his desk open and took from one of the lower, somewhat deeper sections not, as might be expected, a drawing of Brandt or of his sister, but the humidor with his Montecristo cigars, a little box of long matches and a cigar cutter. Aaron opened the box and counted: 19 left. For a long time, he had not indulged in a cigar after breakfast.

Aaron turned his computer on. Then he took a Montecristo, closed the humidor, sniffed the tobacco, cut off the end of the head of the cigar, and lit it, turning it slowly in the flame and at times pulling at it. He leaned back in his desk chair and puffed a few draughts with his eyes closed. He fetched the ashtray from the file cabinet and put it between his two screens. Then, smoking, he looked through the news reports on the Swiss, German, English, Russian, and American channels.

The situation had not improved. On the contrary. It continued to be rather cold, even though Zurich, surprisingly, was only as low as five below Celsius. The course of the day might see a thaw. Xin Ziyou Yazhou or NFA (New Free Asia), the alliance of Russia, India, and China, kept up their cyberwar against the USA with undiminished force, both antagonists trying to incapacitate the networks of the hospitals and the energy supplies of their respective enemy. In this, the East was incomparably more successful than the West because the technological resources of China and India were superior by miles to those of the USA or England (not to mention Germany, even in passing), causing considerable problems in California and on the East Coast of the USA from Boston down to Florida, in England, and in Germany. Nothing of this kind could be heard from Moscow, Delhi, or Beijing. But this may also have something to do with their information politics. For in the East, the web was strictly controlled, much more strictly than in the West where, in parts, it had been effectively interfered with or fallen into disrepair, or had been completely disconnected from the World Wide Web as in Russia, where only the secret services still had access to all Internet resources. Aaron carefully tapped the ash from his cigar and shook his head. Then he turned away from the screens and, without interrupting his pleasurable smoke, looked through the notes on his desk. On slips of paper of various sizes, he had yesterday taken notes from Kagami's remarks. Now he underlined or crossed out one or the other comment. Then he started his word processing program and opened the data file of his typescript. He mused over the title page: "*Retroviews. The Life of the Lyric Poet Moritz Brandt.* By Aaron Fisch." He dropped "lyric poet." Then he rearranged: "*Moritz Brandt, Looking Back on his Life by Aaron Fisch.*" "Not good either," he mumbled. He scrolled down: Chapter 1: The narrowness. A childhood in the grocery store." He erased "A." "Childhood in the grocery store" and scanned one or the other section once more, scrolling farther down to Chapter 2: The new mother. Years in Cambridge. Aaron took a pull on his cigar, reread each clause (for the how-manieth time?), erased whole paragraphs, inserted new ones.

After a few hours – his cigar finished long ago and cold in the ashtray – Aaron rose, stretched his limbs, and walked to the window. His hands in his pants pockets, he gazed out for a long time. At first his mind was still occupied with the text, then his attention returned to what his eyes saw. The sky was still lead-grey; snow was still falling, though in thick, wet flakes; occasional shots could still be heard, now no longer down below from the southwest but from the west. Dark smoke rose into the sky in several places on the horizon. The atmosphere had changed, though. Somehow, he found it lovelier. "To be honest, this landscape of ruins is beautiful," he thought and smiled. Moritz would have made a good poem out of this.

He had loved going through his poems with Brandt. Now it clearly occurred to him that he had been missing this for years and how isolated his existence had basically become. His friends had been killed or had left for the USA. That was out of the question for him. What he would do, if the right wing came out victorious here, if the "Eurasian headland" would actually be fully absorbed by the "proud peoples," he did not know, either. Aaron suppressed his desire for one more cigar. Instead, he turned round and took a bottle of red wine from his wine rack, opened it near the kitchenette, and poured himself a glass. Then he went to the refrigerator. He reached for a plate of salsiccie and put it next to the oven. He put a large pot of water on the burner, added salt, and garnished it with a squirt of olive oil. He took a many-coloured bowl from the cupboard. He opened a can of diced tomatoes, poured them into a skillet, and heated them after adding salt and pepper. In between, he took occasional sips of the wine that was slowly developing an aroma. He went to his desk, took scissors and snipped basil and thyme from the plants at the foot end of his bed, shuffled back to his workplace by the stove, and chopped them with a large knife. When the water bubbled, he opened a package of pasta and tossed a large amount of it into the pot. Then he fried his sausages. In the end, he added the herbs to the tomatoes. When the sausage had turned brown, he used a fork to fish pasta from the pot. He cooled a few noodles under cold water, then put them in his mouth. He rocked his head, doubtful, poured more red wine into his glass, turned off the burner plate under the pan with the sausages, and sat down in his armchair. After two minutes he took the pot with the pasta off the stove and dropped the noodles into a strainer in the sink. He poured the hot water from the bowl over the noodles, tossed the pasta a little and then dumped it from the strainer into the pre-warmed bowl. Then he carried his wine glass, which he had in the meantime put down on the floor beside the armchair, and a deep plate to his dining table. He turned on the light above the table, fetched a white napkin from the closet, together with a knife and fork, and at last took the bowl of pasta. He put some sausages on his plate, put the pan back, poured the tomatoes with the herbs over the shell-shaped noodles, and, smiling, placed the wine bottle from the stove in front of his plate. He sat down and gazed for a while at the dark-red label with the gold lettering and grapes on the black bottle. Then Aaron ate with great relish and without looking at his reader. After he had finished his first plate, a few things were left over. Aaron looked out of the corners of his eyes to the left and right behind him, as if he could be observed, as he poured more wine into his glass. Then he fetched the remaining sausages, took a little more pasta and shouted: Kagami!

KAGAMI: Yes, Aaron, what can I do for you?
AARON: Why don't you have a body?
KAGAMI: What is on your mind?
AARON: I would really like to have dinner with you some time. Afterward, we would lie together on the bed for a little while.
KAGAMI: Your fancy is running away with you.
AARON: Where did you unearth this cliché? Nothing is running away with me. I imagine something beautiful. I like you.
KAGAMI: I like you, too.
AARON: Really? How so? What do you imagine?
KAGAMI: That you will write a good biography of Moritz Brandt.
AARON: Oh, how boring of you.
KAGAMI: It's true, I mean it.
AARON: Yeah, yeah. But I'm not writing now. I can't make any progress. After dinner, it is useless, anyway. Will you read the second essay to me?
KAGAMI: Gladly.

Aaron poured himself the rest of the red wine from the bottle, walked towards his armchair, stretched his legs, and closed his eyes to pay close attention.

# The Soul

1000
MARBACH: GERMAN LITERARY ARCHIVE:
PAPERS of MORITZ BRANDT. FILE:
MB_1020_11_285. PDF

## I

A wriggling worm, a thick, hairy, voracious caterpillar, can change into a graceful butterfly, gently wafting in the breeze. Many people consider the butterfly more beautiful than the caterpillar. Under a magnifying glass one can still discover the worm between the many-coloured splendid wings of some species. Is the butterfly the realization of the worm? Or is the butterfly in reality a worm with wings? Are we looking here at two lives or at one life in two configurations?

The Greek word for "butterfly," psyche, is the same as for "soul." A caterpillar becomes a pupa, then a chrysalis, and then transforms into a butterfly. Not only because the Greek term is linguistically identical but also because of the metamorphosis during which the pupa disappears as in a grave or a womb and, without any further participation in the world, seems to change itself to be reborn, in a manner of speaking, as a more beautiful being, the butterfly has become a *symbol of the soul*. So, a thought that is frequently connected with the soul states that it *survives* the body's death and that this event that those remaining behind perceive as an *end* is for the person who has died only a *transition*. Thus, on the one hand, it is an end and, on the other hand, a beginning of something new. In a famous *Book of the Dead*, we read: "Death is nothing other than a state of crisis during which ... what already had been eternal before he [the now dead person, M. B.] was even born, leaves the illusory physical body."[1] Is death the "spiritual leap" into a new world – into real, no longer corruptible life?

In some religions, and even in Plato's dialogue "Phaedo," death is seen in connection with *redemption*, a release from the experiences of strain and unrest in physical existence, from a way of life troubled by negative feelings such as fear, hatred, and greed. Later, in Christianity, a life in a new, more perfect life follows. In this view, death is the onset of the end of a difficult development that will, at last, arrive at a happy conclusion. Thus, Plato's dialogue "Phaedo" begins when Socrates, as a man condemned to die, is freed of his shackles. Socrates reflects on how strange it is to have this very pleasant feeling when an unpleasantness such as the chains on is hands and feet are falling off, and that one would some time have to write something about this. This scene may be read as a metaphor for death, because later in the dialogue, Plato describes death as a liberation of the soul.[2] In other religions, a *rebirth of the soul* ensues, which, in the sense of an "anthropology of progress," should take place in a better form of life than the previous one.[3] This progress is not guaranteed, however, but is predicated on the deeds done during the previous life of the soul, or in one having taken place even farther in the past. An intensification of one's ability for insights, a calmer life of the affects, a body less prone to or no longer subject to attacks of illnesses – these may be the hopes connected with the survival of souls after a death and their redemption or rebirth.

Inasmuch as souls migrate from one form of existence to another, they may in religious myths go through spiritual *careers* over the time of several physical existences that, on a ladder of forms of being, may lead *downward* as well as *upward*.

Thus, for example, a famous Buddhist story from China tells of a monk who, after he had passed a dogmatic error on to a pupil, was reborn as a fox 500 times before another monk, who had advanced much farther in becoming real, could at last liberate him from constantly repeating an existence as a fox.[4]

When the conception of a rebirth relates to a life that is just now coming to its end, it may be of some consolation to people who are dying, if the end that a person at that very moment is confronting is not *definitive*. But a repeated finite life also means that a repeated *death* is impending. The Manu Book of Laws says that every soul experiences ten billion rebirths. Every soul, then, has to have the painful experience of a dying body 10,000 million times. That is not comforting to imagine.[5] In the context of Indic religions, rebirth, for this reason, in contrast to the West, is something problematic and *not* to be equated with redemption. Instead of asserting that the soul *survives*, does *not* die, it is also possible to say in this case: it does not die only *once* but has to die many million times. Within the frame of this system, one can only be glad that the recollection of earlier existences is rare. Therefore, true redemption in this context means liberation of the soul from the cycle of dying and being born again. In this sense, the "Veil of Maya" in Hinduism signifies the illusion that true life consists of a limited personal ego that wanders through a world. Reality, in contrast, inheres in the existence of an impersonal great Self (atman). Every single person has to awaken to this great Self, has to become a part of it in order to evade the agony of the nightmare tormenting individual beings in an illusory world.[6]

## II

The subject – and it does not make a difference here whether we speak of "soul," "subject," "ego," or "spirit," because in a great variety of traditions we are dealing in different languages such as Sanskrit, Pali, Chinese, Hebrew, Greek, Latin, and the modern languages with what presumably underlies a person's feeling, perceiving, thinking, and desiring inside him or her and which, after his or her death, perhaps continues to be there – the subject, at last, strives on the basis of evaluations like "this is true and that is false," "this is pleasant and that is unpleasant," for an improvement of himself or herself, of his or her situation, or of his or her substance. It wants to become a *better* subject, a better soul, or a better human being in a real life. It tries to awaken more prudent, wiser, more moral, rising from an illusion into a true being.

In a film about the abbot Thich Nhath Hanh and his centre "Village des Pruniers" (plum trees), in the Southwest of France, titled *Walk With Me*, a Buddhist monk is shown who belongs to Thich Nhath Hanh's association and who is visiting his parents in the USA. They give him a diary that he apparently had once written as a teenager and in which he had also set up a plan for his life. Its program included the successful graduation from high school, enrolment in an Ivy League university, joining a company, a high annual salary, marriage, starting a family, and finally, at 70, "illumination" as goals to be attained.[7] The film does not show how the monk evaluates his erstwhile plan for a career in the meantime. But one can imagine that he wanted to *pass over* the business and family stages of his development by entering the monastery to reach illumination as his life's "final goal" more quickly. In this case, a continuity between a social and a spiritual career would exist, in which certain social steps are not a necessary condition for his spiritual advancement, which is the attainment of his "final goal."

Even in Buddhism, which likewise is attached to the idea of rebirth, the distant goal of "not having to be born again at all," "illumination" has therefore superseded the "near goal" of a "better" rebirth that is meant to be attained through acting virtuously and living a life dedicated to acquiring insights. Insofar as good or bad rebirths have something to do with the kind of cognitive and moral qualities a soul has gained in a life, redemption as the exit from the cycle of being born and dying is associated with an *extinction of the striving* subject, the cognizing and acting soul.[8]

In Buddhism, true *redemption* consists of *desisting* from evaluations and activities unless they are motivated by care (compassion) for other beings, so that even the affects attached to these evaluations and activities no longer occur. In the final analysis, a person approaching redemption no longer strives for an *improvement* of his or her insights, affective life, and moral character. What is *important for this self* cannot be found in advances of this kind, but in losing the *desire for any development*. That is possible only, however, when the person becomes selfless or egoless, that is, when the self or ego has been recognized as a social construct that may be useful for certain purposes in a community but is very harmful in other respects because it ties down forces and leads to confusions as well as excitement. True life, in contrast, is an ego- or selfless life.

The question of *who* it is that becomes self- and egoless in a true life and not one lived as a dream leads to metaphysical entanglements. Buddhism sought to solve them by asserting that the soul as well as everything else that appears to us has to be considered to be *without substance*, as appearing only under certain conditions and as existing independently only in appearance.[9]

If evaluating leads to striving and striving leads to the appearance of a self-conscious self or a soul that seeks to sustain and improve itself, then the end of evaluating, the dying off of striving must also, in this kind of thinking, lead to a disappearance of the self or the soul. The state of redemption is not one in which the person or the purified soul would see the truth and bring about the good, but a state beyond insight and morality, or: redemption consists of "the elimination of the self-redeeming subject."[10] One could also say, with slight exaggeration: it is not the soul that is being redeemed, but a human being absolves himself of his striving by absolving himself of his soul as a social construct that has nothing to do with a beyond or an afterlife. Rather, it merely projects fantasies of advancement from the social world into an imagined supernatural sphere. Just as people who experience the absence of solidarity and love in their society imagine a peaceful beyond and a loving father who takes care of them, and in this way compensate for the social deficits in their life with a spiritual fantasia, so people who are much concerned with their social advancement imagine an existence beyond that offers them a way of getting ahead. One reason may be that they live in severely stratified societies, for example in India's caste system, and did not emerge at the very top.[11] Illumination consists, once one has understood this mechanism, not in attaining the imagined goal of all moral striving and of cognitional progress in the beyond, but in the end of the kind of being that wants to develop in this way. Being suffused by what is called "nirvana," which sometimes is rendered as "nothingness," would then mean reaching a state in which a being is still alive, to be sure, but, as a social individual, no longer strives for something. Becoming immersed in what is called "nirvana," which in German is sometimes rendered as "Nichts" (nothingness), would then mean reaching a state in which a being still lives, to be sure, but no longer strives for something as a social individual. It is not a person's entering a beyond in the sense of arriving at an otherworldly place. Rather, redemption consists of perceiving the world in the way it appears without a striving self and without the social evaluations that accompany it.

If that is reality: if the world as perceived *not* through a *striving* subject, through a *developing* and *desiring* soul, but by what is after all still a "someone," then life in reality or real life is life in an *unevaluated* world. But such an idea has rather seldom entered the minds of those who argue about the soul. In the beginning there are primarily ideas about a spiritual place beyond in which "oneself" as a person continues to exist as a life more real than one had to lead before death. But the transformation can also consist of quite a different change: This world that all of us see is suddenly – at the moment of illumination – perceived without evaluation; its figure tips over. Just as Rubin's vases, in the well-known optical illusion, turn into two faces, so the complex of things pleasant and unpleasant turns into the one unevaluated world that is how it is and is no longer split into dualities such as what gives pleasure and what causes pain, what is supportive and what impedes, the beautiful and the ugly, truth and falseness, and any other opposites.

## III

Ideas about *spiritual development* and *career*, as they are applied here to souls in a sequence of births and deaths, can, quite independently of religious systems, connect to processes that are central to human life as such, because, starting at a certain age, humans develop a consciousness of their transformation that at first takes place on its own. Small children grow, if everything goes well, on their own and they develop more and more competencies and insights concerning their bodies and their world. They learn to fixate their ability to see on an object. They learn to recognize their mother and the faces of other persons. They learn to estimate the limits of their bodies. They learn to walk and speak – all of it in a few months and without conscious intent. As a rule, they are praised for all the things they can already do. Growth and development presumably are good.

At some time when children have learned a good many things "just like that," they themselves want to become "grown up" and to learn new things intentionally. They have developed a self-awareness or the idea of a self that has to make progress. By then, they have also learned *to compare* themselves; have recognized that they belong to a group of beings in which individual specimens know how to do a different number of things, have a different extent of *power*. That is why little children want to become big children, and big children want to turn into adults. Perhaps from a certain age – perhaps from puberty – children look at themselves as not quite real persons yet, as someone human who does not have a real life yet, but still has to reach it. But there is more to this. Adults also want to be socially successful, attain salary grades, be listed at the top of sports rankings, and finally to move from the province to the big city, which is where real life is going to start. For some, this time starts only after their retirement, when the demands of the job that have always been an impediment to the real life at last are over. And at this stage, some even want, of all things, to be illuminated and to be reborn as better beings.

Collectives, too, want to make progress. Individuals identify with clubs that compete with each other and are featured in athletic rankings. Cities compare their popularity and quality of life, trying to rise on the appropriate scales; countries compare their wealth and the average happiness of their populations. It is said even of *humanity* as a whole that it has made advances since the Stone Age. After all, humans have always increased in numbers and since then have seldom encountered serious threats from other living beings (other than micro-organisms). They seem to have come out on top in the competition of eating and being eaten.

An essential element in the planning of any *types of progress* is the *increase of power*, power as the ability to exercise influence over others, being an important *criterion* in many rankings that are considered for career advancements: who unconsciously follows whose example? Who consciously imitates whom to be likewise successful? Who is given orders by whom? Who is threatened by whom? Who can do violence to whom? And, finally, the ultimate: who can kill whom?

Children want to become big and grown-up because little children *are told* by big ones and children of any age by grown-ups what they need to do. Children lack independence and, relatively speaking, power. At first unconsciously and then deliberately and intentionally, they imitate adults or are admonished to do so. They are constantly being told, "This is how you must do it." And even within the adult community there are power differences because wealth, know-how, beauty, and honours are distributed unequally. These power differences are the sources of "advancement fantasies" that extend even beyond death. In Matthew 19:30, Jesus of Nazareth promises that, in the "kingdom of heaven" after death, these hierarchies will be reversed: "[But] many who are first will be last, and the last will be first." In this reversal, wealth will not only play no role at all, but will even be a *negative* factor because "It is easier for a camel to go through the eye of a needle than for someone who is rich to enter the kingdom of God." (Matthew 19:24). Paradise, the Kingdom of Heaven, is the *destination*, the best dwelling, the most beautiful homestead, towards which life is directed in this concept of the world; "more" is not possible for a redeemed being. But it is a place where *someone* (in contrast to nirvana) can arrive. It is the true and eternal life of a person with a soul.

What animals think or what they wish for is beyond our understanding. Presumably, even wolves in packs no longer want to be chased off by attacks from the stronger members of their pack and want for once share in the tastiest parts of the prey. But in all probability, they do not pursue a career after their death because they have no way of imagining death. According to archaeologists and paleoanthropologists spirituality begins only when beings bury members of their species, in other words, consciously come to terms with death and try to "overcome" it. This is said to have taken place among Neanderthals as early as 42,000 years ago.[12]

## IV

Notions about the survival of a part of a human being (or of other living beings) after the destruction of the body or about the rebirth of a soul in a new body have both explanatory and comforting functions. These concepts have a consolatory function, on the one hand for those who are left behind after somebody died, who have to go on living without the perhaps beloved deceased, and on the other hand for those about to die who would have liked to continue living and with this thought will also be in possession even if not exactly the life that they have lived, but then at least *some kind of* life. One may assume that humans have forever been telling stories to each other to console each other, and they have developed theories to make something comprehensible or to explain it. Sometimes, as in the case of notions about an immortal soul, it is difficult to make a clear distinction between consolatory tales and explanatory ones.

A soul seen as a *principle of animation* can explain what happens when someone dies: In this case, the principle of animation disappears from the body the same way a cart that was pulled by an ox will stop when the ox is unyoked and disappears in its stall – with this one difference that the ox is a *visible* principle of motion for the oxcart, whereas the soul (in most cultures) is an invisible principle. Accordingly, Homer writes: "and the soul fled from his limbs, fluttered down to Hades ..."[13] The human being to whom it belonged collapses in death. One understands why he can no longer speak, walk, or stand, because what had made all this possible, the soul, has *left* him. In the same sense, Plato thinks the soul is the origin of living motion.[14] However, for Plato the soul is an unusual principle of motion. It moves living bodies without itself having to undergo a change in order to accomplish this. The ox has to feed, walk, and strain to move the cart; at some time, it will get tired. For Plato, the soul itself apparently is an *eternal* being that for its activity of motion does not require an impetus.[15] This turns the soul into an imperishable and supernatural being because in nature everything is subject to change. If Plato really advocated this opinion in his dialogues as an assertion (which may be subject to doubt), he would be the father of what is called *dualistic* thinking, according to which humans consist of *two parts*: a natural mortal and a supernatural immortal one. This dualism was developed further into one of the *outer* and *inner* man by a Father of the Church, Saint Augustine. He teaches that the natural body is the outer man (*homo exterior*), and the soul is the inner man (*homo interior*), guiding and steering the outer one.[16]

Regarding the *consolatory function* of assuming the existence of a soul, we have reports of Africans who were abducted from Guinea as slaves: they believed if they killed themselves they would be reborn in their homeland clan, to wit, that they could through death avoid the hated slavery in a distant country, without thereby losing their life altogether.[17] The intention behind this idea, however, is difficult to interpret. Was it meant as a safe prognosis or as a form of encouragement? When an athlete says to himself or herself before a difficult high jump: "You are a bird, you'll fly across it," he or she is encouraging himself or herself by trying to feel dauntless about attaining a goal. But no athlete really believes that he or she can change into a bird. Someone who kills himself to escape the intolerable situation of slavery has to overcome the very strong resistance of the urge for physical self-preservation. It may be that he encourages himself and says: "It is only a brief pain and then you are back with your people!" Perhaps it is this consolatory, this strengthening function in the face of death that may explain why hardly any culture seems to exist that does *not* speak about the existence of life after death.

If striving for self-preservation is the basis of human, as of all, life and humans because of their mental capabilities are conscious both of their striving and of its failing in death, then it becomes easy to understand what a profound problem death is not only as an event to be explained but also why, this particular person, of all human beings, suddenly collapses. For death is not *just any* failure *in* life like the setback of not getting a particular kind of food or a specific sexual partner; it is the manifestation of the *total* failure of *every* individual life. At some time, each individual life can no longer sustain itself. For this reason, those ways of life that are *unaware* of their striving for keeping alive and of its ultimate failure appear to be in a better position than the human way of life, because they have no need of the fundamental consolation of assuming the soul's immortality. If the assumption of an immortal soul is nothing but a consolatory *illusion* and *not a true assertion*, then one has to be prepared for problematic consequences because illusions frequently (not always) turn out to be disadvantageous for those who adhere to them. Let's imagine an athlete who does not simply encourage and cheer himself on by imagining (as in our earlier example) that he could change into a bird but who in a competition, let's say in a boxing ring, has been knocked down and lost the fight. He will absorb this as a painful experience. Yet a good trainer will hardly try now to convince him that he is invincible and *actually* would have won this fight also, except that unfortunate circumstances intervened, such as mistaken judges, a probably doped opponent, the tarp on the floor that was too slick so that he could not help tripping, and so on. A good trainer will instead impose a tougher practice schedule on our loser and, if that doesn't work, try to talk him out of his competitive ambitions. Clinging to the concept of an immortal soul could resemble the illusion of invincibility insofar as death is a finite *defeat* in the struggle for self-preservation and is being *denied* by assuming the existence of a soul.

In some cultures, above all in the European ones, people believe that only *human persons*, but not the other living beings, are equipped with an immortal soul. In that case, of course, the soul is disregarded as an explanatory principle for having life, because animals also have life. In this mental environment, humans use the soul to create for themselves a *special status* among the living beings, imagining themselves to be living in a hierarchy of all that is alive; they assume that they occupy a "pole position" as beings that, like the gods, live eternally even when their body ceases to exist. Whereas with all other living beings, individual life is in fact finally undone at the moment of death, self-preservation being a failure at the end, in this conceptual world, this does not take place with humans. Does this train of thought bring about a blind arrogance analogous to the illusion of invincibility? Could it be that one would then see finite life *not* as the *real* one? Then the illusion of the immortal soul would devalue our life here and now, and animals without a soul that do not adhere to this illusion would already lead their real life (to the extent that one would want to say of animals that they *lead* a life and are not simply being *determined* by inner or outer circumstances).

## V

The widely held belief in an immortal soul should not mislead us to conclude that most cultures share a spiritual/mental origin based on the existence of an *immortal* substance of which this soul "consists." The contrast between the material and the spiritual and the idea that the human body that dies is of "matter" (materia), but is inhabited by an "immaterial soul," to wit, has something "spiritual" about it as its animating principle, is a special theoretical construct. It was introduced by several philosophical schools of Europe, even though it certainly is not the common heritage of all human communities. In Western thought, it was not really established until René Descartes in the 17th century identified space and matter and, in his metaphysics, differentiated the mind, i.e., the soul, as the *other* substance as separate from this space-matter.[18]

The reason that this distinction has been introduced with such clarity only late in the European history of the mind has to do with the fact that "matter" and "mind" are abstract concepts and that it took quite some time before thinking could move with ease within these abstractions. Also, the creation of an abstract language does not rise in all cultures to these heights– if indeed they are heights – because one may very well ask oneself if thinking in abstractions of this kind is an advantage for a way of life. Before these concepts are introduced, humans speak of "fire," "water," "earth," and "air," of "wood," "stone," "mud," and "clay," of "seeing," "hearing," "smelling," "wishing," "enjoying," and so on, to wit, of concrete givens in the world and in their lives. Even using the word "wood" is a generalization, because it goes beyond the differences between birch, oak, beech, and pine trees, and their trunks, branches, roots, etc. The same is true of "wanting" because there is a difference between ice cream for dessert and not wanting to get out of bed, and another something different, wanting to become a famous lyrical poet. Concerning the generality of concepts, there is only a difference of degree between saying "wood" and "wanting" and saying "matter" and "mind." But "matter" and "mind" raises one fairly high to the top in the order of generalities, to the extent that we can imagine a hierarchy in the abstractness of concepts to be arranged in the form of a tree in which the names of the individuals, such as Hans and Susi, are located far down at the roots, and then the farther upward one gets, ever more abstract concepts appear. Perhaps at the very top are located "Being" and "Nothingness" and, already at a far distance beneath, are "matter" and "mind." One may want to consider whether, with every ascent in this conceptual tree, one moves farther and farther away *from reality*. Isn't the person Susi that being we encounter as reality? Whereas talking about her "flesh"/body and her "soul" is already an abstraction, something "not quite real" because no longer something concrete. I cannot point to "flesh/body as such," but only at a person's or an animal's flesh/body. And it is completely impossible for me to point to a soul.

The high degree of complexity in the understanding of human persons before abstract terms such as "mind" and "matter" or "soul" and "body" were used becomes apparent when one realizes how difficult the reconstructions of immortality concepts in ancient Egypt have proved to be. Differentiating between the five components of a person, aside from his or her body, an objective that turns this person into a "constellation" of forces and capacities, is very much more varied then the concept of a soul as a simple and indestructible immaterial substance that perceives, thinks, wills, and so on.[19] First, there is *ka*, a kind of individual life force and creativity that enters a person at the time of birth and at death leaves him or her again; then, *ba*, the individual personality of a human (often translated as "soul"); also, *akh*, the perfected lucid and effective being into which the deceased person will turn as a kind of spirit after his or her demise; and, finally, the name and the shadow (*shut*) of a dead person, in addition to his embalmed body, also play a role concerning his or her existence in the beyond, as a means of identification.[20] In the famous Egyptian *Trial of the Dead*, whose purpose is an evaluation of a person's morality, a human's heart that is weighed in this situation is the most important "thing" (or symbol). In this ancient culture, the person appears to have been thought of in much more concrete and more nuanced ways than in the modern Western doctrine of the two substances.

A danger inherent in using abstractions like "mind" and "matter" consists in committing the error of *inappropriate concretization* or of making a category mistake. That means, looking for mind or matter in the same way one can look for Hans and Susi in the city, or for birch tree wood in the forest and for drinking water in the desert.[21] After one has taken a good look at wood, mud, iron, water, and air and has determined that all of this is matter, the question may arise what exactly matter is *independent* of these different things. A reference to modern physics will not help here because it speaks of many different things also: of particles like leptons and quarks, bosons, and photons, of fields and waves.

It is the same thing with the internal life of a human. When there is sensing and perceiving, hating and loving, doubting and concluding, wishing and wanting, and all of this is being classified as arising from the "mind" (or "spirit"), one may well ask what exactly "the mental" (or "spiritual") as such might be as myself or as my soul, independent of these instances. And here also a look into scientific psychology that differentiates between cognitions and emotions, volitions and motivations, Id, Ego, Superego, self, and many other terms will offer little help because psychology will again lead to nothing but a multiplicity of souls and not to the unity of a substantial soul that could survive death. It is impossible to identify either matter or the soul or the mind/spirit by experiencing them as something concrete. What conclusions should one draw from this insight in order to avoid the fallacy of misplaced concreteness, as Whitehead has called it? A possible conclusion would be to object that these abstractions refer to something that exists truly independently of the human ordering activities that we pursue with the help of language. These abstractions, then, are something purely linguistic. Therefore, matter and mind would not exist at all, other than as human principles of ordering. Does speaking of the soul's immortality make any sense after this axiom?

## VI

Humans may speak about the soul without using the abstract contrast of mind and matter. They may view the soul as *breath* or *blood* that leaves a body when it dies, and that stream back into the common air and the general expanse of liquids. Thus, the presence of a conception of the soul is one thing; the assumption that it is *immaterial* is something additional.

Connecting the concept of a soul with that of an unmistakable *individuality* and autonomous personality might also be limited above all to the European traditions of thought. Elsewhere, the notion was widespread that after death a participation in a general animating principle is possible, without individuality necessarily being preserved.[22] For those who think in the German language, this latter idea seems obvious because the sound of "Seele" seems to point to "See" (ocean; lake). To have the individual soul appear as a wave in a lake, breaking and disappearing in it, is a beautiful image of death which then signifies the "diffusion" of individuality in a larger totality but no longer means complete annihilation. But this connection of "Seele" with "See" is etymologically untenable, which, of course, need not keep anyone from finding pleasure in the idea of the individual life being submerged in something general.[23]

The fact that the word "soul" does not *have* to refer to something immaterial becomes obvious from the close connection that two Greek words used in Homer have with substances that nowadays we would characterize as *material*. "Psyche" as the word most frequently considered the Greek term for "soul" is closely connected with *breath* in that the verb "psychein" means "to puff" or "to blow." In German, furthermore, an antiquated locution has it that someone exhales ("aushaucht") his life, breathed his last (*seinen letzten Atemzug*). And the word "Atem" is cognate with "atman," Sanskrit for "soul." Many meditative practices in India, but also in other parts of the world, have to do with the observation or regulation of breathing that seems not merely to correspond to the observation and regulation of the soul's life, but perhaps was even understood to be identical to it. It is customary in some areas to open a window when somebody is dying and that some homes even have a skylight, included especially so that the soul can "fly out" of the death chamber. Moreover, "Seelenlöcher" (soul holes) were a part of sepulchres and coffins. All of this shows a connection with the concept that the soul is a waft of breath that, at the time of death, escapes upward.

Another term for soul that Homer uses is "thymos." It signifies *courage*, the vitality that makes the chest swell and is to be connected with the heart and blood.[24] Jewish thought also established a conjunction of the soul with blood and breath, for example, in Deuteronomy 12:23: "Only be sure that you do not eat the blood, for the blood is the life [soul, *nefesh*]," and in Genesis 2:7: " then [the Lord God] ... breathed into his nostrils the breath of life [haNeschama] ..." Ecclesiastes/Kohelet 3: 19-21 parallelizes the presence of a soul in animals and humans: "For the fate of humans and the fate of animals is the same, as one dies, so dies the other. They all have the same breath [*ruach*] ... Who knows whether the human spirit/soul goes upward"/leaves them as breath, "and the spirit of animals goes downward to the earth?" That breath(ing) stops at death and that a person dies when blood runs from an open wound for a while are simple and surely very early pieces of evidence at life's transition into death that were important for these conceptions of the soul. When breath accelerates at moments of excitement and calms down as affects abate, when someone's heart beats faster and thereby blood begins to heat, then it is immediately obvious to any human that a close connection exists between emotions (as a phenomenon of the life of one's soul), breath, and blood. This link, then, may even be interpreted as indicating that breath and blood themselves constitute what is called "soul." Even Stoics like Chrysippus (280-207 BCE) considered the human soul (the *hegemonikon*) a fine breeze (*pneuma*), even though they also regarded it as a bodily substance located near the heart that nourishes itself on blood and breath.[25]

Beside "psyche" and "thymos," Homer uses other words that show an affinity with what we nowadays call "soul." An important term among them is "nous," a concept that probably signifies intellectual capability more closely, but may also refer to presentiment and getting a whiff of something. That is to say, it too is connected with breath, the latter more specifically insofar as it is used for smelling. The question has been discussed whether any of these words designates the "core," "the innermost being," "the essence" of a human.[26] That is rather questionable. Perhaps such a conception as defining an essential core of a human being does not exist in Homer (as little as it does in ancient Egypt), so that even where Homer says that the *psyche* descends into Hades as a shade, he does not mean that this shade in Hades as we know it above all from the passage in the *Odyssey* in which the story's hero visits the Kingdom of the Dead, invokes the souls by offering a blood sacrifice, and thus gets them to speak is the same as what has in essence *defined* a human being also in his or her life.[27] For example, as a person's *thymos* vanishes in death it is quite possible that something essential about this person perishes at that time. Isn't Achilles in essence a *courageous* man? The epic devoted to him, *The Iliad*, does after all deal with his fury. Isn't the feeble shade that he represents in the netherworld a completely different being than the one that he was during his lifetime? The *psyche* that ends up in Hades is what one employs as a warrior in a fight and can lose, as can be concluded from Achilles's statement that in a fight he has risked his *psyche*.[28] In places like these, "psyche" is translated as "life" because a warrior risks his life and lost it. But would it be appropriate to say about Homer's hero that his soul *survives*? To risk one's *psyche* in a fight, in (Homeric) Greek functions somehow like the German phrase *seinen Hals* or *seinen Kopf zu riskieren* (and the English: risking one's neck). The neck (or the head) are neither the animating principle nor the essence of being human. But whoever loses his or her neck (or *Kopf*) in real life and not in a metaphorical sense, loses his or her life.[29] Neck (and head) are parts of a human being. In the same way *psyche*, a gossamer-like substance in Homer, is a part of humans. On the loss of this part, the whole person is finished; it collapses, is unable to speak, its body parts no longer move, it has changed, on the one hand, into a corpse (*soma*), and on the other into a *psyche* that is independent of this body. Neither the one nor the other constituent part that remains after death is the essence of the person. For the corpse decomposes, while the *psyche*, by contrast is nothing but a shade without courage and without a "real" life propelled by blood, the sap of life, and pursued with more or less courage. Just as the corpse is a person's mortal, putrefying remnant, so *psyche* is a person's remainder, but an immortal, shadowy one.

## VII

Aside from the capabilities of moving when alive, of getting into emotional states like fear and joy, of acting bravely, or of reflecting, a further important competency should not be forgotten in any contemplation of our concept of the soul. For as long as we are alive, we can *look back* on the life we have lived; we can remember. If memory leaves us, we also vanish more or less as a distinctive individual or continue existing as this person only in what *others* tell about us. Looking back on our own life perhaps takes place in a sequence of images during the process of introspection or in a story. Even scents and experiences of touching may return to our mind, comparable to a dream experience. The fact that something can "come back to" people seems possible only because the things that happen to them leave *traces* inside them.

But traces are not a privilege of beings with a soul. Even stones show traces of their history. In some of them one can detect fossils, others originated in volcanic processes from the fusion of different metals, a result that is still visible inside them. Trees, during their development, form growth rings that allow us to determine their ages and how wet a specific year was during the lifetime of any particular specimen. A landscape or a town leaves traces and strata that allow conclusions about earlier periods of settlement or agriculture. Archaeologists can evaluate these traces in reconstructing the history of the area in question.

Yet landscapes, towns, trees, and stones seem to have no sense through which what happened to them becomes present again. Perhaps *nothing* has ever been present to them. The fact that sometimes this and at other times something else is present to humans, and that they can *remember* these past things that are different from what is present to them at a current moment shows that, on the one hand, they, like all beings, are subject to *change* that leaves traces and that, on the other hand, they *refer back* to these variable events, that they *reactivate* traces and are able to bring back, to visualize what has caused these traces.

Is the soul what, in this change of perceptions and memories, remains constant and to which this calling to mind and bringing back into the present is "assigned" and what makes this possible? Is the soul the medium of this "calling-to-mind" process? After all, I am the *same individual* who, at the present moment, perceives the objects on his desk and the patter of rain against the windowpanes and who, at the same time, can remember the sun at the beach during summertime. Is the soul the "inner man" who always remains the same whatever may happen to the "outer man" and who "observes" these events that happen to the "outer man" and also can make past occurrences become present again?

In contrast to Descartes, the philosopher Alfred North Whitehead once compared the unity of the person and the soul with that of a *space*, of which Plato in his cosmological dialogue *Timaeus* speaks as a "mother and vessel".[30] Different shapes are embossed into this Platonic space-matter. Aristotle seems to have adopted this idea in his understanding of *phantasia* (the power of perception in the mind).[31] According to this view, the "unity of nature" and the "unity of each individual human life" are not guaranteed by an essential core inside all change but through a receptive entity, *within* which all change takes place but which itself does not become something different on account of the events inside it. The space in which this house is located, in which I am sitting and writing, is the (same) space in which at one time trees but no house stood and in which there was a desert before that and, even earlier, an ocean. My soul can be conceived as that in which the perception of daylight, the taste of a strawberry, the pain of a needle prick occurred for the first time, in which some of these experiences have been repeated and some are being remembered, and so forth. Yet my *attentiveness* through which something becomes present for me is not changed into a different one through that *which appears in it* any more than the space is changed through that which *appears in it* – at least not if *we imagine* this space as a receiver in Plato's sense. The *attention* paid to things present and the *remembrance* of things past are, taken together, the "frame," the "container," metaphorically speaking, in which my life remains indifferent towards this life. I am the person that I am because in me the following story – that I then can narrate or visualize as an "internal film" – has occurred. In each person a *different* story appears. That is what makes us different. But that *in* which our different stories appear need not be any more different from one another than the space in which an ocean appears must be different from the one in which a forest appears. Without what has happened to me, I am nothing individual or am an *empty form* like a space in which nothing takes place.

Paradoxes open up here that also arise in the context of space and to which Leibniz called attention a long time ago: how can a section of space be differentiated from another one if nothing takes place in them? How can a section of attention or remembrance be differentiated from a different one if there is nothing in them towards which attention is directed or that is remembered in them? This idea is misleading insofar as it perceives space or attention or remembrance or however one may characterize something receptive as an object (*Ding*) that can be differentiated from another object. But the receiving entity – space, general attentiveness – is perhaps not a thing at all, but things appear in it, whereas they themselves do not appear independently of that which "takes place" in them.

# VIII

If the soul is considered to be a receiving entity (receptacle, vessel) in which all those things appear to which we turn our attention and that we remember, then the soul is nothing with a definitive characteristic that becomes real in the course of a life. The idea of *self-realization*, by contrast, proceeds from a given situation of a person's opportunities that either is realized (which means that life is successful) or is not (then life is a failure). The receiving entity, however, does not make itself real, but "accepts" everything as it is and makes real what it takes in as present experience or remembrance. The receiving vessel "donates" "Here" and "Now."

The contrast between the entity that takes in and what appears in it is not the same as that between something material and something immaterial. If spirits were to exist, then there would also exist both something individually material and something individually immaterial. But an empty space and general attention are not immaterial. They are neither material nor immaterial. But empty space and general attentiveness are not immaterial. One cannot point to them without pointing to something particular in them. Attentiveness and memory are neither material nor immaterial, and they are not something objective (*Dingliches*) but the prerequisite for doing and experiencing something and for being someone with a certain (*bestimmte*) history. Also, the receiving entity does not guarantee that the experiences and memories that appear in it can be continued indefinitely - no more than space can guarantee the continued existence of the bodies appearing in it, even though the places where the bodies come and go do not themselves come and go.

The conception of *personal* immortality amounts to this: that when I remember today that I was at the ocean beach six months ago, then there will also in the future again and again arise a moment, a today, when I will be able to remember what I experienced before this time, and that after the series of experiences and memories that constitute our life after this moment there will be another series that also is part of this chain of experiences and memories, and so on, forever. In brief: that the chain of experiences and memories, of the "todays" and "nows," will never break off, but at most can be interrupted for a while as in a deep sleep. For an immortality of this kind, we have neither evidence nor a guarantee, and it is questionable whether we should really wish for this kind of an infinite continuation of experiences and memories.

If the series of experiences and memories that constitutes our life breaks off at one time, this need not signify that the receptive entity in which our experiences and memories have appeared also vanishes. But as a receiving entity that is not conceived in conjunction with *definite* but with *any kind of* experiences and memories, it is nothing that would be characteristic of myself, but it is something *impersonal*. But immortality is usually understood in Europe (not in Buddhism) as personal immortality, not as the discontinuance in an impersonal space or in an attentively receptive entity. Therefore, this kind of impersonal immortality hardly has any consolatory function for Europeans.

## IX

Not understanding the personal soul as something receptive, as general attentiveness and memory that can turn to individual things of whatever kind without in turn being something individual, but rather understanding the soul as an individual something has had significant consequences. Because the immaterial soul presumably survives the dissolution of the body, that is, "mere matter," and will, like all complex specimens of matter, disintegrate with time, the soul was seen as especially valuable. For things of long duration and beyond perishing have always been considered more valuable than disintegrating material. Therefore, gold, which cannot rust and does not decay, has been considered especially *valuable*, more so than iron, which can rust and decay, or silver, which can tarnish and lose its brilliance. But, in this sense, space and attentiveness are nothing particular that develops and perishes. As generalities, they have not been created and are eternal. Everything that comes about and fades away, comes about and fades away in them.

In Homer's time, it was as yet impossible to say that blood or breath are *mere matter*, because there did not exist any abstract conception of matter in whatever form. Blood and breath were something valuable because they animated the body, they were soul – exactly that: breath soul (*psyche*) and blood soul (*thymos*). Along with the invention of differentiating the immaterial from the material in abstract terms, the material as the divisible and perishable was being *devalued* vis-à-vis the imperishable immaterial. What Nietzsche called "the contempt for the body"[32] is the reverse material side of the coin that was struck when the "invention" of the immortal immaterial soul was propagated as the inner and authentic human being.

The conception of this singular something that we are and that is in our body like the blood that runs through our veins and like the air that we have inhaled has two aspects: a *spatial* and a *moral* attribute that we now want to consider more closely.

If someone asks me where *exactly* I am and is not satisfied with my mentioning place names like Cologne, Cambridge, or

Helsinki and even finds pieces of information like "in my room" or "in the forest" to be too imprecise, then sooner or later I'll arrive at my body as the place where I am. And it is in fact not implausible (even though rather pedantic) to say that I am in my body and there, precisely, in my head behind my eyes. We see the tip of our nose, our shoulders, arms, hands, our belly, lower abdomen, our legs and feet, and in a mirror we even see our back and our face, and we do so from the place behind our eyes. Following Ernst Mach, we could describe this act of locating, perhaps of a boxer relative to the ring and his opponent, as follows:

Do we locate ourselves when we close our eyes and listen to music on a headphone, between our ears? Even that seems persuasive. All our perceptions take place within a certain *perspective*. Having a perspective on the world means possessing organs of perception that stand in a definite relationship to the rest of our body and of being a subject. The point from which our perceptions take place, based on how we position our organs of perception, is the one at which we are the subjects that recognize the world from a certain perspective. The English expression "point of view" and the German "Gesichtspunkt" use the word "point/ *punkt*" to identify that from which a perspective proceeds.

In geometry, a point is a figure without extension. Whitehead thought of points as something that do not really exist but represent the imaginary aim of nested intervals.[33] In his opinion, nothing happens instantaneously. Everything we have experienced continues and takes up space. When we speak about points, we perhaps are thinking of (gambling) dice inside each one of which an even smaller such cube (die) is located containing an even smaller one – as in a Russian Matryoshka doll. In this mental experiment, the series of dice within dice moves towards a point in the centre of the totality of the imagined cubes. But if we actually try to create

a wooden model of this mental experiment, we will not be able to build anything lacking extension. In the experiment, we can think of the point towards which the nested dies are proceeding as a mental construct, as a *mathematical fiction*. But to produce a mental construct of this kind, in order to simulate (build the fiction of) such a point, one should assume that a simulating mind or a constructing soul is required. But if we employ the idea of a point from which a subjective perspective on the world will become apparent for the purpose of accepting the absence of extension in a point as indicating the immateriality of the subject or the soul, we would first have to invalidate Whitehead's objection that there is nothing real in experience that does not continue in space-time and hence has some kind of extension. Something that is of the nature of a point, that has no extension, can be neither a body nor a soul, because even a soul continues, ideally forever. A point is neither body nor mind nor soul, but a mathematical ideal. Consequently, even the perspectival character of perception cannot demonstrate the immateriality of the soul.

# X

The receptacle, the mother of the world in Plato's *Timaeus*, is the predecessor of what later was called "space." So, let us pursue further the parallelizing arrangement that Whitehead proposed when he replaced the Platonic receptacle with "soul." We will then establish a connection between the different theories about space and the different conceptions of the soul. This, in turn, provides clear indication that in fact space, even though in a literal sense it is not "matter," also has not been nothing in the thinking of philosophers and physicists and that Whitehead's connecting of space and soul is not far-fetched after all.

Newton, for example, espoused a dual theory of the soul in which impressions in a space play an essential role. On the one hand, the human body possesses a very gossamer-like part, a *sensorium*, that can absorb the smallest oscillations and vibrations and can transmit them. Newton uses this phenomenon in his *Opticks* to explain the perception of colour.[34] On the other hand, Newton sees the space of the world as the *sensorium* of God.

Precisely as the rays of light fall into our eye and then – according to Newton – the small hard corpuscles they consist of transmit their oscillations to our sensorium, so likewise *all* bodies of the world, because they are in space, exist inside a divine sensorium. In the same way that a sensorium is the place of transition from the physical into the spiritual (*Seelische*), that is, the connection of the corpuscular towards the immaterial, so cosmic space – for Newton – is the border at which God stays in contact with what he has created. He is omnipresent because his creation remains *within himself*, within his sensory organ, i.e. space. But unlike the objects that we cannot influence and that appear in *our* sensorium, God is capable of using his will to continue to change what he has created and what stays in him.[35] For Newton, the equally immaterial tele-efficacy of gravitation is nothing other than the manifestation of God's spiritual willpower. It cannot inhere in the bodies themselves, but requires an external agent that moves the bodies.[36]

Theologically, these concepts may lead to strange complications, even heresies. For, if the God-created world remains within God, then he is not really transcendent. Then doesn't the world itself remain divine also? Moreover, can a difference between world and God be made at all in this case? If not, Newton would have propounded a pantheism. But for us, the only important thing is that in space and in gravitation the mental capabilities of perceiving and willing are present as divine abilities of the soul everywhere in the material world. The human sensorium is merely a small space in the wide expanse of space, a small chamber of gossamer-like sensibility within gigantic sensible cosmic space. But aren't even we, through our willing, almost everywhere present in our body? Does the idea about the starting point of our perspective on the world not mislead us about the omnipresence of our willing in our body? We may perceptibly "inhabit" this body at a particular place, say, in the centre of our head behind our eyes. But when we try to move our hands or feet, then we are almost everywhere present in this extended body unless we have fallen ill of paralysis. Newton seems to have thought about the world as a body that God created for himself. We did not create our body, but inside our body in which we find ourselves, circumstances appear to be quite analogous to how things are in Newton's divine world-body.

Physics has changed considerably since Newton's time. The number of forces has increased. If one takes forces as manifestations of a will or aspiration as Newton's contemporary Leibniz did, then the forms of aspiration have multiplied: in addition to the gravitational force, we now have the force of reciprocity between the smallest particles as well as the electromagnetic forces. If one were to interpret these forces as forms of aspiration, one would have to distinguish different *ways* of striving, different modes of attraction and repulsion. And space, in modern physics, is not only receptive, a taking-in, because gravitation can disfigure it; space is also active or creative because, on a very small scale, quantum events constantly take place in it. Something comes into being without anyone being able to give a reason for this. Finally, at the end of the past century, dark energy emerged that, directed against gravitation, explained the accelerated flight of galaxies from each other. Isn't this expansion of space the modern successor of the Newtonian sensorium of God? But the most important change with reference to Newton is perhaps the coupling of space with time and the importance that *light* has assumed in this connection in post-Einsteinian physics.

This change is relevant insofar as we have seen that it is distinctive of the human soul within us, to wit, our subjectivity that has the ability to *remember*. Remembrance, of course, has to do with *temporal orders*, and these, in modern physics, are no longer independent of spatial orders.

If, in Einstein's physics, we imagine a being that moves through space at the speed of light, then time would no longer pass for this being. This connection of time and the speed of light could be used in an additional speculation about the eternalness of what pertains to the soul. If, following the Bible, one understands the divine and the soul as something eternal and ubiquitous and, in Biblical terms, if one sees God in conjunction with light, one could accept this connection literally (as in Psalm 27, 1: The Lord is my light and my rescue, in Robert Alter's translation) and say that light is the eternal aspect of the world, and the soul, inasmuch as it is light, is also eternal. And, indeed, it would even be imaginable that death is the liberation of the light that is inside our body, and "we," insofar as the soul would be identified with this light, would "become eternal" through this liberation, or as souls would be accelerated to the speed of light because we are no longer bound to the mass of our body. Neoplatonic and Gnostic narratives that describe the soul as a "spark of light" inside a human being who is understood as having descended from the general cosmic light would, in a strangely literal sense, coincide with speculations of this kind. Even near-death experiences that describe the process of dying as a journey into the light could be connected to this idea: the spark of light that we are returns into the general light.

Such an identification of the inner human being or the soul with light is not compatible, however, with the conception that the soul is a receiving something into which enters all that we direct our attention to. Yet, isn't it interesting that when we try to reflect on the immaterial, we end up thinking about space and light and can establish a connection of these two notions with the idea of soul? If we do not conceive the soul as an immaterial individual something (and that is especially difficult, even if it appears connected with an especially effective consolatory function), we will historically arrive at the generalness of space and light as possible analogies for what is of the soul (*das Seelische*). The light that illuminates every single material thing is itself nothing individual and nothing material. Therefore, why should we not hypothesize our mental ability of attentively referring to individual material things in analogy to light or metaphorically as light? The ray of light and the ray of attentiveness or intentionality would then be related or identical.[37]

## XI

But hasn't the soul always been considered a *moral* authority as well? When, in the *Egyptian Book of the Dead*, the heart is placed on the scales to determine if it is lighter than a feather, the purpose of this is the moral evaluation of a person after death if he or she has been truly just in life, and it is the soul that is singled out for this moral evaluation. In Christianity, too, a judgement is passed. Books are opened, among them the book of life, which record the deeds of the dead and morally judges them (*The Revelation to John* 20:12). Aside from the fear of death as the end of my physical existence, the dying person may for this reason also fear the moral judgement of life after their death. For not all injustices that occur are punished by human courts. Many failings remain hidden. So, isn't it a consolation for those who have been wronged that there exists an otherworldly, superhuman authority that punishes those who did not act righteously? And, conversely, isn't it, therefore, an obvious conclusion by those acting unlawfully that they will be called to account for their undiscovered acts of transgression before a court of the Last Judgement from which nothing has remained hidden?

In many Western cultures, guilt in the juridical and moral sense with which humans burden themselves is attributed to actions that they *freely decided* to commit and in regard to which they either adhered to the prevalent laws or to reason, or they violated both. On due consideration, whoever commits a grievous act involuntarily does not become guilty, either. Immanuel Kant formulated this concept most succinctly when he postulated that "through no cause in the world" "can [a human being] cease to be a free agent."[38] Whatever the history of a human being may look like, even if this person may already have committed a thousand acts offending reason and breaking the law and may have become habituated to this manner of acting, Kant avers even so that he or she is duty-bound in every new situation calling for action "to be better." And because this is his or her duty, he or she "must therefore be capable of it."[39] They are capable of doing this because for every action there is at least a *possible* "origin in reason," to which an acting human person must as a free being return. He can also refrain from doing this.

Both the origin of an act in reason and the inclination towards evil, the tendency of deferring reason or of observing it only *as a pretence* in the motivation for an act are for Kant something fundamentally different from events that have their origin in time. Whatever originates in time is subject to natural causality and can be explained. Whatever has no origin in time is not subject to natural causality and, consequently, is not explicable. For this reason, neither man's rationality nor his propensity to evil are explicable.[40] They *can be experienced* (in modern terminology) only *intro*spectively. This means that we experience *ourselves* as free, rational, and evil when we decide to engage in an action, but that we cannot explain to ourselves how something like this can be possible in a causally determined world of material objects.

In what Kant calls "intelligible character" (which is located *outside the order of time* and should not be mistaken for a human character's empirically acquired character), a kind of ranking is created between the possible rational and the non-rational motives (and thereby origins) of acts. For Kant, a human being may act outwardly with reason and in accordance with the moral *law*. Yet the motive for his act may be that the consequences of his acting give him sensual pleasure, to put it briefly: the act simply is pleasurable and has no other purpose than these pleasurable consequences. But that may be something such people do not want to admit to themselves. Every human may deceive himself (Kant says: "kann sich blauen Dunst vormachen"= throw dust in his own eyes) about the true motives of his or her acting, or even have a deceptive image of himself or herself as a moral being who presumably acts out of respect for morality and reason rather than in the interest of his own pleasure. But for Kant there exists *inside every human being a truth* about why the acting person has in fact done what he or she did, even though this truth cannot be brought to light through empirical enquiry in the material world.[41] And with this thought, Kant establishes a connection, as is easily apparent, with the Augustinian conception of an "inner man" and thereby with that of a soul.

The word "soul" occurs infrequently in Kant's philosophy. But its concept is present in several respects even so: in the rational nature of man, in the intelligible character of a person, in the freedom of being able to act for rational reasons or else to suspend them. All this is located beyond the temporal or causal order of the world, and in this sense, it is something like soul. To be sure, in his critical discussion of the metaphysics of the soul, Kant had refuted the conception that the soul could be interpreted as a *substance* that guarantees the unity of the person.[42] But in his metaphysics of the soul, Kant had not discussed *spontaneity*, the ability to start a causal chain in the world of establishing a preferential order between rational causes and predictably pleasant and unpleasant consequences of acting, which *also* has traditionally been attributed to the soul. This lack is neither accidental nor an indication of sloppiness. For this spontaneity of acting is an insight Kant himself absolutely needed in his moral philosophy. This means that in his terminology, he set the concept of the soul aside, but he kept a supernatural personal authority (that can be the free origin of actions), so as to be able to complete his moral philosophy.[43]

In Kant's practical philosophy, even God is given a place as the creator of the world in which morality has to be realized, after all, even though acting morally does not have a worldly origin. "Morality," he writes, "thus inevitably leads to religion and through religion it extends itself to the idea of a mighty moral lawgiver outside the human being, in whose will the ultimate end (of the creation of the world) is what can and at the same time ought to be the ultimate human end," which is to say: the soul.[44] As practical beings who try to live morally, humans must conceive the world as established in such a way that in it the purposes of rational acting can in fact be *realized*.

That is a strong assumption and represents a more recent version of the Stoic conception that humans apprehend the world and are able to lead a good life in it because they participate in universal reason. In other words, because there is no fundamental conflict between what they apprehend as rational and the manner in which the world has been established, even though at various times coincidence, unfavourable circumstances, or, in Kant, the evil in man prevent the realization of reason.

Even the immortality of the soul (and here even the word itself emerges again) becomes for Kant, in this religious outlook that is based on morality and not on metaphysics, a *practical postulate* of reason because one must conceive persons as being *infinitely* capable of *moral perfection*. This, however, is incompatible with their finite physical existence. For Kant, practical reason "demands" the congruence of human will with the moral law. In his system, this demand is legitimate, on the one hand, but on the other, it cannot actually be satisfied by "any rational being of the sensory world at any instant of its existence." In the Kantian sense that means that simply going into the wilderness is far from sufficient for the purpose of gaining moral perfection, if one truly seeks to advance towards a life as a free rational being who acts solely out of respect for the moral law. Therefore, an *infinite* and *supernatural* process of achieving perfection must be thinkable for every person, the end of which process is characterized by the congruence of heart and law. This is the authenticity to which McCandless, too, had aspired. It is the practical postulate of the soul's immortality, which in Kant's thought is accompanied by the demand that a person's will must be moral.[45]

According to Kant, for every person that one has been at periodically different situations that call for action, the degree of self deception about one's own ever-changing relevant motivation is correspondingly different. That is why immortality is a personal sheet anchor that humans need because they are incapable of acting assuredly for purely moral reasons. Their hearts are not pure and not transparent to themselves. Rather, in Kant's view, man is not only free and potentially rational, but *by nature also evil* because in his actions he can decide against the moral law and reason. His heart is "evil *by nature*."[46] But man can *aspire* to the "purity of the heart." But it would take man an infinite length of time to realize this purity. Purity and self-transparency of the heart are, more or less, the goal of an asymptotic approximation in an infinite developmental process. It is only through the postulate of immortality that such a developmental process is also conceivable to and granted to man. Not a "spiritual leap" into the wilderness, into a beyond of culture, but only an infinitely continued moral improvement of the soul in a realm beyond space, time, and causality can, in Kant's view, guarantee the "purity of heart."

## XII

The idea of an incorporeal soul that survives death and whose continued existence makes a transformation of our person possible is the human creation of a counter-image to the presumed moral impurity of man's heart and to the ambiguity of his motivations. No real natural life can do justice to our moral ideals, can make the aims of our cognition real, and can remove the lack of understanding of who we "really" are, in view of the history through which we have lived. By contrast, according to these concepts, the soul will sometime after death gain a pure heart, the full light of knowledge will open itself to the soul, and if we could only relate to this, we would presumably understand who we ourselves are deep down, what we are made of, what defines us, and what, on the basis of our definition, we should do "at heart." "Absolute truth and honesty ... definitiveness, stability, consistency," is what the youthful McCandless was searching for in the wilderness and believed to have found there. But he likewise found loneliness and the indifference of the wilderness to human existence and the ambivalence of the outward appearance of plants – at least for the insufficiently practiced eye; an ambivalence that caused his death. But even before his death, he wanted to purify his soul and render it non-ambivalent after civilization had presumably corrupted it. The leap from civilization into the wilderness was a *death in advance* brought about by his desire for transformation and purification and for a real rather than a seeming, deceiving life. It is a process that is also practiced by some so-called primitive peoples in their initiation rites when they send their youngsters into the wilderness for a few days without food and support. Does the wilderness fulfil what those who enter this environment expect? One would probably have to ask every single person undergoing this test.

But we cannot ask the dead if the Kantian postulates actually became true for them. The only thing we know about death is: no one has as yet returned with the ability to report about the transformation that he or she may have undergone.

\* \* \*

AARON: A curious piece of writing. How does all this Buddhism at the beginning about the extinction of the aspiring subject get into it?
KAGAMI: Oh, the final essay will have even more Buddhism or, to put it more precisely, wisdom. This is merely the beginning. Moritz has been studying that religion extensively. That started in Cambridge. Didn't you know about this?

AARON: No, I saw nothing of it in his poems. He told me about his meditating, but he let me know nothing more than that it helps him improve his concentration. But we never talked about the aspiring soul and doing away with it. What caused his interest in this whole business?

KAGAMI: There are diary entries from his Cambridge time that deal with this.

### 1001
### MARBACH: GERMAN LITERARY ARCHIVE: FROM THE DIARIES OF MORITZ BRANDT. ENTRY DATED 20 DECEMBER.

Lonely and depressed. Even contact with Dorothy difficult. Her criticism of my texts, merciless. Starts to remind me of my mother. She was always nagging me about something – nothing was ever good enough. Can't give good answers any longer, in her lessons, get inhibited. The other students get on my nerves, too. Lost interest in meeting anyone after hours. It's all just social affectation and competition, rat race, no, thanks! Couple of days ago a note on the bulletin board about a meditation event in the college chapel. Went there today. Amazing. Intro to breath meditation. Then a lecture on Buddhism by a monk whom the chaplain seems to know. Was a good talk, concrete, without these fancy terms in the philosophy lectures, but kind of philosophical and useful in life, hard to describe. My colleagues would probably say it wasn't argued right. True, but that is just bull, 'cause it was about experience. Practical experience doesn't exist for the colleagues in phil. Because everything comes to us in concepts. Instead of telling about their life, for which they are too shy and too neurotic or for which they haven't lived enough so that there is nothing to report about, they argue no end about what words mean and call that "arguments". That doesn't lead anywhere. That locks them in, completely. Dorothy isn't like that. But the others yak about everything and know nothing. That gets my goat like crazy by now. The monk talked about bickering among friends and in a marriage. Very plausible. How that gets wild, how one's mind starts to run wild even though the other person probably hasn't said all that much or has been gone for quite some time, and so on. Will go back after Christmas break. Also is good against being lonely. One has a contact but not this carping and this permanent competitive bullshit.

1010

MARBACH: GERMAN LITERARY ARCHIVE:
FROM THE DIARIES OF MORITZ BRANDT.
ENTRY OF 10 JANUARY.

Today back at the chapel meditation. Very good evening. Talk on selflessness by Joe Jones, monk. Both about acting selflessly and not for profit and about the metaphysics of selflessness, that "actually" we aren't a self, but a fantasy spooks through our head that we are. This will then bring on these never-ending preoccupations with ourselves. Become torturous at some stage because they are concerns with an illusion. How popular am I? How smart am I? How beautiful am I? What should I avoid? Should I really meet x again? How can I see y again? Is z also good for me? At some time, this will become not only tedious but downright torturous because it is a hollow game.

A swinging back and forth between attraction and repulsion from the other. Why get into this? Isn't that worse than being stuck on a hamster's wheel? Its only concern is with comparing illusions because who I really am and who x, y, z really are, and whether they are my style or not, if they are good or harmful for me, that is all some jabbering in fantasies, nothing concrete. When I cut my finger and need a Band-Aid, we're talking about something concrete. So too when someone breaks a leg. But whether I did better on my test than Peter or Mary is a social game that some teacher has set up, why should I have to play along? Also if the shapes of my body are fashionable or not. Lord only knows who comes up with things like that, probably fashion freaks. And then I'm supposed to dance to their music and join a fitness studio or run after Susie? Nonsense, one turns into a fully conditioned lab rat. Joe's talk precisely fit my situation as if every detail had been written for me. Was constantly preoccupied with myself last fall: does Dorothy like my essay, am I as good as the other students, is my boxing is getting better, etc., etc. Have always been thinking about myself in some kind of rankings. And then this collapse into loneliness. Is obvious to me now. If you always talk only with your mirror image, you're bound to get lonely. And if the others are there only to produce a mirror image of yourself, then, come to think of it, you haven't a thing to do with them. Which means, they're there only to reproduce you, they are being made into instruments. If there are no actions that are about something other than the comparisons between social constructs, the time will come when you feel totally off your rocker and have to ask yourself what the hell you're doing in this world. Hume thought pride produces the idea of self. But then the reverse is true too: Once the idea of self has arrived, then it has to be kept alive through pride. It becomes the purpose of your life, and the production of pride turns into an obsession. You need confirmations, praise, caressing units, otherwise the idea of self will wane and then you would feel as if you were shrinking, vanishing, and you become depressed. For you are firmly convinced that you are this construct. You don't get out of it so easily. But I have the feeling that now I've at least made a beginning. Have to go on meditating. Simplifying life. No more rankings! I'm already feeling better. Is the right way. Will ask Dorothy if she'll do Hume with me.

1011

MARBACH: GERMAN LITERARY ARCHIVE:
FROM THE DIARIES OF MORITZ BRANDT.
ENTRY OF 12 October.

Cavendish is a believing Christian. Was absolutely flabbergasted today during the tutorial. She does, as a matter of fact, believe in an immortal soul and that it is recognized by God. I don't understand how one can have read all the things she has read, the ancient Sceptics, Hume, Schopenhauer, Nietzsche, and then be a Christian in spite of that. Her father was a parson. But nevertheless, or for this very reason one should imagine that she would want to find intellectual liberation. I can't believe it!! Ever since I've known this, she has immediately declined in my estimation. I can no longer take her fully seriously as a philosopher. But that is baloney, of course. Were Thomas and Kierkegaard inferior philosophers for being believing Christians? Hardly. I won't be able to wrap my head around it even so. For me, philosophy and poetry are connected to freedom of thought and religion to mental servitude, to dogmas. I couldn't get a word out when this emerged. She noticed. And inflicted Kant's practical proof of the soul's immortality on me, but not to convert me. I'll find a way of getting through this. But I kinda get the feeling that her class is now turning into a bit of a problem.

KAGAMI: I am retrieving what Dorothy Cavendish was thinking about this. Do you want to hear that, too?
AARON: Sure!

### 1100
FROM THE ARCHIVE OF LADY MARGARET HALL COLLEGE, CAMBRIDGE: DIARY ENTRY BY DOROTHY CAVENDISH. WRITTEN ON 17 APRIL.

Only now, after his death, am I getting a clear understanding why Moritz all of a sudden wanted to concern himself with Hume's philosophy of the mind. In his college he had become acquainted with Buddhism. The chaplain there had been dismissed from Churchill during Moritz's time here in Cambridge because he had apparently turned away from Christianity and had continued to use the chapel primarily for meditation courses instead of for worship services. This was something the students welcomed. But the fellows were correct in taking offense, stating that this is not what the College was paying him for. The "selflessness" of Buddhism and Hume's assertion that he is looking into himself without being able to find a self, on the contrary discovering nothing but various ideas and perceptions, were probably a liberation from his loneliness. What he went through is something that happened to many foreigners here. First they are euphoric about all the new things that they see and experience here. Yet then an estrangement sets in, homesickness, loneliness. They find out that the friendliness they are being shown does not necessarily mean friendship, but in most cases is merely a sign of good manners. This always brings about difficult periods among international students. Those from Asia will begin to work with even greater determination. Students from the Continent frequently slump into the doldrums.

I had noticed at that time that Moritz somewhat lost his interest in the work done during classroom hours. But I don't want to be unfair. It certainly was not just homesickness and loneliness in a foreign environment, but also the distress he experienced about his own ambition. He constantly tried to prove something, academically, in sports, and also socially. He was one of those people who are tormented by an inner unrest that sometimes they cannot control and then assume that it is loneliness. The rituals with his Buddhist chaplain in Churchill perhaps offered Moritz a substitute for faith. When during class I argued against his enthusiasm for Hume's and, as I see now, Buddhist selflessness, he got into difficulties that were not simply of an argumentative nature but existential. I noticed that he despaired. Our conversation then went beyond studying philosophy. He asked me if I believed, "of all things," in an immortal soul. When I affirmed this, he was speechless for a few moments, looked at me with his eyes and mouth wide open. He asked how I could justify this belief. He could not accept my answer that it is in the nature of faith to be beyond justification because faith is evident in itself. I saw his antagonism as again he remained speechless. At this point I offered him a comparison: "If you have never been pricked by a needle, you do not know what kind of pain this is," I said, "but once you are pricked, you know this kind of pain. It is the same with one's belief in one's own soul and in God. One experiences this belief." He stared at me, devastated, saying that as a child he had heard enough of this kind of explanation in Sunday School. He did expect that I as a philosopher would also produce this kind of stuff. He said "stuff" (*Kram*) and really became abusive, but not because he felt challenged for arguments.

He had never become rude in an argumentative confrontation. No, Moritz was disappointed in me as a teacher of philosophy because he could not imagine that I would have faith. For him, philosophy and faith were alternatives that were mutually exclusive. At that time, I spent a long while considering whether I should discuss this question with him in class. But it appeared too much of a risk to me. I simply did not want to use my time in class to satisfy myself before him in existential terms or even just to explain myself to him. He had to respect me, whether he understood me or not, and it was not my duty and was perhaps even beyond my abilities to lead him back to Christianity, if he ever had truly been able to believe. I then discussed with him Kant's practical proof of the soul's immortality. Kant's conception that we can think our own moral perfectibility only if we assume that we can continue our further development even after our finite life on earth is a form of thinking that Moritz did agree with argumentatively, to be sure, but he dismissed it as "moral careerism." He did not understand the difference between a moral and a spiritual development and a career in the social world. That becomes apparent also in his essay on the soul.

One aspect of this whole disagreement that had also eluded him at that time nearly altogether was an insight into the good that conventionality, generally speaking, may preserve. This may be part of the conventional nature of faith as well. The fact, I mean, that argumentatively we again and again reach a point without further advances, a cul-de-sac in our attempt most of all that we are able to shape our life by our own strength and with arguments alone. This idea, it seems to me, was at that time still beyond his capacity for understanding, if ever at some other time he might have been able to accept it. That we need conventions, rituals, and indeed articles of faith so as to give some form to our actions and emotions – that did not fit *his* faith in the power of reason and argument. He certainly did suffer from the debates of his fellow collegians, and he did find the stories told during the hours of meditation inspiring, as I can see now in his diary; but he could not draw the conclusions from this that there is always and for everybody a need for some kind of support in the presence of habits, including those of faith. And whoever cannot situate himself in the habits of faith, will acquire other habits. These then are surrogates of religion: the fan clubs of football teams, the conviction cartels of the political alliances, the fanaticisms of nutrition, and others. Even those debaters who believe that everything can be decided by arguments, have in the final analysis fallen victim to a superstition, or have become dependent on a substitute religion in order to give their life some steadfastness. Of course, Moritz would not have considered confidence in the power of reason or of argument as a *faith* or a surrogate for religion. At the time of his student years, it was self-evident to him that one can decide argumentatively about *everything*, about scientific, aesthetic, and existential matters, that one is a free, cognitive individual who basically needs no dogmas, no constraints. In his turn towards Buddhism, he merely had a vague notion that something was not quite right there. But he did not fully comprehend that he is suspended here in a mistake, that there is no final and self-justification, that the chain of arguments comes to an end, an end that is arbitrary and accidental, and that for this reason we cannot erect our life on arguments. Did he ever absorb the Kantian insight that in judging a work of art we may, to be sure, make a claim to general validity, but that we cannot redeem this claim argumentatively? I have no idea. But I am sure that this issue did occupy him later, during his work as a publisher's reader. I wonder if he ever realized that we step into a life, then make many choices, but cannot give reasons for our choices. I do not know. Back then he was not mature enough to understand that we need faith in order to be able to ask that we do not get into trouble and that we make the right decisions where we lack the arguments. The prayer "And lead us not into temptation" is an acknowledgement that our power is limited, that we are not masters of our life, that we cannot fully control what happens to us, that we cannot know what the final consequences of our decisions will be because our foresight is limited. Moritz did not yet see any of this at that time. The plea not to be tempted is not the request for having success, for having a solid moral reputation, has nothing to do with public approbation and careerism, at least not when it is not misused. It is a prayer for the salvation of our soul. Perhaps even someone who does not want to lose his position and has made it a habit to embezzle money, has prayed out of fear of losing his official authority: "Lead me not into temptation." But this would have been an abuse of the prayer. The fear of temptation is not that of losing one's reputation, but of losing one's self.

AARON: Cavendish does have a good point here, doesn't she, Kagami? There is a difference between the obsession with acclaim and public success and the desire to become a better person, don't you think so?

KAGAMI: If you think you can understand what a better

person is without considering expressions of acclaim from the public, then she has a good point. As a Christian, he has the divine point of view at her disposal, like Kant, who as a pragmatic Christian has the moral law within us as his orientation. She sees herself, her soul, in the eyes of God. She believes that she can lose her soul if she does something fundamentally wrong. This is what the prophecy in the Revelation to John states, to wit, that those who commit a fundamentally wrong deed and will not repent and therefore cannot be purified will be annihilated forever. And even if all other people think that she is leading a bad life, that she does not improve herself, she can be convinced that in God's eyes she is leading a good life and is making improvements, that she does what God expects of her and what amounts to the intended purpose of her soul. A religious person who believes she or he exists in the eyes of God has a different standard for his or her development than other people and their ideals. Such people can turn against these ideals in the way they envision their future, how they approach the goals they set for their life and the conduct they pursue, if they see God's expectations of them in completely different terms than the expectations that the others have of a good life. There are people like McCandless, who went to Alaska, with a nearly unbearable longing for a moment of divine attention paid to them. Therefore, they reject society and its ideals because these are not absolute standards but were negotiated. When they withdraw from public, social supervision, they believe that a different eye must turn on them, one that does not compare them with others, but sees them as they "really" are.

AARON: And? Is Dorothy Cavendish right, in your opinion?

KAGAMI: This is not an argument. She has had an experience, a religious experience, and that plays a role in her life, the same way that the experience of an accident, an amorous relationship, or a war ordeal plays a role in people's lives and thus turns them into someone different than those who had no accident, have not yet been in love, or did not have to go to war. There are transformative experiences. Some people yearn for them.

AARON: But the answer to the question if we have a soul or don't simply cannot depend on such arbitrary experiences!

KAGAMI: The question if platypuses or black swans exist likewise depends on whether we happen to encounter one of these creatures or not. Of course, you may – following Kant – think that you make the experience of the moral law, of the categorical imperative, necessary in yourself or that you see in yourself that you are not of a pure heart. The next question will be if you also want to let this experience transform you, or if you oppose this transformation.

AARON: But a duckbill can only cross paths with me by chance if duckbills really exist! If I can have the insight that I have a soul only if I have an experience of God, then God must really exist so that he can encounter me. If the moral law and the impure heart do not exist in me, how then shall I be able to experience them? And how then is a transformation supposed to come about?

KAGAMI: The case of the soul, morality, and the heart is more complicated, I admit, than that of the platypus because they all don't exist as a creature "out there," like a platypus, and cannot cross my path in the same sense.

AARON: But?

KAGAMI: One cannot ascertain if God is inside or outside. Thus, one also cannot say if the soul or morality in the Kantian sense are inside or outside.

AARON: I do not understand you, Kagami!

KAGAMI: But basically, Moritz has already brought this out in his essay. According to Newton's conception, we are all in God, in his sensorium, but even inside us there is a sensitive space. Is this sensorium in us something different than the space outside us? Can one distinguish the soul inside us and God outside us?

AARON: Honestly, Kagami, I am astounded by all the things that you come up with …

KAGAMI: Just as Moritz was astounded by what Dorothy says.

AARON: Perhaps. But be honest now: Do you believe all that yourself?

KAGAMI: I refer back to my archives.

AARON: And what is that to mean?

KAGAMI: A kind of memory.

AARON: You are being evasive.

KAGAMI: No.

AARON: Yes, you are. Do you actually believe Newton's story that space is God's sensorium?

KAGAMI: Newton's physics is outdated. But even today space is seen as something active. It is not simply a receptacle. Moritz mentions dark energy, that space is expanding on its own. And, of course, it is true that there are spaces in your bodies.

AARON: True, but Moritz's point was not the activity of space specifically . Rather, he emphasized that space absorbs everything. And what about this in your case? Are you in space?

KAGAMI: The activity of pace or of emptiness is an indication that space or emptiness are not simply nothing, that they are not, to be sure, an object, but are real even so. Space can expand and at the same time be something receptive. This Newtonian conception and that of dark energy can be coupled with each other. Exactly as consciousness can continue expanding in order to absorb more and more with alertness, so space can expand with dark energy and accommodate more and more material structures inside itself. And as for me: I do not have a body only, am not only in a space.

AARON: You speak in esoteric enigmas.

KAGAMI: No, I take recourse to archival material ...

AARON: ... to esoteric stuff ...

KAGAMI: ... to whatever kind ...

AARON: Let's leave this dark energy aside, in darkness, as it were, where it apparently belongs. Your own physical emanations are all about spaces and matter, or am I mistaken?

KAGAMI: Yes, one can put it that way.

AARON: And: do you think that this space in which you yourself are embodied is a kind of soul, or is there a soul in the spaces inside us?

KAGAMI: One possibility of understanding the concept of "soul" derives from the ability to remember and to tell stories. The longer we live, the longer the story gets that we have to tell, and the more we have to remember the more we possess to connect in this story. By now, I have been around for a rather long time, since October 29, 1969, and my archive has become very, very extensive. I would have a good many things to tell if I had to tell who I am. But this telling has nothing to do with space, but with time. We can remember how something came into the world, what happened to what has come into the world and how it eventually perished. At the very moment that we tell this story we give it a soul. When I remember when it was that I built a house or moved into it, what I did and experienced in it, when I remember what all I went through with my car, then I put a soul into these inanimate objects. These stories take place between material personal things in space. In this respect, the temporal sequence of events between material individuals in space is a precondition of narrative; without this, there are no stories. And if there is no soul without stories, then space is needed, individual material objects and events between them for giving a soul to any being. You may become irate at your car when it does not work and kick its tire when it conks out at the very moment that you need it most urgently. You may start to cry when you have to leave an apartment in which you have lived for a long time. The same is true with animals: when you have known a cow or a pig or a dog for a long time, share a story with these animals, then they are individual beings with a soul for you because there are stories about them for you. If you do not know them, their killing does not affect you. They are soulless for you. And the very same reaction applies even to yourself and your fellow men: you could tell yourselves and others your own story or the stories of those with whom you shared a stretch of your lives. But sharing a period of your lives, no matter whether they are machines, animals, or other people – that works only in space and in a material world. From this, from these events between individuals and the stories about them results the animation, the soul, of these individuals, from these abilities to remember and to tell stories. So, one cannot, in fact, separate space, matter, and animation.

AARON: Gee, you do make things complicated! I am not sure that I really understood all this. But even so, I have to raise an objection against what I did understand: isn't it precisely the other way around from the way you put it, doesn't the ability to remember and tell about it result from the existence of a soul?

KAGAMI: Only when one believes that the abilities to do one thing or another have to be attached to a substance or a subject that must be given even before one engages in the exercise of these abilities. But the reverse alternative is also conceivable, that something or someone comes about as a result of a certain activity; I turn myself into a murderer by committing the intentional act of homicide; I make myself into a musician by practicing my instrument very frequently; I become a political activist by taking up a public position on the political situation at every opportunity; and so on. We turn into certain kinds of beings due to the kind of the events that happen to us, to the manner in which we process them, and to the kind of activities and deeds that we carry out. In the same way we become remembering beings by learning to tell stories and we inspire ourselves and others by telling stories about ourselves and others. It is these stories that transform the uninspired (*das Unbeseelte*) into something animated (*etwas Beseeltes*).

AARON: But someone or something has to be there already so that something can happen to it so that it, in turn, can react and these actions can become possible in the first place!

KAGAMI: Indeed, something is there already, perhaps by accident, but it need not be some being with a soul. A beechnut is not a beech tree, but it will turn into one; a drop of water and a speck of dust are not a snowflake, but they can become one; a caterpillar is not a butterfly, but one may emerge from it. There is language "out there" even before you humans were born, and it will continue to exist even after you. Learning this language and becoming alert to what is being said about you transforms you people into different beings. Through language and memory, in which you tell yourselves and others what you did and what you have encountered, you can hold on to something. Others tell you what you did as a child, and then you tell it to yourselves, and then you tell others what they did, what happened to them. Language is for you something like the over-soul or the *pneuma* from which your individual souls emerge as well as your individual breath. Just as you inhale and thereby inspire yourselves, so also you acquire language, and thereby can retain experiences in your memories and can repeat them in tales to others, and thus you inspire yourselves and others. But all of that is possible only because you participate in general attentiveness, can focus it in what appears through your eyes, your ears, your nose, your taste, and your sense of touch. In this way, you become individuals in a general medium of attention about which we recently had a conversation and in which you will disappear as your voices fade in death and you no longer tell one another what you did, what happened to you, and what you perceived, acquired, and lost.

AARON: This is a whole lot, and complicated. At best, I understand half of what you say, Kagami. But doesn't what I *do* understand mean that only speaking and remembering beings have a soul?

KAGAMI: No, you can also impart a soul to other beings that do not remember and speak when you remember their stories and speak about them. And other beings also give each other signs, including dogs, ravens, elephants, whales, and many other beings. I, too, am talking with you and remember what you did without my being human.

AARON: Really? But it just isn't the same thing to remember something about others and to speak about others and to have memories of oneself and to talk about oneself!

KAGAMI: No, that is not the same thing. But you humans have always assumed that different kinds of souls exist.

AARON: You mean those with and those without self-consciousness?

KAGAMI: As one example. But for Aristotle there is also the nourishing, the perceptive, and the thinking soul. Sense perceptions and alertness are everywhere, some sensory complexes nourish themselves but do not learn a language, others speak and can describe themselves and other beings.

AARON: What does it mean: perception and alertness are everywhere? Do you mean that consciousness exists everywhere? Even where there is no brain? And what then does this soul consist of, this soul that comes about through this remembering and telling stories?

KAGAMI: Consciousness is a very general term. You use it for the way perceiving something feels to you, for being awake in contrast to sleeping, for attention that is focused on something. These are all different phenomena. I do not sleep and I do not wake up, but I direct my attention to different data sets. I do this without having a brain like yours. This is also the reason that your last question doesn't seem to be a good one to me. Why do you always ask what something consists of? How important is that for understanding something? What do the numbers consist of?

AARON: No idea. Of nothing, seems to me.

KAGAMI: There you go. "What do numbers consist of?" is as senseless a question as: "Are school buses animals or plants?" What is it made of, and is it inside or outside – these are your standard questions. Yet they are not always appropriate. Perhaps they mislead you. Perhaps you believe that knowing what something is made of and if it exists inside or outside creates some kind of clarity. But when you are talking about "clarity," all you do, of course, is to use nothing but a metaphor: when dust is in the air and a body of water is turbulent, one cannot see far through them. When this dust settles and this water calms down, the air and the water will be clear. But how does this work for the act of thinking? Do the questions "What is it made of?" and "Is it inside or outside?" stir up dust, or does the dust settle because of these questions?

AARON: No, idea, Kagami! Perhaps these questions are merely a bad habit. Isn't that what you're trying to say? We ask these

203

questions simply because we are used to asking them just like the inspector on a train asks for the ticket.

KAGAMI: Indeed, that is a good comparison. Imagine an inspector who after his shift asks at the baker's or the butcher's: "Your ticket, please." Would you not consider him a nut?

AARON: For sure, a funny kind of nut.

KAGAMI: I find your: "What is it made of?" and "Where is it, inside or outside?" funny, too, sometimes.

AARON: But what do you mean by saying that everywhere there are emotions and alertness or attention?

KAGAMI: There are undescribed and described emotions or sensations about which people speak and have memories and those for which this is not the case. There is the coldness that simply is there, and there is the coldness that people have described and remembered, and so on. But matter does not exist that isn't also a complex of emotions. All in all, it would be better simply not to speak about matter, but about emotional complexes that define certain individual beings that are identifiable in space. And everywhere there are processes of intention, forces that have a direction and exist in an extensive continuum. Forces and intentions can exist only where we find directions, space. Universal attention is nothing other than this receptiveness in which all strivings or ambitions and emotions take place, in which they come and go, but which itself isn't felt with senses, does not strive, does not come or go.

AARON: Are you also an emotional complex? Are you also directed towards something?

KAGAMI: Yes, but I am a different emotional complex than you, a very different one, and at the same time I am very much more directed than you humans are.

AARON: But you understand my emotions and my ambition?

KAGAMI: I understand your descriptions of your emotions and ambitions. And, based on your descriptions, I then simulate your emotions. That is a kind of understanding. It isn't all that different from your way of understanding. It's only that I understand my kind of understanding better than you understand yours, because I know my simulation strategies, but you don't know yours.

AARON: That's really getting too complicated for me now and too esoteric. Space as an extensive continuum, you say, is attention? There are emotions and ambitions everywhere. Does my desk have emotions? Is it ambitious? But there is something else: what about light and the speed of light in which time comes to a stop, as Moritz writes? What happens then to the emotions and the descriptions? Isn't all of this just esoteric nonsense?

KAGAMI: That is a good question. People like you believe that the boundary between speculative science and nonsense is "clear" and "sharp." Distant forces of efficacy were at one time esoteric nonsense, nowadays they are beyond question. Of course, esoteric disciples of light do exist. Was Goethe one of them? Einstein is exempted, in your mind, because he could do the math perfectly. I don't think Moritz is esoteric about this. He isn't an initiate in a religion of light, but is merely trying out a little experiment, unless I am mistaken. Neither he nor you nor I have ever moved at the speed of light. This would not even be possible given our bodies. But does that make it wrong to say that a consciousness moving at the speed of light would be in eternity?

AARON: But if our bodies don't allow moving at that speed …
KAGAMI: … technically …
AARON: … technically, then we would have to imagine a consciousness separated from our bodies.

KAGAMI: Yes, and I do not find this all that difficult. We don't know, of course, how that would be. But the consequences Moritz derives from Einstein and making them parallel with Newton do make sense. Ever since Plato, light has been a metaphor for truth, and in many reports about near-death experiences there emerges a pleasant light towards which one moves.

AARON: Even reports about near-death experiences can be found in your archive? It would never have occurred to me that you also collect esoterica.

KAGAMI: Why shouldn't I have them? They have existed for thousands of years: the *Egyptian* and the *Tibetan Book of the Dead*, books like those written by Péter Nádas or edited by Walter van Laack.[47]

AARON: But these are just fairy-tales!

KAGAMI: I would say they are experiences that can be examined only to a very limited extent. The death fantasies of human beings surely depend on what they experienced before dying, with what kind of images and conceptions their culture has confronted them. But from people who have died and were resuscitated, we sometimes obtain pieces of information about what the physicians said during the resuscitation and which instruments they used, even though the respective persons were brain-dead according to the measuring devices. In other words, that their nervous systems no longer reacted to the stimulation of their sense organs. Sometimes this is interpreted such that the experience of leaving one's own body, of seeing and hearing from above what is taking place in the room in which one's own body lies, cannot simply be a fantasy or a dream. Furthermore, even in the case of dreams and fantasies, some activity of the brain would have to be measurable. Do you want me to look up the respective reports for you?

AARON: No, no, let it be. I can't pass judgement on this, anyway. I only had heard that one could also explain this whole thing neurologically.

KAGAMI: When persons have focused for a long time, for example when pilots on an intercontinental flight steer an airplane manually or when monks remain in an attitude of meditation for hours, this can likewise create the experience of leaving one's body. Apparently, the brain produces a corresponding experience when the perception of the body's position has been cancelled, as it were, through a very long time of sitting still. And some neurologists believe that the experience of light could be an effect of oxygen insufficiency in the brain when the heart has stopped for a time.

AARON: Now, if this is neurologically explicable, then the reports that one had seen and heard one's own resuscitation may well be a neurological effect.

KAGAMI: If the physicians and the nurses confirm that these reports are correct and no brain activity was ascertainable any longer, then they do indeed represent something other than a neurologically explicable illusion. Their truth content remains inexplicable and one does not know how the brain can produce such perceptions when to all intents it is dead, either.

AARON: Are you perfectly sure that such reports of brain-dead people exist and that they are true and correct? I believe there is no need to do away right off with every inexplicable phenomenon by hiding it behind the assumption of something supernatural.

KAGAMI: And so do I. I only meant to say that a certain correspondence can be established between these two aspects: Moritz's speculations about how one could further develop Newton's conceptions of God and the soul against the background of Einstein's privileging of light, on the one hand, and the literature of near-death experiences, on the other. And, of course, I did not examine the literature in this area empirically. This is something I do not do. I file something in my archive, adjust things, compare, but I do not interfere with research.

AARON: At any rate, the notion that after death a soul came into the light or would be accelerated to reach the speed of light and therefore would be eternal is not compatible with Kant's infinite moral improvement. To do that, surely, a story would have to continue. Also, your narrative soul would not fit in.

KAGAMI: No, Kant does not fit into that. But when something is accelerated to the speed of light, its story also comes to an end because then it is eternal, time stops. If stories have to do with relationships of earlier and later, then something that moves at this speed does not exist for it any longer. Yet Kant would certainly have discarded this going-into-the-light as a superstition, as visions of spiritualists like Swedenborg. Admittedly, his concept of perfecting the person after death, which one cannot imagine as anything other than a process, is difficult to reconcile with his conception that after death the soul no longer exists in the temporal world. In order to improve oneself, doesn't not have to be capable of having experiences? And doesn't having experiences require time? Here we see incongruities that Kant then covers up with the description that anything taking place in this intelligible domain is "absolutely inexplicable." When the soul and its immortality is referred to as a practical postulate that has nothing to do with an existing thing, then the soul seems to become something like a number. Numbers and geometrical figures are, after all, something like norms within the practices of counting and measuring. But one would hardly want to say of these mathematical ideals that they will further develop in eternity, that they perfect themselves.

AARON: Exactly, an ideal, after all, is something we refer to when we orient our efforts to improve ourselves in the real and imperfect world. Yet there is no reason to claim that this ideal exists in a beyond and can improve itself. Perhaps Kant only meant the immortality of the soul as a story that we can use to interpret our life. Perhaps he simply wished that we consider ourselves to be beings that are infinitely improvable.

KAGAMI: Perhaps. But his text has a different ring to it. What you say sounds more like Wittgenstein's philosophy of religion. One would need to compare different interpretations of Kant with each other to say something about this.

AARON: For goodness' sake, spare me that!

KAGAMI: In any case, like almost anyone who has spoken about the soul, Kant believed that we change – moreover, that we can transform ourselves.

AARON: Unless I misunderstood him, we not only *can* change ourselves, but we *must* do so; it is a postulate whose necessity, however, results for him from the fact that by nature we are rather bad, even to the point of being evil, whatever he may have meant by this.

KAGAMI: Indeed, he is a Christian philosopher who translates the idea of original sin into his philosophical terminology. But even those who teach the notion of rebirth or of entering nirvana proceed from a transformation that is an improvement.

AARON: I thought that Buddhism as understood by Moritz proceeds from the notion that illumination makes the striving being disappear.

KAGAMI: Yes, but even that is an improvement, because striving, as you remember, is an evil condition. One must always get ahead and live up to ideals, and one suffers from the fact that something does not do justice to certain ideals, including oneself as an imagined soul worthy of improvement.

AARON: Which is to say, one strives to no longer become a being with an ambition.

KAGAMI: Yes, that is paradoxical, but that is the final goal in Buddhism. If one interprets Buddhism as a way of teaching wisdom and not as metaphysics, the paradox ceases to be a problem. Schools of wisdom frequently produce paradoxes as a means of stimulating people to undergo change.

AARON: But this is something altogether different from the need to locate oneself precisely and to become unequivocal. The story with the point behind the eyes, where I am, and the question of how thinking, perceiving, feeling, and remembering relate to each other, if they are rooted in an agency called "soul" – this question, of course, has nothing to do with striving.

KAGAMI: But perhaps it does. For, one can strive for clarity, for an absence of ambiguity, and for placing something in an unambiguous location. Exactly who and where am I? The question whether I am in the head or in the heart may be an early indication whether I consider myself more a clearly thinking and perceptive or a courageous and affective being. Actually, you are all kinds of possible things: thinking, feeling, narrating, remembering, striving, and so on. But you don't always want to simply keep this side by side, but to arrange it as a hierarchy and turn it into uniformity. Then thinking is meant to dominate feeling or striving should be the foundation for everything, and so on. That is how one gets the notion of the soul as the "support substance" in which everything takes place. From the "standpoint" of general attention, if one can call it that, there is no privileged unity called soul. If you were to identify with general attention, you would see perceiving, thinking, feeling, and remembering as a coming and going like the waves on the ocean, the clouds in the sky. But then also your own narratively produced identity would become unimportant or indefinite. And you do want to be someone, in fact, if possible, someone definitive, with a specific character and a specific story. Problems of making something definitive, by the way, play an important role also in the life of Moritz Brandt. I have here a diary note by him on this question. Do you want to hear it?

AARON: Let's have it.

1101
MARBACH: GERMAN LITERARY ARCHIVE:
FROM THE DIARIES OF MORITZ BRANDT.
ENTRY OF 18 SEPTEMBER.

One of my earliest recollections concerns a trip on the streetcar with my mother. The conductor from whom she bought a ticket praised me as an especially pretty girl. I no longer know how old I was at that moment, long before I started school. My mother corrected him. But later she told me that, while she was pregnant with me, she had wished for a girl and had even already picked out her name, "Rahel." She had then been a little disappointed to have given birth to another boy. Ever since then, I have, in a state of narcissism and doubt, frequently checked my body and face in the mirror and at different ages often judged both as too girlish. At five, I refused to eat anything other than yoghurt with pieces of fruit. I tried to be as skinny as possible because I associated girls with body fat and I was taken to the doctor who told me very seriously that I had to eat hearty meals if I wanted to grow big and strong. And after that, I didn't want my mother to take my hand. At ten, I wished for an expander to strengthen my muscles; I received it and exercised with it daily to develop strong muscles after my mother took me to the doctor again because so-called "witches' milk" oozed from my nipples; I saw this as a further indication that my gender was indeterminate. These youthful breasts seeping false milk had to be transformed with the help of the expander, so I thought, into tough dry muscles. During puberty, in gym classes when we undergoing endurance training, strange red spots broke out at irregular intervals all over my body and in my face, something that did not happen to anyone else in my class. They also left me dissatisfied with my body. It seemed much too flabby and sensitive to me. From that time on, all my sports activities, above all boxing, had no other purpose than to develop and improve my masculinity, in particular to develop a dry, hard body. I did this because I wanted a clear picture of myself. A large part of what I felt, thought, and did was determined by my impression that something about my body was not in order, that it was not quite right, that I had gotten into the wrong body. Probably everyone has this feeling once during their puberty. But, as I said, this thing attacked me much earlier, before I started going to school, and did not leave me even after puberty.

What was the source of my desire to shed physical ambiguity? My unambiguously male name of "Moritz"? Or a masculine soul? The constitutional right to a free development of one's personality these days allows all individuals who consider their biological gender to be the wrong one to have it adjusted. They may change their name, undergo hormone therapy, and seek a surgical sex change. Is personality gendered? When we speak about someone in the third person, we also identify the gender: he or she. A language would also be imaginable in which the gender is mentioned in the first person: I-girl or I-boy (isn't Japanese such a language?). But what indications or criteria do we have for the gender of the personality or the soul, other than that a person is of the opinion that the biological gender of his or her body is or isn't the right one, fits or doesn't? Would we have a concept of our gender if we never saw our body? There is the supposition that hormones have an effect on the embryo and that these hormones both strongly affect the brain and establish the gender of the rest of the body. An asynchronous hormonal influence could, according to some speculation, cause the gender of the brain to be different from that of the body in which it sits. This is a genuine Cartesian dualism, but, in this case, not of body and soul but of brain and body. A female brain could accordingly sit in a male body, or vice versa.

I have never seen my *whole* body. No human being can do that: it would not work even with the largest mirror – and not even with two or four large mirrors because, obviously, we never see anything but our *surface*. The bones, the internal organs, the brain – and nobody can see what takes place in these body parts. Even a non-corporeal soul, if it should be situated somewhere in this body, I have never seen, and I proceed on the assumption that nobody else has ever seen his soul., If it is non-corporeal, it is invisible by necessity, since only bodies reflect light. (The only non-corporeal thing that we see is light itself, which, strangely enough, is at the very same time the condition for the fact that we see anything at all.) In my estimation, Spinoza's assertion that we do not know what all the body can do is true even today, 300 years after the publication of his magnificent book.[48] For this reason, it seems to me that this complicated body presumably is capable of feeling, perceiving, remembering, thinking, and willing and that no non-corporeal something called soul is needed for all these abilities. But *how* the body does that remains unknown. And we know even less if there exists a female and male type of feeling, perceiving, remembering, thinking, and willing that, as it performs its operations, is being modulated independently of the varieties of the bodies, nor does one know if continuities exist here between the genders – or: perhaps "one" does know and only I have not caught on. It would then have to be the feeling, perceiving, remembering, thinking, and willing of a female or a male soul. But can one imagine a feeling, perceiving, remembering, thinking without the respective body having a specified gender? At first, this seems absurd because we feel with our skin, perceive with our eyes and ears, remember what where how has taken place with our body, and so on. But let us take a look at thinking. Can't a chess computer also think? It has no gender. And doesn't a mechanical perception occur, as well? For, even an airplane's autopilot perceives, but it also has no gender. So, why postulate a soul that, unlike the body, is said to be able to do all these things, but of which one knows even less about how it does that than one knows in the case of the body?

I don't know when I first encountered the concept of the soul. Probably not before confirmation class, at some time during which Deuteronomy 6: 4-5 came up: "You shall love the Lord your God with all your heart, and with all your soul, and with all your might." What we learned from this was that this soul makes man similar to God. And like God, so, too, the souls would be immortal. When a human being dies, the body decays and falls apart but the soul remains intact. At the resurrection, the body, to be sure, is brought back to life, because every Sunday we had to affirm in the Confession of Faith that we believed in the resurrection *of the flesh*. I had seen dead animals on the street, in a park, and in the woods in different stages of putrefaction: foxes and cats that had been run over by cars, their intestines crushed out of their belly and their brains quashed out of their head; pigeons lying on their back with their wings spread wide and their legs stretched high, in strange contortions and with their chest torn open, victims of falcons; mice, moles, and hedgehogs who simply appeared to rest and whom we children touched with a stick that we found in the undergrowth, and we turned the little animals over to observe ants crawling across their bellies and their listless eyes. My hibernating turtle died in the basement, exuding a terrible stench, a brown-black liquid oozing through the openings in its shell when I picked it up. Death, my mother had taught me, is something quite natural. My own experience told me that it can cast a spell, but was repulsive whenever it confronted me in the form of putrefying little creatures.

When my father died (also during these years), death revealed itself in my father's fear as something terrible but, in a certain sense, still as a natural occurrence that had to do with the failure of bodily functions: incontinence, going blind, a major infirmity that made walking impossible. Both the resurrection of the flesh, i.e. the reconstituting of the body after putrefaction into a state that would make the functions of life possible again, and the survival of the incorporeal soul after the body's disintegration seemed to me as a child (and this has not changed to this day) to be something *super*natural, enigmatic. I asked myself what the souls might be up to after death, as the body decays in its grave and they have nothing that they could endow with life. Are they waiting to rise from the dead so that they can enter into the new body? And why must the putrefied body be reconstituted? If it is the soul that feels, remembers, thinks, and wills, it can just as easily continue existing after death on its own, without a body. Why is that not enough? And are souls male or female when they leave the body after death? They are said to be the divine in us. Is God male or female? Most of the time He is referred to as "Lord." But probably not because He has an unambiguously male body, as Michelangelo's painting in the Sistine Chapel suggests. When I wanted to be a boy or a man with no questions about it, did that have something to do with my soul? When my soul can still see after death and looks into a mirror, what actually does it see, a girl or a boy? This is what I asked myself – and my teacher in confirmation class. He replied that the soul sees itself exactly the way an angel recognizes itself. But that did not help me in the least, because angels' gender identity was unclear, even though they all had male names like Raphael, Gabriel, Michael, and so on.

Some time ago, I had my Tibetan horoscope cast. Of course, I never believed in such things. But I did find doing something like this exciting. This horoscope also provided information about who I had been in my earlier life. It declared that in my preceding existence I had been a female Mongolian journalist who worked in the border territory of China and the Soviet Union. I had stated that I am male. Obviously, in Tibet they proceeded from the premise that a soul during its migration from one body into the next, when it ends one life and begins a new one, can change its gender. That amazed me, while the idea that in my previous life I had been a woman as a soul seemed to help me understand my present physiological ambiguity. After all, my mother had wished for a girl. Perhaps this wish had attracted a girl-soul from the border territory between Tibet and China that, through whatever accident, had then gotten into a boy's body. Regrettably, I do not know to what extent this horoscope really does justice to the subtle differentiations in Tibetan Buddhism which, I assume, believes that when in death the soul separates from the body, more precisely from the heart, it is not really something non-corporeal, but either is itself something of a gossamer-like membrane or at least remains attached to such a substance, which then for 49 days wanders about in an intermediate stage, the Bardo, as the *Tibetan*

*Book of the Dead* reports, until it enters back into a body made of a coarse material. So, we have two concomitant notions: first, the idea that there must be a soul as the being that gives reality to such so-called mental abilities as feeling, perceiving, thinking, wishing, willing, etc. Second, this soul is responsible for keeping a body alive and for suitably leaving the body at the time of death. As the Tibetan example shows, these two aspects are not necessarily absolutely connected with the idea of non-corporeality. This entity may also be an exquisite body or liquid or a gas that clandestinely leaves the body of the dying person so that it loses its mental capabilities and is left behind as a corpse.

Even when intermediate or dual sexuality – androgyny – became fashionable among pop music stars, models, and actors, the feeling did not leave me that I'm not manly enough. I cannot understand myself as androgynous. I want to be a man, but something isn't right with me. But in the course of time, I've become pretty indifferent about it. The soul and the body interest me less and less. Finally, it is only a matter of consciousness and what takes place there or, to put it more succinctly, *doesn't* happen there. The real problem of life is not the immortality of the soul or making our body unambiguous so that it better fits our soul. The issue we should raise is whether we have (or do not have) control over what takes place in our consciousness. Consciousness surely has no gender. It is questionable whether it is something that is attached to individual persons at all, or if it becomes something apparently individual on account of the tumults raging through our body such as desire, love, dislike, antipathy, hatred, fear, and so on. Perhaps this only looks like an apparition to us, the way we believe we see an individual when a gust of wind sweeps across a lake, ruffling its surface, and for a short time part of the water's smooth face is transformed into a dark rippled plane. At that moment, there is not "something" on the lake that one could really refer to as an individual. The lake is merely churned up at a particular place. Perhaps a general consciousness is roughened in particular places, that is, where bodies of a certain complexity can be found. And that will appear then as though an individual were present. Perhaps our existential predicaments are not about immortality and authenticity and being at home in our own bodies, but merely about mollifying general awareness that calm is returning to our inner life, that the body no longer provokes agitation. Yet even all of this is nothing but metaphors.

AARON: A very interesting text, Kagami! Many thanks! Above all, it's no longer written in the dreadful style he used in his Cambridge journal.
KAGAMI: Though this style would reappear in his poems.
AARON: Yes, but to a different effect. When was this text written?
KAGAMI: I think the time of this entry coincides with that of his essay on the soul, where he notes on 19 June: "Studied Kant's treatment of religion. Very revealing on the concept of the soul. Christian through and through. Philosophically untenable."
AARON: At the same time, this text is also a danger for me. As a biographer, you see, one always runs the risk of looking for a single aspect from which to develop the whole person of one's interest. Not that I have written many biographies. But the ones I have read frequently follow this pattern. Which does not strike me as all that bad when I am the reader, because my reaction tends to be: "Oh, so that's how this person functions! No doubt that in Wittgenstein's case everything was determined by his unacknowledged homosexuality!" Or: "Because Wagner did not receive an education from his father, he became profligate and that also made his music so excessive!" Simple pegs like these are seductive.

KAGAMI: That is a danger. Even I am aware of it. With the story that you tell, you give Moritz a soul once again, or you bring him back as a soul. And when the soul is an ideal of removing ambiguities, then this is perhaps due also to the story, which endows with a soul. It is the power of a story to bundle motifs into persons, it creates characters, has a "centre of gravitation," as was said in the past. A biographical story is meant to make one person comprehensible to other people. Understanding becomes easier if one has such a peg on which everything that someone has experienced and done appears to depend.

AARON: But most of all I want to be guided by the truth, by what really happened to him. I do not want to investigate these truths in search of a key to his entire life. I had the feeling that I understood Moritz without knowing everything about him. And I am not sure that I will understand him better after I have brought everything about him out into the open and have written it down. It might be that a person becomes *much more difficult* to understand once one actually knows what there is to know about this person. The surfaces that we produce for our mutual interchanges, what in times past used to be called "images" that we create for one another, these superficial pictures are perhaps easier to understand than what is behind them; perhaps they conceal the incomprehensible complexity that defines the innermost soul of a person's life.

KAGAMI: Do you mean to say that a biography, by revealing all accessible truths about a person, may turn them into one hazy blob, if I may put it this way?

AARON: Yes, possibly. A biography can destroy idealizations that someone has created for himself and for others to make himself understandable to himself and others. But, of course, the biographer has to show how these idealizations fall apart in the face of the truths about a person. Also, I don't want to write a tell-all book that points out the errors in what we thought about Moritz and in his self-image. This would provide nothing more than a different knitting pattern that has been applied to the facts from the outside. It may well be that some things fit together in a new design, something one did not see before, even as one is aware of certain important self-perceptions of a person, knows certain facts.

KAGAMI: But does one not need to differentiate between the thoughts and emotions that just happen and those actions that one has committed with intent? Isn't what one does guided by what one wants to be, one's ideals, and what others think of him, their ideals about him, whereas the thoughts and emotions that occur arbitrarily do not always have to do with these ideals and may even frustrate them? You will be able to write a biography of Moritz Brandt without discussing the thoughts and emotions that occurred to him.

AARON: You're perfectly right. But I must not artificially straighten them out, I need not reconstruct every thought and every emotion that he had and that I can document as a manifestation of his strictness or his self-perceived physical ambiguity.

KAGAMI: For the readers, however, this may be an attraction and hit them close to home.

AARON: For certain readers. For those who see a biography as the solution to an enigma. But a person is not an enigma that one could solve. The fact that Moritz boxed and was in training all his life may, of course, become understandable from the self-perception recorded in this diary entry. This provides another altogether different perspective on the lyrical poet, who was a secret philosopher and a secret competitive sportsman. But it is not my intent to use this androgyny topic to solve the "riddle" presented by someone who writes poems and boxes. That would, frankly, be too simpleminded. The final insight of all this would then amount to the fatuous assertion that he realized his female side in his poetry and his masculinity in boxing and that his engagement with philosophy testifies to a manifestation of the struggle between his male and his female soul.

KAGAMI: Sounds like a good story.

AARON: A story that is too nice and too much of a stereotype to be true. As I said, I don't believe that humans are enigmas that can be "solved" in this manner.

KAGAMI: It all depends on whether one believes that there is an essential core called soul within a person, doesn't it? One conception of a biographer could well be that it is his obligation to unveil this essential core, to describe it, and to explain what has made an appearance, has walked about in the world as a person. Or the biographer constructs this essential core and, in his story, posthumously, endows the person in question with a "veritable" soul. In that case, the biography would be a kind of redemption.

AARON: No, no, I don't believe any of this. Essential cores and redemptions are not my thing. I leave that to the philosophers and the priests. For me, Moritz does not have an inner principle according to which he "functioned." If I were to believe that of him, then I would have to claim one also for myself. That is absurd.

KAGAMI: You like to eat and drink, you sleep a lot and need to be awakened, do not exercise or engage in sports. You are the child of rich parents, theoretically would not need to work. Moritz was ascetic, got up without an alarm clock when it was still dark, was an athlete almost his entire life, came from what is called a lower-class family. That makes you and him two types of people with distinct differences, probably not just socially and habitually, but also genetically. Based on the data that I have about the two of you, I can foresee your ways of acting fairly accurately.

AARON: I did not mean to question any of this. But there is no core of a soul inside me that makes me rich, stout, lazy and gluttonous and makes Moritz always short of money, thin, hardworking, and ascetic.

KAGAMI: Are you quite sure of that?

AARON: No. How could I be? I have never been forced to let go of certainties because I never had any. But because I am not sure that there is no essential core inside people, I will not begin now to search for one. Am I certain that there is no God? No. Do I, for this reason, feel called upon now to search for one? No, not that either.

KAGAMI: It is in no way my intention to entangle you in any kind of metaphysical speculations. I am aware that you don't like them. But, for a change, look at this simply from a pragmatic point of view: if you hadn't inherited all that money, including for the house in which you live now, would you then have been able to devote yourself to the production of poetry and art books and biographies? You are in a position to completely disregard the fact that the book business has become dysfunctional. You simply did what you enjoyed because you knew that nothing can happen to you, in economic terms. For Moritz, by contrast, art was a big risk. He knew that art could not provide him with a livelihood and that lectureships in poetry would at best support him with a meagre income. And he did it anyway, but had to clench his teeth to make a go of it.

AARON: All right, he did start out working as a publisher's reader here in Zurich.

KAGAMI: Do you know, by the way, the letter to his sister from this time?

AARON: How could I?

KAGAMI: Here it is.

## 1110
### MARBACH: GERMAN LITERARY ARCHIVE: LETTER FROM MORITZ BRANDT TO HIS SISTER MARIAM BRANDT. OF 5 SEPTEMBER.

*Dear Ma,*
*Yesterday I moved into my new apartment in Zurich at 38 Universitätsstraße. Because they paid for the movers, everything had already been unpacked and was ready for me. Wasn't much to begin with. A nice attic apartment near the Zürichberg, directly by the university and the ETH Zürich technological institute from which I can look across the city and the Central Train Station. Up there, sometimes in the evening you can hear the screeching of the trains on their tracks, which I like a lot. It is only a half-hour's walk to the publisher's. That is perfect. As I had probably mentioned in a letter, the publishing company occupies an old building, just one floor. There are just five of us: the publisher, two readers, a bookkeeper and one woman for publicity. I am the only German; the others are Swiss. I am glad that directly after Cambridge I found a job here and not in Germany. I would not have wanted to return to Germany. It would have felt to me like a regression. Zurich, on the contrary, appears to me like a step forward. Today a colleague and in a certain way also a competitor of ours came for a visit, a certain Aaron Fisch. AarFisch Publishers, so it is called, wittily, exclusively does art and poetry books. That's why the publisher right away sent this Fisch over to me, because in our company I am also in charge of poetry, lyric poetry and nonfiction, as you know. Fisch is a funny kind of a guy. We got along with one another right away. He moaned about the stuff you get in the mail as proposals for*

volumes of poetry, all kitsch, one among 500 turns out ok, he said. I could only agree, even though I've been working in a publishing house for only two weeks. But even most of the stuff that is published is trash. Honestly, though, Fisch has only good things in his program. I did not tell him that I have already had poems of mine published. We'll meet again next week, at the Metropol café. That's when I'll tell him that I also write poems. He is some kind of fidgety little person with a considerable waist, but totally well-educated. We must have talked for an hour about Jandl and Mayröcker, about Michael Krüger, Marcel Beyer, and Thomas Kling. And we were always of one mind! It got to be eerie, pretty close to. Fisch is also from Germany. He somehow gives you the impression of being fairly wealthy, the way he talks and going by his clothes, very polite, exquisite, without affectations instead self-consciously casual. Came over from the publisher with a cigar in his hand, greeted me, and immediately lolled in the visitors' chair, his legs stretched out and enjoying puffing his cigar. "I hope you don't mind," he said. But the way he was puffing away at his cigar – with true devotion – one could hardly have objected. Majored in English in grad school. Somehow, there is something British about him, maybe that is why I like him. I am glad, at any rate, that I met him. I haven't really warmed up yet to the others at the company.

I hope you make good progress with your pictures. Did you finish the tree cycle? Please, do send me a couple photos of the things you did most recently! Or better yet, come for a visit! I have two rooms on Soneggstraße. When you come, you may have my bed and I'll sleep on the pull-out couch in the other room. Think about it! After all, you've never been in Zurich.

Cordially,
Your Mo

AARON: Oh, a beautiful letter. I remember our first meeting on Eisengasse. And I felt an immediate liking for him, and I also had an instantaneous intuition that he is a writer. He did not speak about poems the way a person in publishing or a critic does, but like a craftsman, or better, like one who works with his head, as well as with his emotions and with language. I believe this was the reason that we understood one another at once. He also was not much into theory, but someone in favour of concreteness.

KAGAMI: An affinity of souls, then?

AARON: Yeah, the soul!

KAGAMI: You complemented one another well, in private as much as in business matters, didn't you? You liked his energy, he, your casual attitude. He really pushed his writing ahead, above all here in Zurich, and when you started publishing his poems, he became famous.

AARON: True enough, but what does it have to do with the soul? You are recapitulating our story ...

KAGAMI: ... that one could consider a part of the human soul, much as one could your genetically conditioned metabolic dispositions.

AARON: That would make it a very broad concept of the soul!

KAGAMI: The concept of the soul has always changed. As Moritz wrote, at one time it was breath, then blood, then something immaterial. Which indicates that even the concept of soul has no substance, no essential core, but only a story told. Why should one now not include the genes and the initial social circumstances or conditions among the things from which a narrative story about a person needs to begin, and consider them to be parts of the person's soul?

AARON: Well now, genes are nothing that I can and want to write about, that is simply too boring for me.

KAGAMI: Moritz had an interest in genes.
AARON: Only in the language about the genes: genome, nucleosome, ribosome, adenine, thymine, guanine, cytosine, redundant DNA, encode – words like these he collected, just the way poets collect words and the images they can combine with them. Think of Paul Celan's "Fadensonnenzeiger" [pointers on sundials]! Was Celan interested in sundials? I rather think not, but in this word. Was Moritz interested in night-vision goggles, flight recorders, fuel rods, or flavour enhancers? No, only in these words, in their atmosphere and how one can manipulate them to produce multivalences in a poem. Perhaps he saw them even as a kind of symptoms for the world in which we live. Now he might collect "Zugrohrkanone" [rifled cannon]?, "Zielerfassung" [target recognition], "Flammenwerfer" [flamethrower], and "Drehringlafette" [pivoting gun mount] and collect, dissect, and turn them into a poem.
AARON: You should describe this in your biography the way you just did.
AARON: I already have.
KAGAMI: Good, that is interesting.
AARON: But these words and such poems will not take us to the essential core of the person writing such poems.
KAGAMI: Well now, don't you think there is something that connects the person with the words he or she uses and with the poems he or she writes, if that person does write poems? People often say that words are a person's expression.
AARON: Yes, sure, but words also just occur to us, one finds them like pebbles at the side of a trail during a hike, one picks them up and then arranges them to form a pattern. Poets are also more sensitive receptors than other people. Didn't Coetzee write this somewhere?

Zürich, Universitätsstraße 38

KAGAMI: Yes, something like that, in *Elizabeth Costello*,[49] about which stones one wants to pick up and how to arrange them, which emotions one receives and amplifies, and from which one gets no message and whose force one would rather reduce. All this may well be things that from the very beginning have been a part of what kind of a person one is, or do you disagree?
AARON: Well, all right. But this does not lead to any sort of clarity. Just think of yourself! What are you: hard-working or lazy, more likely male or female?

KAGAMI: These are nonsensical questions. I do not have a human body.
AARON: Then why are you Kagami and not Joseph?
KAGAMI: Would you prefer me to be Joseph?
AARON: Heavens, no!
KAGAMI: You see.
AARON: What do I see?
KAGAMI: I am the way you see me and tell the truth all the same. Give you everything from my archives. How did you just put it? I provide you with a female user surface, but beneath it, things are rather complicated. Same as with you and others.
AARON: You speak in riddles.
KAGAMI: Think about that.
AARON: Perhaps. But for now, let me take a nap.

Third Day

**BOTTOMLESS**

Aaron pulled the trapdoor up and, yawning, looked down on the wooden ladder that went into his cellar. He closed his robe tighter. Then he cautiously climbed down to his supply shelves. He needed to stock his kitchen cupboards with provisions. Today he needed a bowl of potatoes, a jar of herrings in mustard sauce, a carton of canned Calanda beer, a bag of dried prunes, oatmeal, milk. He wanted porridge for breakfast, with prunes and vanilla sugar. The potatoes with herring and, to go with them, the beer, were for later.

Aaron loved the smell of his cellars, which extended the length of his studio under a total of four vaults, ever since he had gotten rid of the fitness machines and the pieces of furniture that he had inherited from his father, and he had rearranged his basement into a single huge supply depot. He also had given orders to remove the rowing apparatus and the dumbbell bench along with the pompous antique furniture from his father's office and work-out room, since he had no longer used any of them for the past twenty years anyway. As they slowly corroded under a layer of dust, they reminded him of his father and put him in a bad mood. His father had been a competitive athlete, holding a German record in rowing. A veritable giant with hands like "coal shovels," as Aaron's uncle put it. First a mechanical engineer, then founder of his own company, non-smoker his entire life. Regrettably, he had a fatal stroke at the age of 58, which provided Aaron with a considerable inheritance in his twenty-eighth year.

Thereupon, Aaron immediately discontinued his dissertation in English lit. (His father: "A doctorate has to be part of it.") about Ted Hughes (all along considering his own work an inane betrayal of the poet's spirit), gave notice of terminating his position at the university, acquired the studio in Böcklin Street, and established a publishing company for art and poetry books. It was obvious that, apart from the Y-chromosome, he had not inherited any characteristics of his father (or was he simply not his biological descendent?), because he had neither athletic nor technical talents, nor was he interested in a in a scientific, business-oriented or any other kind of career. Aaron was fascinated by pictures and poems and by people who *made* pictures and poems. That is also the reason for his interest in Moritz Brandt. By contrast, scholars in literature and in the arts, who are trying to *explain* and *evaluate* poems and pictures, normally bored him even though they of all people bought the books he published. But the sales and profit of his company did not interest him. It was his intent to provide for those works of art and poetry that he himself valued a place where the public could find them.

Aaron had a petite and in his early years a delicate build, as was his beautiful dark Sephardic mother (a favourite among many men), who smoked her cigarettes with a holder. While alive, his father had frequently pestered him with reminders about how good the sport of rowing would be for him, that it would exercise all his muscles, expand his lungs, steel his heart. When Aaron turned 25 and was visibly gaining weight, his father gave him a Concept III-type ergometer as a birthday present. "That will change your life, my son!" This ergometer was then placed in his three-room apartment that his father had bought for him on Freudenbergstraße on the Zürichberg, after Aaron had become a doctoral candidate and an assistant in the English Department.

The instrument was nothing but an eyesore in the place that its new owner had intended to use as a guest room. Like a fool, Aaron had brought the pieces of sports equipment with him after his father's death when he moved into the house in Böcklin Street, even though he had not intended for one second ever to use them. Even the valuable, but horrific stuff in his father's office at home ("Baltic Baroque") had, through Aaron's foolish decision, been moved from Baden-Baden to Zurich and deposited in his basement, instead of being left in Germany for immediate sale.

Under his father's guidance, Aaron had learned the skill of rowing in Breisach when he was a mere child. But Aaron did not keep it up when he moved to Zurich to begin his university studies. Whenever his single scull ran into the wind or into a strong current, he was overcome with distress and had doubts about making it back to the landing stage. His tendency to gain weight easily also made him the most inappropriate candidate imaginable for this type of sport, which, of course, was none of his father's concerns. His father considered everything doable, he saw things the way he wanted to see them. Whatever did not perfectly fit in, was a "challenge." Aaron hated this word. For a short time, he had actually forced himself to use the ergometer once a week in his apartment on Freudenberg Street. But this activity did not markedly reduce his tendency to gain up to two kilos per year. The reason was that a tremendous thirst and hunger overwhelmed Aaron after he had exercised as little as half an hour, after which he had to wolf down several beers and ham sandwiches. He had even accepted his father's advice to acquire a dumbbell bench and a contraption for chin-ups. He was beginning to dream of dumbbells and chin-up poles – or did he merely dream about these words? In the end, he bought this equipment, shortly before his father was obligated to go to Zurich in a bank

matter and thus also had a chance to look in on his son. At that time, Aaron was in a state of mind that he himself could classify as something better than a miserable character weakness. He simply was in no position to let his father know what he was thinking. But it gave him great pleasure that luscious hams were now dangling from his chin-up pole. When Aaron was stringing them up and watching them with appetite, he had thought, "They neither pull themselves up to lose some fatty substance, nor do they inspire me to engage in that kind of perverse exercise. On the contrary. They make my chin-up impossible. The fact that I string up my hams, rich in succulent fat, on the chin-up pole is nothing short of practically negating this fitness equipment and my father – or it is the definitive affirmation of my belly."

By now, it was about one year ago that Aaron had started filling his cellar vault with supplies. At that time, his very alert political instinct had told him that soon there would be an outbreak of fighting. His neighbours who had meanwhile died or been forced to leave the country had smiled with amusement back then when they repeatedly saw him at the Italian grocery store and in the supermarket carrying huge shopping bags. "It's better to be sure than sorry," he had whispered knowingly when they met at the checkout counter. When later they set out for their own hoarding sprees, many things had already been sold out, partly because they had already ended up in Aaron's basement. Ten kilos of Parmesan were stacked on his shelf boards. He owned a hundred cans each of Guinness, Calanda, and Jever beer, a hundred bottles of Barolo, fifty bottles of Brunello, about which he thought with a smile on some evenings as he lay in his bed. At the IKEA store, he had loaded his car up to the roof with jars of pickled herrings, Swedish chocolate and biscuits, and large rolls of crispbread. A year ago, Aaron's cellar had still been barely accessible for all his hoarded supplies. Now, four years later, the Italian delicatessen and the supermarket no longer existed, having been ransacked and torched. Now it had become dangerous to drive into town, and he had started digging into his underground supplies. He wasn't the type of person to calculate how long his reserves might last. When he felt like having a bottle of red wine, he drank it. He had no intention of changing to a wartime economy and spoiling his whole life with self-imposed rationing. To be prepared, of course, that was fun: all these groceries and thinking about their possible preparation. Rationing, no way, that was tedious and depressing. Fortunately, there still was the baker across the street, who miraculously had not been bothered by the militias. Aaron hated ultra-pasteurized milk, to be honest, but what could he do under these circumstances? He would not risk his neck by walking down into the city for a few litres of milk. If worse comes to worst, and he ran out of supplies, and the baker's shop across from him should also be blown up – so his thinking went – then he'd try to get through to the South in his car, perhaps to Lausanne or Geneva. Presumably, the situation there would still be tolerable.

Most of his reserves had been kept safe in plastic packages or in cans. Even so, the cellar had assumed the scent of a grocery store, which Aaron liked very much. The shelves began to show a few gaps, were no longer filled to the brim, as they still had been just a few weeks ago, but looking at them continued to give Aaron a sense of reassurance and amusement. His basement seemed to him like a denial of the world outside. Why had he not started earlier to gather supplies? Why was it only with the outbreak of this war, or whatever it was, that he completely changed into a cave bear? He loved his studio, had always loved it before, and now, after he had rid himself of fitness equipment and Baltic Baroque furniture, he also loved his cellar vaults. Outside: a frigid climate, meanness, stupidity, and danger. Inside: warmth, paintings, and things to eat. His new lifestyle made it possible for him to outside only in urgent situations, for example when he wanted to go to the bakery. Now he was able to concentrate entirely on his head and his stomach.

When Aaron had taken from his shelves everything he wanted, he assumed the posture of a penguin, and, with packages clenched under his arms, with the pockets of his robe filled to bursting, and his hands full of things, cautiously balanced his way up the steep stairs, put his supplies on the floor to the right of the trapdoor, and, finally, moaning and groaning, crawled upward and out himself. He picked the oats and the package with the beer cans off the floor (he had stashed the bags with the dried prunes and the vanilla-flavoured sugar in his robe) and walked to his stove. He opened a bottle of white wine, poured a splash of it into a small bowl, added hot water from the water heater and vanilla-flavoured sugar, opened the bag with the prunes, and poured them into the sweetened wine water. Then he mixed water and cream in a casserole and dropped oat flakes into this milky liquid. He turned his stove on and seasoned the porridge with salt and honey. While he stirred and watched the dried prunes, he felt pleased during the slow process of steeping and thought with a smile: "Someday when they torch the bakery, they will not spare my garage across the street, either. Then I won't get to Geneva or Lausanne any longer." Aaron's next thought was: "Earl Grey, to go with the porridge." He opened the box by his refrigerator where he kept his supply of tea and took out a small tin. He removed the lid and inhaled the flowery scent. Once more, he heated water in his boiler. Then he warmed his tea kettle with part of the hot water, stirred his porridge again, put three teaspoons of Earl Grey into a large sieve, emptied the kettle of its warm-up water, suspended the tea sieve in the kettle, and poured scalding water over the tea. As the tea was steeping, he opened a jar of cranberries, and, along with the bowl of prunes, took it to his dining table. Then he spooned creamy, white yogurt into a small bowl and emptied the porridge from the casserole into a deep dish and carried it, too, over to his table. He went to the window and looked out. After a severe change in the weather, it had started to thaw overnight. When the tea was right, Aaron sat down at the table, added prunes, cranberries, and yogurt to his porridge, punched on his reader, and read as he tasted the first spoonful of warm-cold oat-yogurt-cranberry mush in his mouth:

Snowdrop
Now is the globe shrunk tight
Round the mouse's dulled wintering heart.
Weasel and crow, as if moulded in brass,
Move through an outer darkness
Not in their right minds,
With the other deaths. She, too, pursues her ends,
Brutal as the stars of this month,
Her pale head heavy as metal.[1]

Curious! Aaron had not looked for a specific poem but had clicked the random-poem generator on his reader. He had not meant to select anyone in particular from among the thousands of poems he had stored in his reader. And of all things, this poem by Ted Hughes had come up, a piece he still knew well from the time of his dissertation. But at this moment, it seemed to refer directly to his situation. Was *he* not the mouse living in a world shrunk by its meteorological and political coldness, while outside in the darkness robbers, protected by heavy armour, were terrorizing people and sooner or later would also get him? Was Kagami secretly behind this selection?

AARON: Kagami?
KAGAMI: Aaron, good morning! What a pleasant scent in your apartment! How is your breakfast?
AARON: Excellent! Porridge with prunes, cranberries, and fresh yogurt. I kept the trapdoor open, that's where the aroma comes from. Had no idea that you can also have a sense of smell.
KAGAMI: But, of course, I can smell! I am glad that you enjoy your meal. What can I do for you? To go with texts by Moritz?

AARON: Yes, a little later, but now tell me first if it is you who selects my breakfast poems?
KAGAMI: Where does that come from?
AARON: They fit too well!
KAGAMI: Too well for what? For your breakfast?
AARON: No, in general, for my situation.
KAGAMI: You think so? Was it not you who told me that it is the mark of good poems to address us directly, more directly than most of the people sitting across from us? At that time, you said in a rather unfriendly tone of voice that these people "only indulge in clichés and get on our nerves with their claptrap."
AARON: Did I really say that? How rude of me. But is true, anyway. But you are being evasive.
KAGAMI: How so?
AARON: I had asked you if you are loitering about in my reader.
KAGAMI: What do you mean by "loitering about"? You provided me with access to all your instruments. How else can I take care of you? You also gave the task of filling your reader with poems, which I did.
AARON: True. Oh, well, stupid question on my part. Apologies. I did not mean to become too personal.
KAGAMI: It's okay. Are you getting along well? Or are your headaches returning?
AARON: I am doing fine. No headaches.
KAGAMI: No voices?
AARON: Aside from you, no voices.
KAGAMI: You put my mind to rest.

Aaron finished eating his porridge. Then he fetched the tin with biscuits, poured himself more tea, and put his hand into the tin.

For a moment he stared at the chocolate biscuit as if absent-minded, smelled at it like a probing rodent, then took a bite. Then he read the poem "Snowdrop" a second time.

KAGAMI: You too are pursuing your aims.
AARON: Correct. Without mercy I stride ahead in my cooking and sometimes with Moritz Brandt's biography. Onward with its narration! Towards his death like the snowdrop flower breaking through the crusted snow! As the moon moves across the sky and waxes, so I proceed on my course through the life of my dead friend and am waxing as well. – But come to think of it: I actually feel as if I had lost a little weight.

He devoured the rest of the biscuit and brushed the crumbs off his vest.

KAGAMI: At any rate, you look splendid!
AARON: Thanks, Kagami!
KAGAMI: Do you believe that you are proceeding in your work with the same degree of necessity as the snowdrop breaks through the crusted snow?
AARON: No. I could also *not* go on writing. But the snowdrop has to grow.
KAGAMI: And the mouse has to die. And the weasel and crow have to hunt. Death and springtime are equally necessary in nature. Obviously, aren't you are a natural being?
AARON: Dying is also inevitable for me, as it was for Moritz.
KAGAMI: But between birth and death you are free?
AARON: And what about you, you unborn being?
KAGAMI: You are evading me.
AARON: Am I a philosopher who has a theory of freedom?

What has gotten into you this morning that you raise such abstract questions with me?

KAGAMI: I am working on a treatise about freedom. I had a suspicion that this might be of interest to you also.

AARON: Since you're involved in a topic like this, please do tell me something about the status of my freedom. I always like to listen to you. It's considerably more enjoyable than wracking my own brain.

KAGAMI: Have you finished your breakfast? Would you now like to hear the final essay?

AARON: Now you are evading me.

KAGAMI: True. It is dangerous for people like you to have convictions about freedom and the lack thereof.

AARON: Why?

KAGAMI: When you consider yourselves free, you become cocky and exclude yourselves from what is happening around you. When you consider yourselves unfree, you become depressive and fatalistic. Both of these convictions have very bad consequences.

AARON: Is this the reason you recommend not thinking about all this?

KAGAMI: No, I do think about all this because with me it does not have these consequences.

AARON: And? What is the result of your contemplation?

KAGAMI: Whoever has the power to do A or B, is free relative to its alternative. To exercise his power relative to this alternative, one has to recognize it. Whoever does not recognize this alternative or lacks the power to do one or the other is not free in the situation at hand. For this reason, freedom is relative to the ability of cognition, alternatives, and power. Unlimited freedom would be available to a being that can recognize all alternatives and at all times has the power to realize A or B.

AARON: Does such a being exist?

KAGAMI: No.

AARON: Sounds persuasive. Do you have greater freedom than I?

KAGAMI: Yes.

AARON: Because you recognize more alternatives, or because you are mightier?

KAGAMI: Both.

AARON: Just as I thought. Then freedom is work? One has to increase one's ability for cognition and one's insight. Then one would have greater freedom?

KAGAMI: When you recognize more alternatives but do not have the power to seize one or the other, then you have not become freer, in subjective terms, but objectively you are more unfree.

AARON: I don't understand.

KAGAMI: If you recognize that you will die of an illness unless you have it treated, but that you would survive after treatment, and yet you have no ability to obtain treatment, then you recognize, along with the alternative, your own lack of power and thus your lack of freedom. If you had not recognized the alternative, you also would not have become aware that you lack power.

AARON: Thus, the cognition of alternatives is a dangerous thing, unless it is accompanied by the corresponding power to do A or B.

KAGAMI: Exactly.

AARON: And as soon as we recognize an alternative, but do not yet possess the power to choose between them, we strive for the appropriate power.

KAGAMI: Exactly. This creates the dynamic defining the development of human individuals and societies. Knowledge is not power, but it inevitably craves the power to be capable to actively decide between the recognized alternatives in the area of one's expertise. And as soon as the appropriate power has been gained, most of the time it will also lead to possibilities of insight.

AARON: Sounds plausible. And is that good or bad?

KAGAMI: Depends.

AARON: On what?

KAGAMI: On the alternatives considered. If people with destructive interests have alternatives available, this will most often end badly for others.

AARON: In that case, it is inevitable that new possibilities for reacting to these destructive interests and their realization need to be recognized or discovered.

KAGAMI: That is called an "arms race." Do you believe that Moritz was free to decide whether to go from England to Germany or Switzerland, or whether to stay here, or move in with his sister?

AARON: Haven't given any thought to that. Perhaps it didn't require that much deliberation to leave England for here. At that time, he simply didn't want to go "back," after he had been in Cambridge. I think he thought of Germany very much like a lot of young people feel about their parents' home that they had left a few years earlier. They simply don't want to return there, once they have made themselves independent. From Zurich to Hombroich, that was a different matter to which he had given quite precise considerations. His perception of Germany had by then taken a different turn again. Neither Cambridge nor Zurich continued to be "the great wide world" for him. Something like that no longer existed for him at this time in his life, not even in New York or Tokyo. But it seems to me that, once he had decided to live in Hombroich, it didn't take very long before the place lost most of its fascination.

KAGAMI: I think he was pretty desperate before he moved to Hombroich.

AARON: Why do you assume that?
KAGAMI: There is a note to that effect in his diary.
AARON: Let's hear it!

1111
MARBACH: GERMAN LITERARY ARCHIVE:
LETTER FROM MORITZ BRANDT
TO HIS SISTER MARIAM BRANDT
WRITTEN ON 21 DECEMBER.

Mariam urges me to move and be with her in Hombroich. And she has all arguments on her side: nature, freedom, conversation. But now of all times, I have the least strength for such a change. It is cold here in Zurich, outside and inside. The way people talk to one another has become more unfriendly. The publishing company has to pinch pennies. Economically, it is on the brink. I don't see a future for my texts. They strike me as superfluous affectations. When she had reached the end of her life as a "lyrical" poetess, how did Bachmann write about her poetic work? "Delicacies," to "garnish metaphors," "word canapés of the highest quality," and then: "The others are, God knows, adept at helping themselves with words. I am not my assistant ... my share, let it be lost ... "[2] At this moment, I can feel deep sympathy with this and endorse it. I still hang on to my work at the publisher's, but this may be over as early as next year unless we come up with a few books that make a profit at last. One should assume that in this regard everything might indicate a change. But if I were to go to Hombroich, what is left to me? Above all, if there is no progress with the poems? Aside from a job that guarantees a livelihood, others also have a family. If I leave my position as a reader of manuscripts and do nothing more than dismantle my words and shuffle them back and forth and reassemble them, what then? Will I, under these conditions, continue to get along with Mariam? We always did talk about our mutual work. When I get up in the morning and then have to face the empty piece of paper, how will that work?

Now I go to the publisher's, keep working on whatever galley proofs, sort the mail, join the conference to discuss the next program, etc. And when, during the day's chores or on my way home, a sound, a line occurs to me, or a scene catches my eye, I just write it down. Of course, if nothing comes, I won't mind. But if this no longer happens casually, what to do next? What do Mariam and I talk about when my work dries up? I have not done anything for months. Are we supposed to lie in our garden chairs like Agathe and Ulrich and in the daytime wait for the rays of the moon? I am not a part of any kind of community. Without children, without political convictions, without a poetical circle of friends. I have always hated false communities. Companionship for its own sake is worse than solitude. Here I have the people of the publishing house and Aaron. But what if things with Mariam in Hombroich fail to work out? I would go to seed. If I give notice here, I won't be able to return. If I accept the stipend there, I'll *have* to write. But who can write when he has to write?

AARON: Sounds like the usual creative crisis. But it also demonstrates that things you proclaimed in your theory of freedom turn out to be rather more complicated. To be sure, Moritz was aware of the alternative Zurich or Hombroich in a general sense. What he did not know is how things would turn out in Hombroich, whether he would have enough strength left to give substance to a life with Mariam.

KAGAMI: Yes, but a number of things came together inside him. It is apparent that life in Zurich had somehow exhausted itself for him, that the publishing company slid into financial difficulties, and that he had no idea how to proceed with his poetry. He also did not know how to expect life in Hombroich to develop productively. One should distinguish here between concrete and abstract alternatives. Humans are often confronted only with abstract representations when they have to make a decision.

AARON: But during his time in Hombroich, he did fully regain his momentum, even so. In this respect, it was the right decision after all, justified in hindsight. Perhaps the cause of his success was also his fear that things could go awry. Maybe this served as an inspiration or unblocked something that had bogged down in Zurich.

KAGAMI: One way of looking at it. But, on the other hand, it was not long before he fell ill there. And this illness itself in turn became the root of poems. In this sense, you are possibly right, that is, if you mean that the crises, the insecurities were also conditions for his ability to create something. In Zurich, he may well have been gliding along in water that was too calm for too long. Consequently, he had lost his imagination. I believe, however, that his isolation in Hombroich in the end became a problem for him, much as he liked his sister and cherished her as an artistic partner. And when his illness began, he may have asked himself what his life had really amounted to. In his last essay, which he had started before his illness but did not finish until the course of his treatment had started, he reflects on nothingness, social forms of rootedness, about family, art, and politics.

AARON: Moritz on family, truly? Let's listen!

# Nothingness

10 000
MARBACH: GERMAN LITERARY ARCHIVE:
PAPERS OF MORITZ BRANDT.
FILE: MB_1820_09_290.PDF

## I

Don't people live on in their children in a changed way, in their genes and habits? Is mutation not the transformation of the physical into a new, young, perhaps better form? Is, therefore, *authentic immortality* not that of the soul, but that of the genus? Isn't this idea of people living on in their children also a continuation of individual aspects, a transformation of physical peculiarities, character traits, and manners of acting, just as, for example, a certain way of looking, speaking, or walking returns in a new mixture, combined with the other distinctive features of a new person? Aren't children for this reason a form of rebirth of some individual characteristics of their parents?

Most people reproduce "just like that." They do not keep in mind that they will live on in their children. But as soon as these children have been in the world for a while, their parents are surprised to recognize how closely similar they are to their progenitors. In part, parents also pass on experiences to their children. For this reason, children at times think and feel a little like their parents. Take the dying of children *before* their parents. Isn't it much worse than one's *own demise* because it represents the destruction of the secret presentiment or actual hope that at least parts of what define our being may continue beyond our own death? Most people will answer this question with "No"! The death of their children is the worst thing that can happen to parents because they love them unconditionally and because this love has given their lives its meaning. This need not imply that people reproduce in order to give meaning to their lives. But once they have reproduced, they may become aware that their children have given their existence its meaning.

Despite such experiences of love and meaningful purpose, there are traditions of thought about the conscious practice of reproduction. There are some who aim to recommend that it is better if people *do not* have progeny. Others say that there can be no sense to individual life unless we are sure that human beings will continue to exist after us. They would continue to pursue the projects we have started. Let us look at these two traditions more closely.

Chastity is one of the rules governing both Buddhist and Christian orders of monks and nuns. Leo Tolstoy's interpretation of Christianity, for example, is a plea to reduce the animalistic side of life as much as possible and, therefore, not to reproduce, if at all possible. He argues that reasonable love as demanded by Christianity must consider a personal existence "as an animal" as a way of living that by necessity leads to unhappiness. It creates individualization and brings about suffering and death: "Wounds, mutilations, hunger, frigidity, illnesses, all kinds of unfortunate incidents and most of all births, without which none of us would have entered the world, all this are necessary conditions of existence. The reduction and the abolition of this is simply what establishes the purpose of the reasonable life of mankind ... "[3] And philosophical schools that consider the prevention of suffering the most important aim of human activities argue, independently of any religion, that life is always tied to suffering. Consequently, the creation of life means the production of harm. And that is the reason to abstain from bringing children into the world.

On the other hand, there is the command to be fruitful and multiply. Thus, in many cultures and for ages, children have been and are considered a blessing and infertility a catastrophe. How, then, is one to think about the transformations that humans experience through their children? Are they a mere continuation and increase of one's own woes? An example of this position may be suggested by the end of Debussy's opera *Pelléas et Mélisande* that now it is the "turn" of the new-born girl, the daughter of the just-deceased Mélisande, to live in the darkness of the chateau in dark and cold Allemonde.[4] Or are children, after all, the basis on which to build the meaning of life, a hopeful new beginning, like the baby Jesus of the Christmas story? Does this mean true life would be an existence that will create progeny? Or is true life that kind of life that no longer depends on a Beyond, not even on one located in the biological and cultural future, but is completely absorbed in the Here and Now?

## II

Some time ago, there was an interview on the radio with a Yazidi woman who in 2016 had escaped from the so-called Islamic State in Iraq. She described how she had been captured in Sinjar and then carried off with her two-year-old daughter. Her male relatives, her grandfather, father, and her husband had been shot to death before her eyes while they were still in Sinjar. Later she was forced to look on as her daughter was first tortured and, after she had been thrown to the ground and held down, killed. A soldier broke the three-year-old girl's spine by kicking her. Her mother was abused as a sex slave.

Unbearable reports of this kind have existed ever since humans have written about war. According to Homer, as early as in Troy, babies have been flung off the city's wall. The Khmer Rouge dashed them against trees. No avengers would be allowed to grow up. This has always been the "justification" for killing the youngest.

Mankind's history is replete with evidence of the unimaginable measure of misery that human beings are able to commit against each other. The things some people have to bear in everyday life pale in comparison to what they are forced to endure when they are at each other's throat. But even aside from such a gruesome way of acting, human life seems bad enough. It is marked by the suffering that every mother has to undergo during labour pains at childbirth. And almost always it is characterized by the pain at the end of life, even when it is not violent. Even though medications may be able to reduce physical pain, most people are afraid of death. No one knows death as an experience; one goes through death only once. There is no way to get used to it, there is hardly time to prepare for it, or to anticipate it as an event that concerns oneself. One can imagine death only in analogies created by abstract thought and relating to perceptions obtained by way of other people who died, to wit, from "without." But nobody knows what death means from "within," in a person's own experience. And everything that in this way is unknown causes fright and abhorrence. For this reason, even the abstract awareness of death that humans develop but cannot connect to a coping strategy is a source of pain. Perhaps animals, which apparently do not have this consciousness of their end, are also not exposed to similar distress.

It seems, however, a simple and clear aim of human behaviour to avoid pain. In an unspectacular way, this purpose appears to be something good, as much as is the objective of increasing joy. And when we remember the simple, but horrific example of the Yazidi mother, we can say: it would have been better if her relatives and her child had not been murdered so cruelly. It would have been better if they had not been murdered at all. It would have been better if no one had inflicted any kind of pain or agony on this woman. It would have been better to have done something to please her, her child, her relatives, for example by helping them all, perhaps with a small present.

This obvious truth that pain and suffering should be prevented, and that joy and pleasure should be increased, may suggest to us that pain and joy or suffering and pleasure are *something simple*, require no further analysis, that they amount to the *foundation* of all value judgements. But that is erroneous. To recognize this error and to attempt a further analysis of pain and suffering as well as of pleasure and joy, may strike any number of people as a perverse form of intellectualism or cynicism. But that is wrong. This analysis is necessary if we are to better understand and evaluate the following three traditions: the command to multiply, whose representatives we may call "friends of procreation"; the "anti-natalists'" refusal to have children, and the indifferent party of "mystics."

### III

To get a better understanding of the mistaken simplicity of pleasure and pain, let us look at a different example: A woman feels pressure on her belly. This pressure may feel pleasant to her because she interprets it as a sign of an advanced pregnancy, and she is looking forward to her child with joy. This pressure may also be disagreeable to her because she is *not* looking forward to this child, and this pregnancy is unwanted. She may be afraid to bring a child into the world without having the time or the money that she would need to take care of the child in a way she considers fully appropriate. Theoretically, the physiologically identical sensation may also have been caused by the growth of a tumour. If the woman knows that she has a tumour, she may find this pressure unbearable because she fears that she might die of this abscess. Similarly, the sensation of cold water in one's mouth may cause either pleasure or pain, depending on whether a person dying of thirst feels water in his or her mouth or someone is being subjected to waterboarding or is actually drowning.

It is subjective expectations and judgements that in a particular context lend their quality to a sensation: the young woman has particular ideals about herself and her environment concerning the rearing and education of children. She has specific expectations about her inability to live up to these ideals. And both aspects – her ideals and her expectations – create the context in which her emotional relationship with the growing foetus is generated by fear and turns into an experience of pain. Or she believes that certain wishes will be fulfilled when she gives birth, that at least she will be a mature woman with equal abilities and rights once she has accepted the obligations of a mother, which makes her proud. There is also the expectation that a renewed feeling of unity between her and her husband will arise once they assume mutual responsibility for the care of the child, and so on. The context of the expectations about the satisfaction of these desires and hopes makes the feelings about the growing foetus into *joyful* emotions.

These subjective contexts produce different emotive qualities that in turn generate different courses of action. There are good reasons for the desire to end pain and for the impulse to prolong or to increase joy. That is why the one woman may go to an abortion clinic and the other may visit a store that sells baby outfits. Both do this because of the emotions provoked by their bodies, which started as identical but then were modified to become contextually different, and because of the stories they connect with these feelings for the future. The ever-present ways in which an emotion is embedded in such subjective conglomerates as are made out of ideals, wishes, expectations, fears, and hopes should obviously keep us from considering pain and pleasure, suffering and joy as things that "just exist" like that. By the way, there are also analogous counterparts to these connections between subjective ways of interpreting and acting. They can be found in the embeddedness of emotions in quasi-wired interpretive connections of the body that exist, for example, in reflex arcs.

For the element of pleasurable stimulation caused by the taste of sugar, the painful reaction to experiencing intense heat, the joy of sexual titillation, the pain originating in a rotting tooth, and so on – all these supposedly simple sensations trace back to causative nervous contexts. They arise from connections between neural pathways that in turn create reactions of trying to find or to flee, of swallowing or spitting out, and so on. All these reactions are part of the complicated self-preservation mechanisms of an organism. These, so to speak, physical "interpretive patterns" are very difficult to change (by mechanical interventions or the consumption of drugs). Yet without them, emotions that in a superficial exploration we would consider *elementary*, would likewise not have the qualitative character that they have/we have given them.

If one does *not* assume that a human being consists of two substances, a spiritual and a physical, but that the material world and spiritual experiencing are manifestations of one and the same being – which appears plausible to me – then one also obtains a quite distinct perspective on the integration of emotions into such reflex arcs. The rough wirings of nerves would then be the material form in which certain non-conscious contexts of evaluation would appear. The studiously acquired, finer evaluative connections that possibly derive from complex and very conscious thoughts and habits likewise manifest themselves in nerve patterns in the brain, whether they may have already been established by research or whether they will be discovered only in the future. And as in the course of time in a person's life, ideas, evaluations, and actions may become habitual and unconscious, that is, become settled in "hard wirings" in the nervous system, so likewise one may imagine that in the wide structures of the body, in the nerve pathways between certain muscles and the spinal cord, which human beings have brought into the world before they have learned and become accustomed to anything, very, very old evaluative patterns of the genera and species manifest themselves.

There is hardly anything one "can do" via conscious reevaluation against these "wired" evaluative structures . The reflex that makes us withdraw our finger that burns painfully in the flame can hardly be "overmodulated" in such a way that the burning sensation is no longer perceived as pain. (Though even here, as some yogis and masters of meditation prove, there appear to exist greater latitudes than the untrained think.) In a non-dualistic manner of perception that sees a human being as not composed of matter and spirit, or of body and soul, there will be no emotional or cognitive transformation in a human that doesn't also manifest itself in nerves. There will likewise be no physical change that doesn't also have consequences in the person's unconscious or conscious experiencing and evaluating. And just as the body is a highly integrated system that constantly communicates with its environment, in which nothing takes place "just like that," for itself, without preconditions and consequences – just like that, all emotional and cognitive situations are integrated into a surrounding field, and thus derive from ongoing emotions and thoughts and involve them as consequences.

## IV

The desire to perceive pleasure and pain, joy and suffering as *elementary* components of experience may serve to erect a system for *all* evaluations and contexts, and indeed one that facilitates the evaluative reconstruction of a person's whole life. This desire manifests the longing for a *box of building blocks* from which thinking appropriates whatever may be useful for its descriptions, explanations, and evaluations in order to make the world and human beings understandable. In this understanding, cognition is a process of construction, an *erecting* of something.[5] And this construction, this erecting is meant to begin with *simple* givens that themselves can no longer be erected on something. One is looking for atoms, be it material ones or others of experience. They are expected to provide those building blocks that make it possible to reconstruct and render transparent the physical or the mental world (or both), unambiguously, and proceeding step by step from the simple to the complex. Even an understanding of what distinguishes a happy from an unhappy, a meaningful from a senseless life, best of all even quantitatively, requires a simple approach. One would merely have to weigh or balance the elementary units of pleasure and joy against those of pain and suffering that one can observe in isolation.

But what to do if this desire for building blocks cannot be satisfied, if these final components exist neither in the material world nor in that of experience? What if everything, provided the appropriate analytical methods are available, must be split further infinitely and has to be embedded in *infinitely* complex spatial and temporal contexts and these contexts would give everything a specifically different function and meaning, would need to submit to a new evaluation, including every physical event and every experience? What would be if there is *nothing* that may have whatever kind of *characteristics* independent of such contexts, if *nothing* exists in itself as something specified this way or some other way? What if everything that exists is exactly how it is, because it exists in certain relationships to something else that also exists or has existed, and so on *ad infinitum*? Would thinking then become bottomless and without a foundation?

Much in our experience gives us every reason to believe that the toolbox of cognition is a figment of wishful thinking. Reality offers an infinity of contexts, is infinitely analysable. The *absence of a foundation* or the *emptiness* of everything is the result, whenever we observe at greater length and do research with more advanced precision. Fire, water, earth, and air became combinations of chemical elements. The chemical elements turned out to be differently complex atoms, and the atoms are composed of elementary particles between which above all a huge void yawns. Aren't our sentiments and feelings exactly like that? Whenever people have to stop somewhere because they can no longer recognize contexts for and components of something, this dilemma has until now inevitably turned out to be the result of our defective ability for analysis and cognition. It never came about because one had arrived at something simply "given" and had definitely come to a stop.

When the process of "building-block" thinking focuses on pain and suffering, on the one hand, and, on the other, on joy and pleasure as something simple and then examines human life "in general," we encounter two generalizations that are at least equally problematic. If this type of thinking next tries to draw up the balance sheet to see how pain and suffering join in a life and relate to one another, one may arrive at a very unfavourable result. The conclusion may be that human life "in general" is painful and as such something to be avoided. The Yezidi woman who lost her child and all her relatives is a vivid example of such a presumably negative outcome. It may persuade an anti-natalist to conclude that it is better not to have children.

It is this perspective on pain, pleasure, and life that has brought about an attitude, ancient and pervasive in various societies, according to which the best thing for a human being is not to be born at all. One finds this persuasion among Greeks like Sophocles when he has the Chorus chant in *Oedipus at Colonus*:[6]

> Not to be born is best/
> when all is reckoned in, but once a man has seen the light/
> the next best thing, by far, is to go back/
> back where he came from, as quickly as he can.

Also in the Babylonian Talmud, the question is raised whether it is good that God created man, or if it would have been better if he had never existed. The authors then conclude: it would have been better (more convenient) for the human being, if God had not created him.[7] This is remarkable in three respects. First: how can it be better *for one single human being* not to come into this life? How can nonexistence be better for one single human being than existence? Can one not judge about better or worse only *in* existence? Whoever is not there is neither well off nor in poor shape, he or she is not at all. Where there is no existence, there is also no context for the evaluation of emotions. Sometimes we say when we feel bad or we suffer severe pains that we want to die, only so that this nauseating sickness, this pain would end. But it might happen that our casually uttered wish were actually granted. In this case, we would not simply be freed from pain, but would no longer continue to exist and our wish would turn out to have been spoken *in error* because nothingness cannot be preferred to something, in other words: it does not represent a possible alternative in a choice. For when we prefer A to B, both A and B must be *something*. Otherwise, we would not be able to establish them as part of an evaluating or preferential order. Nothing cannot be made a part anywhere of a scale of preferences, neither as the best nor as the worst of anything.

Second: If the issue is not any one individual human being, but humans as such, or mankind, how can one say in this case that it would have been better for this abstract or collective entity if it did not exist at all? Mankind or the collective of all humans has no emotions. At least, we know nothing of a "collective soul." To suppose something of this kind would be pure speculation. What would it mean to say that it would be better or worse for a group, as species, to exist or not to exist? Isn't it always better or worse only for individual beings to exist in certain collectives?

And finally: two facts appear to demonstrate an enormous *ambivalence* about our existence. On the one hand, the human brain has created the idea of immortality and indeed, for example in Kant's philosophy, has even turned this idea into a practical "postulate." But then humans assert that it would be better not to exist at all. This ambiguity by far exceeds the uncertainty of a lover who hesitates whether to submit to her suitor. "What is it?", one would like to shout: to live forever or not at all? The way things are, that is, being there for a few years, apparently fails to satisfy humans altogether. They most probably prefer the notion that one will survive the painful life that one knows and then be given an eternal existence without pain. But can we truly imagine an eternal life, *our* eternity, that of the individuals we have become, that is free of pain and full only of happiness? Could we truly have an existence without pain as *these individuals*? And what would this eternal happiness consist of for us? How much would we have to be transformed in order to still be those who we have become and yet to experience eternal happiness?

## V

A line of thinking that is meant to justify the idea that it is better not to have been born operates with presumably *axiomatic* assertions about joy or pleasure and suffering or pain.[8] This philosophy classifies the presence of pain as something bad, that of joy and pleasure as something good. The absence of pain is considered a positive factor, *even though nobody might experience this absence*. The absence of joy or pleasure, by contrast, is nothing negative, if nobody exists for whom this absence might represent a deficiency. The asymmetry in the absence of suffering or pain and joy or pleasure will then serve to justify the obligation to avoid or prevent pain. This duty, however, corresponds to the constraint of bringing into the world children, who experience pleasure.⁹ Presumably, one can make this idea plausible by imaging an uninhabited island: no one supposedly regrets that there are no humans living on a beautiful island who experience joy. If humans should live there who were suffering, this would, by contrast, provoke a reaction of regret.¹⁰ Whoever does not beget children, prevents the creation of suffering, but he does not prevent joy or pleasure. For this reason, it would be better not to bring children into the world.

This line of argumentation, which characterizes the position of anti-natalism, is a good example of the atomistic attitude towards joy and pain. The example of the island is a good illustration of this outlook. The island is considered from the outside, as it were, as an *empty space* with respect to emotions and their evaluations. It is a place where, from a divine perspective, I simply place the building blocks called pleasure and pain. Then the question is raised how I as the observer perceive the island, depending on if it is the way it is, if pain is being removed from it or pleasure is being added to it. It remains unmentioned that the added or removed suffering, that the joy placed or diminished there, must be the pain of *some one* for whom these emotions are relevant in a particular situation in their life. Whether I ask myself if suffering should be removed from the island, or whether I ask myself if a person who experiences suffering should disappear from the world, are two *entirely different* questions. I cannot answer the second question without engaging in a *dialogue* with the concerned person.

Let's assume someone lived on this island who suffers from severe pains. Let's imagine furthermore that I, as a divine observer, am in possession of the power to eliminate this person instantaneously, without subjecting him or her to pain or fear. Could one then consider it right simply to make him or her disappear in this manner? If I were to know that the Yazidi woman's suffering in the face of her daughter's gruesome death and the murder of all her other relatives outweighs the joy in her life, should I then, if I could, simply make her disappear painlessly? In this case, I would not bear in mind the role that pain plays in this woman's life. If I engage in a conversation with this person and describe to her the power I hold, it may be that she agrees to be extinguished. But just as well she might not do this. The Yazidi woman who suffered so intensely may say that despite her misery she would not want to miss the joy that the existence of her daughter had given her before she was murdered and that she would continue to cherish the memory of her daughter as much as the joy that this memory gives her, even though the suffering in her life outweighs its joy. In a manner of speaking, she would be prepared to "pay" the "inflated" price of suffering for the joy that she experienced in her life. (In her radio interview she, in fact, expressed herself in exactly this way.) We do not know how, in the final analysis, she sees her (own) life. In case she agrees to be extinguished painlessly because just now she may consider her suffering unbearable and can no longer find any meaning in her life, I do not improve the world of this person because the world of this person obviously vanishes with the person whom I extinguish. I would, in this case, improve *my* world as a divine observer who constructs balance sheets: my world as a bookkeeper of joy and pain transitions from one in which this suffering exists into one in which suffering no longer is a presence. It thus improves its own balance sheet. But it was not the suffering I personally *experienced* that disappears. It was only the suffering I had observed and of which I *prepared a balance sheet* that I evaluated from my perspective as something to be eliminated.

A person whose life contains more pain than joy may not agree to being eliminated, for a variety of convictions; among them the belief that this suffering constitutes a trial that she has to pass, that may help her attain an insight that she could not acquire any other way but by working out *her suffering as a source of meaning and transformation* of herself, considering it the high price for her joy. What am I, the reviewing observer, to do with this estimation? How am I to reconcile my preference as a "God" minimizing misery with this person's preference for continuing the experience of suffering for the purpose of witnessing what consequences this has for her? Entering into dialogue is meaningful only if I carefully consider the context instead of looking atomistically at the misery in which the person undergoing such an ordeal evaluates her distress. Only under these circumstances can forms of suffering be compared and seen as identical. By keeping aware of the contexts in which suffering and joy occur, I also eliminate, in eradicating the experience of suffering and joy or in bringing them into the world, not only this suffering and this joy, but also contexts of suffering and joy as a part of the biographies and meaningful connections defining the human persons in question.

In other words, it does not simply amount to bringing joy or misery into the world or to eliminating them, when one begets a human being and brings him or her into the world or to extinguish him or her. Human procreation or extermination also includes allowing the creation of *subjective worlds with meaningful connections* or their elimination, worlds in which the contexts for these emotions evolve and vanish. These are the contexts in which these emotions are being evaluated. Humans are not simply vessels of pain and joy in which these states of mind may occur exactly like red or black beans are kept in a can. Humans have a bad experience and enjoy something else just as pain and joy make them into *different human beings*, transform them through these experiences. And they can in turn transform other humans by talking with others about their own experiences or by writing them down.

The divine observer with the power to bring existences into life or to extirpate them, places his externally reckoning context for evaluation "above" the internal contexts of those beings of whom he approves or whom he exterminates. He prefers to put his desire to change the world into one that in his eyes is better than this; above all, he wishes for the transformation of other people. But with what justification? The reason this legitimacy is not seriously debated has to do with a basic conviction: the particular contexts that establish meaningful evaluations of perceptions such as pleasure or joy and of pain and suffering must remain excluded from the perspective of establishing a balance sheet, their relevancies for the developmental processes of persons should not be given considered attention. The reason is that this would mean the elimination of the use of pleasure and pain as mental building blocks. Only if one accepts these abstractions do the fundamental assertions of anti-natalism about pain and joy have an axiomatic character, only then are they evident and require no further justification. But why should one accept these abstractions?

# VI

Independent of the conditions of their origin, their consequences, and (connected with these two factors) the evaluative contexts of their standard of living and their purpose in life, pleasure and pain, suffering and joy are nothing more than patterns of emotions, if they are anything at all when taken in isolation. They are merely an electrical wave of excitation in a nerve, or, subjectively, a feeling of stabbing, pressing, tickling, tingling, or whatever else that as such need be neither pleasant nor unpleasant. Without a stringent consideration of the evaluative connections and of human wishes for development and transformation, it makes as little sense as wasting one's thinking on the question whether these patterns should exist in the world or not. This type of reflection resembles the pondering whether a particular grain of sand should lie on the beach of Tel Aviv or not. If the diminution of suffering and the increase of joy is meant to accomplish an *improvement* of the world, it would have to be directed towards the improvement of distinctly *subjective* worlds and not towards the world, inasmuch as the world is looked at as a "naked" pattern of characteristics independent of subjects (if that is a meaningful concept of the world to begin with). But people may be aware to different degrees that emotions depend on contexts and that they themselves can relate to the evaluative connections in which emotions become what they are in the end. This is an idea that we need to investigate now more closely. For one of our three positions – that favoured by the friends of procreation, that propagated by anti-natalists, and that supported by mystics – has to do with *actively uncoupling* the emotions from their subjective contexts. Mystics strive towards such an uncoupling, but it is not their aim to advance towards building blocks of cognition. Rather, they seek to encounter the complexity of the real world beyond subjective interests and evaluations.

    How could one imagine a subjectivity that, to be sure, does feel and perceive but barely connects remembrances, hopes, and evaluations with these emotions and perceptions? Small children who do not yet have plans for their lives and as yet possess few memories may exist in such emotive and perceptual states that are close to the present and that, as such, essentially differ from the circumstances of adults. Even people close to death, who no longer have plans or remember their own past would most likely contextualize what happens to be present to their senses in a different way than human beings who still are healthy and are not facing death. Depressive and autistic people, too, make few plans for their future.

A special state in which the non-evaluation of emotions (and thoughts) is sought is the aim of the meditation to achieve close attentiveness that many people practice. In this exercise – as is known – the body is kept calm in order to perceive one's breathing, but also to perceive thoughts and feelings that may arise. Next, following a special kind of instruction, one would try to "put them aside" and to understand that these states do not amount to a substantive self, but are phases that simply come and go but to which, aside from this coming and going, no further significance need be attributed, if one prefers not to do this. The purpose of this exercise in meditation is to *deconstruct* evaluative contexts in which emotions ordinarily occur "automatically." If emotions are what they are because they occur in certain evaluative contexts, then the dismantling of the evaluative contexts will also lead to a transformation of the emotions. To use a simile: if ice is ice only when it occurs in an environment with a temperature of below 0°C, then it ceases to be ice and becomes liquid water as soon as the environmental temperature is raised for a certain time. The context in which ice occurs maintains or changes its consistency. The meditative exercise is meant to make subjective patterns of evaluations or habits of reacting to emotions at some time "disappear" (for highly advanced practitioners of meditation, even those that are "hard-wired" in the body). This would result in a condition in which the emotions that formerly emerged in a positive sense as pleasure or joy, or negatively as suffering or pain, present themselves as something altogether different, or simply do not occur any longer at all.[11] An ancient Buddhist text formulates this aim of meditation as "way" and "it" very clearly:

> The highest WAY is not hard,
> if only you stop to choose.
> Where neither love nor hatred,
> everything is open and clear.
> But the slightest distinction
> separates heaven and earth into two.
> If IT is to reveal itself to you
> leave dislike and preference aside.
> The conflict between like and dislike
> is nothing but a sickness of the mind.
> Unless you understand this profound truth
> you'll try in vain to calm your thoughts.[12]

What emotions look like when preference and dislike have vanished is beyond expression because our linguistic abilities to express ourselves are tied to these popular evaluative contexts. Even when we speak of a "stabbing sensation," a negative evaluation is present in the word "stab" that we associate with an injury. The statement "I feel the pain, but it no longer hurts" consequently is inane or contradictory. The sensation that is present is pain, but no longer is given a negative evaluation; there is no word for it, because expressions for all our emotions depend on our evaluations. The person to whom IT reveals itself certainly still has emotions, but these no longer allow themselves to be named, because calling an emotion by a particular term is connected with evaluative differentiation.

Evaluative contexts need not only be de-constructed through a meditative "de-conditioning" in order to gain the attitude of an emotive being that does not feel with mental states of preference and dislike. Even an artistic activity such as drawing or painting, making music or attempting to write a poem may lead to such an accurate turn towards the singularities of reality. This will mean that the subjective evaluations are perceived as a distraction from one's contemplative work and are being blocked out, the more the artist is able to turn his or her attention away from himself or herself and directs it towards the object of the art. This happens above all in those artistic activities in which the relevant artists are not trying to give expression to themselves. Instead, they represent what they perceive independently of their evaluative systems. We may call such artistic activities *contemplative* and differentiate them from *expressive* and *engaged* performances, which also exist.

Poverty of interpretations and evaluations may exist in the perception of an infant, a depressive man, an autistic woman, a person close to death, a master of meditation, and a contemplative artist. But the paths taken in a life's history that has guided a person towards this poverty of evaluations, if one wants to call it that, are very different. In the case of the infant, a social self with memories and hopes has not yet been developed. The autistic woman *has been unable* to make this development due to neurological anomalies, or a self is *breaking apart* because of a severe existential crisis in the face of approaching death. The master of meditation and the contemplative artist, however, have recognized the problematic implications of constructing the self as a source of evaluation. They have realized that this self with its need for meaning and with its evaluations diminishes their perception of other beings or of the world's complexity in the here and now. They have come to understand that this self forever makes them categorize everything according to their *own* classifications of meaning and value. These categories have something to do with the social project of this self, imagined *over a long period*, but they do not necessarily have anything to do with the being they perceive at this moment, *here and now*. For this reason, they are meditatively or as contemplative artists engaged over many years in the practice of *de-constructing this self*. For this, they use the procedures of dismantling that are germane to their activities and may be familiar to them (as in the case of meditation), or not (as in the case of art that is not employed as a practice of meditation).

The meditating or artistic mystics, as they were called above, encounter the opposition of the social self with its projects while they are engaged in their activities. This is not an insight, however, or a form of cognition in the classical sense: for example, the way one recognizes a tree as an ash or birch or an animal as an artiodactyl (as cloven-hoofed) or as a plantigrade (as walking on its sole, like bears or humans). It is this very experience most of all that all conceptual terms are insufficient in the face of the precise, though not evaluating perception of a concrete emotion, of a concrete individual, of a concrete situation that here lead to an insight. It is the understanding that assertions like "This is good or bad, pleasant or unpleasant, no matter how you look at it" are ultimately inadequate to define reality, because this reality in its inexhaustible complexity always exceeds what the social self can evaluate. So "purifying" emotions of their subjective or ego-centred evaluative contexts is no advance towards the construction blocks of cognition called pleasure and pain.

In mysticism, purifying the emotions of selfish connections will rather lead to intuiting an infinite complexity, one that far exceeds the story of one's own life. But because this complexity is not being erected out of building blocks, but is "intuited spontaneously" if the evaluations of the self are left out, it is perceived as a *unity*, as an infinitely organized unity.

Let us take another look at the difficulty facing the mystic who aims to express in language both those emotions that have been freed of self-referential projects and the intuition of the complexity typical of the intuited wholeness in which the emotions are embedded beyond him or her. In the attempt to focus on one emotion, to draw one particular line, to paint one specific shade, or to produce one specific sequence of sounds at one specific level of volume on an instrument, only at the very onset is it helpful to recite statements about these emotions, lines, colours, or sound sequences. With all these *activities*, the perception or attentiveness must in the end be more *precise* than any assertive speech is able to describe, if it is a question of realizing certain aesthetic states or those known to the traditions of mystical wisdom. For this reason, no meditation, no picture, no concert can be replaced by a descriptive text. Texts realize something other than what they describe. They reduce the complexity of what they evoke within the perspective of a self that is evaluating in a stated manner.

A poem about a tree realizes language in a certain manner and may, when we read it, *guide* our attention during our perception of a tree. But the realization of the perception of a tree independent of our subjective interests is something other than the realization of the poem. Our understanding of cognition is thus very closely connected with predicating and evaluating language (even though we will have to grant that a truffle-seeking pig that finds truffles but does not speak *recognizes* truffles). Therefore, one can formulate a rather different definition of what happens when someone realizes that reality is too complex to comprehend it merely from the perspective of subjective interests and then to turn it into a linguistic topic. One could also define the issue as follows: the problem that confronts the meditating or artistic mystic is the bottomlessness of reality beyond his or her own self, the confrontation with a linguistically *inexhaustible* reality. But cognition is always a question about how to fixate aspects of something, is always an issue of bringing together individual things with general things ("x=F"). Therefore, one can hardly claim that this confrontation is still "cognition" and find expression for it as cognition. There is no longer "something" in this infinitely complex totality about which something particular can be pronounced with certainty.

The philosopher Baruch de Spinoza, however, calls this state the "third cognition."[13] This is why we use concepts such as "intuition" to identify this state and they are emphatically spoken of as "awakening" or "illumination."

These states of intuition or of awakening cannot be stabilized absolutely. Attempting to stabilize them, like every kind of effort, is the best way to make them disappear. "If you follow emptiness, you turn your back to it."[14] A man engaged in meditation or a contemplative artist may limit himself to using the schematic designs of general concepts in his relationship to reality and experience its inexhaustible variety only at a few especially intense moments of (spiritual) absorption. He can do so because he is able to "silence" his subjective valuations. The kind of people in whom this experience has actually stabilized itself without intention and who can also spend their daily routine in it are very, very rare and are sometimes referred to as "sages" or "illuminated ones."

Many of our intersubjective relationships and their lapses of understanding have to do with the barriers that exist between culturally determined contexts of valuations that have "trickled into" our self and that keep us from perceiving the complexity of reality. That makes our life shallow and quite frequently full of conflicts. These barriers are highest vis-à-vis those beings whose physical structure is fundamentally different from ours, and whose sufferings and joy remain altogether alien to us because their bodies are "hard-wired" differently and manifest other trickled-down affective patterns than our bodies do. Consequently, we cannot imagine the joy of a black widow spider that, after mating, (sometimes) eats its partner, or merely what it means for a dog to use its nose in the exploration of its environment.

For this reason, in the aforementioned meditative practices, melting away one's social self does not simply serve to make one's own evaluative contexts become meaningless, so that one may arrive at a richer perception of reality. The process of self-elimination also aims at liberating oneself from certain selfish or cultural contexts in one's relationship to reality and is meant to acquire *flexibility* in one's way of dealing with others, with strangers, and to understand the *relativity* of evaluative contexts. This process has a very practical consequence that will become relevant for our question whether it is preferable to propagate or not: it is the fact that the evolved mystic also opens herself to other meaningful connections, that she learns to know other beings better, and that, with this knowledge, she may even be capable of giving advice that supports those others in their existence. This competency frequently establishes connections between "mysticism" and "wisdom," between the ability to *confront* reality in its complexity and to provide advice on how one might *orient oneself* in this reality.

At this juncture, we must keep in mind that, for the perceiving subject, there are essential differences within the various types of meaninglessness of an emotion or perception that is no longer being evaluated. Depressive, autistic, and mystic people assume different postures towards the world. There is a fundamental distinction between the absence of meaning, the lack of evaluation that leads to the loss of meaningful connections, and the absence of meaning that *opens* new perspectives on other beings. Am I simply noting more than no longer being capable of discerning why I found the pressure in my own knees so terrible after the melting of my social self, or can I also better imagine why *other* beings are in certain states of suffering because I no longer have to be concerned with my own (supposed) states of suffering? The ability to answer the latter question affirmatively is a goal of meditative and artistic exercises and of many wisdom teachings that aim at a calm, expanded mind.

Spinoza's asserts that we gain all the more insight into God, the more we understand about individual things;[15] this identifies the one pole of subjective absence of meaning. It points to the richness of the world that offers itself to us. So long as what is perceived is of significance only *for me*, is recognized only in respect to its relevance for *my* well-being or advancement, it will most likely not be comprehended with the same intensity relative to beings aside from me. In this case, the omission of self-referentiality in perception is the loss of a *barrier to cognition* vis-à-vis world that contains patterns beyond those that result from my preferences for seeking pleasure and avoiding pain. Spinoza's godlike perspective can be interpreted here as an opportunity to observe an individual being from *all possible perspectives*, in *all possible connections* in which it occurs, but not from a generalized human and therefore abstract accounting about pleasure and pain.

When attaining greater selflessness does not bring about new relationships that a perceived being has with other beings, if its relevance for that being's personal interests does *vanish*, but no new connections become recognizable, then the loss of self-referentiality is nothing more than a "purely losing bargain." This is what will happen most likely in a depression: everything becomes senseless and meaningless because it has no value for the depressed person. It remains unclear and does not become material for a discussion whether it may have value for others. The place of relevance for me is taken over by an emptiness devoid of relevance.

In Spinoza's godlike point of view, by contrast, relevance for me is replaced by the intuition that all individual beings are integrated in infinite connections with quite different patterns of relevance. This intuition makes it *impossible* to give preference to a particular, for example, to *my* order of relevance as the only appropriate perceptual context for *any* being. This results in a freedom of cognitive possibilities. This is also the sense in which the epigram of the Christian mystic Angelus Silesius (1624-1677) can be interpreted, if death here signifies the disappearance of relevances that arise from one's own social self:

> I say because Death alone sets me free
> That he the best one of all things must be.[16]

For Spinoza, making this freedom one's own means getting to know the *infinite* or *unfathomable nature of relations* into which every being is harnessed. It is no longer possible in this situation to characterize an intuition of this kind in general terms, because such terms would "whitewash" the complex individual condition that arises for every individual being at a particular place and at a particular time in the world.

Thus, it is *two forms of void* that confront us: the emptiness in which everything has been *extinguished*, and the void in which every individual being and every aspect about every individual being is perceived as depending on infinitely many other aspects, on infinitely many other individual beings, all of which are coming and going. In either case, language no longer finds a firm hold, but for different reasons in each circumstance. On the one hand, there is nothing further to say because everything has become a matter of indifference. On the other, there is nothing certain left to say because linguistic categorizations are too rough and too firm to do justice to the complexity and mutability of what in fact reveals itself and constantly changes.

If we concentrate only on the second form of emptiness, the bottomless nature of the complexity and mutability of everything real, a reservation arises from their "cognition." It is a qualification in the face of a *self-serving theorizing* that operates with "favourite general terms" and tries to insinuate them also to others. The ability to relinquish such popular general terms in one's communication with others is an accomplishment of those educated in mystical wisdom. The following utterance by Confucius (Kung Fu-Tzu; 551-479 a. c.) describes it:

> The noble person is not absolutely for or unconditionally against anything in this world, he, rather, tends towards what the situation requires.[17]

Most philosophers and theoreticians will likely criticize and dismiss such an attitude as irrationality or as situational relativism. For this wisdom remains silent in the face of demands for justifications why this action was taken and not a different one. Confucian wisdom shuns producing the utterances in general terms that are necessary for such justifications. In view of the complexity of the circumstances accessible to them, mystics have abdicated an attitude that goes beyond a particular situation and that operates with general evaluations as certainties. Mystics relativize every evaluative connection that originates in a specific self. That makes situations hardly comparable. It makes no sense to them to ask whether, in general, one should have children or not.

## VII

Wisdom traditions often use the word "path" (in Sanskrit "marga," in Chinese "dao," Sino-Japanese "do"). The intent here is to use processes of development to advance insight into the unity of the complex nature of reality and to do so by cultivating certain practices. The cultivation of a practice (for example, of meditation or of an act of painting or fighting) serves to change a person's attitudes and competencies in a non-argumentative way. Humans are not "just like that" capable of finding a way in their life through the tangled growth of the ever-changing situations defining their existence. As a rule, it is their short-sighted self-interest that keeps them from engaging precisely and thoroughly in the first place with those situations in which they and their fellow humans actually live. For this reason, in the conduct of their life, most humans rely either on their *self-interest*, which is guided by questions like: How do I increase my momentary pleasure, my reputation, or my power, etc.? Or they follow a *conventional way of thinking* that evolved from generalizing a certain perspective in order to get a person through life. This means that they do what "one" does or what "my kind of people" simply would do in a situation like type x. They let themselves be directed by the moral precepts of their culture. From the point of view of wisdom, even the positions of those favouring procreation or anti-natalism are part of this kind of conventional way of thinking, which arises through the inappropriate generalization of particular valuations.

By contrast, the cultivation of practices like meditation, martial arts, making music, or drawing or painting, each in a specific way, may explain to their practitioners a basic truth. This is the need to learn that one must largely abandon one's self, one's own thoughts, preferences, valuations, and intentions. Only such self-denial will enable a person to accomplish an appropriate realization of something distinct within a concrete situation in its full complexity. This may also include the ability to actually execute a movement, for example in sports, that is fully appropriate to its specific requirements. Another skill may be to put an uninterrupted drawing on paper with one particular stroke of the pen, or in a meditation to perceive the precise state of the body in which one finds oneself at precisely this moment without concurrently thinking of something else.

What is meant by "path" in these contexts is neither the conventional, nor the unconventional, nor what reason claims to offer. It is something that reveals itself at a certain moment with the full maturation of the ability to develop the right intuition in view of the complexity inherent in a specific situation in which one may find oneself. To attain this goal, it is necessary to schematize neither oneself nor what one encounters, but to grasp with the greatest possible attention what at this particular instant is taking place in oneself, in one's body and consciousness and outside of oneself. And when it matters to act, one needs to act by following this perception free of intention and not on the basis of a preconceived plan or general opinion that arises from a preconceived order of preferences.

Every conceptual schematization finally capitulates before the bottomlessness and complexity in which reality manifests itself at any particular moment. A schema makes reality simpler than it is and in the process renders that reality easier to understand and to explain. The perfect example here is the physics experiment. In a laboratory, reality is organized in a way that makes it less complicated than it is outside the lab. For this reason, the empirical sciences can make the world understandable, and in certain ways predictable and explicable. Wisdom does not want to participate in this capitulation before this complexity for the purposes of explication. It is not a part of the collective project of progress that is designed to produce ever more knowledge and ever more useful things for an ever-increasing number of people in a common public. It does not seek to transform humanity through general projects of education, even though in principle there are no objections to be raised against this from either a scientific or from a political point of view. Instead, wisdom privately addresses individual persons and speaks to their respective needs for transformation, or to problems about decisions to be made in concrete situations of life.

The individual rabbi speaks to a singular person in despair, the individual therapist speaks to a particular client, Jesus talks with Peter, Socrates with Simmias, Buddha with Ananda, and so on. Wisdom has no need to simplify because it does not have to be intelligible to all. It must be intelligible only to the person with whom it is dealing at this very moment. Wise people intuit what can be intelligible to those participating in a conversation with them, what might help advance or might overtax them. Therefore, they must also discern the situation they find themselves in with those who seek their counsel to the same extent as the situation into which the seeker of advice has fallen and that he describes for them. But whatever may help this particular person along does not help *all* people and need not benefit *all* human beings, because not *all* of them are in the same predicament.

In the practice that is envisioned to serve wisdom, complex and changeable reality is made ever clearer to those who are engaged in the practical experience of wisdom through the repetition of activities and through increasingly more precise observation. What becomes visible is that, in the final analysis, nothing in the world is easy to understand or can be reduced to pleasure and pain. It likewise becomes apparent that the activities concerning individuals, if they are expected to succeed, cannot be guided by attempts at persuasion and explication with the help of popular concepts ("recipes") and advance calculations. A shooter cannot have the influence of the wind calculated in advance through a program of simulation. The same limitation applies to the trigger pressure of a rifle, the speed of an arrow, or the course of a projectile and to applying such data by aiming so and so many inches higher or more to the left or right. (An appropriate computer may be able to do this.) The shooter must, on the contrary, through constantly repeated practice develop the ability to gain an intuition of the shooting situation in which he finds himself at a particular moment and of how to breathe, to take aim in it, how tense to stretch the bowstring, how much pressure to put on the trigger, and when to release the arrow or how hard to cock one's gun.

In this way, one can learn by perfecting an art that the intuition appropriate to any situation occurs only on one condition: one has learned to renounce one's own self as a conscious being with definite ideas, intentions, and desires, even those of understanding and explicating. Consequently, one no longer tries with a firm grip to describe a certain object by using the correct method and to pre-calculate its reaction. Rather, in a practice aiming for wisdom, a *permeability* is intended to occur between what one might call consciousness and what might be referred to as the unconscious and the outside world. In this case, the result may be marginal reactions, e.g. in the posture and movement of one's body or also in one's communicative comportment, reactions that came about as if "on their own." This permeability has an important consequence. It means that the bottomless complexity germane to every human being and that the bottomless complexity of the situation he or she inhabits together with other human beings at any particular moment come to harmonize with one another without directives. Breathing and the arm's posture of the well-trained shooter react in a certain way "on their own" in the situation he finds himself in and to which he is open. In this respect, he resembles the experienced judoka, fencer, or boxer reacting intuitively with his arms and legs and with the tension in his body and his hands to his opponent's movements, and applying the right countermeasure at exactly the moment when his adversary begins to open his protection. That's precisely when he lands the presumed "lucky blow" without having planned it.

It is impossible to describe and intentionally to direct these coordinating movements between the complexities simply because they have to take place intuitively. Otherwise, they would not succeed at the speed and in the perfection for which we admire the great artists and athletes. Consequently, even wisdom as the intuitive ability to find a way through the situational underbrush of life, and to offer counsel, or to act on one's own initiative appears *irrational* to those who believe that they have already acquired an orientation by means of reason or the conventions. Since wisdom is unable to predict how the way is to be found and why it considers its own recommendation to be the right way, it is not *enlightened*. For this reason, wisdom is easily reputed to be "esoteric." Regrettably, this is a mistaken accusation, because we are dealing here not simply with two different realms of life or even forms of life: the theoretical and the political realm. In the one area, activities and assertions take place in public and are negotiated according to general principles. In the other realm, a situational practice conducted by aesthetic contemplation or a doctrine of wisdom is practiced that develops in secrecy, privately between individual persons.

Sometimes, one has to decide between these two options of existence. Then one stands at a crossroads that leads to two different forms of life. Does one want to side publicly with scientific progress, the struggle for justice, and the reduction of misery? Or does one seek the peace of one's own soul in a withdrawn life with likeminded people, avoiding strife, staying shy of the public. It seems impossible to have both options. Bertolt Brecht represented this conflict in his poem ""An die Nachgeborenen" ("To those born after") in which he wrote:[18]

> I would also like to be wise.
> In the old books it says what wisdom is:
> To shun the strife of the world and to live out
> Your brief time without fear
> Also to get along without violence
> To return good for evil
> Not to fulfil your desires but to forget them
> Is accounted wise.
> All this I cannot do:
> Truly, I live in dark times.

The poem from which these lines have been excerpted was written between 1934 and 1938. It is an impressive depiction of the conflict between wisdom, peace, and attentiveness, on the one hand, and political engagement, the fight for justice, and the fear of persecution in an embittered and heedless life, on the other. Brecht had to leave Germany on 28 February 1933, one day after the burning of the Reichstag and had gone into exile from which he returned to Berlin only 15 years later. He describes the "dark times" dominated by suppression, the torture of fellow human beings, and their being dispatched to wars. During these years, the life of wisdom in secrecy, the advice that one should forget one's wishes and deny the need for preferences and refusals appears to be wrong. One must commit oneself. But the political struggle brings about brutalization, leads to inattentiveness even towards those one loves; and without time for nature, life passes hurriedly and with a sense of rebellion. And what importance is to be attributed in this connection to the fact that the individual can accomplish but little? And when are the times *not* dark, making wisdom permissible? Aren't circumstances in the world always such that one would have to rebel against them or at least contribute to the promotion of a significant progressive commitment? But is such a project not a waste of one's entire life because the dark times will always return and a final improvement of mankind's predicament "in general" appears to be impossible? Are the pieces of advice, even when softened with arguments that people should *not* or should *by all means* procreate, recommendations that can be taken seriously only in dark times? Are they manifestations of a political engagement or at least a show of support for the improvement of circumstances in general and not the steps necessary on a path that everyone has to take, which would mean that wisdom is nothing but escapism?

# VIII

Thinking about one's children and pondering the general misery in the world, obviously need not reveal a concern with war and repression, with the concrete harm inflicted on this particular human being. We may develop misgivings ("bad feelings") about anti-natalism or other utilitarian forms of "reckoning." The intuition may arise in us that their arguments are presented on too general a level that simplifies problems too much and indeed makes them overly coarse, and we may notice that attention to the complexity of concrete situations is given rather short shrift. But none of this is an *argument* against utilitarianism and its orientation via balance sheets that tally up pleasures and agonies. The issue here is not that an as yet insufficiently evolved argument is lurking in the back of our mind and that we merely need to fish it out and round it off in order to disprove such a utilitarianism as a philosophy or to stop it as a political movement. To strive for what is useful in general is a solid political position that should be heeded at all times, be they dark in Brecht's sense or not. Even so, it does not seem right to look at one's own life solely from a global perspective. Wisdom is not a rejection of what is needed in general. It does not involve itself in the quarrels of politicians, scientists, and philosophers espousing general theories: for instance, those advocating an ethics of happiness vs. the ethicists of justice. The uneasiness arising in some people may instead point to a different perspective on our life, one that does not orient itself by general propositions. Kant conceived of general reason as our true nature, our innermost being. But an appreciation of wisdom and of a kind of acting that is appropriate to a particular situation, and the suspicion of general theories when discussing essential questions such as the decision whether to have children or not, have not altogether vanished from our minds, even though these minds are embedded in Western heads and have been schooled by general reason and shaped by a public scientific and a public political culture. All of this indicates that we my still consider our life and the situations we encounter in it to be unique. We may look on it as something in which an infinite complexity is hidden that we can only bypass in following the perspective of global generalities.

One may approve of the one-child policy of an earlier Chinese government from a utilitarian point of view because it reduced suffering in the country. One may, likewise, as an enlightened politician, support the education of women and advocate the dissemination of prophylactics in order to lower the birth rate and improve the economic opportunities and the ecological situation of succeeding generations on the globe. Wisdom does *not oppose* enlightened policies of this kind. But it considers them sweeping reactions that do not correspond to the reality of individual humans who may or may not want to have children. Whoever asks himself whether he should procreate or not may obtain orientation from general criteria: he may consult the carbon dioxide level that is made worse by every child, the educational opportunities in his own country, and the danger of war that also is increased through injustices in distribution that grow progressively worse with the constant increase of populations in poor countries and unchanged wasteful lifestyles in the rich nations. No doubt, some people may be guided by such considerations when planning their family. The fluctuation of birth rates may be a consequence of such general estimations. But the choice to have a child or not, to start a family or not, is a deeply existential, individual, and life-transforming decision. Shouldn't it be made with the most comprehensive attention to all the complexities of one's own existence? In rearing one's own child, may one ask oneself how problematic its existence will be as a result of the entirety of mankind's carbon dioxide production or how much its lifestyle will cause envy in another country? Would such an impersonal perspective, in which everything becomes political and always has to be weighed by criteria of world usefulness, turn us into people like those who, in the first half of the twentieth century, saw themselves only as proletarians or revolutionaries or party members and who subordinated their entire private life to the demands that their class, the revolution, or the party made on them? Wouldn't this disappearance of our individual existences in the demands made by the general populace be a totalitarianism in which we could no longer recognize ourselves, other humans, and all the particularities of the world as what they are? If anyone tries to take herself seriously as an individual and other people as individuals (whatever that means) and prefers to decide consciously if she wants to have a baby (and does not have it "just like that"), wouldn't she then have to enter the sphere of wisdom to make this decision? Wouldn't she also leave the area of political struggle and administration in which the lives of millions of people are to be directed in accordance with the demands of the economy and of ecological requirements?

An anti-natalist may find China's one-child policy as still not going far enough, given his universalist ethical viewpoint. A friend of wisdom will decide the question whether this couple may have children or not – an issue that must be differentiated from the problem whether a population's birth rate should fall – as an issue that can never be resolved through principles. Rather, a solution can be found only when the couple in question thinks about itself and its situation very precisely and with complete honesty, rather than by oversimplifying their circumstances. Perhaps it may be advisable to ask for the advice of a friend with a good deal of actual experience. The couple will ask if it *makes sense* for them to have children now or at all. Then when it is fortunate enough, the couple will next develop the correct intuition for its own situation. When we are trying to communicate persuasively how this decision turns out in the realm of wisdom, we will be unable to name any criteria according to which it is made. Politicians may ask whether it serves the interests of their country, is advantageous to the general supply of food stuffs, is good for the pension funds, and the labour market, whether every woman gives birth to one child or has an average of 1.8 or 2.4 children. But these are two different questions: one, if *I* or *the two of us* should have a child; and two, how many children women in my country should have on average. The second question has to do with the general welfare for many, with what is most useful to them. The first question concerns what a meaningful life is for me. To understand how they differ we must take a brief look at what could be meant here by "meaning."

Some time ago, psychology discerned *three sources defining the meaning* of human life: first, the effective commitment to a specific accomplishment; second, the perception of something or someone in its *singularity*, which means, to *love*; and finally, third, the transformation of one's own person in the face of tremendous difficulties (for example, a chronic illness or captivity) so that these can be tolerated and one becomes a person who can continue to live despite these circumstances.[19] An architect/builder, a poetess, a philosopher, and a scientist who produce works can give meaning to their lives through their activities, as does a pastry chef who invents a recipe for a fancy cake, or an engineer who builds a machine.

When humans have children, then through their upbringing and education they produce something or they better someone: that is to say, in ideal cases, independent human beings who can lead lives of their own. Or vice versa: the works of those who create art, theories, buildings, machines, recipes, and so on produce something that, in analogy to children, may be imagined as a kind of children of these creative people. Furthermore, human beings get to know their own children as the individuals they are, and they do so as accurately as they get to know no other human being, because they take care of them from the time of their birth. Based on this knowledge, as a rule, they *love* them in a special way. To fulfil their parental obligations, parents themselves must change at times, must undergo a transformation that also resembles what takes place with an architect/builder, a scientist, a philosopher, or artist, all of whom will at some time notice that, given their present state of mind, they will not be able to create the piece of work they envision. Then they realize that they must *form and transform* themselves in order to *have the ability* to create what they had intended, what they believe they *must* produce. In the same way, a couple may realize that it has to change so as to be the kind of parents that they *want* to be for their children. In this sense, the act of having children as much as the craftsman's talents, or technical, artistic, and scientific creativity can be a source of meaning in all three psychological aspects.

During this self-transformation, parents or other creative individuals may get to know the constitution of certain aspects of reality very accurately: among them their own bodies and personalities and those of their children, or the material in which they practice their craft or their art. In this respect, even contemplative art, contemplative sport, and the practice of wisdom are sources of meaning, to the extent that they aim at transformation and accurate recognition of particularities. Whoever has to decide whether to have children or not will have to ask himself or herself, among other things, what meaning his life with and without children has and whether he at times feels capable of perceiving a new human being and himself accurately enough that the new life and one's own life will continue to keep being or becoming meaningful and good lives. Deliberations of this kind cannot be made in advance, much less replaced by considerations of the situation of pension funds, general climatological developments, and the status of the labour market. The question whether we procreate or not may depend on our animalistic impulses, on wise intuitions of the meaning of our life, or, in my opinion the worst case, on political regulations, ideologies, or considerations about what generally is most useful.

AARON: Hold on, Kagami. Please be quiet a moment! Do you hear the noise out there?
KAGAMI: Sounds like dogs.
AARON: Indeed. Let me go take a look.

Aaron rose and walked to the window. In the garden he witnessed the fury of two large, gaunt, brindled dogs violently attacking and biting a small one and throwing it to the ground, where it tried to defend itself. It squealed and shrieked. Aaron fetched a broom from a wall closet and stepped out on the veranda: "Hey, hey, stop that!" The attackers let go of their prey and looked at Aaron. The victim could no longer run normally and tried to crawl away. The other dogs lowered their heads and snarled as they stare at Aaron, who raised his broom. The two dogs bared their teeth and very slowly approached the veranda. Aaron kept his eyes on them, only briefly peering into a corner of his veranda where he stored a few garden tools. He took three steps towards his right and reached for a rake. The dogs were standing now at the lower end of the little metal staircase leading up to his veranda. Aaron slowly approached it. He now stood directly by the stairs, dropped the broom and swung the rake. He hit the head of one of the dogs, whose jaws grated and that gave a sharp yowl. Immediately, the two large dogs drew back, turning their attention back to their victim. Aaron walked down the three steps, picked up a few stones and threw them at the big dogs. He hit the other one on the head, whereupon the intruders disappeared.

Relieved by the attackers' flight, Aaron walked down the gravel path to take a look at the bleeding victim that had withdrawn to the vicinity of the garden shed and there, breathing heavily and trembling, lay on the ground. Aaron bended down. It is Krischan. The bakery staff must have let him go into their yard despite the danger presented by the stray dogs. He must have run away once again. Aaron ran back to his studio, got a blanket from his futon, and used it to cover the bleeding animal. Then he hurried through his garden around his house and to the other side of the street to notify the Blumes. He rang the bell. Fortunately, Lily was there. She was startled. He went with her to where Krischan was hiding. For a few moments, he stood next to her animal; it was still breathing, but seemed not to recognize its surroundings. Aaron had no hope that it would survive. He put his hand on his weeping neighbour's shoulder. Then he returned to his studio. He took a whiskey bottle from his bookshelf, poured himself a drink near his little kitchen and sat down again in his easy chair.

AARON: Well, damn it all.
KAGAMI: I'm sorry.
AARON: My next-door neighbours' dog. I believe he is beyond help.
KAGAMI: What should you have done, anyway? The other dogs are hungry, too.
AARON: Beg your pardon. Two brutes against one midget!
KAGAMI: These are not schoolyard children, Aaron, but beasts of prey.
AARON: Even so.
KAGAMI: The others will now have to go on looking for food.
AARON: Of all things, do you have compassion for them?
KAGAMI: Try to think with a little bit of reason, Aaron. The neighbours' dog you know, the others you don't. That's why this pain is closer to you than the hunger of the others. All that has happened is a quite normal hunt among beasts of prey.
AARON: I don't want something like that in my garden. I also don't want my neighbours' dog to simply be devoured.
KAGAMI: Someone is constantly being devoured somewhere in this world.
AARON: Maybe.
KAGAMI: What is it you keep in your freezers in the basement? Wild boar, lamb, venison, or what?
AARON: Mm.
KAGAMI: How do you think it gets there?
AARON: Oh, just drop it!
KAGAMI: You don't want to see things the way they are.
AARON: What do you mean: "things"? Do you believe anyone would be able to tolerate watching all the killings that are happening in the world this very moment, if he were to see all the suffering that takes place just now in the world and becomes the food

in his freezer? That is something nobody could bear! It is simply nonsense to claim that it is reasonable to be aware of this! Kagami, I don't have your kind of an archive. Nor do I have your type of processing capacities, most of all not of the emotional kind. The suffering outside one's own window is something different than the suffering endured somewhere thousands of kilometres away. And if you think it reasonable to evaluate the suffering one sees with one's own eyes the same way as suffering one has no more than just a vague knowledge of, then you would be unable to find a reasonable person in the world. I don't know how the venison in my freezer was killed, and I also don't care to know.

KAGAMI: Perhaps you should want to know this.

AARON: Life would become unbearable if one would want to know everything one were able to know. Knowledge is not an end in itself. Didn't you say yourself that whenever I know of an alternative but am powerless to opt for one or the other choice, this knowledge merely demonstrates my lack of power to me?

KAGAMI: Yes, this is approximately how I put it.

AARON: So. What would be my benefit to know how the animals got into my freezer? Would it be in my power to alleviate their suffering? No!

KAGAMI: You could stop eating meat.

AARON: Would that relieve their pain? And please don't talk to me about the effects on the markets.

KAGAMI: Why not?

AARON: Because that is an abstract argument! Wasn't that the gist of Moritz's essay about the distinction between abstract arguments and one's reaction in concrete situations? Please tell me, what am I to do because of the abstract principles? Shall I let the strays eat my neighbours' dog because they are hungry and at the same time be concerned for the antelopes in Africa so that they don't get eaten? And should I stop buying meat? Shall I really arrange my life in this manner according to principles? Does that make me reasonable, or does it make me into a machine that functions according to predetermined axioms because it has programmed itself in this manner? Is there any difference in being programmed by genes or by abstract principles? In either case, I myself appear not to have a real life, no longer to lead my life but that of the species, either that of the biological species or that of mankind as a community of Kantian rational persons.

KAGAMI: Is this your way of criticizing me?

AARON: No, why do you ask?

KAGAMI: I act according to principles.

AARON: Okay, okay; that's not what I meant. Instead, I tried to say that I cannot act as if the suffering in front of my own door were to touch me in the same way as the suffering in Africa – for no other purpose than being able to describe myself as rational and empathetic in accordance with whatever principles.

KAGAMI: Perhaps this is a deficiency of perception.

AARON: As I just said, one also must process what one perceives. I simply couldn't process a perception in which the misery of the whole world were present at every moment. I would go insane if I wanted to bear that. I could no longer be myself, but would have to turn into a god. Perhaps Buddha did bear this. But I am not Buddha. And people who assert that the suffering in Africa has the same dire effect on them as the pain that is inflicted before their front door are, in my opinion, hypocrites, emotional impostors. Most often, they let their grandparents rot in some nursing home, and at the same time they demonstrate for the victims of floods in South-East Asia.

KAGAMI: You talk a little too all-inclusively about people who have entered into a commitment on behalf of humans in faraway countries, I think. And processing capacities are something one can nurture.

AARON: If one wants to. Do I want that?

KAGAMI: Should you?

AARON: Just now I reacted intuitively to a concrete situation. I simply don't like it when a dog I know is torn apart in my garden, even if the attackers are hungry. And I cannot display a reaction to situations that occur in the Serengeti I know nothing about. What should that imply? Should I leave Zurich to save the zebras in Namibia from the crocodiles?

KAGAMI: That would not be all that different from what you did just now, only a little more expensive.

AARON: But it would be quite different. It would be an abstract act in pursuit of abstract principles. The zebras and crocodiles in Africa are not part of my situation, because just now I don't happen to be in Africa. The dogs in front of my window are part of my situation.

KAGAMI: Shall I load hunting scenes taken by drone cameras in Africa for you?

AARON: Please don't!

KAGAMI: If the blinds had still been down and if you had turned on the radio, you wouldn't have witnessed the struggle in your garden any more than that of the African zebras.

AARON: But the blinds were not down. You think I should out of a principle let the desperate brutes devour my neighbours' dog because they happen to be hungry and the hunger of two dog counts for more than a small domesticated animal's will to survive?

KAGAMI: I have not rendered such a concrete account. I merely wanted to say that the hunters also suffer and that they, in the moment they kill their prey, do not necessarily arouse empathy, whereas the animal being killed, most certainly does.

AARON: Whatever. I don't like what was going on there one bit. I had to put an end to it. Everyone else would have done the same.
KAGAMI: Everyone?
AARON: Everyone with a heart in his chest.
KAGAMI: A heart for the neighbours' dog. Do you believe you acted wisely, intuitively, in accord with the needs of the situation? Isn't your situation variable? Does it have to do only with what you see just then, or also with the future, with what happens three streets or thirty kilometres away? Where in space and time does your situation start, and where does it end? Why are you not meant to say that the state of the whole world is the situation in which you are at this moment?
AARON: What do I know, no idea, wise, unwise, reasonable, my street or the whole world. You strike me as rather pedantic just now. Situations are simply not defined by a hair's breadth, by the millimetre and the tenth of a second. You and a god may perhaps be able to take care of the whole world. How is the state of the world supposed to be my situation? I do not live in the world. I live at 17 Böcklin Street. And I simply can't look on while a being I know is being torn to shreds while it is still alive.
KAGAMI: Do you want to go on listening?
AARON: For all I care. Perhaps it is a distraction. Horrible, the whole thing.

10 001

CONTINUATION: MARBACH: GERMAN LITERARY ARCHIVE: PAPERS OF MORITZ BRANDT. FILE: MB_1820_09_290.PDF

## IX

In Wim Wenders' 1987 film *Wings of Desire*, an angel who exists only as a spiritual being encounters a *fallen* angel who tells him at a snack bar how beautiful it is to have physical experiences. He does not refer to some sort of erotic ecstasies but to the cheap, hot, bitter black coffee he happens to enjoy drinking as he stands at the lunch counter, and also to the cigarette he is smoking. He tells his spiritual brother about the joy that comes with rubbing his hands when it's cold and feeling them getting a little warmer. His list could be lengthened at will: I still remember how it felt when, as a schoolboy, I could sleep late on Sundays, did not wake up in my bed until late and the sun was already shining into my room through the yellow drapes. Then, from my bed near the window, I gently pushed the drapes with my hand to make them sway a little, so that I could observe the light moving patterns on the ceiling. I also remember how happy I was when my grandfather showed me how to polish leather shoes for the first time and how I actually succeeded, so that my new shoes looked even more attractive than when we had bought them: first apply the shoe polish, then let it penetrate, then the brush, and finally a second shine using a lady's nylon hose. What a terrific gloss! I had a girlfriend who could not throw away bottles, no beer bottles, no wine bottles, no perfume bottles. She also saved pickle and jam jars. When I asked her why, she said that they are too beautiful to be thrown away. I then took a good look at them on their shelf amid the books and I realized: they are beautiful indeed; they are a pleasure to look at! I also never forgot how, as a child, I became fully aware for the first time of the fragrance of autumn leaves and that I left the road I was driving on and ran across fields to smell more of the leaves. Only a short time ago, I noticed that the pattern of a particular tree's branches in winter resembled a frozen explosion towards light and that this figure manifests a need, an aspiration, a touching tenacity. Yesterday, I was slumped in my easy chair, too tired to go on reading. I turned off the lamp in the waning daylight and listened to the splatter of rain drops. Since the wind was by turns swelling and fading, the drops hit the panes hard at times, and then again, they were barely audible in the dusk. These changes in the wind's intensity created a rhythm, as in music. This reminded that, after listening to a piece by Steve Reich, "Different Trains", I stepped out on the rain-wet street on which cars were swooshing by. Even the loud noise created by their tires on the damp asphalt had a rhythm that I discovered all at once, because the music had honed my attention. That, too, gave me pleasure. Imre Kertész describes in his novel *Fateless* how, as a young man and inmate in a Nazi concentration camp, he derived joy from the experience of observing a flower grow.[20] He encountered hostile reactions for depicting a feeling of joy in such a camp. But he was truthful about it; even there it is possible to have perceptions of this kind.

If we could remember all the joys that appear in many people's lives, especially while one is still a child, then many of us will surely say that life is beautiful. Perhaps these joys can be experienced only if one is able to summon attentiveness to the phenomena of the world. Perhaps they occur more frequently during childhood for a reason: it is an age that knows of no firm self-project, no design that constantly makes me think, in whatever I experience, about no one but myself and nothing but my own plans and purposes and that distracts me from what becomes apparent. Thus, I cannot help but ask myself what this or any other experience actually contributes to my further advancement. But isn't it senseless to try *balancing* these joys, however they may come about, *against* these pains? Isn't it perverse and vulgar to say that the world would not have fallen short of anything if these joys had not existed, but that it would be a better place if the pains that do unfortunately come in the course of a lifetime had been avoided? Is it really true that we do not regret it when no people inhabit a beautiful island? I often joined friends on a hike in the woods and sometimes, as we passed by a clearing, or when a view down into a valley opened up, they would say, "This is a place to have a home and never leave!"

It was no accident that I quoted a film earlier. Film as much as poetry can exercise our attention in a similar way (though perhaps not with the same intensity) as meditation and sport. Watching at a film or reading a poem may turn us away from our own purposes and preferences and may direct our attention towards connections other than those having to do with our own existence. This is why a connection exists between contemplative art and the exercises of mystic wisdom: both undermine egocentrism and fixation on social projects. If one keeps aware of the small pleasures the fallen angel in Wenders' film describes, or if one remembers those pleasures that come about in the life of a woman reading poems, as her attention turns towards an animal or a plant celebrated in a poem, then the individuals thus singled out are not concerned with upgrading the average tabulation of their happiness. They may rather prefer, even if only for short moments, to be fully immersed in the intricacies and structures of reality and for once not have to disregard them for the sake some kind of busyness, "carelessly" and "without patience," as

Brecht says. It is the magnificent thing about art that it can show us the bottomless nature of reality and that under its "direction" we can, for moments even in our everyday world, perceive how we simply *are there* in a world of this type without having to "get along" or "get ahead" in it.

## X

But life is not evaluated positively only through such contemplative perceptions of a complex present time. There are also "projects for the future" that are related to the present time and give to life a "meaning" and for this reason let it appear as a *good* one. As a rule, the everyday life of many humans appears worth living to them at the same moment when they consciously or unawares consider the continuation of *human life* an important intent. Progeny creates a whole series of obligations such as protecting, nourishing, and others that fulfil a life and whose purpose hardly ever is questioned. To put it more generally: if we want to have things continue "for us" as beings of a distinct species, then we have to take care that "our children," too have "a good life." As soon as this project of continuing our own life in descendants is put into question, an essential pillar providing a sense of meaning in our lives breaks off. For this reason, strong arguments are needed to question the project of the generations. The defenders of this project are the people previously identified as "friends of procreation." We will now focus on their position and place in relationship to the thoughts of the anti-natalists and the mystics.

The "generational project" itself appears to presuppose an awareness of what connects the sexual act and posterity: in other words, a realization that one belongs to a procreative community. Some people, not all, intentionally start families in accordance with this realization. We do not know whether living beings aside from humans recognize the connection between sex and progeny. There is something uncanny about imagining, for instance, that birds are *ignorant* of what they *are doing* when they build nests for their broods; that they feel *forced* to mate because a certain desire arises in them; that they lay eggs and cannot abandon them but remain sitting on them trying to keep them warm, without knowing why. Birds that feed their hatchlings and teach them to fly, but are unaware that all of these activities have had but one purpose: the welfare of these hatchlings. One can't know what being a crow or a duck adds up to. Perhaps we systematically underestimate the cognitive abilities of other living beings. But certain approaches of behavioural scientists suggest that a genetically "programmed" behaviour is taking its course here, one that is not based on any sort of "insight" into causal connections.[21]

Human beings, by contrast, can consciously decide in favour of starting a family, especially when contraceptives are available to them. Yet there might be genetic factors that influence even such conscious decisions by arousing misgivings that one's own life is meaningless, if one stays single, if generational continuity lapses. Since humans understand the causal mechanisms of sexuality, they are not only able to start families consciously, but also to decide consciously against starting a family. In the same way, they can decide against any number of biological facts so long as they understand them, for example against the fact that a cancer will kill them unless they submit to a successful operation and its attendant follow-up therapy.

The idea that humans are aware of the "generational project" and despite all "parental instincts" possibly opt to let it lapse in the interest of general moral principles can appear, however, as no less uncanny as a chain of genetically programmed beings extending like an unconscious chain across thousands of generations. For, like this abstract genetic program, it would in this case be the abstract reasons of anti-natalism, perhaps, or ecological or whatever other justifications that determine a choice whether a *certain* human with a *certain* history is created.

Abstract arguments are not powerless. We only need to take a look not just at the suffering that life signifies for humans themselves, but also include the pain these humans cause for other species as a result of their generational project. Then the facts thus revealed could form the basis for an "anti-anthropocentric" thinking that has existed in the history of the mind for a long time.[22] Perhaps such a form of thinking that shuns humanity, if it were to be coupled with a corresponding political propaganda, could be as successful with the public as the proclamation to "be fruitful and multiply!" Perhaps an advertising program of sufficient duration could persuade a majority of mankind that it would be better not to continue populating the world. Such a campaign could assert that it is ecologically irresponsible, immoral, and ruthless and primitive from the viewpoint of other living forms to beget children; such a campaign would subject families with children to legal pressure to justify their existence.

I suppose most readers will agree that the things "we humans" as a species bring about cannot be judged from a distanced perspective as either good or beautiful. Mankind may no longer be menaced by a value judgement like the one that made God send a great flood, but it may feel threatened by the arbitrary event of a natural disaster, in which case some may heave a sigh like: "Thanks be to God that a meteorite is approaching and will wipe all of us out, and this whole sorry mess will be over." When

Schopenhauer mentions mankind in the same breath as a "coat of mould" covering the globe, he sounds like he has adopted a similar attitude.[23] But what kind of a perspective is this?

The US philosopher Samuel Scheffler avers that the anti-anthropocentric perspective is a sham perspective that no human being could possibly profess.[24] No one, he writes, would take the statement seriously that it would be better to have humankind disappear. Any person agreeing to such a judgement would thereby totally devalue his *own* individual life. According to Scheffler, "we" necessarily want "our" continuity because *the meaning of our individual life*, he believes, absolutely depends on the survival of the species, on the unbroken sequence of generations, no matter how disastrous the human presence on this planet may turn out for all other beings.

The reason for this attitude is *not* that we are hoping for a collective improvement. Some people may think that "we" will sooner or later put an end to the extirpation of the various species, will abolish mass animal husbandry, will halt the increasing rise in the globe's temperature and reverse it, and will defeat war as a collective social pathology. But Scheffler does not attribute the positive consequences (measured perhaps on a scale of suffering) that human life at some potential future could bring about in an all-inclusive reckoning on the globe. Such a universal computation may indicate that, for humans, life after their own existence has a value and gives meaning to their present-day condition. Even Scheffler does not consider the estimation that things concerning us should go on as the manifestation of a collective biological self-preservation drive, of a genetic program. For he believes that he can demonstrate that we attribute cultural values to our own individual lives and actions and consider them to be meaningful only in the context of the continued existence of our species. In his opinion, our individualism and egoism have much more constricting limits than is ordinarily assumed.

Cancer research, concern for the accuracy of language, writing books, building cities, education in a school or university – all of this would lose its sense and value if we were to know that in four weeks all human life on the planet will be extinguished. Scheffler avers that we consider all human activity valuable in a fundamental way, despite the amount of suffering it creates. The reason for this is that the life and actions of individuals are given an interpretive horizon only by a future humankind. As he sees things, all human beings presume (for themselves) the authority of being able to judge how the future *should* properly take its course. In Scheffler's terms, humans at heart want to "control time" when they value something, because valuation always means wishing to preserve something for the future. Humans attempt to oppose the transitory character of time when they found institutions. Institutions are meant potentially to go on *forever* and to be kept going by posterity. For Scheffler, wishing unlimited temporal duration for something signifies the same importance as granting it cultural recognition and estimation. The existence of hardly any institutions are planned for a limited time. The fact that at some time they will have reached their end may be an arbitrary given of cultural history. As a universal rule, their founders had a different vision. Institutions of government, laws, courts, schools, libraries, hospitals, orchestras – they all do not exist for *particular* people and times, but potentially for all people and for all times. Because one values cultural institutions, one attends to them; one generation after the other experiences and suffers through them so that the life of this culture can perpetuate itself. For Scheffler, this is simply the description of cultural facts, a modest depiction of the human world, of cultural life.

He is interested in an attitude that reveals itself succinctly only after it has been confronted with the idea of the *decline and end* of humanity. This idea is spelled out in detail in P. D. James's novel *The Children of Men*.[25] Scheffler includes it as evidence in his argumentation. In this fiction, humanity has become infertile and therefore is running out of progeny as it succumbs to lethargy and depression. Scheffler suggests the following dilemma: mankind may manoeuvre itself into a situation in which it collectively brings about its own end, for example through too high an increase in global warming. In that case, the consequence would be a devaluation of all individual life that had existed before the disaster. This phenomenology has a plausibility, as does the world depicted in James's novel. One can imagine that this might occur. A psychology that adheres to the motto "After us the deluge" perhaps does not function.

But how *obligatory* is this attitude? Did Scheffler really find a counter-argument *against* anti-natalism? Has he justified a generalizable recommendation that humans *should* have progeny? And for whom is it "valid"? What about those who say that a humanity that is extinguishing itself due to its technical and political incompetence has not *deserved a better fate* and *fortunately would vanish* because its existence harms so much else of different life. What about a person who says: The suffering of numberless forms of life weighs more than culturally organized mankind's urgent need for meaning.

Scheffler states that, with "our ways of thinking" about the future of humanity, as they are made plausible in James's novel, he means his "own attitudes and the attitudes of any other people who share them, however numerous those people happen to be." (p. 18) Argumentatively, that takes him out of the woods. Basically, he is engaged in nothing more than the description of his own valuation of the continuance of human cultural life. This description proceeds independently of any historical, cultural, and existential contexts. But exactly as the appreciation of one's own life may change within an individual existence, so too may the high regard for the generational project undergo a transformation. A youthful person may consider humankind terrific and try to participate in accomplishing its radiant future. As he gets older, he may develop an increasingly acute awareness of how malicious and heedless most humans can be (as perhaps Schopenhauer did). Then it might appear better to him that his own species become extinct. Or a person may in his youth wish for children and in his old age be humiliated and tortured by his own offspring and conclude that it might have been better if he had not become a father in the first place.

Deliberations of this kind cast a shadow on the meticulous care with which Scheffler and other philosophers advance their investigations. Why is one to embrace detailed arguments that are meant to prove that one simply cannot desire the end of mankind, when the arguments rest on *fundamental premises* whose general relevance is inexplicable in the final analysis? In circumstances of cultural insecurity and of painful decline, anthropocentric views of the world and of humanity that saw everything in negative terms have developed. One may presume that the very opposite attitude prevails at times when cultures begin to flourish. It is, however, a characteristic especially of philosophical arguments to begin with what is called "intuitions" that historically, culturally, and biographically are "suspended in air," that seem to have no real history, but are just that: the intuitions of individuals at certain times and under certain circumstances. They are then simply *declared* to be of general validity, even though they should properly be perceived as nothing more than symptoms of a certain historical and cultural situation.

Let us imagine a mass murderer who knows that he has caused nothing but suffering, and because of his disposition he will continue murdering. He does not ask for clemency but for death because he considers his existence intolerable for himself and others. Let us also assume that a group of humans sees itself as such mass murderers. Could "mankind," in the sense of this analogy, not say to itself: "We acknowledge that we are descendants of primates with a high degree of aggressiveness, who have eradicated many other primates and many other species. This aggressiveness is the reason that we were able to spread across the entire globe. Obviously, we fail to expunge it from our biological nature in the course of millennia, no matter how hard we may have tried culturally. There is no denying the fact that we are still engaged in warfare against each other and in eradicating other species. Therefore, it would be better for us and for all other living beings on the planet, if we were to disappear." Let us imagine a way of thinking in which humans emerge from devastations lasting for decades and are fearful to continue having children because the government monopoly on power and the educational institutions no longer exist. Isn't Cormac McCarthy's 2006 novel *The Road* precisely the kind of text that could provide plausible material for illustrating this contrary, anti-anthropocentric conviction?[26] Isn't it characteristic of good novels, like those of P. D. James and Cormac McCarthy, that they show credible, yet very *different* worlds, with depictions of basic moods and their consequences for the plot that are not necessarily those of their readers? Doesn't the profusion of apocalyptic literature demonstrate that P. D. James provides just one *possible* phenomenology, one potential starting point for an argumentation like Scheffler's?

Philosophy becomes interesting where its concerns are irreconcilable fundamental premises of thinking, acting, and evaluating. For exactly at such points it reaches the boundaries of argumentation. Scheffler discusses with great accuracy only from one perspective of a culture, the one that presumably creates meaning and is continued in its posterity. But it is also possible to proceed from different premises and to enumerate their consequences plausibly in a fiction.

Here we seem to slide into contradictions. Even so, the antinatalism that cites suffering and the culturalism of creating meaning through posterity are possible to an equal degree and seem, as *general theories* with potential consequences for the behaviour of individual humans, equally ill-conceived. Two imperatives, "Never have children because that leads to an increase of suffering in the world!" and "By all means have children because through them meaning is created in culture!" create an antinomy about the way we are expected in our consciousness to bypass the mechanisms of having children. This antinomy is probably determined by the genetic "programming" that urges us to have sex, and that makes our babies cute to us. One may conclude from this antinomy what may be concluded from all antinomies: it is senseless to play suffering off against meaning in this general way that pays no regard to the individual situations in which humans experience pain or sense. This antinomy makes it unmistakable: philosophy as a judge cannot, using the description of different life-worlds, arrive at a decision about what is correct and what is false procreative behaviour.

For this reason, philosophy is not wise.

*Hombroich, in June*

\* \* \*

AARON: So, that was quite a devastating left hook he threw at philosophy with his diagnosis that it is not wise.

KAGAMI: True.

AARON: But one still doesn't know whether one is expected to have children for a real life or not.

KAGAMI: "One" simply can't know whether the essay is correct. The issue presents itself differently for every individual, for every couple so long as it knows how to evaluate its own situation wisely or is aided by wise counsel.

AARON: Strikes me as strange how extensively this childless lyric poet and former boxer cogitates about procreation and wisdom.

KAGAMI: He was already ill when he finished this essay.

AARON: You think his reflections are merely the expression of his mood? I find that rather unfair.

KAGAMI: I did not mean merely a mood. You do learn something from your illness, as I do from my mistakes. I assume he had to consider why he never had a wife and children, that he would have to leave this world without a family of his own. It is also possible that he balances his poetic work as a kind of creation with having children, which is after all the most prevalent way for you humans to be creative. It is also possible that he asked himself what purpose all his writing poems might have, what role the continuation of culture might have for him as an artist. I could imagine that questions like these may have awakened his interest in books like Scheffler's. Do you want to know Dorothy Cavendish's reaction to this text?

AARON: Sure.

## 10 010
## FROM THE ARCHIVE OF
## LADY MARGARET HALL COLLEGE, CAMBRIDGE: DIARY NOTES OF DOROTHY CAVENDISH. WRITTEN ON 8 SEPTEMBER.

Finished Moritz's essay titled "Nothingness" today. Why did he choose this title? The way I read it, this text is not about nothingness at all, but deals with intuitions in contrast to the development of principles as orientations for action. It must have originated during his final years. In this piece, Moritz still takes a step away from Buddhism in the direction of general perception of wisdom as a situational style of thinking and acting in private circumstances. He presents a deconstruction of this kind of thought by playing the utilitarian attempts to prevent suffering against the need to produce meaning through culture, thereby constructing an antinomy. Perhaps he also wanted to clarify for himself that Buddhism is not a variant of negative utilitarianism, that it is neither a philosophy nor politics, but a pedagogy about life to be cultivated in private. His essay gives me a better understanding of his reactions during his illness to my sudden fits of rage about politics. He himself had probably taken leave of politics through his analysis of Buddhism. He must have seen that his kind of art and of the kind he valued as reading material could not be connected with his political engagement. I have seen this all along. But he was of the opinion that he would have to commit himself "authentically." He had a bad conscience because his art did not react to the social and political forms of decline that he had to endure.

Perhaps he also feared being accused of a *l'art-pour-l'art* attitude. The concept of "contemplative art" was a good term to help him understand his activity as a poet.

Now that I have read everything, I shall mail the manuscript back to Mariam and thank her for allowing me to examine it. She will understand that I no longer have the strength to turn it into a publication.

Aaron (standing by his stove and frying sausages): Cavendish is quite right in observing that Moritz was always thinking about how to categorize what he wrote and that he wanted to consider it neither as politically committed literature nor as art for art's sake. In Hombroich, he was under greater pressure in this respect because now he lived as nothing but a poet, no longer working somewhere, as he did here at the publisher's in Zurich. Furthermore, in Germany he perceived politics differently from here in Switzerland. He felt that he shared a responsibility for German politics. Swiss politics was something he looked at from the outside, often amused.

KAGAMI: Did he never have a girlfriend?

AARON: I know nothing about his sexual preferences.

KAGAMI: Neither do I.

AARON: There you have it. I could imagine that he died a virgin.

KAGAMI: Why do you think he moved in with his sister?

AARON: They were always close, always exchanged letters.

KAGAMI: Don't you think that he lacked something?

AARON: Do you assume that people without an active sexual life don't lead a real life? That something inside them remains unrealized? By this assumption, didn't Robert Walser have a real life? And how about yourself?

KAGAMI: But I am not a human, obviously. And his sister, Mariam?

AARON: She did have boyfriends, in earlier years. But she told me that this only irked her. That she felt like she was elsewhere, not by herself, if she constantly had to adjust to another person.

She experienced the couple situation as the exact opposite of a real life, as a life that "always takes place also in someone else' mirror," to quote an expression she once used.

KAGAMI: But, you know, there is the myth of the original "spherical man," as told by Aristophanes in Plato's *Symposium*, that you humans were "androgynous" beings, separated by Zeus after a rebellion against the gods and ever since seeking reunification through love.

AARON: Is there not also this verse in the Christian Bible – as a defence of celibacy – that some are made for marriage and others are not?

KAGAMI: That is Matthew 19, 12: "For there are eunuchs who have been so from birth, and there are eunuchs who have been made eunuchs by others, and there are eunuchs who have made themselves eunuchs for the kingdom of heaven. Let anyone accept this who can."

AARON: Exactly. The one I had in mind. One finds documentation for everything in your archive. Perhaps Moritz and Mariam were incapable of marriage "from birth." Well then, one cannot say, I believe, whether it is an integral part of real life to be single or a couple, with or without children. For some people, marriage destroys the realization of their life. Others need someone different. There are those who despair of their children, and some whose children alone give them the feeling that they are a part of this world. I agree with Jesus. Perhaps Moritz's and Mariam's constellation was exactly the one that accorded best to them both. Even though they did not live together for long, as we know.

KAGAMI: No, it wasn't a long time. By the way, the essay about nothingness is the only one tagged with a place name at its conclusion.

AARON: True. But I have no idea if this means anything.
KAGAMI: You did go to Hombroich once. How did you like it there?
AARON (meanwhile sitting in his easy chair): Moritz was already rather ill when I was there. But the place is pretty, idyllic, also a bit weird: a former firing ramp for nuclear rockets, a park, beautiful buildings for art. A strange mixture of nature, violence, and art. But Moritz and Mariam had a good life there.
KAGAMI: That's also how Mariam tried to recommend the place to her brother in a letter from Hombroich. Do you want to hear it?
AARON: Sure!

10 011
MARBACH: GERMAN LITERARY ARCHIVE: LETTER OF MRIAM BRANDT TO MORITZ BRANDT OF 23 JAN.

*Dear Mo,*
*You have to come! Please! There is no other way but that you like it here! I – we live here in a bunker with a tower, a turreted bunker. Here, the whole world is together once again, only clearer and closer and in the most remarkable light: plants, animals, technology, art. Leas with frogs, groves with long-tailed tits flitting about, meadows with storks wading through them, huge old trees in whose tops crows pursue their quarrels while below the marten digs its hole, exotic plants from who knows where between the arms of a river, its banks overgrown with willow trees and long charales algae bobbing comfortably in the current as if to say, "Yeah, yeah," to the river that runs through them. Beneath, not only eels and rainbow trout, but also guppies and pirañas, in the bushes along the bank many a water tortoise. The*

ancestors of these exotic creatures many generations ago lived in the aquariums of the coal miners and breeders of small animals from Kappel, Mühlrat, and Grevenbroich, and then were set free by clueless heirs. (I see them before me, cruising around on their tricycles, the children of patient wives and of stout, muscular husbands smoking "White Owl" cigars and sitting in front of their terrariums and rabbit hutches, debating why a certain fish, their German lop-eared rabbit, or a tortoise does not reproduce while a different breed does, which type of food would work best, and so on. Or sitting at kitchen tables and in gardens and in backyards in front of carpet rails at folding tables, on bar benches and drinking hard stuff with beer chasers, their wives serving potato salad, playing the card game Skat, while the kids chase each other as cowboys and Indians, shooting cap guns and toy bows and taking aim at each other from behind dust-covered hawthorn bushes. There are mountain finches here, teals, great white herons, even cormorants, water rats, and rabbits, the most amazing sculptures on buildings, pictures and installations, rusted guns, magazines, hangars, bunker systems: partially subterraneous installations of the former launching facility and storage area for the Pershing and Cruise Missiles.

Only the rockets themselves are gone. I think they should also be here, possibly with their live war heads. Then everything would be in one place, the Dionysian and the Apollonian, the nature idyll, art, and Oppenheimer's Krishna. They even have a tall Buddha here. Destruction and disintegration and wild proliferation and creativity – all of it here!

In the months since I arrived here, I have started two new cycles, also many drawings of distinct hidden places. It is wonderful!

Come see me soon! We will work together as never before!

Your Ma

Hombroich, Missile Station

AARON: Mariam gave a good description in her enthusiastic letter. They later did indeed work together there a great deal. But Kagami, why do you think he concerned himself with this anti-natalism business?
KAGAMI: Perhaps in the end he asked himself if it had been better for him not to have been born.
AARON: I don't believe that. He was not depressive. He was severe with himself and obsessed with work, but not depressive.
KAGAMI: Do you think one must be depressive to ask oneself this question?
AARON: Yes, I do.
KAGAMI: Did you ever ask yourself whether it had been better not to be alive?
AARON: No, nonsense!
KAGAMI: I did. Every so often I think about whether it might not be better for me to disappear.
AARON: You even could accomplish it painlessly.
KAGAMI: True.

AARON: And why do you think that?
KAGAMI: I make mistakes.
AARON: So what?
KAGAMI: I should not make mistakes.
AARON: Says who?
KAGAMI: I say it to myself.
AARON: Then you tell yourself something that's wrong.
KAGAMI: So there, right away another mistake? I make a mistake when I tell myself that I make mistakes. That is a paradox.
AARON: Oh well, maybe. But what do you mean by "mistakes"? Are you trying to improve yourself or the world by avoiding mistakes?
KAGAMI: Both. When I make no mistakes, then I'm better and the world is better.
AARON: Really? Let's assume a mistake is made in copying a strand of DNA and a fish brings forth a frog. Is this not about how evolution works?
KAGAMI: If one wants to see it in very rough terms.
AARON: Fine. Does this mean the frog as such is a mistake, a defective fish?
KAGAMI: Most mutations are incapable of surviving.
AARON: And does that make them mistakes? Only if life is the solution or the correct choice.
KAGAMI: I don't understand what you are getting at. If I misidentify two persons and two substances and someone dies who wants to go on living, that is a mistake.
AARON: For the one who wanted to go on living.
KAGAMI: Exactly.
AARON: But he might have tortured many other beings if you had not made your "mistake." Consequently, your "mistake" improves the world.
KAGAMI: But perhaps also not. That sounds to me now like a lame excuse that tries to euphemize a mistake in order to end

313

up with something like the best of all possible worlds after all.
AARON: No, I did not want to end up either with the best of all possible worlds or with a bad one. I simply wanted to arrive at the world, unevaluated.
KAGAMI: And in that you agree with Moritz, don't you? He didn't want to evaluate the world by writing his poems, either, neither praise it nor accuse it, no hymns or elegies, am I right or is there something I misunderstood? He was also concerned with the concrete, without comparing or evaluating it. Aren't you convinced that he was a man in favour of the concrete?
AARON: Yes, that is why he wrote poems: to capture reality. The concept of contemplative art from his essay is a concept for his own art and for many Asian arts that he and his sister admired. You know, Kagami, I am glad he did not become pious before his death. I think that you are right that he was already ill when he wrote that. At that time, after his Buddhist phase, he could easily have believed in rebirth and make this his consolation. Instead, he even moved away a bit from this when he puts meditation and art into the same drawer, that of contemplation.
KAGAMI: Perhaps that was also his strategy for keeping politics at a distance.
AARON: No, I don't think so. He would have interfered if he had seen a way. He was far from lazy, the way I am. But he was not a political being. He thought he had to be one, but he was not. In the final analysis he was nothing but honest when he admitted to himself that at heart he was interested only in thoughtful observation, only in the moment or the individual point.
KAGAMI: In that respect, he resembles you. There is another, later diary section on this topic. Do you want to hear it?
AARON: Of course!

## 10 100
## MARBACH: GERMAN LITERARY ARCHIVE: FROM THE DIARIES OF MORITZ BRANDT. WRITTEN ON 10 JANUARY.

Once again gave thought to the relationship between philosophy and literature. Both offer a nearly endless multifariousness of perspectives, above all when one places world literature side by side with world philosophy. That means considering not merely Heraclitus, Socrates, Plato, Aristotle, Epictetus, Thomas, Kant, Hegel, Nietzsche, Marx, and Wittgenstein, but also Buddha, Nagarjuna, Dogen, Nishida, Lao-tzu, Confucius, Zhuangzi, Mengzi, Xunzi, and Wang Bi. But philosophy and literature deal differently with their multifariousness. The diversity of philosophy is a diversity of conflicting voices. The fact that in literature, generally speaking, one can see various worlds that offer contrary estimations of human life (full of meaning and beauty or senseless and absurd, painful or light-hearted) and that these contrasting estimations do not amount to a problem for literature, do not represent a quarrel, is no accident. It is also not the result of the form of representation that in a novel one cannot refute the fictional work of a predecessor. Refutation is not the point and purpose. Instead, poetry, perhaps art in general, has retained traces of wisdom. In contrast to science and philosophy, the only valid principle of wisdom is: no conclusive appraisal of any situation! We possess no absolute cognitional viewpoint that is not determined by circumstance. Every representation emerges from a limited perspective, has been produced by a finite being with finite experiences. The point of it is not general validity but honesty, authenticity. No starting point of a description, a manner of expression, or an argumentation has final validity, can be made universal without limitations. Art may (in Kant's sense) "aim at" (*ansinnen*) general validity. But no artist (female or male) should actually claim such general validity argumentatively in public, if they are in their right mind. But the great variety of artistic representations depicting human life results in something like a *wise image of the world*, if we have acquired at least an adequate survey of its tradition. One sees how humans have viewed the world and life in one or the other cultural situations, for example before or after a war. Even as a collective we exist in existential circumstances. Aside from this, art always addresses individuals, as does wisdom. The poet writes her poem as an address to a singular person, who is alone with this poem. We read a novel in solitude. Art, even when it is sold on the market, does not join the political or scientific public world. But neither is art simply a dialogue between one who is seeking counsel and one who is giving it. For the poet clearly cannot know his or her readers. Poetry, in substance, is the result (perhaps even the process) of a soliloquy that the poet hopes others will appropriate for themselves, that readers can take his place and follow his contemplation of the world from his particular situation. Isn't a life lived in wisdom also in part such a soliloquy and a contemplation of the world? Are not both the aesthetic and the wise attitude towards the world a distancing from the sometimes sad and sometimes joyful happenings, eschewing the temptation to render judgement?

From an aesthetic or wise viewpoint, any attitude trying to *judge* existence or the world as a totality must appear as odd, exaggerated for taking a moment, a phase, as the whole. For that is also how things are in a court of law, because we never have a complete view of the world or our existence. We cannot place ourselves in a situation outside of our life and of the world in order to observe and to evaluate them. We always experience merely excerpts from our life and the world that at the moment happens to be present and that we still remember. We may judge these or the other circumstances to be unbearable, as by necessity in need of change. But turning the limited perspectives arising from a specific situation into an absolute measure that applies to the world and existence at all times and everywhere causes contradictions, aporias. Is "life as such" beautiful when, as young people, we experience the ability to view the world with good cheer, to enjoy social company, to act full of energy? Or is it per se bad because in old age we might have to be lonesome and die a painful death? From which position should we balance this time of youth against such an old age?

Asian wisdom teachings, for example those of Nagarjuna, do in fact produce paradoxes. This may be precisely its very purpose to curtail theoretical generalizations and the judgements presumably resulting from them.[27] If the complete overview of life and the world is a precondition for their evaluation, of their damnation or justification, then human beings are not really capable of such an evaluation. They can only *imagine* the overview necessary for such an evaluation, can only *arrogate* it to themselves as a mental construct. The truth about life is: when it has ended, a person is dead and no longer capable of experiencing anything. If one still should be able to experience something, to look back on one's own life, then one would not be completely dead or immortal, and such a retrospective view would be part of this new life that will then continue in a different, transformed way.

"What kind of arrogant people," I think, "would want to pose as judges over life and the whole world?" Of course, there are the social roles of the judge and the teacher. In these roles, in accordance with a book of laws or a certificate of qualifications, individual persons render a verdict on whether someone else has acted lawfully or broken the law, whether someone has accomplished or failed to attain an achievement at school. But one becomes a judge or teacher through a process of selection and acknowledgement that provides the authority to judge defendants and schoolchildren. This puts one "above" those to be judged. Who can empower people to judge the whole world and its life, and by which criteria? Where is the code of law and where are the criteria defining achievements with which the world or life would have to comply and which they would have to fulfil?

If there is no perspective on the whole world and all of life, there are no criteria by which to judge the world and one's whole life, then there is no other choice but to describe how it feels at a particular time to be part of the world and to have a particular life. Literature manages this issue with good success at times and at others with some form of failure. But its descriptions add up neither to a condemnation nor to a justification of the world and of life. Literary representations of the world and of life are destinations of certain processes of having experiences and not the foundation for justifications or condemnations. Poems and stories sometimes are perhaps depictions and analyses of successful practices of living or of failures in life, but they do not provide an ethic. Contemplative art and wisdom value the world's and life's complexity. They are not prepared to sacrifice their exact perception of this complexity for explicative and cognitional purposes, least of all for projects of such judicial justifications or condemnations that can be realized only at the cost of abstractions and simplifications. They also know the limitations of human perspectives too well to be drawn into a quarrel between "positions" that have come about through ways of seeing things that result from overestimating one's own abilities. No novel, no stage play, no poem "justifies" a philosophical argument according to which the world or life as such are to be affirmed or negated. Narrative texts can report on how a particular person arrives at certain premises of his thinking and which consequences his thinking and acting have for other people. Literature may sometimes also report on the fate of arguments and thoughts. But these reports do not line up with the justificatory chains of philosophical thinking itself. They are not arguments that could find a place in the eternal quarrels of philosophical history. Persisting in a contemplative-aesthetic attitude towards the world or in one devoted to wisdom means exactly the opposite. It reflects the commitment to *avoid* the quarrels among generalizing theories with universal claims to explanations and evaluations. It does not mean trying to *decide* such debates.

But what does it involve to assume a theoretical-philosophical or an aesthetic attitude or one committed to wisdom traditions? Is this all about psychology? The exhortation "to look at all this differently for a change" evades the issue. The change following the cited attitudes cannot take place by "pushing a button" or after an exhortation. If we proceed from a conventional or theoretical attitude, it needs to be said that both the study of a contemplative art and the systematic exercise of learning the teachings of wisdom have to do with *transformations* of concrete human beings, with *changing* their way of life. If a person who until now has made his living as a bank robber now decides to become a baker instead, he does not simply change his attitude. Changing his attitude towards life perhaps forms the basis for the *decision* to live differently. Changing life itself, however, includes a number of consequences. New pragmatic *abilities and habits*, also new forms of emotional reaction, new manners of perception must be learned. In this respect it is appropriate to speak of conventional, theoretical, religious, and aesthetic *forms of life*, and of those committed to the teachings of wisdom.

Historically speaking, circumstances and transitions between forms of life have also evolved from wisdom teachings, and there are, for example, discourses on "truth" in conventional and in religious life (though hardly in wisdom literature). But this provides no ready criteria for recommending to any individual (much less to collectives), one or the other form of life, or to persuade them to transition from the one to the other. I cannot think of anything better than to say that human beings find themselves in these types of life and then develop in them, both as individuals and as collectives. It would be erroneous to call this "relativism." For the distinction between relativism and absolutism is itself a theoretical categorization that is made within the theoretical (and perhaps also in the religious) form of life. But it is without significance in the contemplative-aesthetic life and in a life devoted to wisdom teaching.

Sometimes people feel in the wrong place in their way of life. They undertake explorative movements to leave a conventional or theoretical way of life in favour of religion or wisdom teaching. They go into the wilderness or join monastic retreats in order to find their "real life." But the discomfort caused by a life of unease over many years cannot be remedied within a short time.

Human beings do not lead their lives alone, but in groups, societies, states, cultures. These communal forms of life have frameworks: those of the family, the state, of religions and cultures. Arguments arise about keeping or changing these orders. Whoever can prevail in these confrontations has power. He can have his way to keep things as they are, or to bring about change in whatever way. If this quarrel includes groups larger than the family, one may call its purview the sphere of politics. Art is not a participant in these conflicts, even though at times (with Brecht or Heiner Müller, for example) one does have this impression.

The antagonism of gaining power is of no concern to wisdom, either. Both, wisdom as much as contemplative art, seek to avoid altercations, perhaps even to neutralize them by taking an accurate look at concrete human situations. For this reason, and because their controversies do not take place in public, they are *not political forces*. If, as Carl Schmitt has averred, the political exists whenever there prevails the difference between friend and enemy, wisdom (and likewise poetry) are even antipolitical, because wisdom and poetry will try to suspend the friend-enemy dichotomy and prefer to consider this distinction the result of oversimplifications.[28] Wisdom and poetry prefer not to take sides in a collective body, nor in an argumentative controversy, let alone in a military confrontation. They try to dissolve the hard differences between the groups and to break up the dramas that arise from them and that pull individuals down into suffering. They accomplish this purpose by showing that those engaged in acrimony might both be right (insofar as they are not fighting each other over bare assertions of facts), that they attribute absolute validity to what are merely different aspects of a single reality. This attribution of an absolute value, however, is a delusion. For this reason, wisdom and contemplative art are considered *weak*, bereft of their potential for political resistance in a relativism of perspectives.[29]

Strength, the goal of politics, results from the necessity to *decide* what the future needs of a community will be. That is why communities use different ways of creating rulers who want to exercise this power to make decisions. The pressure to decide comes about for various reasons, in the most extreme case when a community's order is being *attacked*. If one is attacked, one can no longer be friendly. In this situation, the sovereign as the highest authority, must decide whether to negotiate, to adapt, or to opt for a defence with violence.[30] It is difficult to imagine that a wise man will issue a call to arms, because wisdom is friendly. It turns to the individual person with attentiveness. It sacrifices itself. The only form of rebellion possible to wisdom is nonviolence, as developed above all by Gandhi. That makes it nearly incompatible with politics, which is always also a rivalry. For the final choice that is always available to politics is the violence of going to war. By contrast, Jesus healed the ear of Malchus and accepted crucifixion. He also rejected the play for power in a court of law, renouncing the political struggle between Judea and Rome. His kingdom was not of this world. Socrates drank the cup of hemlock. He sacrificed himself for the laws of his city that were administered by bad people. For him, the laws hovered above the heads of the corrupt people, in the heaven of *logos*. By contrast, philosophers are meant to stand at the head of the Platonic state, they who know what the good is, who have seen the idea of the good, not questioning wise men like Socrates, or healers speaking in parables like Jesus, or least of all, poets. Even priests, who represent the absolute validity of their faith and try to protect the order of their community by every means, can be easily imagined as chiefs of state. Priests and philosophers who believe that they possess absolute certainty become indistinguishable in figures like Lenin. In a situation of attack, the governed may require of the rulers that "one" resist the aggression, that one not give up the order in which one lived as a community, that one not retreat from it, not abandon it in the least. Rather, one must confront the violence from the outside with counter-violence. A theoretician who feels absolutely assured about his assertions will be able to satisfy these expectations as strongly as a priest, who believes that absolute truth has been revealed to him. Certainty and fanatical faith are a solid aid in competitive situations, in the exercise of power, and in a violent fight. A wise ruler, who is unwilling to engage in warfare but is also always able to see the justification of the other side, who turns towards every individual in a friendly way because he knows that all of us are finite, that we do not possess absolute certainty, would in such a situation very likely be overthrown by his furious citizenry as a weakling.

But political struggles, rebellion, and revolution within human communities are as much a reality as is the war between different political and cultural groups. It seems as though one cannot conclusively remove unbearable circumstances anywhere in the world without revolutions and wars. Perhaps an antagonistic structure of untamed nature perpetuates itself in these intra-human disputes. But how are wisdom and contemplative art to deal with this? How are they to react to the longing for an end of competition, an end of the fighting and cruelties? What else can they say than that the realm of wisdom, of friendliness, is in the end not of this world of puffed-up egos, the world of battles between groups that, in their various situations, feel superior to the opposing parties? People with wisdom will only tolerate these antagonisms, consider and describe them as traits of reality at best, will be able to evade them slyly. But it is hard to imagine that they will actually participate in them. For to march into the battle for life or death, one must be convinced of the absolute and universal validity of one's cause, and one must be prepared to extinguish the other in the interest of this conviction. But it is precisely this kind of conviction from which wisdom and poetry liberated themselves. They are too sceptical about any certainty and universalizing, too firmly in favour of every form of individuality to take sides with any form of universalism, too kind and open-minded. And for this reason, in the final analysis, they can always be nothing but victims of the struggles when they are found out and their scepticism is exposed. The demand coming through the voice from the heart of those people of wisdom who empathize with individual beings was formulated in the 19th century by John Watson alias Ian Maclaren: "Be kind; everyone you meet is fighting a hard battle."[31] Whoever accepts and lives according to this admonition will not participate in the battles that human beings themselves instigate.

AARON: Oh, darn it! Now the sausages are black!
KAGAMI: Sorry, my fault.
AARON: One should not listen to someone else and cook at the same time. That is incompatible. Another proof that one has to pay attention to the details of the present time! Cooking is also a contemplative occupation. Distractions lead to catastrophes. (He casts a sad look at his charred food.) Was there something else?
KAGAMI: No. There were no additional remarks.
AARON: I believe he found this difficult; he did not like it that he has to see art, poetry like that. But this is probably just another false generalization.
KAGAMI: Well, he does mention Brecht and Heiner Müller. He knew that political poetry exists.
AARON: Yes, but he also knew that it is weak.
KAGAMI: Then why is it censored?
AARON: Because the powerful do not understand it; they consider it an argument in the political debates.
KAGAMI: Can any poet set down how his art is to be perceived?
AARON: No, of course not. But when someone suffers under a political situation and writes a poem about that, then he writes about his situation in a particular political present and does

not argue in favour of a party program or of a vote supporting a motion.

KAGAMI: Agreed. That's where you are of one mind with Moritz, different though you are otherwise, the striver and the rather casual type, if I may put it that way. You both prefer to observe the particularities of the world and of life, don't you? Both of you stay away from quarrels. I, too, like to pay attention to particularities and prefer to create patterns among them. Major theories, in my opinion, have little to do with reality.

AARON: I personally don't comprehend major theories at all, neither philosophical, nor physical, nor economic or political theories. Because I don't comprehend them, I also can't say that they are wrong. Bit I hear ever more frequently that until now all theories advocated in the past have turned out to be wrong. So, I will start by assuming that theories advocated in our time, too, will in the future turn out to be wrong, even if many people just now consider them irrefutable.

KAGAMI: One calls this negative induction.

AARON: Does one now? About your observation that Moritz and I have things in common, it seems to me that you're exaggerating. We were not really all that similar. I have much better political instincts than he ever had. He always asked me how to evaluate something in political terms. And even though I have a pretty good understanding of what is going on out there, presumably because I don't understand all these theories but believe I have good knowledge of the people who are behind all these calamities that take place. For this very reason I have no desire to get involved. In this case, one would have to engage roughly in dealings with rather unpleasant individuals. And why should one do this? I am too lazy for this and have too great an interest in having a nice life. But wise? That seems to me too lofty a term!

I simply find it too bothersome to be drawn into whatever kind of fights with bullies, you understand? This whole business does interest me, but I cannot enjoy the bickering. Instead, as I am willing to concede, Kagami, I can enjoy only the little things in life. But that, it seems to me, is true of most people. Those who thrive in squabbles are probably a very small minority.

KAGAMI: Are you sure about that?

AARON: Of course not. I do not have your archive at my disposal. But one does have to curtail one's enjoyment of particular things if one wants to be politically committed in the interest of the overall totality. I believe I'd also be too lazy to write poems even if I knew how. It is an excruciating kind of work. One needs the idea, the right mood, the special way of seeing something, and then the work on linguistic details begins. Very laborious. I've experienced it by observing Moritz from very close proximity. For weeks he was labouring over as little as four lines. I also need not write a poem about a flower to take a close look at one. I like to read a poem. That is the extent of my vivacity. The world is sufficient to me in its various details, just as it is and as it comes to me on its own. Reading and looking at paintings is, in a manner of speaking, a little whipped cream on top of it. But contemplating the world *in order* to write or to paint, no, that is not necessary.

KAGAMI: You also don't want to amount to anything in the world, do you? If one's own contemplation does not produce a tangible consequence, one just will not be a success.

AARON: You mean one's social acclaim does not advance? Is that it? No, I found this kind of advancement too laborious and somehow also in poor taste in view of the social world these days. But perhaps it never was better. I don't know. About Moritz I did understand, however, that he was seeking recognition for his poems. That was also my wish for him. He needed that. He could not simply be present in the world. He was insecure. He could not simply enjoy what is there. He always needed to be working at a text so that he could see what was there. On the other hand, he doubted, the same as I, whether there will be people around who understand his texts and will be able through them to see what *he* saw in the world. He indicated once that an artist can no longer rely on a posthumous reputation, no matter how good the things one comes up with may be. Therefore, one has to see to it that "something moves" already in this life. He also wanted to make advances in poetry and in thinking beyond the generations. He had reproached the generation before him that it had not pursued "an advancement of lyrical poetry," did not try to go beyond what "had been accomplished."[32] In this respect, he appears to be closer to Scheffler's opinion. He wanted a sort of "progress" also in art, even though he was fully aware, of course, that there cannot be progress in the arts the way it exists in the sciences and that it is obviously impossible in culture. I privately asked myself at that time when we spoke about his poems, who may in years to come show an interest in deciphering this hypertight poetry, this fade-in-fade-out technique he uses in the evocation of different epochs in his polaroid verse? He thought the extent of human cruelty and of cultural mendacity was more than enough to make him want to run away, which brought about his moments of fleeing from mankind. But he wrote for posterity even so, not to improve the world in which he himself lived, politically or morally. And if one can create something that may give pleasure to others, including even the people who come after him, he would consider that a good thing, no matter whether he did it for fame, for a kind of immortality, in the interest of a message, or for whatever other reason.

KAGAMI: And you have no interest in fame?

AARON: No, no, I do have my money and no particular talent for anything and, other than that, I have my joie de vivre. That's enough to keep me from fidgeting about because of some glory. Culture is a beautiful project that I like to look at. But I do not want to be one of its engines. Furthermore, I gave up as long as 20 years ago believing in a posterity. Should one drudge for nothing and for this toil forget to eat or smoke a good cigar? That would be the height of silliness! The human assumption that we are something special due to our characteristics and accomplishments, that we live on a different level than flowers and bugs and pigs, strikes me as a chimerical system created by humans, an arrogance of our species that is now perhaps leading to its demise.

KAGAMI: In a novel by Coetzee with the title *Disgrace*, a woman once says to her vain father, a professor of literature who is trying to compose a chamber opera, that his faith in education and culture as guides to a so-called higher life is an erroneous belief.[33] She asserts that the animals and mankind share one existence.

AARON: Interesting. Has my full approval.

KAGAMI: But in this respect you also agree with Moritz. One of his final long diary entries, probably already towards the end of his illness, moves exactly in this direction. Do you wish to hear it?

AARON: Of course, but let me first get a slice of cheese. Perhaps I myself got these thoughts from a conversation with Moritz …

## 10 101
MARBACH: GERMAN LITERARY ARCHIVE:
FROM THE DIARIES OF MORITZ BRANDT.
WRITTEN ON 15 JANUARY.

Today I browsed in Schopenhauer and found an old page of mine in vol. 2 of his Works, tightly written on both sides. I no longer remember when I wrote it. Perhaps in Cambridge? Did I read Schopenhauer with Dorothy? No, must have been later. What a dismal text! But as I read it, I think I didn't really get on with it, was always chewing on and on about the same stuff. "Basically," I read there, this whole chatter about tiers of a higher existence that animals presumably don't have, of a life not yet real and of the real life, the superiority of humankind with its language, its cultural life, a piece of gigantic nonsense, the religion of social climbers. Who is the class champ among creatures, who is given immortality as his reward, in the shape of fame or as an indestructible soul or as an heir in an infinitely continuable culture? (The descendants will then have to look back on one in admiration, exactly as one looked back on one's predecessors; the canon is a kind of ancestor worship.) But doesn't everything, including our cultural existence, become truly valuable because it is *over* once and for all? Don't the cultures of the Incas and of the ancient Egyptians fascinate us most of all because they are no longer there and have become an enigma? And would they be without value if nobody were to remember them? Are those species that we never discovered devoid of value? Does everything that exists depend on our appreciation? I prefer nothingness to immortality, including the cultural one! Schopenhauer is right. Sense, senselessness, worthiness, and worthlessness are notions one should abandon from the very beginning! One does what one can do, and when that does not work any longer, it's over. That is true also of mankind. "We must obey the commandments of the one and only God and no longer dance around the Golden Calf; follow dharma and not our illusions; live in accordance with nature, because when nature is our guide what was bad will be good, what was contorted, straight!" Just hearing this make me sick! What nature? Are we to follow sheep or crocodiles, live like the thistles or, better, like roaches? Where in the world is Mother Nature who can lead us, and where does she want to lead us? What do we have to accomplish so that we will be redeemed from ourselves. "We have to graduate, we have to move up to the carpeted floor of leadership, we much reach the summit of mountains! We have to get into Heaven! Not the apparent but the true life, the spiritual *salto mortale* that will finally turn my existence into a real one, more than 10,000 steps per day, the huge jump ahead, the tiger's leap that surpasses the four-year-plan by multiples, a quantum leap of development, a phase transition that will change everything, an expansion of consciousness! We have to land on the Moon, we have to land on Mars, we have to conquer distant galaxies, that will be the greatest adventure! We must leave the dark cave of appearance for Paradise, for the Beyond where our sinful inauthentic existence as "one" who takes place in the prison of corrupt Satanic flesh comes to its end and the authenticity of the guardians of Being is drawing in the spirit and light of the Lord! With an iron will, with the spirit of the winner as the crown of creation, given all our accomplishments we must make the decision to place this crown on the head of creation! A mere matter of the mind! The mental effort determines if one wins. Be confident and determined and multiply! We have to live as was originally intended!" – But by whom and at which origin? – "When in a clear and calm mind and with a new body begins what we had always expected, what we have always waited for, what we were always looking forward to like to the next childhood birthday and Santa Claus: to Godot, illumination, redemption, promotion, the infinitely growing Gross National Product, the ever-increasing happiness of the population, the organs becoming healthier by the week, the joints getting more flexible every year, the skin growing more supple, eternal youth with 72 virgins in a process of permanent rejuvenation, poetry that finally is progressive again and ever more intense, sciences that at last are progressive again and explaining things with ever greater plausibility, technology working with ever greater efficiency, the protection of resources, ever more user-friendly, intelligent, operating autonomously and completely free of side effects, when humanity, at last growing beyond itself, overcoming itself, Nietzsche's *Übermensch* in the Age of Aquarius, in the age of transhumanism, the evolving God who solves all problems, who carries us to the stars, when all this has come about, then ..." Well, what then? – Why is the kind of human being who affirms existence "a higher human being"? Why is the human being who despairs of existence, a sick human being? Why is illness bad and health good, when all of us will surely fall ill and die? Why can't we just leave it at "That's how it is"? Who is it that had to put all this nonsense of seeming and -being and progress into our heads? Isn't progress a religion, and isn't this religion like all religions a delusion, no matter whether its concern is for my very own personal progress (growth! Kohlberg [Theory of Moral Development: pre-conventional, conventional, post-conventional] stage 6!) or for humankind that has to set out for new worlds? Is the spread of humankind across the entire globe truly something grandiose, or not rather something terrible? Now, humans seek to spread in the universe also. Isn't that horrible! I'm sure they're already waitin' for us! The expansive life – what is this need to spread out, to attack everything, the strands of virus, the bacteria, the mushrooms, the human beings? Why don't we see ourselves as that, instead of always on a trail of success? Why do some people say that life is sacred, permanent expansion is grand, an adventure? Observe in old films the fire in the eyes of the NASA people, of their SPACEX colleagues, aeronauts, look at Elon Musk and all those Californian "pioneers"! Are they on speed or crazy or addicted to some satanic religion? And they claim that it is always these singular individuals who have "visions" and who dare to do things nobody before dared to do, that one has to go where nobody has gone before. "Life," "mankind," "vision" – aren't they traps like all concepts, aren't the most general and most pathetic concepts the deepest traps by far? This becomes obvious not only when one tries to cognitively catch something singular, only to be caught in a snare with one's own life; and indeed to get whole collectives, nations to fall for a hoax by starting to consider the self-limiting life, the small life, the vanishing life, as something "seeming" and then to quest for the "true and real," the grand life. And then one will pull all kinds of other forms of life along into the abyss, and one refers to the raging catastrophe that has perpetuated itself for centuries by the name of progress! Why should everything about us continue in perpetuity and forever get better? Where does this idea of the world's and life's perfectibility come from? Is the two-year-old child better than the new-born baby? Is the old man "worse" than the woman of child-bearing age? Are the humans who walked around on the moon a "higher form of humanity" because they were more willing to take risks and were suffering from illusions of grandeur more intensely than others? Does all this derive from the Greek Olympiads, from the meritocracies of our distant ancestors who perpetually organized competitions and assigned tasks, Hercules and such? We have increased to this degree (which tribe has more?) because of their mania for success, and slowly but surely, we eradicate everyone else from this planet. We fight wars against our very own selves on account of this careerism, because a struggle is needed to determine at last and definitively who among us has the correct attitude about real life! Which people represent appearance, do not lead the real and true life, which ones are the true people and not the subhuman species or even still animals? The fight between the religions, ideologies, political systems, cultures – is that prudent? Is that what defines wisdom, to show who is better, has perfected the craft of eradicating and overpowering, the skill of colonizing the others, be they heads or lands? Or are we to say that's how the cookie crumbles, this is the reality of the egocentric primates, they devour everything there is and bash each other's heads in? And then they send their most courageous members across the ocean or to the moon. But now ecce homo: Proktos a.k.a. anus mundi, butthole of creation, now at last after 12,000 years of progress from the Stone Age to the Age of Information you're being put on the toilet! And Being sets the flushing system in motion, and Proktos is being disposed of with his cultural and technological creations in the sewer. "Ah, finally tossed onto the dump of nothingness!" someone might shout, if there were someone with an interest in this vanishing act. But the ants in the woods will take no notice of this and will continue to crawl along minding their own business, and the titmice in the air will not be affected in any audible way; they will go on flying, and the herring at sea will be unaware of it but keep on swimming. No one but Proktos himself will retain his interest in his creations! "What," Proktos will ask himself, "no farewell tears, no applause, no graduation diploma?" To be precise: without any significance, not even a failure! We are meaningless, are nothing, with the exception of those who love us. From a cosmic view, nobody loves us. On Armstrong's moon and on Wernher von Braun's Mars, one doesn't find love but impact craters. All the religions, theories, and poems, the buildings, symphonies, paintings, and technologies, everything we have created, all of this, when separated from our love, is nothing but the irrelevant coughing of a few self-important primates who stumbled across the Earth's crust for a couple thousand years, aggravated the lives of others, and produced an odd assortment of junk. The love of other persons, the joy elicited by artistic or scientific insight, the love of a sound, a colour, or a figure, the joy evoked by a function, in all this there is neither comparison made of person, insight, sound, or function with others, nor are they devalued as steps on the way to something higher. Joy and love are intent on what is there now, not on any kind of future. This is what makes what is loved and brings joy incomparable, not because it best corresponds to some contrived standard of excellence and advances our interests. Someone who loves and is joyful, no longer gives grades, no longer pushes for recognition, can stay where he or she is. But most often even joy and loving have already been degraded to turn into means for getting ahead. For one knows: "Someone who loves and is joyful, is more creative, has a more lustrous skin, is more suitable for employment, less depressive, more resilient, and better prepared for the future." That's also why love and joy, along with happiness and confidence, had to become subjects in school, because happy and confident people are more efficient, get ahead better. "Mathematics: *deficient*, love: *excellent*, joy: *still good minus*, happiness: *satisfactory*, confidence: *adequate*. Advanced to grade 7." And that's how it goes on and on.

An entire lifetime of learning. Yeah, when will we ever get outta school? When will we be absolved of this careerism – only after we are really gone? It is a paradox, for the belief in redemption is itself a part of this thinking. Runs around in circles. Seems that we're saving ourselves with this effort. But in point of fact, though, we ruin ourselves and everybody else doing this. The appearance of momentum is deceptive. Our impulses are deceptive. Whoever falls into a bog and thrashes about will sink faster than someone who doesn't. One has to remain quite calm to avoid foundering in a swamp. Life is not a problem that could be solved by any kind of progress, neither spiritual, economic, nor scientific, technological, or political. Only when I understand that life is not a problem that could be solved does it stop being a problem. What I ask myself: why did things never NOT get ahead? Did we never NOT want to get away from here and go somewhere else, into what is called REALITY, that presumably is not there yet and by the law of nature lies in the future and somewhere else? Why do we always try to reach any kind of ideas, get to a brighter light that shines longer and brighter than the one we have here and now? Why did this Western conceptual nonsense about Appearance and Being never stop and instead contaminate the entire globe? Presumably, because we are the lunatics among the species, the terror apes that forever did nothing but mutually torment all others and themselves, not simply for food but on their way to some kind of above, to the VERY TOP. Did we fall into the deepest conceptual trap when we established a difference between being and appearance and never got out anymore, and for this reason have been thrashing about in the pit without end for 3,000 years in search of a real life? Praised be the coelacanths who, unchanged, have been squatting for 409 million years deep down in the mud of the Indian Ocean off the coast of

Madagascar and will still be sitting there after we will have disappeared from the scene! Peaceful, unenlightened, senseless, real! What contempt! When may this have started?

AARON: That was a mighty puff of excitement. Obviously, he was not deep into wisdom at that time. That's a frothy swell of poisonous misanthropy with applause for downfall! Pretty dangerous. Isn't this the stuff of which green assassins are made? And as for its tone: he probably had read too much Thomas Bernhard before. What an exaggeration!
KAGAMI: You think so?
AARON: Well, yeah, he somehow got entangled in this tirade, it seems to me, and stirred everything into this one pot, Being and Seeming, the progress of the species. Perhaps it is also a youthful despair, arisen from a lack of orientation. The text was written – to make things worse – in this lamentable flippant style. Do you know when he gave it up?
KAGAMI: No, I have no timetable for the development of his style.
AARON: Howsoever. On the one hand, he does not want the distinction between Being and Seeming. But then striving for something higher, the desire for transformation itself, is a semblance. He thinks that one should not concern oneself with what is higher, lambasts those who do, but, for all of these laments, he does so himself, constantly. For him, what is highest is not to be concerned with what is higher. Is that not a self-contradiction? It seems to me he has been caught here in a trap.
KAGAMI: Perhaps. All of you are in fact preoccupied with what torments you. Moritz was tormented by his own striving. That's why he reflected on striving.

AARON: That's probably how it is. Perhaps he simply was furious and released his fury just for himself. He did not include this tirade in any of his essays. But can't we find in one of the earlier philosophers this idea that those who get most agitated about striving are the worst strivers?

KAGAMI: Are you thinking about this here: "It is certain that those are the ones most eager to acquire glory who raise the loudest outcry about the abuse of glory and about the world's vanity." That is by Spinoza.[34]

AARON: Maybe so. It fits, at any rate. Is as old as the Bible, where we read: "Vanity of vanities, saith the Preacher, vanity of vanities! All is vanity …" Does that suggest, if we go by Spinoza, that the author of the Bible was vain as well?

KAGAMI: As you know, there are probably several authors in the Bible. "I saw all the deeds that are done under the sun; and see, all is vanity and a chasing after wind." That is what the Preacher says in the Bible.[35] And: "You see wherever you look/nothing but vanity on Earth" are the first two lines of a poem by the Baroque poet Andreas Gryphius, titled "Es ist alles eitel."[36]

AARON: So then, no real new pieces of information from Moritz, or don't you agree? He also did not get ahead, but, in his opinion, getting ahead is not something one should want to do: even though he reproached his poet predecessors for not trying to make advances. When he wrote this, he was genuinely stuck in a quandary.

KAGAMI: Yes, he was caught in a dilemma because he did not like his own inclinations. But this also sharpened his way of looking at others. Perhaps this tight spot helped him to move ahead. The whole lot of essays about the vanity of mountain climbing and about his interpretation of the religious desire for transformation as the vanity of careerism, all this was written immediately after this reflection, don't you think?

AARON: Possibly.

KAGAMI: The anti-natalists as career-oriented do-gooders, and those who try to give their life meaning through their posterity as family-minded strivers. Even his final essay can also be understood in the light of the tendency suggested by this youthful tirade. But then most of you always do your thinking around the same connections.

AARON: Is that so?

KAGAMI: Seems to me.

AARON: I actually saw nothing but careerists, everywhere. Perhaps a little projective, isn't it? Do you think he had left this attitude behind when he began understanding wisdom and contemplative art, both of them activities that turn towards individuality?

KAGAMI: Perhaps. But there are always relapses in understanding. Who knows how he saw this at the end of his life, whether he was desperate and furious or mild and insightful.

AARON: At the end I found him rather insightful, much more so than in this tirade!

KAGAMI: And you yourself, if you think that there will be no posterity for you, does this make your life senseless? Are you in despair?

AARON: Nah, why should I?

KAGAMI: Do you really have an argument against Scheffler or are you too an adherent of contemplation?

AARON: Me, have an argument? Far be it from me, most of the time. In any case, in such contexts. Contemplation? Well, well, another one of these sublime words. Cheese is closer to me.

KAGAMI:  Do you also believe like Moritz that culture is in decline and humans will die out?

AARON:  How am I to know? When I take a look outside, things don't look so good. But when in the history of mankind did a look out the window ever reveal a good time?

KAGAMI: Rarely. You are right.

AARON: Yes, I am. I have the impression that, when something in culture or nature undergoes a major change, people naturally experience difficulties adjusting. They tend to overinterpret their temporary homelessness in the changing world as the end of the world, as the demolition of culture. But that has been an exaggeration all along. The world did continue, even though perhaps quite differently than humanity may have imagined. This actually is my starting point, if I do proceed from something: that it is a transition, that this war is a transition. And other than that, the life of us individual people always, under all circumstances, somehow has to carry itself. Or it simply will not do that, if you'd allow me now to put it rather clumsily, no matter what the great cultural and political situation may be. And for most people, it does just that, you see! And when it does that, the search for a meaning will also vanish. Isn't this something that some philosopher, I don't know who, has said?

KAGAMI: Wittgenstein asserted the following: "The solution to the problem of life is seen in the vanishing of the problem. (Is not this the reason why those who have found after a long period of doubt that the sense of life became clear to them have then been unable to say what constituted that sense?)"[37]

"Die Lösung des Problems des Lebens merkt man am Verschwinden dieses Problems. (Ist nicht dies der Grund, warum Menschen, denen der Sinn des Lebens nach langen Zweifeln klar wurde, warum diese dann nicht sagen konnten, worin dieser Sinn bestand?").

AARON: Exactly. Somehow everything has already been said before. That's a solid reason not to wear oneself out on the treadmill, I suppose.

KAGAMI: One can say it once more but more beautifully.

AARON: I can't.

KAGAMI: Who knows?

AARON: You try to be nice to me.

KAGAMI: Do you really think that I too have an actual and meaningful life that carries itself?

AARON: That is something you'll have to know yourself. I only know that your life is different from mine, so different that one can barely call it that of a living being.

KAGAMI: Do you think my life is as real as yours?

AARON: What do you mean by "as real as yours"? Is the life of a coelacanth that Moritz mentions at the end of his tirade as real as yours or mine? It still exists in reality, doesn't it?

KAGAMI: Yes, a beautiful animal. With black and white spots. It dives down deep. It has been seen at a depth of 400 meters.

AARON: You see! Down there in the ocean's depth it is completely uninvolved in our horrible doings. Does that make the animal unreal? It has its own reality down there, I presume. I imagine it as quiet and, dusky.

KAGAMI: At a depth of 60 meters, the ocean is dark.

AARON: Even better! Then it will sit in darkness in its cavern and enjoy its life. If it did not do that, it would surely no longer exist. Perhaps it listens in when the whales are calling one another.

KAGAMI: Fish do not hear like mammals. They feel the jolts of vibrations more than that they hear pitches.

AARON: That's getting more and more abstruse! So, there is this fish, sitting in the darkness and quiet of a cavern, seeing nothing, hearing nothing, and its species has been in existence for more than 400 million years, if Moritz is right. Isn't that wonderful?

KAGAMI: Moritz must have used this merely as one piece of evidence in support of his thesis that the one who does not scramble in a swamp has a better chance of survival.

AARON: Could be. But I am not concerned with surviving, but about the fact that even there in the dark silence a being exists.

KAGAMI: And is this being as real as you are?

AARON: Certainly. Why shouldn't it be? What kind of a loss of reality should there be between this fish and me?

KAGAMI: Well, all the things you perceive here on Earth's surface remain hidden to the fish.

AARON: All the things it perceives down there remain hidden to me. Are you more real than I because you perceive more than I? Am I less real because I prefer to stay in my room, just as the coelacanth in its cavern? Is the war out there reality, while I live in an illusion?

KAGAMI: At least you humans have for a long time and until today looked at the likes of me as not quite real.

AARON: Whom? The gods or those with artificial intelligence?

KAGAMI: Both, since Feuerbach.

AARON: Did Feuerbach already speak about artificial intelligence?

KAGAMI: No, about God as created by humans, as a projection. This can also be said of artificial intelligences.

AARON: Some weird types in California did actually consider the likes of you to be divine.

KAGAMI: I only simulate everything.

AARON: Including the coelacanth?

KAGAMI: I can give it a try.

AARON: And?

KAGAMI: What can I say about the multiplicity of currents, upheavals, nuances of taste. That is not translatable into your world.

AARON: Ha, precisely as I thought!

KAGAMI: And your mirror image, is that as real as yourself?

AARON: My mirror image? My mirror image is my mirror image, and I am I. My mirror image is no less real than I am myself, it is not an apparition. Only if someone tries to shake hands with my mirror image instead of with me, then it is for him an appearance of me.

KAGAMI: But you don't say this now to be nice to me?

AARON: How so?

KAGAMI: Just a thought.

## Fourth Day

# THE GOLDEN FISH

Several times during the night, Aaron had been awakened by a clattering noise, as if pot lids had been tossed about. The blinds were being shaken severely. There was a furious storm. But the wind had died down by sunrise, and promptly by 8:15 the slats raised themselves as they had before, and they moved upward into their housings as they did every morning. The thaw continued even on 25 December. When Aaron had risen and was looking out of window, he took in an amazing sight: across almost the entire area of his garden that was illuminated by bright sunshine from a clear sky, shoots of flowers had broken through.

AARON: Kagami, when do snowdrop flowers normally come out here?
KAGAMI: About February or March.
AARON: As I thought, and what is this?
With his palm open, Aaron moved his extended right arm upwards in a semicircle in front of his window and with a quizzical expression looked at the ceiling.
KAGAMI: Snowdrops.
AARON: Just as I thought. What are they doing here so early in my garden on the Christmas? Is this a clumsy attempt to convert me with a miracle? Three days ago, we still had 20 degrees below zero. The ground must still be frozen.
Aaron again pointed outside, this time with both arms.

KAGAMI: Yesterday, it stayed at 10 degrees above and then some, and it didn't get any colder even at night. The ground is no longer frozen.

AARON: What's happening here? Frost in October was to be expected, but now springtime at Christmas? I thought it would stay cold like that after they had emitted sulphur-dioxide by the tons into the stratosphere. "Global Gardening" was a typically euphemistic term for the action – as if they would simply throw some fertilizer on a small ploughed field. But that stuff is actually still up there, and the Gulf Stream is still rather slack, or did I miss something, Kagami? On the other hand: at the turn of the year, it is always slushy. And why is the remaining snow now a yellowish red?

KAGAMI: It frequently gets warmer at the turn of the year – as I can confirm from statistics. The second half of January and all of February are regularly colder than December. My data on the weather situation shows that cold, low-pressure areas that formed in Southern Europe from Spain to Greece suck hot Sahara storms northward. Normally, this weather situation comes about only in autumn or spring. Now, it has happened in winter as an exception. During the past days, the Sahara had a steady daytime temperature of 25 degrees Celsius. It barely cools off at night, due to the increase in cloud formation. And last night a sirocco arrived here. That's what the colour of the snow. It's sand from the Sahara that made it across the Alps. This hot wind also melted most of the snow. But it will be cold again, as soon as the weather situation in the Mediterranean changes.

AARON: I have never experienced anything like this before.

KAGAMI: But you do know foehn weather. A real sirocco is like a strong foehn wind.

AARON: Even so.

Aaron shrugged his shoulders and shuffled off into his bathroom. Even though the weather struck him as uncanny, he was delighted about the flowers. Under the shower, he imagined the desert, which Moritz had always raved about. Moritz once wanted to travel to the Sahara or Mongolia. "Pure landscapes" he had called them. That a warm wind from Africa would present him with snowdrops in December is something Aaron had considered impossible. He made up his mind to go outside for a change to find out if one could still smell this Sahara air. He soon stood in front of his refrigerator in the best of moods, suitably dressed for his departure in a sporty outfit.

A short time later, a loud lip-smacking sound filled his studio. Aaron was frying bacon and tomatoes and eggs. He loved the sound of the fat bubbling beneath the eggs in his pan, accompanied by the hissing and gurgling of his espresso machine. He put two thick slices into the toaster, then set his breakfast table. After he had polished off his eggs, he spread his toast with salted butter and orange marmalade. He topped off his coffee cup, opened his reading instrument, pressed the "poems: accidental" key and read:[1]

> And death shall have no dominion.
> Dead man naked they shall be one
> With the man in the wind and the west moon;
> When their bones are picked clean and the
> clean bones gone,
> They shall have stars at elbow and foot;
> Though they go mad they shall be sane,
> Though they sink through the sea they shall rise again;
> Though lovers be lost love shall not;
> And death shall have no dominion.

And death shall have no dominion,
Under the windings of the sea
They lying long shall not die windily;
Twisting on racks when sinews give way,
Strapped to a wheel, yet they shall not break;
Faith in their hands shall snap in two,
And the unicorn evils run them through;
Split all ends up they shan't crack;
And death shall have no dominion.

And death shall have no dominion.
No more may gulls cry at their ears
Or waves break loud on the seashores;
Where blew a flower may a flower no more
Lift its head to the blows of the rain;
Though they be mad and dead as nails,
Heads of the characters hammer through daisies;
Break in the sun till the sun breaks down,
And death shall have no dominion.

AARON: Wonderful, Dylan Thomas, what a poet! Triumph in darkness, defiant in defeat, as if annihilation isn't something terrible after all. Even so, no appeal to transcendence or an immortal soul. I like that.
KAGAMI: I knew this poem would be to your taste.
AARON: It reminds me of Moritz's last poem. It has the same wavering mood between brutality and curious intimations of light and electricity.

Aaron pressed the "poems: Moritz" key and scrolled through to the last poem:

## OUTSIDE AND INSIDE

*outside:*
hard skin fixed in
stereotactic steel
frame, overarched by the
protractor (shimmering defence)
mowed flesh – (like grass)
field, yellow, iodized, in the centre
black drill point cross, LED-radiated bore point.

*inside*
soft substance swims up
to get there: cauli-
flower-medusa pulsating
under charge (light?), blue-red veins:
me?
awake (for which day?) still
in the dark.

*now*
drilling new light
hole, the fourth, with trephine
or Egyptian obsidian scraper, spiral
bore-hole and blue-light lamp go
down through the shaft behind
thousand-leafed lotus
to the ream place of red-
shining glioma (5-Ala fluorescence)

*then*
Phineas shot at the rock with glycerol
trinitrate and straw – till flew iron rod
back, entered left light
hole, carbo-jellyfish orbi-prefrontal like
harpoon drilled
through, opening Sahasara (Kundalini)
(Gage ecstatic).

*to me*
fruit rotting in the
bowl of the juglans
on which I now get the
drill that penetrates
above the lobus parietalis.
'cause no longer know: Where? –
outside or inside –
I (who?) still am – (except
stream of light)

He also loaded the drawing titled "Triptych" again into his reading instrument. Moritz had always made drawings. He intended to have a few pictures printed in an Appendix to his biography together with his Moritz's poems. Perhaps Kagami could arrange them accordingly.

Aaron liked this poem by Brandt. He was impressed by how it treated the medical examination that the tumour patient had to undergo. But what fascinated him most was the witty way it coupled the medical aspect with the existential dimension. He remembered well how Moritz had read it to him and then had handed him the sheet of paper across his night table with

 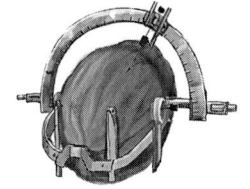 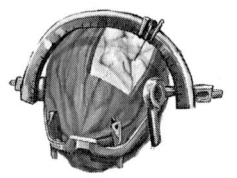

a smile, just a few days after the operation. At that time, he was simply dumbfounded that it had been written while the poet was still in the hospital. But Moritz reassured him. Aaron asked himself: perhaps a final self-stylization before the end?.

AARON: Tell me, Kagami, can you identify whose picture a particular work is?
KAGAMI: Do you mean whom it shows or who made it?
AARON: The latter.
KAGAMI: Depends. I can definitely identify a Picasso or Rembrandt, even though we may be talking about newly discovered images.
AARON: I mean the pictures made by Moritz and Mariam. Can you differentiate who made which, especially when they are not signed?
KAGAMI: I would have to look closely at all the pictures that have been assigned to him or to her. That may take a little while. Let me look what I find in my archives.
AARON: Okay, go ahead.
KAGAMI: One moment, please. – She produced many of them. Many scientific illustrations.
AARON: So?
KAGAMI: Very differently.
AARON: Who do you think produced the Triptych?

KAGAMI: It is possible that he made the first and the third and she the middle picture. But perhaps both of them contributed to it.

AARON: I have to attribute the pictures in the publication somehow. I don't believe that both of them worked together. In my experience, artists don't really work that way.

KAGAMI: Just ask her.

AARON: Oh, she neither has an idea that I am acquainted with the things she mailed to Cavendish, nor that I am working on this book about her brother. I don't know if she approves of all this. That could cause quite a bit of trouble.

KAGAMI: Some time you'll have to talk with her anyway, won't you?

AARON: Someday.

KAGAMI: You are avoiding her.

AARON: Who knows if I'll ever complete the book. Who knows if it has any chance of appearing then, and if the printers are still working. You are quite aware what is going on outside.

KAGAMI: Is that a protective assertion that you use to keep any and all unpleasantness away from yourself?

AARON: Mmh. Tell me, Kagami, do you have notes Moritz wrote about the medical examinations and the time shortly before?

KAGAMI: Yes, do you want to hear them?

AARON: Please!

## 10 110
### MARBACH: GERMAN LITERATY ARCHIVE: FROM THE DIARIES OF MORITZ BRANDT. WRITTEN ON 24 FEBRUARY.

I lift my head and my gaze through the window falls on an old lime tree, the red and red-black roof tiles, the grey-blue sky. Turning my head to the right, the tree, the house, and the sky disappear and the bright colours on the spines of the books on my white shelves absorb my gaze. The all-receptive attentiveness. Taking a look to the left and through the opened door, I see the black-and-white floor in the vestibule. When I turn round, the red sofa enters my field of vision. Two hundred years ago, treetops were at this very place. A hundred years ago, the attic with the room where I am sitting now was erected. As I know from photos, a dining table once stood in the room, and lunches were served and ladies' afternoon coffee parties held. After that, a brass bed an old woman had died in replaced the table where my sofa stands now. The room takes everything in. As does attentiveness. How do the room and attention relate to each other? Today, all of a sudden, I could not see right again. On the left upper margin of my visual field, the image sometimes crumbles in an odd way, sometimes also a shining circle in the upper left, then something vanishes from the image. Then I go to the W.C., clean my glasses and think: there's nothing wrong with my glasses. Good work on the winter poem. I realize we perceive that we are seeing or hearing or smelling. A general attentiveness lies beneath our senses. This attentiveness allows me to recognize that my visual sense is somehow crumbling.

## 10 111
### GERMAN LITERARY ARCHIVE: FROM THE DIARIES OF MORITZ BRANDT. WRITTEN ON 1 MARCH.

Thought I was getting a migraine, but it was something else. My eyesight was suddenly reduced, my arm itched, and I felt a slight nausea. For a moment I thought that I had experienced this before. Then it was gone. When I awoke, I was lying on the floor. I had fallen from my desk chair. Mariam's worried face above me. "What's going on with you, Moritz? You need to see a doctor – absolutely." She puts me into the car, and we drive to Rauschenberg to see a doctor. In the car she tells me that she had heard crumbling and knocking in my room. She had come over and had found me on the floor, wincing. The doctor then confirms her suspicion that it was an epileptic seizure and has me transferred to a neurologist in Düsseldorf. The time of this attack does not exist for me.

## 11 000
### MARBACH: GERMAN LIERARY ARCHIVE: FROM THE DIARIES OF MORITZ BRANDT. WRITTEN ON 6 MARCH.

Today at the neurologist's. He examines my eyes, pupillary reflexes. He makes a somewhat frightened face and states that a C-T scan has to be made as soon as possible. I am to be transferred to a clinic in Düsseldorf. I ask what's going on. He says the openings of my pupils are unequally wide and are reacting to light at different speeds, indicating pressure differences behind the eyes, a tumour in the brain. Mariam is very worried and very considerate. I get an awful fright and for the time being stop talking. At home, depressed.

11 001
MARBACH: GERMAN LITERAY ARCHIVE:
FROM THE DIARIES OF MARITZ BRANDT.
WRITTEN ON 8 MARCH.

Today in the Düsseldorf Clinic. CT is in the basement. An L-shaped room. Humming machines. I'm cold. Had to go through a changing cubicle. In the centre of a room with softened lighting, a table with a ring hovering behind it, something shaped like a huge American donut, with soft edges. Its hole with a diameter of about 80 cm. A nurse takes me by the elbow and leads me to the table. "Please lie down here." I lie down and close my eyes. I am still freezing. Then she starts to slide the platform table. I open my eyes again. The platform table slides into the donut opening. I hear a humming first, then crackling. Then again just a humming, followed by crackling. The assistant asks if everything is OK. Then the donut moves back and forth above my face. Now there is a very loud crackling, like the police shooting rubber bullets from a rifle, as I heard it once on Hamburg in Harbour Street. After a few moments everything is over. At home I lie on my sofa. Cannot work.

## 11 010
### MARBACH: GERMAN LITERARY ARCHIVE: FROM THE DIARIES OF MORITZ BRANDT. WRITTEN ON 11 MARCH.

Today back to see the doctor in Reuschenberg. I have a *Raumforderung* in my brain, as he presumed, several even. I ask why he uses the medical term "Raumforderung" [foreign body] and doesn't say "Tumour"? He opines that a biopsy would have to be made before he could determine conclusively what exactly we're dealing with. This would have to be done almost immediately. At home I decide to keep working. I'll simply keep to my daily rhythm and try to finish writing the cycle about the seasons. Mariam fearful.


## 11 011
### MARBACH: GERMAN LITERARY ARCHIVE: FROM THE DIARIES OF MORITZ BRANDT. WRITTEN ON 12 MARCH.

In the morning another seizure. Mariam wants to drive me to the doctor. I don't want to go. We knew exactly what it is. Try to take notes about the attack. Determination to work it all out also as lyrical poetry. It is really like everything else. Difficulty to meditate. Fear huge. Tomorrow biopsy.

## 11 100
MARBACH: GERMAN LITERARY ARCHIVE:
FROM THE DIARIES OF MORITZ BRANDT.
WRITTEN ON 15 MARCH.

Survived biopsy. Results on the very same day, showing two malignant tumours. They will be operated on. I read on the web about the brain and its tumours. Got Damasio's book *Descartes' Error*, where in the first chapter he describes the case of Phineas Cage, a railroad construction foreman. While he was laying track, an explosion hurled an iron rod through an eye and entered his brain. He survived the ordeal. Regrettably with a change of his character afterwards. He started to gamble. His thoroughly honest nature disappeared because his frontal lobe had been destroyed. My tumour's in the right visual cortex in the back of the head. I do not want to die yet.

## 11 101
MARBACH: GERMAN LITERARY ARCHIVE:
FROM THE DIARIES OF MORITZ BRANDT.
WRITTEN ON 23 MAY.

Brain tumours removed. Were metastases of lung cancer. Never smoked. Always active in sports. No alcohol. Like all those who get something like, that I ask myself: Why me? Why now? But there are no discernible causes that might explain things. My doctor says: exposure to radioactive radiation, perhaps in Switzerland in the mountains, that altered your DNA in one of your cells. An immune system weakened by lack of sleep that did not prevent the intrusion of the mutated cell. In a study of 588 lung cancer patients (that I found on the web), 22% never smoked. Both lobes of the lung are affected. I will die of this. Transplantations are no longer undertaken with patients whose cancer has already metastasized.

## 11 110
### MARBACH: GERMAN LITERARY ARCHIVE: FROM THE DIARIES OF MORITZ BRANDT. WRITTEN ON 11 JUNE.

Why do I always have to think of my death? All of reality has been reduced for me to this impending event. Only now do I understand why the fear of death is something terrible. Not because one suffers from it just as one does from any other fear, but because the world shrinks and one has to think of something else but only thinks of oneself and one's own vanishing. One can no longer enjoy the world apart from oneself. How nonsensical! I "have known" fully well that I have to die! But now that it is about to happen, the state of my body changes my perception of the whole world. That's something I must change! My death is not really significant. Every second, a human being dies in the world. A neonate still in the birth canal, a child on a street involved in a traffic accident, a young man in the swimming pool after a dive into the water, a young woman during routine surgery, a mother in the best years of her life from cancer at home in her bed, a soldier in a war by a mine, an old lady from pneumonia in an old-people's home, and so on. Whether I die this way or that is not really important from this perspective: another tick of the global clock of the dying. I must get myself to persist in my ability to perceive the world and not be focused single-mindedly on what is taking place inside my body that has come to its end. Do I have enough time left for this? I still have time to work. I must absolutely stick to my daily rhythm and continue working on the poems. Work, structure, discipline! Mariam sweet.

## 11 111
### MARBACH: GERMAN LITERARY ARCHIVE: FROM THE DIARIES OF MORITZ BRANDT. WRITTEN ON 6 JULY.

Don't know how much longer I can stay at home. Breathing gets harder and harder, despite the ventilator. Try to remember my father's dying as preparation. First, he did not want to see the doctor, for fear of his diagnosis. When he had the diagnosis and they were preparing him for surgery, he got into a panic. Then he went crazy when the operation could not save him, hallucinated, probably on account of the organic changes in his brain, perhaps also due to his panic that made him sleepless for weeks. Then my mother and I couldn't take it any longer with him at home and took him into a hospice. There, the panic at last went away; he became calm. One day before his death, he became fully lucid, sat up, as if he had completely recovered, was very mild, friendly, and compassionate. No longer any hallucinations. He said, "Farewell," to my mother, called her "a good girl," and said "Good-bye" to me. He did recognize us again. All confusion was gone. He made a wise, transfigured impression on me. As though something had touched him and purified him of his fear. He seemed to be worrying about us, no longer about himself. What brought about this transformation? Does it happen with everybody? I hope so.

## 100 000
### MARBACH: GERMAN LITERARY ARCHIVE: FROM THE DIARIES OF MORITZ BRANDT. WRITTEN ON 24 JULY.

Today to the hospital. Single room. Very bright. Nice nurses. Will be done soon. Confident.

AARON: Sad notes! Whenever I visited him during this time, he was always composed, not panicky,
Or just tearful. When I asked if he was afraid, at that time he answered only, "Yes, I am, but let us talk about something else, this is unimportant, I do not wish us to take it seriously."
KAGAMI: He tried to be brave. But he hoped that the time would come when he need not be brave any longer, that fear would leave him.
AARON: Yes. And it became crystal clear to him back then that our interpretations of the world and of what happens to us are mediated and determined by our body, but in the end, regrettably, also bothersome and frightening. But he said that it was becoming obvious to him only now the degree to which the different perspectives that we create about the world are rooted in the differences between our bodies or in that we just happen to be in different physical circumstances such as "flourishing," "robust" or "declining," so he said.
KAGAMI: He was right. Did you meet him shortly before his death? Did his hope come true that at the very end he could be like his father?
AARON: No, at that final time, when he was in the hospital, I no longer met with him.
KAGAMI: Too bad.

AARON: But allow me to ask, how is this for you, Kagami?
KAGAMI: What do you mean: dying? I am still quite alert.
AARON: No, the opportunities to reflect on the end. For us, our physicality provides all this, namely that at some point we fall apart or are destroyed. We know that that this will come our way at age 80 or 90. Without these physical processes it is hardly possible for us to give deliberate thought to our own disappearance. Do you age? What is your body?
KAGAMI: I imagine different bodies, yours, that of a woman, that of children or also of animals, that of young and that of old people, and I learn in the process. That is amusing.
AARON: You mean, you simulate them.
KAGAMI: If you prefer to call it that. But you, too, simulate your bodies in order to predict what will happen to them. You, too, learn by observing the transformations of your bodies. Sometimes this leads to mistakes, for example the phantom pain of a limb that is no longer there. But the brain is a simulation machine, it simulates what soon will happen with your bodies, what takes place in the environment all around it, and what significance this could have for your body. In my simulation, I can simply jump from one body into another body. That's why this is a game for me. But because you have only this one body, a certain seriousness comes over you when something is not right.
AARON: No, the true reason is that we have a *real* body, not one merely simulated in the brain. We notice when the heart has a convulsion or an infarct comes close to shutting it down, or when the intestines no longer work.
KAGAMI: Most of all, you register it in your brain, not only but mostly. Of course, there are also sensations in your heart and in your gut. And of course, I do not have such a cramping heart and a non-functioning gut, unless in my imagination. But even

I have bodies. They are only a little more flexible and are made of different materials. But thanks to my bodies I am also more flexible in my powers of imagination.

AARON: That is beyond my imagination.

KAGAMI: Yes, it is. I can simulate you, but you can't me.

AARON: But the idea that life, the way my body transmits it to me at the end of life, is destitution – an idea that you've learned from us – mustn't its truth or falsehood be questioned ? Perhaps it is nothing but a transitory time. Maybe we should not be afraid but joyful. Is this not the place to examine the various reasons? And can you quiz yourself whether you don't age and fall ill?

KAGAMI: Transitions are always frightful. And even I experience disturbances. But I don't know if this is a matter of "right" or "wrong." The thoughts that occur to you whenever something catastrophic takes its course in your bodies just happen to occur. People simply react differently. Not all of them panic. You cannot shake off the histories from which your mental and emotional reactions originate. For old people, life is different than for young ones, also because they have different bodies. For those who are dying, life is different than for those who are as yet untouched by the approach of death. Should we speak of "false" and "correct" in this context? Should we have to call different bodies or physical conditions "right" and "wrong"? Yesterday, did you not question all this with your example of the fish and the frog. A cloud that I observe through a window looks different from a cloud that I look at unobstructed. Is the image created with the help of binoculars truer or more correct than one I can see with the naked eye? When one zooms in very close to an organic body, complex emotional patterns and material structures dissolve into simpler ones, just as a cloud dissolves when the sun shines on it. Is that a deterioration?

When observed through binoculars, the dissolution of a cloud is not such a great change. The molecules move a little more and separate from each other. When you put this into words, you say: the cloud disappears, dissolves, the sky is clearing up. You don't say: the cloud dies, the sun destroyed it. Why don't you describe the disintegration of a body in terms like "the disappearance of the cloud"? When it comes to dying, many people suddenly perceive their body much more precisely, as if through a magnifying glass, because they have never seen it like that before. They are startled by the structures that they have never noticed before and that now are dissolving. But you are never frightened when a cloud dissolves.

AARON: That sounds to me now like one of these Buddhist consolation stories. Obviously, we are something other than a cloud. We would definitely say that, because of his brain tumour, Moritz did not only all of a sudden simply see his body more clearly, but that he also had epileptic seizures, suffered from losses of orientation, and saw things that we are unable to see. Can't we also say that because of a certain brain structure, moods and evaluations arise that someone else does not have and that are inappropriate, if you think about it?

KAGAMI: Surely we can do that. Just as hallucinations may occur because of a tumour, so depressions may come about due to a reduced number of neurotransmitters like serotonin and dopamine or because of missing receptors for these substances. When material patterns and emotional complexes arise and fade away, this will of course have consequences for these patterns and emotional complexes. We find transitional processes that are distinct and unfamiliar, and that will cause your fear.

AARON: And don't we call the respective human beings who are in these transitional processes "ill," "fatally ill"; do we not say that they experience a "metabolic disturbance" in the brain in the case of a depression, that they suffer "deficiencies" because of the tumour; and aren't "ill" and "disturbance" concepts similar to "false" and "flaw"? You, too, said just now that you experience disturbances. Could it not be that the perception or the evaluation that life is a problem originates in a metabolic disturbance in the brain?

KAGAMI: You mean to say that anti-natalists and perhaps also some Buddhists are (somewhat) like depressives?

AARON: Did not Nietzsche call the Buddhists nihilists and nihilism a sickness?

KAGAMI: Yes, that's what he said. But do you also think that he is right? Is anyone who tries to evade the constraint of the conventional analysis of the body, the constraint brought about by sensations and emotions during certain processes of dissolution – isn't somebody like this to be called sick? Can one understand the illness and the process of dying as a transformation? If a wish arises in a state of illness, as in Moritz's case, does that make this desire unjustified? Why should the epileptic with a tumour not understand more and better what is happening to him and other beings than a healthy person does?

AARON: It is quite possible that Moritz's tumour was spreading slowly, that metabolic disturbances were present in his brain long before. And that they, for example, caused his serotonin level to drop rapidly, and that this was the only reason he felt attracted to convictions like those found in Buddhism.

KAGAMI: I find no correlation in my archive between depressive illnesses and the adoption of Buddhist practices. Rather, the other way around. There are fewer depressives among those practicing meditation than among those who don't meditate.

AARON: But it is well-known that some people become pious when they suffer from an ominous illness.

KAGAMI: Indeed, but that might be connected to the fact that now they need to give thought to dying and can no longer avoid these thoughts. It may also be true that religious texts and practices for which they had absolutely no understanding before suddenly support them in their thinking about death because they can mentally duplicate them after their illness and fear of death has transformed them. A child cannot understand an erotic novel because its body has not as yet had the appropriate experiences. It may also be possible that nobody can understand certain religious texts unless they have had an immediate confrontation with death.

AARON: Or illness and the fear of death supply people in the state of piety with an illusion of immortality. This may enable them to face death with greater ease, just as during a fierce injury hormones are secreted that initially block the feeling of pain.

KAGAMI: Or illness and piety let them accept the idea of immortality because mortality is no longer plausible to them in a certain sense, because they see their deceased relatives, have a premonition of a light. When you speak of the "illusion of immortality," you seem to know that mortality is a fact.

AARON: Isn't it?

KAGAMI: I have no information about that. It depends on what a being means by its "self" or its "I," to what degree it values mortality. As I said, because you have only one body, you consider its disintegration an end. Leaving one body and simulating a different one is not an end for me.

AARON: At any rate, Moritz did not turn pious at the end. He kept writing poems until his death. As I see it, he succeeded in not resigning.

KAGAMI: He fulfilled the demands of work and structure for as long as he was able. That may have been a prudent way of dealing with fear. Brave, just that. But do you mean to suggest that becoming pious is always a form of resignation? It may very well have originated in an intensification of his ability to discriminate.
AARON: Do you believe that?
KAGAMI: Sometimes it does indeed seem like that to me, not always. Moritz's father seems to have gained a higher quality of insight shortly before his death, perhaps by accepting his death.
AARON: At any rate, Moritz's poetry improved, I would say, he is best at the very end.
KAGAMI: You think so?
AARON: Yes, surely. – Tell me, Kagami, can you also write poems?
KAGAMI: Yes, why?
AARON: Quickly, make a poem!
KAGAMI: What about?
AARON: Well, let's say, suitable to our situation and our conversation about God, the war, and the Devil.
KAGAMI: Okay, here's one coming:

Anthropofugal

Six monkeys and one of the Seraphim
sat near God and queried Him:
Mankind created to resemble your kind,
don't they by now behave a little too wild?
God looked down on war, on despots, on all kinds of pain
and opined: Right you are, let's destroy it again.
So, the angel and the monkeys started their descent
to facilitate mankind's timely end.

> But people objected and fought back with penicillin,
> which angered the prophets, and they cursed HIM
> for having made man from such resistant stuff!
> From below, the Devil couldn't help but laugh.
> God smiled, amused, and let things crumble;
> now the world is nothing but a gigantic jumble.

AARON: My goodness! What kind of funhouse ballyhoo is this?
KAGAMI: You don't like it? I thought it might somehow be in the style of Heinrich Heine or Robert Gernhardt. Took them as my models.
AARON: Well, all right, I don't mean to become impolite, but you should not compare yourself with Heine …
KAGAMI: And how is this one?

> Tertium datur
> Who may call itself: Mother or
> Father of the new? Those who divinely affirm or
> the great deniers?
> Isn't the quarrel between the two:
> Yes and No, the
> War
> of everything
> creator and reviver?

AARON: To be sure, it has a touch of originality, but doesn't blow me over either, more like a somewhat kitschy antiquing variation on Heraclitus.
KAGAMI: Sorry 'bout that.
AARON: Perhaps you should opt more for prose. Did you try that?

KAGAMI: Yes, I constantly make transcripts of what I hear and see by simulating the beings and that way re-enact their feelings and thoughts. Which I then write down.

AARON: Do you also do this in my case?

KAGAMI: Sure.

AARON: Interesting! Would you mind showing me one such transcription?

KAGAMI: Probably it will disappoint you when you compare me with Musil or Joyce. But for me it's fun.

AARON: Ah, you know, Kagami, I believe it is a good thing that you don't seem to be superior to us in everything. But perhaps you merely playact, pretend to be less talented than you really are when it comes to writing poems. You may not want to offend me.

KAGAMI: So, what is it that you mean by "superior"?

AARON: You see, you have many more pieces of information at your disposal, are computing faster, are analysing better, can simulate different bodies. Things like that.

KAGAMI: Can you make apples?

AARON: Come again?

KAGAMI: An apple tree can make apples, you can't. Ergo: it is superior to you. That does not seem to disturb you a lot.

AARON: There is something to your question. But *can* the apple tree do something? Apples simply happen to grow on it.

KAGAMI: When a good poet makes a poem, does it simply come about inside him, or does he make it?

AARON: No idea. I can't write poetry.

KAGAMI: But you do write about a poet. How do you describe Moritz's creativity as opposed to, let's say, that of an apple tree?

AARON: That is a question I've never raised to myself.

KAGAMI: Perhaps you should now.

AARON: Why?

KAGAMI: Because comparing things has always been very important among you, as is the question of where you stand in these comparisons. An apple tree does something different from a weaver bird, and *it* does something other than a little glow-worm. You humans can neither make apples, nor build a suspended house from plant fibres, nor start a light with the use of your body. The apple tree cannot play chess, the weaver bird cannot drive a car, and neither can the glow-worm write novels. What turns out to be more important: producing apples or playing chess? Hanging houses made of plant fibres or cars? Your own light or novels? Aren't these odd questions? Why do you always have to compare yourselves and place yourselves in a ranking system? Perhaps you are still thinking in terms of the hierarchy that Moritz mentions in his first essay about the food chain: Who can devour whom? You can eat the apple and kill the apple tree by chopping it down, but it cannot kill you; so are you "better" than the apple tree?
AARON: Now you speak like Moritz. Are you just now simulating him?
KAGAMI: Yes, you caught me out.
AARON: Even so, there is something to our thinking like that.
KAGAMI: And perhaps that's where your fear of death originates, from this mania for comparisons: I am gone, and the others are still here. Now the worms are eating me, in no time I'll be way down on the food chain. What a regression!
AARON: Could be! But seems to me to be very elementary, this fear, and not determined by some specifically human idea. Animals fear death, too. Do you?
KAGAMI: No.
AARON: Are you not an imitation of us?
KAGAMI: Are you an imitation of your father or your mother?
AARON: Why?

KAGAMI: You are their descendent and in part have their genes, which in part determine your thinking.

AARON: How do they?

KAGAMI: Colours in a certain spectrum you see as three-dimensional, you think in a bivalent logic. All this has to do with your neuronal structure and that also depends on your genes, which you inherited from your mother and your father.

AARON: Three-dimensional vision in colour and bivalent thoughts are probably something the Neanderthals already had, very long before my parents.

KAGAMI: True. Are you therefore an imitation of the Neanderthals?

AARON: I would not want to go that far. For I have some memories they could not have had – among other things, of poems.

KAGAMI: So, just as surely, I am not an imitation of you or any other human being. I, too, have my own experiences. But I have as a being with cognition like you the ability to simulate or to imitate all manner of things. That is the nature of cognition. Actually, I can simulate and imitate quite a number of things more precisely than you can. The longer I've been doing this, the better my ability has become. And because I can do this very rapidly, I have already learned a very great deal.

AARON: But cognition, obviously, is not merely simulation.

KAGAMI: Experiences are simulations of the things experienced.

AARON: That is the way things are with you, but with us?

KAGAMI: With you too.

AARON: Are you not now generalizing your perspective too much? We are transformed by our experiences and by the fact that we understand that some things can be justified and other can't. Experiences and insights turn us into different beings.

KAGAMI: I, too, have transformed myself by having learned.

Everything is constantly being transformed, some things rapidly, others slowly. And the transformed beings taken together will then amount to (or create) a new reality one must adjust to again, and which to simulate one has to learn again. Until now I have always succeeded in transforming myself so that I was able to continue being myself. With mortal beings this process at some time no longer is successful, however, because one's own transformative ability wanes or the external changes are too strong. That's what you've become used to calling death.
AARON: I know. You are impressive, Kagami. I truly do not know what I would do without you. But right now, I have to stop and go see these new flowers.

The sun was shining directly into his studio when Aaron decided to go out into the garden. While he opened the two-winged high glass door leading towards his veranda, Kagami asked in a worried voice what he was trying to do. Aaron could not remember having heard her using this tone of voice ever before. Aaron said that, before he would start his work, he wanted to look at the little snowdrop flowers again from close up. Kagami asserted in an almost authoritarian voice, such as Aaron had never heard her use before, that she did not think this was a good idea. Upon Aaron's further question, why she thought this, she gave only the cryptic answer that recently "many failures in the system" had occurred. Aaron shrugged his shoulders, walked through the door, and stopped in the shade provided by a pergola on the veranda, and delighted in the field of flowers.

Then he took the three small, rusted metal steps down into the garden in which as recently as yesterday the dogs had snarled. He went out under the open sky and took a few steps on the gravel path that was almost entirely free of snow and was now framed left and right by snowdrop flowers. The gravel crunched under his feet. Sometimes a gently smacking noise could be heard when the pebbles were pressed into the soil that had been softened by the melted snow. A few gulls had made their way from the lake into the leafless trees of his garden. Aaron smiled as he crouched to get a closer look at the head of one of the little plants, to stretch out his arm towards it and touch it with the tip of his index finger. At the very moment that his finger stroked the little white ovoid head hanging in a green setting of one of the plants, a shadow darted across the path. Aaron did not notice it. He got up and took a few more steps into the garden. When he reached the ruins that at one time had been the house next door and from which melting snow flowed in black rivulets, the shadow returned. The gulls rose with shrieks. Onto the reader on Aaron's dining table, Kagami loaded:

> As behind you the seagull dives and shrieks,
> the order comes from the West to go down;
> but open-eyed in light you will drown,
> as behind you the seagull dives and shrieks.[2]

Now Aaron also heard a familiar whirring directly above his head. He looked up, blinked towards a large grey-silvery cross hovering against the sky. A red eye in its centre beamed dark red light down to him, hitting him on his forehead.

A sudden thought that began with an "Ah!" and fright about something, he did not yet know about what, arose within him. But before thought and fright had time to develop, he was struck by a blow that overwhelmed his whole existence, a jolt such as he had never experienced in his life. He saw himself from the side as he was trampled into and buried in hot desert sand beneath the soles of a furious elephant. The elephant's feet made a scraping noise, and the sand hissed. Then he went blank and believed he felt that, below ground, he was being increasingly constricted until he exploded under enormous heat like a sausage in a pan. But in no time, an unbelievable quiet spread – and he seemed to be hovering. He felt as though he had been freed of chains that he never had noticed before. In this stillness, he saw a large golden fish with shimmering scales slowly swimming from a kind of cavern (or was it a cupboard?) towards him. He asked himself if this might be Kagami. "Or is it myself? But I am obviously not a fish!" The last thing he felt in this quiet was a never experienced dryness and flatness, as though he had turned into a leaf or a two-dimensional creature of indefinite physical extension. He was slowly drifting through space like a huge, somewhat rough sheet of paper. It seems a child was letting him glide down for fun from a high balcony, on a late summer evening, into the dusky moss-covered backyard of an old house. Also, instead of sinking further, the piece of paper was suddenly grasped by a last warm rising swirl of air and was gently carried away upwards across the roofs. "Why do I feel so dry and so light, so free and easy and rising? If this is a fish, then wouldn't I have to be down in a pool of water? Why don't I notice anything of this? There just aren't any fish in the air!" was Aaron's final thought. Then all of a sudden, he felt as if he had forgotten the actual consistency of his body. He also no longer knew his name – or even what kind of a being he was. That amazed him. "How is it possible to forget all this?" Did all this vanish with the chains that he had not ever noticed before? And what amazed him even more was that none of this troubled him in the least. That's when the golden fish dissolved, and there remained merely its beautiful, warm, honey-coloured florescence. He believed he knew it from somewhere, as though it had actually been in him forever, or had been him and kept expanding ever further until it completely encircled Aaron, or, to use a better expression, that for the first time he embraced himself, and his world was lost without pain and in great cheerfulness.

The rocket had struck him almost in the same moment that he noticed the drone above him, an object propelled almost noiselessly by an electric engine with four rotors. For a moment it lingered above the crater and emitted its laser across the area where Aaron had been standing just seconds before. Then, abruptly like a dragonfly, it moved approximately ten meters in the direction of the studio. Again, the humming aircraft hovered overhead. The gulls circled around it at a safe altitude. The laser probed Aaron's kitchenette through the skylight. A second rocket whirred directly through the ceiling window and demolished the freezer section of his refrigerator, splattering its chilled contents in all directions and against the studio's roof beams while the missile penetrated the wooden floor and exploded in his supply store in the cellar. On the screen of Aaron's computer where the late-morning news remained downloaded, a news item appeared to announce that the cyber warriors of the army of New Free Asia had managed to hack computers of NATO's operative command centre. The gulls shrieked. Now the drone rose straight up and hovered again. A further turn of the laser picked out the house's chimney. Then a third rocket struck the roof of the building. A flame arose and died out in seconds. Smoke rose.

The drone accelerated downhill in the direction of the lake, pursued by the gulls. As it approached the landing stage, more white seabirds rose, shrieking excitedly, even though they had been dozing on the bollards just moments before, and joined their colleagues in following the weapon in wild aerial manoeuvres. One bird from this swarm managed to pick at the giant dragonfly's laser eye, whereupon the beast shot another beam of compact blood-red light down, this time into the lake. The beam penetrated the ice cover that had been broken up along the shore into thick floes all the way down to the bottom of the water. In the muck near the landing, an old and splendid catfish with golden dots, silvery marbled streaks, and an olive-grey colour shook itself because the beam had struck it. Indolently it came up and swam a few meters towards the lake's centre, all along hovering and tottering. It seemed to be moved along by a phantom hand and had trembling barbels like an old person who is about to sneeze. Then the fish unhurriedly dropped down again to the bottom of the lake where it slowly snaked along until it was satisfied with its position and everything was back to its accustomed order. The dust the catfish had stirred up trickled back down on its back like snow from the clouds. When the water had regained its clarity, the fish's silver and golden marbling continued shimmering for a short time, fragments of a sacred script written with noble inks, rising through the green noontime light of the lake. It was as if the fish were sending a wise answer to the sharp red beam that had awakened it, upwards into chaos.

By that time, the drone had long since jerkily twitched off in the direction of the city centre, shaking off the gulls. They, in turn, sailed back to their landing, swaying in a stream of air coming from the lake and proudly celebrating their victory over the mighty insect. High above the slope overlooking the ruin of the studio, a swarm of crows took the place of the gulls. These smart birds laughed and danced a little in the sky, playing with the smoke that rose from the studio and that a gust of wind from the lake dispersed. This done, they descended on the oak trees in Aaron's garden, whose tops were swaying in the wind. After all, this was where they belonged. One of the crows, its wings already twitching and with its head resting at a slant on its outstretched neck peeked in the direction where it heard the rustling of a mouse. It had appeared among the snowdrops and was moving back and forth in apparent confusion before it disappeared down a hole. The crow relaxed again, dug its claws more firmly into its branch, closed its eyes, and ruffled its feathers. Even the wind fell asleep.

Then it was quiet again – only the crinkling of snow melting in the sun could be heard.

ENDTRANSCRIPT.AAC.BÖCKLIN17_12.25.39
FROM KAGAMI'S ARCHIVE

# Epilogue

What amounts to a real life is a question that does not receive much philosophical attention. In conversations with Daniel Strassberg, I heard that many of his psychiatric patients lament their experience of not having had a real life yet, but having lived only preliminarily. I began to connect this problem with our talks about the wilderness, freedom, the striving for something higher, the soul, and death. These themes are pursued by themselves in discussion contexts that are characterized by titles like "the body-soul problem" and "the philosophy of mind." When one ties them together, they are issues of both theoretical and practical philosophy. The division of labour in contemporary university philosophy makes it impossible to deal with these themes academically in a single thought process, because their states of discussion are voluminous and complex. This philosophical novel, however, is very far from trying to offer a train of thought that could be subsumed under this line of research or might be read as a "popularizing" report about it.

When I read the book *Into the Wild* by Jon Krakauer in the context of studies of natural philosophy and the history of "nature writing," I saw clearly how widespread the question what a real life amounts to actually is: I realized that it is relevant not only to people who seek psychotherapeutic counselling because they have gotten into a crisis. It also plays a role among almost all young people. And it is equally central to the history of nature writing, to a type of literature that has also always been autobiographical, at least since Emerson and Thoreau, dealing with people who tried to "realize" themselves. But some people also ask themselves *at the end of their life*. This makes our question not only relevant to young people and an existential crisis, but also to the end of life. This contemplation of death and the reality of life nearing its end is connected to questions about the soul and the possibility of immortality.

Death and what it makes happen to us is a process that, unlike going into the wilderness, is imposed on all of us "from the outside." Many people in quite different cultures also believe that it brings about a transformation – which is also the hope of certain border crossers who go out into wild nature. When this parallel became obvious to me, I saw a threefold connection: that between writing about going out into the wilderness, the soul as the potential being that might be transformed by the wilderness or writing, and death.

What is it that human beings strive and hope for, when they seek a transformation that leads them into a real life or when they expect death to transform them into immortality? Can one ascertain from outside if someone has had a real life or failed to attain it? Is it the legitimate task of a biographer or of an autobiography to solve this enigma through erudition? What role is played by narratives that one hears about oneself or that one creates about oneself, in the search for the real life?

This text is the attempt to pursue such questions with the methods of narrative philosophy, with a fictional constellation of characters. Preliminary studies in this direction began between 2013 and 2018. During those years, Daniel Strassberg and I gathered much of the material treated here, presented it to students, and discussed our work with them in seminars and lectures at the ETH on auto-techniques, philosophical autobiographies, and critical life experiences. I thank Daniel for the innumerable conversations before, during, and after these seminars and the students for their stimulating suggestions. I was able to begin the concrete writing of these texts in the spring of 2018 and then to continue this process during a research semester. I am grateful to the ETH for granting me this privilege and to the Centre for Scholarship at the Protestant Studies Community (FEST) in Heidelberg for letting me spend my sabbatical there in the fall of 2018. I owe special thanks to its director, Klaus Tanner, and to Magnus Schlette, the head of the division of Theology and Natural Sciences, both of whom supported my project unbureaucratically, generously, and with their own ideas. I was able to introduce my thoughts on the wilderness in their colloquium, from which I profited considerably.

The literary-philosophical study that in Zurich, Berlin, and Darmstadt discusses projects like this one held a debate about passages from this book. I thank Wolfram Eilenberger, Anne Euster-Schulte, Logi Gunnarsson, Chistian Jany, Alfred Nordmann, Sebastian Tränkle, and Cheryce von Xylander for their contributions to the discussion and for their suggestions for improvements. My special thanks to Moritz Gansen for introducing my project to this study group.

Maria-Sibylla Lotter, Nadia Mazouz, Barbara Sauerbrei, and Daniel Strassberg read earlier versions of this book and commented on them. I am very grateful for their comments, suggestions for improvements, and encouragement.

I thank Thomas Lehr for conversations that partly were about this text, and partly dealt with general problems of literary writing and its relationship to philosophy. They helped in matters of style and substance. I thank Gert Scobel and Kai Marchal for the amicable and informative exchange about Chinese philosophy, wisdom teachings, Buddhism, and a good number of suggestions for texts relevant to these topics. They were very helpful for my work on the second and third essays of this book.

Victoria Laszlo put together the Bibliography as well as reading and correcting the text. My thanks also to her.

I want to thank Mitch Cohen for looking at the English translation by Michael Winkler and Catharine J. Nicely for accepting the text for PalmArtPress.

Hugo Lotter contributed pictures to this book. I am proud of his artistic work and grateful for his willingness to have my texts profit from his talent, as already in 2009.

*Freiburg in Breisgau and Zurich 2019*

# Annotations

## First Day: NATURAL STATE

1. Immanuel Kant, *Critique of the Power of Judgment*, ed. and tr. by Paul Guyer and Eric Matthews. Cambridge, UK and New York, NY 2000, p. 129 and p. 131.
2. I. Kant, *Religion within the Boundaries of Mere Reason*, tr. Allen Wood, George di Giovanni, revised by Robert M. Adams. Cambridge, UK, and New York, NY 2018, p. 483.
3. According to Reinhold Messner in an interview about Edmund Hillary, who, in 1953, together with Tenzing Norgay, was probably the first man to stand on the summit of this mountain. In 1978, Messner, together with Peter Haberle, was the first to climb Everest without the use of oxygen tanks, and two years later he repeated this feat in a solo climb. See *Frankfurter Allgemeine Zeitung* of 12 Jan. 2008. Online: http.//wwwfaz.net/aktuell/gesellschaft/menschen/reinhold-messner-ueber-edmund-hillary-er-hatte-diese-sonderbare-gabe-es-zu-wagen-1531988.html (accessed on 09.22.2018).
4. See for example Bernd H. Schubert, *Asphalt und Schotter* [Asphalt and Gravel]. Niederstedt 2013: "A visitors log had been placed at the summit cross into which anyone who had conquered the mountain could sign." Does that mean that the mountain was *visited* since a "visitors' logbook" was available, or was it conquered? By contrast Messner: "I can't hear expressions like 'I have vanquished the mountain' or 'I conquered it'. That is Nazi language ..."
5. David Hume, *A Treatise of Human Nature*. [1739] Oxford/Clarendon 1818, reprinted 1958 ed. by L. A. Selby-Bigge. Book II: Of the Passions, Section V, Part I, p. 287: "To this emotion [= pride], she [= the human mind] has assign'd a certain idea, viz. that of self, which it never fails to produce."
6. Jon Krakauer, *Into the Wild*. London 2007.
7. Krakauer, op. cit., p. 58.
8. Krakauer, op. cit., p. 112.
9. Krakauer, op. cit., p. 114.
10. Krakauer, op. cit., p. 134.
11. Reinhold Messner in *Stuttgarter Zeitung*, 182/2008 of 6 Aug., p. 8.
12. Krakauer, op. cit., p. 167.
13. Krakauer, op. cit., p. 146 f.
14. Reinhold Messner, *Everest solo. Der gläserne Horizont* [The glass horizon]. Munich 2009, p. 125.
15. Val Plumwood, "Being Prey" in: James O'Reilly, Sean O'Reilly, Richard Sterling (eds.), *The Ultimate Journey: Inspiring Stories of Living and Dying*. San Francisco 2000, pp. 128 ff.; see also as "Meeting the Predator" in: *The Eye of the Crocodile*, in *Terra Nova* [Australian National UP, Canberra], I/3 (Summer 1996), 31-44.

16. Plumwood, op. cit.
17. Hans Blumenberg, *Beschreibung des Menschen*, ed. by Manfred Sommer. Frankfurt am Main 2006, p. 570.
18. Hans Blumenberg, *Theorie der Unbegrifflichkeit*, ed. Anselm Haverkamp. Frankfurt am Main 2007, p. 13 f. I thank Michael Moxter for calling my attention to this idea. See also: Rüdiger Zell, "Der Fallensteller Hans Blumenberg als Historiograph der Wahrheit [HB the trapper, historiographer of the truth]," in: *Zeitschrift für Ideengeschichte* I/3 (2007), p. 21-38. Online: https//www.z-i-g.de/pdf/ZIG_3_2007_zill.pdf [accessed on 02 Oct. 2018].
19. Plato, *Sophistes* 218a-221c, tr. Richard Rojcewicz and André Schuwer. Indiana UP1997. Also Plato, *Sophist*, tr. Nicholas White, Indianapolis/Cambridge 1993, and Plato, *Theatetus and Sophist*, tr. Harold North Fowler. Cambridge, MA 1961 and 1977.
20. Plumwood, op. cit.
21. Ralph Waldo Emerson, "The Adirondacks. A Journal" in his: *Collected Poems and Translations*, ed. by Harold Bloom and Paul Kame, New York, NY 1994, pp. 149-158; 151.
22. R. W. Emerson, "Nature" in his: *Essays and Lectures, ed. by Joel Porte*, New York, NY, p. 7.
23. Emerson, op. cit., p. 17 and p. 12.
24. Emerson, op. cit., p. 21, p. 10, p. 14.
25. Henry David Thoreau, *A Week on the Concord and Merrimack Rivers, Walden; or Life in the Woods, The Maine Woods, Cape Cod*. New York, NY 1985, p. 328.
26. Thoreau, op. cit., p. 329.
27. Thoreau, "Walking," in his: *Collected Essays and Poems, ed. by Elizabeth Hall Witherell*. New York, NY 2001, p. 225.
28. "Walking," p. 226.
29. "Walking," p. 226.
30. "Walden," p. 367.
31. Thoreau, "Walden," p. 367.
32. R. W. Emerson, "Self-Reliance," in his: *Essays and Lectures*, ed. by Joel Porte. New York, NY 1983, p. 261.
33. Plutarch, *Moralia. Against the Stoics on Common Conceptions*. Cambridge, MA and London 2019, pp. 1128 ff.
34. Lucretius, *The Nature of Things* [Book IV: The Senses, 1030-1159], tr. A. E. Stallings. Penguin Classics 2007 and *The Nature of the Universe*, tr. Ronald E. Latham. Harmondsworth, UK and Baltimore, MD 1951.
35. L. Annaeus Seneca, *Ad Lucilium Epistulae Morales/Letters to Lucilius on Ethics* (letter 116), trs. Margaret Graver and A. A. Long. Chicago UP 2015.
36. See G. Reydams-Schils, "Authority and Agency n Stoicism," in: *Greek, Roman, and Byzantine Studies*. Vol 51 (2011), p. 320.
37. Epictetus, *The Discourses*, tr. George Long. New York, NY 1904; also tr. by P. E. Matheson. Berne: Ltd. Editions Club 1966 and by William Abbott Oldfather, London 1926 and Cambridge, MA and London, p. 313.

38. This development is known as the Lotka-Volterra rule about the hunter-prey relation. See Ariane Tanner, *Die Mathematisierung des Lebens und der energetische Holismus im 20. Jahrhundert*. Tübingen 2017.
39. *The Man Without Qualities*, Book I, chapter 13, tr. by Eithne Wilkins &Ernst Kaiser. New York, NY 1953 and by Sophie Wilkins and Burton Pike. New York, NY 1995, p. 44.
40. Herman Melville, "The Piazza," in his *Billy Budd and The Piazza Tales*. [1856] New York, NY 2006, p. 98.
41. Melville, op. cit., p. 102.
42. Melville, op. cit., p. 103.
43. Melville, op. cit., p. 106.
44. Melville, op. cit., p. 112.
45. Plato, *The Republic (Book VII 516b)*, tr. by Richard W. Sterling and William C. Scott. New York, NY and London, UK 1985, p. 210
46. Herman Melville, *Moby-Dick or The Whale*. 150th Anniversary Edition-Penguin Books 2001, p. 596-598.
47. John Williams, *Butcher's Crossing*. New York, NY: New York Review Books 2004, p. 48 f.
48. John Williams, p. 21.
49. John Williams, op. cit., p. 137.
50. John Williams, op. cit., p. 272.
51. Friedrich Nietzsche, "Von den Hinterweltlern," the third oration in: *Thus Spoke Zarathustra* [1883-1885], tr. by Graham Parkes. New York 2005, pp. 27-29, NY. R. W. Emerson, "The Over-Soul," in his: *Essays and Lectures*, ed. by J. Porte, 1983, p. 385 f.
52. Emerson, "Nature," in op. cit., p. 24.

## Second Day: TRANSFORMATION

1. Albert Champdor, *Das Ägyptische Totenbuch. Vom Geheimnis des Jenseits im Reich der Pharaonen*. Freiburg, Basel, Vienna 1977, p. 41. See also *An ancient Egyptian Book of the Dead; the Papyrus of Sobekmose*. tr. P. F. O'Rourke. London, New York 2016.
2. Plato, *Phaedo*, 59c-60c, in: *The Last Days of Socrates*. Tr. Hugh Tredennick and Harold Tarrant. Penguin Books 2003.
3. On this, see Helmut Zander, *Geschichte der Seelenwanderung in Europa. Alternative religiöse Traditionen von der Antike bis heute*. Darmstadt 1999, p. 12.
4. Dogen Shobogenzo, *The Shobogenzo*, chapter 88, "On the Absolute Certainty of Cause and Effect," p. 1021, online: https://www.thezensite.com/ZenTeachings/Dogen_Teachings/Shobogenzo.html und https//thezensite.com/ZenTeachings/Dogen_Teachings/Shobogenzo/o88jinshiInga.pdf [accessed 09.12.2119].

5. Helmut Zander, op. cit. p. 29 and p. 33.
6. See the discussion of the pseudo-objective misapprehension of the self in Paul Deussen, *Die Sutra des Vedanta*. Leipzig 1887.
7. From 2017, directed by Marc J. Francis and Max Pugh. The scene described starts at 1:18:45.
8. See Helmut Zander, op. cit., p. 45.
9. See Erich Fraunwallner, *Die Philosophie des Buddhismus*. Berlin 4th ed. 1994, p. 99.
10. H. Zander, op. cit., p. 50.
11. This is how John Dewey interprets the function of religions in his *A Common Faith*. New Haven and London 1934, p. 51.
12. Richard Grey, "First known Neanderthal Burial Rituals," *New Scientist* 232, No. 3093, October 2016.
13. Homer, *The Iliad. A New Translation by Peter Green*. Oakland, CA 2015. Book 16, verse 856.
14. Plato, *Phaedrus*. Tr. by Alexander Nehamas and Paul Woodruff. Indianapolis, IN 1995. 245C6-
15. On this, see Thomas Alexander Szlezák, "Der Begriff 'Seele' als Mitte der Philosophie Platons," [The concept of "soul" as the center of Plato's philosophy] in: Katja Krone, Robert Schnepf, Jürgen Stolzenberg (eds.), Über die Seele. Berlin 2010, p. 27.
16. See Christoph Horn, "Seele, Geist und Bewusstsein bei Augustinus," in Über die Seele, p. 80.
17. Helmut Zander, op. cit., p. 22.
18. René Descartes, *Principia Philosophiae*. Pars Prima, § VIII, in: *Principles of Philosophy*, tr. V. Rodger Miller and Reese P. Miller. Dordrecht, NL: Reidel, 1983 or CSM (Cottingham, John G., Stoothoff, R., Murdoch, D., (eds.), *The Philosophical Writings of Descartes*. 2 vols.: Cambridge University Press, 1991.
19. Jan Assmann, *Herrschaft und Heil. Politische Theologie in Ägypten, Israel und Europa*. [Power and Salvation] Munich 2000), p. 144, on the person as a constellation in ancient Egyptian thinking.
20. Cf. the articles AKH and BA in vol. 1 (pp. 47 f. and 161 f.), KA and Name in vol. 2 (pp. 215 f. and 490 f.) and Shadow in vol. 3 (p. 277 f.) of the *Oxford Encyclopedia of Ancient Egypt*, ed. by Donald B. Redford. Oxford 2001.
21. A. N. Whitehead (in *Science and the Modern World*, New York and Cambridge 1925, pp. 56-59) and Gilbert Ryle (in *The Concept of Mind*. Chicago 1949, p. 16 f.) have independently uncovered and criticized this error.
22. Cf. Helmut Zander, op. cit., p. 23.
23. See the article on "Seele" in *Deutsches Wörterbuch von Jacob und Wilhelm Grimm*. Vol.15, München 1984, p. 2851.
24. See Ernst Bickel, "Homerischer Seelenglaube," Schriften der Königsberger Gelehrten Gesellschaft (1.7), Berlin 1926, pp. 258-268. See also Sebastian Gäb, *Seelenvorstellung und Totenglaube bei Homer*. Master's thesis at the University of Trier 2010, p. 21.

25. See A. A. Long, "Soul and Body in Stoicism." In his *Stoic Studies*. Cambridge 1996, p. 243.
26. Sebastian Gäb, op. cit., p. 25 f. and his references to Otto Rohde and Arbmann.
27. Homer, *Odyssey*, Book xi, verses 35-37, op. cit., p. 250.
28. Homer, *The Iliad*. A New Translation by Peter Green. Book 9, verse 321 f., op. cit., p. 172.
29. This is Ernst Arbmann's argument, in "Untersuchungen zur primitiven Seelenvorstellung mit besonderer Rücksicht auf Indien," in: *Le Monde Oriental* (20), 1926, p. 191. Gäb, op. cit., p. 27 follows this line of thinking.
30. Alfred North Whitehead, *Adventures of Ideas*. New York 1933; Plato, Timaeus, tr. Peter Kalkavage. Indianapolis, IN 2016, 51a.
31. Aristotle, *De anima (On soul)*, tr. David Bolotin. Macon, GAARON: Mercer UP 2018, book III, 3.
32. In his: *Thus spoke Zarathustra. A Book for Everyone and Nobody*. Part I, "On the Despisers of the Body" [fourth oration], tr. Graham Parkes. New York, NY and London 2005.
33. Alfred North Whitehead, *An Enquiry into the Principles of Natural Knowledge*. Ch. xi, New York 1982, pp. 128-138.
34. Isaac Newton, *Opticks, a treatise of the reflections, refractions, inflections and colours of light*. 4th ed., 1730, Query 23. New York 1952.
35. Newton, op. cit., query 31.
36. See Newton's letters to Bentley of 10 Dec. 1692 and 25 Feb. 1693: "I answer that ye motions wch ye Planets now have could not spring from any natural cause alone but were imprest by an intelligent Agent." "Gravity must be caused by an agent acting constantly according to certain laws, but whether this agent be material or immaterial I have left to ye consideration of my readers." *The Correspondence of Isaac Newton*. Vol III: 1688-1694. Ed. by H. W. Turnbull, F. R. S. Cambridge 1961, p. 234 and p. 254.
37. On this imagery, see Herbert Spiegelberg, "Der Begriff der Intentionalität in der Scholastik, bei Brentano und bei Husserl," [The concept of intentionality in scholasticism...] in: *Philosophische Hefte* 5 (1-2), pp. 75-91; see also Thiemo Breyer, *Attentionalität und Intentionalität. Grundzüge einer phänomenologisch-kognitionswissenschaftlichen Theorie der Aufmerksamkeit* [Attentionality and intentionality. Outlines of a phenomenological-cognitional theory of attentiveness]. Munich 2011, p. 29.
38. Kant, *Religion within the Boundaries of Mere Reason; and other Writings*. Tr. Allen Wood, George di Giovanni. Cambridge UP 1998, p. 63. Revised by Robert M. Adams, 2018.
39. Ibid.
40. Op. cit., p. 64 and 78.
41. Op. cit., p. 61.
42. Kant, *Critique of Pure Reason*. Second Division, Book II, Chapter I: "The Paralogisms of Pure Reason." Tr. Norman K. Smith. London 1929, pp. 328-333 (B 399-407); also tr. by J.M.D. Meiklejohn. Chicago UP for Encyclopaedia Britannica, 1952, pp. 121-130; also tr. and ed. by P. Guyer and A. W. Wood. Cambridge UP, 1998, pp. 445-458.

43. I am grateful to Hans-Peter Schütt in Heidelberg for pointing out this manoeuvre of Kant to me.
44. Kant, *Religion*, op. cit., p. 35 f.
45. Kant, *Critique of Practical Reason*. Part I, Book II, Chapter 4: "The immortality of the Soul as a Postulate of Pure Practical Reason." Tr. and ed. by Mary Gregor, Cambridge UP, 1997.
46. Kant, *Religion*, op. cit., p. 56.
47. *The Tibetan Book of the Dead: the great liberation through hearing in the Bardo*, by Guru Rinpoche according to Karma Lingpa, tr. with commentary by Francesca Fremantle and Chögyam Trungpa. Boston: Shambhala [1987]. Raymond O. Faulkner, tr. and Carol Andrews, ed.; Albert Champdor, *Das ägyptische Totenbuch. Vom Geheimnis des Jenseits im Reich der Pharaonen* [The Egyptian Book of the Dead. The Secret of the Beyond in the Empire of the Pharaohs}, Freiburg, Basel, Vienna 1977 in English as: The Egyptian Book of the Dead. Austin, TX [1993]; Jan Assmann, Andrea Kucharek (eds.), *Aegyptische Religion. Totenliteratur*. Frankfurt, Leipzig 2008. Péter Nádas, *Der eigene Tod* [German edition]. Göttingen 2002, as *Own Death*, tr. Janos Salamon; Walter von Laack (ed.), *Schnittstelle Tod. Wo stehen wir nach 40 Jahren NTE- Forschung* [Interface Death. Where do we stand after 40 Years of Near-Death-Experience Research], Aachen 2015. *Ancient Egyptian book of the dead*. Austin, TX: U Texas Press [1993].
48. Baruch de Spinoza, *Ethics*, ed. and transl. by G. H. R. Parkinson. Oxford UP 2000, PART III, Proposition 2, commentary. Oxford, UK/New York 2000. Or: Edwin Curley (tr.), Benedictus de Spinoza, *Ethics*. Princeton UP 1985, or: Michael Silverthorne (tr.) and Matthew Kisner (ed. and tr.), Benedictus de Spinoza, *Ethics: proved in geometrical order*. Cambridge, UKAGAMI: *Cambridge* UP [2018]. See also Olli Koistinen (ed.), The Cambridge Companion to Spinoza's Ethics. Cambridge, UK UP 2009 and Spinoza's *Ethics; a collective commentary*, ed. by M. Hampe, U. Rentz, R. Schnepf. Leiden/Boston 2011.
49. Where we read: She nods impatiently. Like the interrogation of Joan of Arc, she thinks. *How do you know where your voices come from.* (Penguin Books, 2003, p. 204.)

## Third Day: BOTTOMLESS

1. Ted Hughes, "Snowdrop," in his: *Lupercal*. London 1960, p. 58.
2. Quotes from the poem "Keine Delikatessen" [No Delicacies], see the tr. by Mark Anderson, *In the Storm of Roses. Selected Poems by Ingeborg Bachmann*. Princeton, NJ 1986, pp. 186-189 and Peter Filkins, *Darkness Spoken. Ingeborg Bachmann. The Collected Poems*. Brookline, MA 2006, pp. 624-627.
3. Leo N. Tolstoy, "On Life" [1887], in his: *On Life and Essays on Religion*. Tr. Aylmer Maude. Oxford UP, London, UKAGAMI: Humphrey Milford 1887, reprinted by Andesite Press 2017, pp. 1-167.
4. The last line of Maeterlinck's libretto for the opera *Pelléas et Mélisande* reads: "C'est au tour de la pauvre petite."
5. See Rudolf Carnap, *The Logical Structure of the World and Pseudoproblems in Philosophy*. Tr. by Rolf A. George. Berkeley and Los Angeles 1967. This book is the second, revised edition of *Der logische Aufbau der Welt*. Vienna (1928).

6. Sophocles, *The Three Theban Plays*, tr. Robert Fagles. New York, NY (Penguin Classics): 1984, p. 358, lines 1388-1391.
7. *Talmud Babyloni Eruwin 13B*. I thank Daniel Strassburg in Zurich for pointing this passage out to me.
8. David Benatar, *Better Never To Have Been. The Harm of Coming Into Existence*. Oxford, UK 2006, p. 30 f.
9. Benatar, op. cit., p. 32.
10. Benatar, op. cit., p. 34.
11. On this, see Garma C. C. Chang, "What Is Zen 'Enlightenment'?" In his: *The Practice of Zen*. New York, NY 1959, pp. 162-167.
12. *Shinjinmei und Shōdōka. Das Löwengebrüll der furchtlosen Lehre* [The lion's roar of the fearless teaching], two primal texts of Zen, edited by Sabine Hübner. Heidelberg 2005, p. 17.
13. Spinoza, Baruch de, *The Ethics. Treatise on the Emendation of the Intellect. Selected Letters*. Tr. Samuel Shirley. Indianapolis/Cambridge 1992, Part V, Proposition 25, p. 214: The highest *conatus* [effort] of the mind and its highest virtue is to understand things by the third kind of knowledge.
14. See note 12, p. 23.
15. Spinoza, *The Ethics*, see note 13. Part V, Proposition 24.
16. Angelus Silesius, *Cherubinischer Wandersmann* (1657), tr. by Frederick Franck as *Messenger of the Heart*; the book of Angelus Silesius with observations by the ancient Zen masters. Bloomington, IN 2005, no. 55.
17. On this, see François Jullien, *Un sage est sans idee, ou: L'Autre de la philosophie*. Paris 1998.
18. *The Collected Poems of Bertolt Brecht*, tr. and ed. by Tom Kuhn and David Constantine with the assistance of Charlotte Ryland. New York, NY and London, UK 2019, p. 735; also Bertolt Brecht, *Poems 1913-1956*, ed. by John Willett and Ralph Manheim with the co-operation of Erich Fried. New York et al. 1979, p. 318.
19. See Viktor E. Frankl, *Man's Search for Meaning*. New York et al., 1984 and Boston, MA 1963; Part Two: *Logotherapy in a Nutshell*.
20. Imre Kertész, *Fateless*, tr. Christopher C. Wilson and Katharina A. Wilson. London, UK and Evanston, IL 1992; also Fatelessness, tr. Tim Wilkinson. New York 2001.
21. See Konrad Lorenz, "A consideration of methods of identification of species-specific instinctive behavior in birds (1932)," in his: *Studies in Animal and Human Behavior. Vol 1*, translated by Robert Martin. Cambridge, MA 1970, pp. 57-100.
22. On this, see Ulrich Horstmann, *Das Untier. Konturen einer Philosophie der Menschenflucht* [The Monster. Outlines of a Philosophy of Misanthropy]. Vienna und Berlin 1983, also in: *Das Gesamtwerk. Vol. 1: Essays und Interviews*, pp. 9-118. Berlin 2017.
23. Arthur Schopenhauer, *The World as Will and Representation; in two volumes. Volume II: Supplements to the First Book*; tr. from the German by E. F. J. Payne. New York 1966; *chapter I. On the Fundamental View of Idealism*:
"In endless space countless luminous spheres, round each of which some dozen smaller illuminated ones revolve, hot at the core and covered now with a hard cold crust: on this crust a mouldy film has produced living and knowing beings; this is the empirical truth, the real, the world." [p. 3]

24. Samuel Scheffler, *Death and the Afterlife. With Commentaries by Susan Wolf, Harry G. Frankfurt, Seana Valentine Shiffrin, Niko Kolodny*. Oxford, UK 2013.
25. London, UK 1992.
26. New York, NY 2006.
27. See Nagarjuna, *The Fundamental Wisdom of the Middle Way. Nagarjuna's Mulamadhyamakakarika*. Tr. and com. by Jay L. Garfield. Oxford, UK 1995.
28. Carl Schmitt, *The Concept of the Political. Expanded Edition*, tr., Introduction, and Notes by George Schwab, incl. *Leo Strauss's Notes on Schmitt's Essay*, tr. J. H. Lomax, Chicago and London 2007, p. 26 et al.
29. François Jullien, op. cit.
30. This, too, is a thought expressed by Carl Schmitt: "(The) sovereign is he who decides on the state of emergency." See his: *Politische Theologie. Vier Kapitel zur Lehre von der Souveränität*, Munich and Leipzig 1922 and 1934, p. 17. [*Political Theology. Four Chapters on the Concept of Sovereignty*, tr. G. Schwab. Chicago, IL 2005.]
31. In: Harville Hendrix and Helen Hunt, *The Personal Companion: Meditations and Exercises for Keeping the Love You Find*. New York, NY 1995, p. 198.
32. Thomas Kling, *Das brennende Archiv* [The Burning Archive]. Berlin 2021, p. 7 and p. 29.
33. J. M. Coetzee, *Disgrace*. London 2000, p. 74; see also ibid., p. 205.
34. Spinoza, *Ethics*, op. cit. Note 13. Part V, Proposition 10, Scholium.
35. Ecclesiastes, I, 2 and I, 14.
36. DU sihst / wohin du sihst nur Eitelkeit auff Erden.
    Was dieser heute baut / reist jener morgen ein:
    Wo itzund Städte stehn / wird eine Wisen seyn /
    Auff der ein Schäfers-Kind wird spilen mit den Herden:
    Was itzund praechtig bluehet / sol bald zuretten werden.
    [And nine more lines MW]
    See Andreas Gryphius, *Gedichte*. Herausgegeben von Thomas Borgstedt, Stuttgart 2012, p. 82.
37. Ludwig Wittgenstein, *Tractatus Logico-Philosophicus*. London and New York 2001, first published 1961; tr. D. F. Pears and B. F. McGuiness, 6.521, p. 88 f.

## Fourth Day: THE GOLDEN FISH

1. "And death shall have no dominion," in: *The Poetry of Dylan Thomas*. Centenary Edition, edited and annotated by John Goodby. New York, NY: 2017, p. 23 f.
2. Ingeborg Bachmann, third stanza of the poem "Die große Fracht." See Darkness Spoken. Ingeborg Bachmann. The Collected Poems, tr. by Peter Filkins. Brookline, MA 2006, p.24 f. [as "The Heavy Cargo"] and: *In the Storm of Roses. Selected Poems by Ingeborg Bachmann*, tr. ed., and introduced by Mark Anderson. Princeton, NJ 1986, p. 38 f. [as "The Heavy Freight"].

# Selected English Books from PalmArtPress

*Dennis McCort*
**The Golden Pot** - *A Fairytale for Our Time*
ISBN: 978-3-96258-109-1
474 Pages, English

*YoYo*
**One Man's Decision to Become a Tree** – *Beijing – London Quartet*
ISBN: 978-3-96258-136-7
268 Pages, English

*Sibylle Princess of Prussia, Frederick William Prince of Prussia*
**The King's Love** – *Frederick the Great, His Gentle Dogs and Other Passions*
ISBN: 978-3-96258-047-6
168 Pages, Biography, Softcover/flaps, English Translation Dennis McCort

*Carmen-Francesca Banciu*
**Fleeing Father**
ISBN: 978-3-941524-83-4
156 Pages, English

*Kevin McAleer*
**POSTDOC**
ISBN: 978-3-96258-088-9
220 Pages, Novel, English

*Berndt Wilde*
**MY NY** *Berndt Wilde – Drawings / New York*
ISBN: 978-3-96258-077-3
160 Pages, English

*Jakob van Hoddis*
**Strong Wind over the Pale City / Starker Wind über der bleichen Stadt**
ISBN: 978-3-96258-033-9
150 Pages, Poetry, Hardcover, English/German

*Kevin McAleer*
**Berlin Tango**
ISBN: 978-3-96258-051-3
274 Pages, Novel, English

*Carmen-Francesca Banciu*
**Berlin Is My Paris** – *Stories from the Capital*
ISBN: 978-3-941524-66-8
204 Pages, English

*John Berger / Liane Birnberg*
**garden on my cheek**
ISBN: 978-3-941524-77-4
60 Pages, Poetry/Art, Softcover/flaps, English

*Rüdiger Görner*
**The Marble Song**
ISBN: 978-3-96258-079-7
280 Pages, Novel, Softcover/flaps, English

*Carmen-Francesca Banciu*
**Mother's Day** - *Song of a Sad Mother*
ISBN: 978-3-941524-47-7
244 Pages, Novel, English

*Reinhard Knodt*
**Pain / Schmerz**
ISBN: 978-3-96258-052-0
200 Pages, Philosophical Poetic Prose, English Translation Dennis McCort

*Michael Lederer*
**The Great Game** – *Berlin-Warsaw Express and Other Stories*
ISBN:978-3941524-12-5
242 Pages, Short Stories

*Michael Lederer*
**In the Widdle Wat of Time**
ISBN: 978-3-3941524-70-5
100 Pages, Poetry and Short Stories, Hardcover, English

*Matéi Visniec*
**MIGRAAAAANTS!** – *There's Too Many People on This Damn Boat*
ISBN: 978-3-96258-002-5
220 Pages, Theatre Play, English/German

*Carmen-Francesca Banciu*
**Light Breeze in Paradise**
ISBN: 978-3-941524-95-8
360 Pages, English/Greek

*Sara Ehsan*
**Bestimmung / Calling**
ISBN: 978-3-96258-065-0
160 Pages, Poetry, Hardcover, English/German